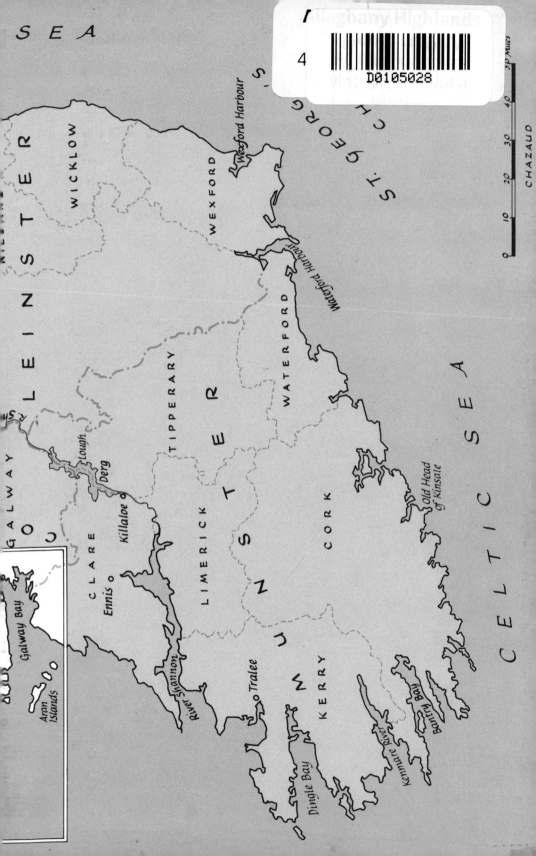

Grania

GRANIA

SHE-KING
OF THE IRISH SEAS

BY MORGAN LLYWELYN

Crown Publishers, Inc. New York

Copyright © 1986 by Morgan Llywelyn

All rights reserved. No part of this book may be reproduced or transmitted in any form or by any means, electronic or mechanical, including photocopying, recording, or by any information storage and retrieval system, without permission in writing from the publisher.

Published by Crown Publishers, Inc., 225 Park Avenue South, New York, New York, 10003

CROWN is a trademark of Crown Publishers, Inc.

Manufactured in the United States of America

Library of Congress Cataloging-in-Publication Data

Llywelyn, Morgan,

  Grania: she-king of the Irish seas.

  I. Title.

PS3562.L94G73 1986   813'.54   85-29975

ISBN 0-517-55951-X

10 9 8 7 6 5 4 3 2 1

First Edition

For Charles
Forever

PROLOGUE

Dark upon dark stones, Rockfleet. Seen from outside, the square stone tower was forbidding. Like some dark, stout, weathered woman, it stood defiantly without even a softening veil of ivy. But within was a different atmosphere. Fires burned brightly on the hearths, old tapestries glowed on the walls. The fortress could offer warmth and something of beauty to the few who gained admittance.

The woman came bounding up the circular stone stairway two steps at a time, as always. The feat was risky, for the stair was narrow in order to repel invaders, but she did not hesitate until she reached the chamber doorway. There she paused, surprised by the pounding of her heart.

She pressed one hand to her chest for a moment and it eased. The sea called to her through one of the narrow oblong window-slits and she started across the room, only to pause again with the color draining from her face. A stab of pain shocked her. There was a brief, coppery taste in her mouth that she recognized of old. Trying to ignore it, she made her way across a floor carpeted with fresh rushes and sank into a cushioned window embrasure, her eyes turning out of habit toward Clew bay.

People might think her aged and past her prime, but she had never lost the seaward perspective. Survival and action were the imperatives of her existence. The laws of the land, like the land itself, were obstacles to the unrestricted movement she craved.

She stirred restlessly on her seat, clenching her hands on her knees, gnawing her underlip to will the pain away. She would get up soon. The ability to pick herself up and go on, no matter what, had always been her greatest strength. War and murder, impoverishment and imprisonment—wild currents had swirled around her all her days, dragging her down again and again. Yet she fought her way back to the surface still able to laugh, still able to wring satisfaction from life. She would do it this time, too.

I am as sound as new rope, she insisted silently. She took one hand from her knee and made a fist to pound against her thigh, testing the muscle. It did not seem possible that the rich tide of her life might finally be ebbing.

She moved deeper into the embrasure and leaned on her elbows so she could see through the loophole to her boats at waters' edge below. Guns had been fired through that loophole—yes, and she had fired them, and could again, in defense of those boats and this fortress. Her flag flew from both. Not an English flag but an Irish one, the banner of Grace O Malley, as Elizabeth Tudor had called her. Gráinne Ni Mháille. Granuaile. Grania.

"When the time does come for me to die," she wondered aloud to the empty room, "will anyone remember me as the Tudor woman will be remembered?"

She listened to the silence echoing from the stones. No. Probably not. Yet she had spent much of her life gaming with Elizabeth Tudor and winning, sometimes.

Sometimes.

She was not one to count her losses.

Bards were outlawed in Ireland now, on the brink of the seventeenth century, so who would there be to tell her grandsons' grandsons the truth of what she had done and been, of her struggles to hold her place in an increasingly hostile world? She had survived the destruction of civilization as she knew it, but who would chronicle that survival? There would be only biased accounts of her exploits in the records of the English and the wild tales her own countryfolk delighted in spreading.

Chuckling in spite of the pain, she recalled the most recent story that fierce, funny man had heard somewhere and brought back to share with her. Inlanders were saying she slept in this very chamber with the hawser of her galley passed through a loophole and tied to her body. If anyone tampered with her ship, according to the story, the tug of the rope would warn her at once so she could plunge down the stairs, brandishing her pistols.

The chuckle became a full-throated laugh and she threw back her head to surrender to it. The pain retreated in response. What an absurd story, she thought. Every lapping of the water would have tugged on a rope fastened that way, and the turn of the tide would have dragged her out of bed. She had to admit it made a grand tale, though; one she would never spoil with a denial.

But she understood that the reality of her life was more unlikely than any storyteller's creation. She was a woman who had defied every convention and rebuilt more than once from wreckage and rubble. She had lived fully according to a pattern of her own design and meant to do so until the end.

No more laziness, she commanded herself. With an effort she stood up, straightening her spine in increments. There. She planted her feet wide apart and drew a deep breath, then glanced around the chamber for the ledger in which she recorded all business transactions, legal or not.

At first she could not find that precious compilation of so many small victories. If it fell into the wrong hands it contained enough information to hang her, and she knew just whose fingers itched to tie the knot around her neck. But when she searched a second time, with a lighted candle, she found the roll of papers had fallen down behind her sea chest. Seizing it with a sigh of relief, she riffled through to reread the last entry, fish and a few kegs of gunpowder and two men with an English price on their heads hidden under canvas in the bottom of her galley. They had paid well, and the gunpowder was stolen so it represented pure profit.

I am what they call me, a pirate, she mused. And several other things too, for have I not lived many lives in one? And known more than one man . . . her lips curved in a smile, remembering. I've taken what I wanted, but I've also done the best I could for those who depended on me. Some call me an ally and some think me a traitor because they do not understand that.

He understands, though, she told herself as his familiar step sounded on the stair. She had fought the pain back, it would not dare attack her again this night. There were years left, surely. Surely . . .

She strode to the doorway and called down to him, "Go and get some more turf for the fire and bring up the last of the good ale, and be quick! When you get back here I may give you a hug to crush your bones."

He would return the embrace in full measure, she knew. They were two strong people.

Waiting for him, she put the ledger aside. For once the details of trade had lost their fascination. Pain, with its intimations of mortality, had given her the desire for a different kind of accounting. Tonight she wanted to sit with him and just watch the fire on the hearth and talk of the old days, the wild days. The spectacular days. She felt compelled to examine the details of her past and decide if her life had really been a tragic one, as many might say.

Or a triumph.

part one

donal

1

The fire was only a spark at first. Anyone who saw it could have extinguished it. But no one did.

In the darkest watch of the night, a sailor from the forecastle had crept to the rail and glanced around nervously, making certain he was unobserved. From beneath his tunic he had slipped a small metal case, a pierced-brass body warmer given him by his wife. Her man suffered chills and fever but had insisted on going on this voyage anyway. Their cottage overflowed with children, and a crewmember's portion of the profit the captain so generously shared would support the whole family.

The sailor had concealed his illness as best he could when he came aboard, for he meant to haul his share of tackle. But soon after they set sail his bones began shivering in their envelope of flesh. When the ship anchored off the coast for the night, he sneaked below to the brick cooking hearth, bedded on gravel ballast in the hold, and stole some hot ashes for his warming pan. Wrapped in flannel and pressed against his chest, the warmer offered welcome comfort.

He knew he was breaking a cardinal rule of the sea. None but the cook was allowed access to the hearth, for fire was the terror of timbered sailing ships. When his pan cooled, the man had surreptitiously emptied the ashes over the side and replaced them with a hand fishing line and some bobbers, innocent equipment most seamen carried in packets on their persons.

He was so concerned about being discovered he did not notice that a small coal among the ashes was still warm. As he pitched it over the side, the wind caught a living spark and blew it back inboard, dropping it into a coil of tarred rope in the waist of the vessel, out of sight behind the ship's boat.

The sky paled and the wind calmed, then freshened, making the great sails creak overhead. The half-hour glass, made in Venice and so fragile the ship carried several spares, was turned and turned again. The watch bell sounded. Seamen exchanged places. Some went to their hammocks in the forecastle or their favorite corner of the deck where they could brace themselves against the pitch and roll of the ship; others, rubbing their eyes, went shuffling to the break in the poop to relieve themselves and then lined up for a meal of oatcakes, cheese, and onions. A fresh lookout was posted fore and aft, and the ship's boy made his way to the captain's cabin, carrying a meal in a wooden bowl. The anchor was hoisted, the ship under way.

And in its hiding place the spark grew a little red tongue and began tasting the frayed fibers of its rope nest. The waist of the caravel was low and often awash in a high sea, and the rope was far from dry. But the tiny fire was stubborn; it meant to survive.

A fair wind was blowing by now, and the caravel was an eager ship. Accompanied by two galleys, she was on a trading voyage intended to follow the southern coast of Ireland as far as Wexford harbor, having originated northwest of Galway bay. Wool and tallow from Iar Connaught waited in her holds for eager southern customers, and the clansmen of Iar Connaught waited just as eagerly for the goods she would bring back in return.

The older crewmen were hard at work manning halyards and tending tacklings, while their younger, more agile mates served as foremastmen, furling and slinging the foresail as needed or scrambling aloft to tend the great fore-and-aft lateens that furnished the ship's principal motive power. On a tossing deck, footing was precarious enough, but for a foremastman aloft, with bare prehensile toes clinging to ratlines or muscular torso stretched out along a yardarm, life was uncertain from one heartbeat to the next. A misstep, a lost handhold, and the sailor could be pitched headfirst into the sea. In common with seamen everywhere, the crewmen of the caravel were not swimmers. Their trust was in their ship and captain . . . and their God.

On the morning watch, the youngest apprentices scrubbed the decks with seawater carried from a tub amidships. Keeping that tub filled was hard work, and dangerous, because the boys had to lean far out in order to lower their leather buckets into the sea, and if the caravel wallowed it was easy enough to go overboard. Once the tub was filled there was no danger but the tedium of the task, which the apprentices relieved by singing and joking as they worked, sweeping the planking with coarse brooms and taking up the remaining moisture with mops made from rope-ravelings.

There was always one boy who held his mop to his head so the ravelings lay like curls against his cheeks, while he pranced and played the girl and the others cheered him on. The decks rang with laughter and the old seamen scowled, but their eyes twinkled with memories of their own as the lads frolicked. The apprentices were mostly red-cheeked young Gaels from the hills of Connaught, with a taste for adventure. The sea had not yet turned on them, and it was a fine thing to be part of a bold venture off the coast of Ireland on a summer morning.

One freckled boy, naked except for a pair of woolen trews chopped off at the knee, trotted up to the tub to refill his bucket for deck swabbing. He hesitated, wrinkling his nose at an unfamiliar smell. He was a rawboned, merry lad, and the sea was new to him. Until he came aboard for this voyage he had never been off dry land, and he did not yet know what sights and scents were commonplace to a four-masted caravel under full sail. But instinct warned him the odor of scorching rope and charring wood was wrong here—terribly wrong.

Taking another sniff, he tried to isolate the smell from that of salt and tar and bilge. "Something's burning," he said tentatively. He did not want to make a fool of himself over nothing. The men who sailed on ships such as this—ships that sometimes engaged in piracy as well as trade—were the cream of their profession, hardbitten and courageous. They would make life miserable for anyone who acted timid, crying false alarms.

But the smell was growing stronger.

Then a shrill voice screamed, "Fire! *Fire!*" The boy did not realize it was he who screamed. He stood rooted to the deck, staring in horror at a sudden banner of red flame leaping above the ship's boat and dancing in the seawind.

"Fire!" cried a dozen other voices at once. There was no hesitation, because every man on board knew what fire could do at sea, where there was no way to escape from it. Men came swarming from every direction, ripping off their clothes to beat out the flames, shoving the boy aside in their hurry to get at the mop water in the tub. Somebody grabbed the bucket out of his hand and filled it and then threw the water at the fire in one smooth gesture, and the boy heard the fire hiss. But one bucket was not enough to drown it; the contents of the depleted tub were not enough to drown it.

The fire took a deep breath and roared.

"Send for the captain!" shouted the boatswain's mate as he began trying to haul the ship's boat, his particular responsibility, out of the way. The waist of the vessel was crowded, and there was little room to work. Other men joined him and grunted and tugged until the boat scraped forward, but the fire billowed into the cleared space like a beast released from a trap. It had already ignited the far side of the ship's boat, and from there was reaching for the mainmast.

"Keep it out of the rigging!"

Sailors pressed forward, beating at the flames, as an acid, tarry stench seared the nostrils. The rising wind encouraged the fire to leap higher, snatching at the lateen sails.

An inferno was being born. It exploded savagely, driving the men back. If fire got into the sails the ship was lost; falling spars and burning sheets would set the whole caravel ablaze.

There was more to fight than fire. Panic rippled through the crew, and they reacted reflexively, without plan, running from this spot to that and getting in each other's way. The country boy who had first spotted the fire had no idea what to do, and no one was able to tell him. He looked longingly toward the gunwales and imagined plunging into the cold sea. Drown or be burned.

His eyes dilated with terror.

"Look out, boy!" cried a voice roughened by years of shouting commands. Hands gripped his shoulders and flung him violently to the deck just as a burning shroud snapped overhead and whipped through the air.

The apprentice was thrown forward. His cheekbone struck planking, and stars of pain shattered in his skull. He heard the vicious whoosh of the blazing line as it passed over him. He heard the scream of agony as it hit another man full in the face, searing his eyes.

"Get up now, you're in the way lying on deck," demanded the boy's rescuer. He recognized that voice, for he had heard it often since coming aboard, giving orders or requesting information or whooping with a great wild peal of laughter. Everyone knew the distinctive voice of the commander of the fleet and captain of this ship, a being with one foot already planted in legend.

The commander grabbed the boy under the arms and hauled him upright, where he stood shivering and speechless, mouth agape.

"You could thank me," he was told. The eyes that met his were the shifting color of the sea, but he caught a glimpse of laughter in them.

"Th . . . thank you," the lad stammered, hating himself for his awkwardness.

The fire would not wait for formalities. The commander could not waste time with an apprentice while the greater life, that of the ship itself, was threatened. She turned away abruptly to take up the battle for the caravel, and the boy stared after her, blushing crimson.

"Gráinne Ni Mháille," he whispered in Gaelic. "Grania."

The commander of the fleet was tall and lean, taut-muscled. The English would translate her name as Grace, but she was no milk-skinned girl in a laced bodice. Aboard ship Grania, in her early thirties, wore a man's sleeved shirt, a fustian jerkin, and worsted trews. Her coarse black mane was knotted at the neck to keep it out of her way. Heavy eyebrows cut a straight line across her strong-boned face, and her complexion was weather-beaten, squint lines framing the eyes. At a glance she could be mistaken for one of the Gaelic warlords who still struggled to hold their native Ireland against the encroachment of Elizabeth Tudor's England.

To the boy she had just saved, Grania was beautiful. His awed gaze followed her until she plunged through a wall of smoke and disappeared; his shoulders prickled where she had touched him.

She could not help seeing the admiration in his eyes, but she had been thinking of her ship; nothing else mattered just then.

✠

The caravel had been Grania's special joy since the day its keel was laid to her order in the shipyard at La Coruña, the same Spanish port from which the first Gaels had set out to colonize Ireland two thousand years earlier. The chief shipbuilder had personally conducted the formalities of turning the completed vessel over to her new owner, because he was an old friend of Grania's father, the redoubtable Gaelic trader Owen O Malley. Dubhdara, in Gaelic—the Black Oak.

Everyone for miles around came to the harbor at La Coruña to admire the black-hulled ship, graceful as a tern, with her spars of golden wood gleaming in the sunlight. Adhering to tradition, the wives and children of the men who had built a caravel for Dubhdara's daughter threw armloads of flowers into the water; there were bonfires of celebration, and singing.

The old master shipbuilder told Grania, as she took possession of her new vessel, "The ships I build are demanding children. You cannot abuse or deceive them or they will find the weak planking in you and split you wide open. But if you treat them well, they will support you handsomely in your old age."

This was not Grania's first visit to Spain, for she had come on trading voyages with Dubhdara, but it was her first caravel, and she thought it the most beautiful vessel ever launched. She had worked hard to acquire enough money to commission it; she had earned every timber and line herself. Herself.

The caravel belonged to the general family of round ships but had narrower quarters and was faster than many of her contemporaries, better fitted for maneuvering. Grania's new ship had a square stern, fore and aft castles, and a foremast raked well forward, giving her a jaunty look. Her cargo holds were capacious, and her forecastle bulkhead had been pierced for cannon. She was a serious ship, a cargo carrier with teeth.

Dubhdara, who relied primarily on galleys, as did most Irish seafarers, possessed a caravel or two for voyages to Spain and other distant ports, but nothing in his fleet was as fine, as modern, as Grania's new flagship.

"Mine," she had breathed with delight as she took possession.

Before they were outlawed entirely, the few remaining bards sang in her honor in the peat-smoked meadhalls of Ireland:

> *By rock-ribbed Connaught my swift vessels glide,*
> *Like swans they are breasting the full-flowing tide.*
> *Warships and Gaels all ready to sail,*
> *To sweep the salt sea from Cape Clear to Kinsale.*

Warships and a warrior woman to lead them: the numerous songs sung of her were repeated across the west country, from the time she took command of that first splendid caravel.

✠

And now the very survival of the caravel was threatened. Flakes of wood ash fell like bitter rain. Greasy particles of burning hemp writhed in the air like tiny blazing snakes and clung, stinging, to human flesh.

The first mate caught sight of his captain and ran to her side. "What are your orders?" Tigernan wanted to know as he rubbed the smoke from his eyes.

"If we bring her up into the wind," Grania replied, "we might be able to drive back the fire and contain it."

Tigernan shook his head. "We can't bring her about—the running rig's already too damaged. And many of the shrouds are burned through. We could be dismasted by the next real gust of wind. As for the helmsman . . ."

"I know, I saw him aft, with his hands like cooked meat and his mustache half burned away. But we have to save the ship. And if we can't use the sails . . ." She tilted her head back and gazed aloft, narrowing her eyes. "If we throw them overboard with the rigging still on them, they won't be burned and we can retrieve them later," she decided swiftly. She raised her voice to a commanding bellow. "Dowse all sails and pitch them into the sea!"

Tigernan repeated her order, a necessary precaution aboard ship, where a misunderstood command could lead to disaster. The crew immediately began lowering the sails, foremastmen swarming up the ratlines on the windward side to free the sheets from their yards.

Grania watched the big lateen sails being thrown into the sea. They lay outstretched upon the water like the wings of a fallen swan.

She blinked hard, then shouted the next order. "You there, find every bucket or bowl or cask on board, get them over the side and filled with water. And you to the forecastle; those other men to my cabin. Strip out every piece of material that can be used for beating the flames. And hurry, it's gaining on us!"

Putting word to action, Grania pulled off her own jerkin and shirt and whirled bare breasted to lash at the fire.

Yet with every blow she struck she felt a thrill of fear. She had watched from the shore of Clew bay as burned bodies were washed in by the tide from a ship that blazed and sank within sight of land, a doomed ship not one survivor escaped. The story was commonplace enough: a mast struck by lightning or a lantern carelessly handled. But the memory of those charred, twisted bodies stayed with Grania a long time, and it came back now in a sickening wave.

For one moment her mind was blank with terror. Then she gasped and beat at the flames with redoubled effort, submerging memory in motion. Fear had to be set aside or it would swamp her —and the caravel too.

With an effort, she made herself slam doors shut in her mind. She could be afraid later, when it was over.

The two galleys accompanying the caravel were aware of the disaster by now. Their aghast crews rowed closer to attempt rescue of any survivors, for no one doubted the vessel must sink. Even a massive greatship could go to the bottom in no more time than it took to turn a half-hour glass, once fire took hold of her timbers.

The first galley to reach the caravel stood well off her starboard bow, mindful of the undertow with which a sinking ship dragged down everything around it. The few seamen who noticed the waiting galley made no effort to signal it closer. As long as their commander stood among them, smoke-blackened and fighting, they would not leave her.

A sooty pall stained the sky.

Even under Grania's direction, there was much confusion and wasted motion. One man reeling back from a gout of flame caromed into two more, causing all three to fall across a hatch grating in a tangle of legs and profanity. The fore topsail, ripped too impatiently from its yards, crashed down onto the deck, burying men beneath heavy canvas that immediately began to smolder. In frantic haste those nearby struggled to lift the sail over the side, but one unfortunate fellow got tangled in the rigging and went with it, screaming all the way down to the water.

His voice could not be heard above the din of disaster.

Standing with her back to the mizzenmast, Grania was beating at the fire with a rhythm that had developed a life of its own. Swing the arms, strike down, flap the scorched fabric to clear it of sparks, and lift it again. It was like reefing sail; she could lose herself in the physical act. Just fight and fight, the fire would not get this ship. Not *her* ship. . . .

She became aware of someone close beside her, beating the flames with a broom. From the corner of her eye she glimpsed the young apprentice she had saved earlier. The boy gave her a shy grin, a flash of teeth in a smudged face.

Grania's mind slowed, distorting time. Her body continued to function automatically, and she saw her arms lift—ever so slowly —then bring the cloth down as if there were all the time in the world. Time enough to muse on a universe where no ship was burning and no death hung like a raven in the air.

In such a universe, the apprentice had once stared at her with his mouth hanging open and a blush rising up his pimpled neck. Reflected in his dazzled eyes had been an image of embodied myth. Gráinne Ni Mháille as the warrior goddess of Gaelic legend.

She could not help being amused. In her own version of reality, Grania saw herself as a plain woman toughened by need and circumstance. The courage and daring that had already made her famous on the west coast of Ireland were a form of callus, built up layer by layer to shield hidden fears and wounds.

But the apprentice with his worshipful face had demanded she be responsible for his truth and live up to his image.

"What sept are you, lad? What clan?" she shouted to him.

"I am called Fergal, of the line of Owen, clan O Flaherty," he called back, choking on smoke. "From the region of the Twelve Bens," he managed to add, for a man must locate himself by place as well as by blood.

"You are far from home, then," Grania said. Boy with a face and now a name and family, from a place she knew. She would have to see that he got back to the Twelve Bens safely.

A fearful cry rang out. "The fire is belowdecks!" Grania responded with an oath. But at least she and Fergal had made progress; the flames in their area were almost extinguished. Leaving the boy and his broom to finish the job, Grania hurried down the companionway to the lower deck to determine the extent of the fire for herself.

A billow of smoke greeted her, accompanied by the scurrying of rats fleeing from the hold below. Her first mate had followed her; she felt his hand on her arm. "You could be trapped if you go any farther," he warned.

She shook him off. "Come with me then, Tigernan, and be the eyes at my back. I have to see how bad this is, because if the fire eats through the hull we're lost."

"We're lost anyway," he tried to tell her. "The ship's afire from bowsprit to poop."

"Burning, perhaps, but not yet sinking!" Grania snapped at him. "Follow me, and be careful." She headed for the ladder down to the cargo hold.

Tigernan hurried after her naked back, trying without success to overtake her in the cramped spaces belowdecks. He had obeyed her orders in many a rough sea and tried to interpose himself between Grania and many a danger—but as usual, she was too quick for him.

There was heat in the cargo hold, but no flame. If the trading wool they were carrying down there had been burning, Tigernan thought, the stench would have already sickened everyone aboard.

"The fire's still above us," Grania said with relief. "We may yet save her. Go back up, Tigernan, and bring me a party of men to fight the fire wherever we may find it. Hurry!"

Belowdecks was a luridly lit nightmare: hot, suffocating, with air thick enough to swim in and too murky to see through. The fire sped through the ship in thin lines, following the pitch and oakum used for caulking seams. But Grania was right, it had not yet reached the lowest levels; there was a remote possibility they could stop it.

All sense of time was lost. The commander and her crewmen were trapped in a burning box, and the only way out was through. The fire was no sooner extinguished on the gun deck than it was discovered in a companionway, and must be pursued with haste, with prayers, with desperation.

The only way out was through. Through the smoke, through the flames, beat them down, beat them back, the fire must die so humans could live.

They passed the point of exhaustion. Muscle and sinew could give no more, yet somehow they did. Step by step, even to the base of the capstan-shaft, the fire was challenged and defeated.

When Grania at last led her weary but victorious men up from below, devastation greeted them.

The masts stood like charred trees, festooned with black spider-webs of burned rigging. The fire had reached as far as the forecas-tle, and smoldering sea chests were still being tossed overboard by men too tired to try to salvage their contents. The ship's boat had also gone overboard, blazing down into the sea with a shaft of steam to mark its passage. The seamen who had stayed topside to fight the fire there were scarcely recognizable now, devoid of clothing and singed black. Some lacked hair and eyebrows; everyone was blistered and beginning to feel the pain.

But the caravel was still afloat, and where there had been flame there was only smoke and sizzle.

"Signal the galleys to come alongside and take off the seriously injured," Grania ordered. "Then we'll assess the damage."

The ship was listing badly to port. It was soon apparent she was too burned to be controllable, for without the use of her sails a caravel was helpless. She would have to be towed to the nearest safe harbor if she was to be salvaged at all, and Grania's men were beginning to suggest rather loudly that it would be best if everyone got off the ship.

But their commander refused. "I sailed out with her, I go back with her. You can leave if you like, so long as a skeleton crew remains with me to handle the towing. Tigernan, there was an apprentice—Fergal O Flaherty, from somewhere near Ballina-hinch. Find him for me, will you? I want to be certain he is all right."

The galleys pulled alongside and began taking off the injured, men hurrying up a boarding ladder to receive the broken and un-conscious as their mates passed them over the rail. Someone brought Grania a mantle. Only then did she realize she was naked above the waist.

She rubbed at her sweated skin with her palm but only suc-ceeded in smearing the greasy soot that clung to her. Shrugging, she threw the cape across her shoulders and pulled it over her breasts. She glanced up and saw a sailor staring at her.

The man quickly looked away again, but not before her laughter singled him out. "Aye, look at me, Ulick McAnnally!" Grania challenged him. "When next you are ashore and someone tells you Gráinne Ni Mháille is really a man, you'll have an answer for them!"

Fergal was brought to her. The boy was coughing incessantly, but his eyes lit up when his commander called him by name. "I'll see you get safely home," Grania assured him, "and when you are well again you have a place on my ship at any time."

He turned away as a spasm wracked him. Grania saw his shoul-ders flinch from the pain. Perhaps his lungs were seared. The youngster might never be fit to sail again—he might not even live to become a man.

She put her hand on his shoulder and felt how narrow the bones were, how young. She leaned close to him and whispered, for his ears alone, "Everything hurts, Fergal. All the time. Start with that and life won't be able to disappoint you."

She could tell that he did not understand, though he drew his singed eyebrows together in an effort at concentration in spite of his pain. But someday he might recall her words and draw some strength from them. It was little enough to give him for having thrown away his health in her service.

Every muscle and bone in Grania's body ached. When she moved she thought she must creak like the ruined superstructure of her ship. She too was burned and battered. But still afloat. Still afloat. She lifted her chin and surveyed the wreckage around her, already seeing it repaired, the caravel refitted, new paint, clean crisp sails bellying with a following wind . . . *ah, you lovely creature!* Then her eyes moved beyond the ship, scanning the far horizon.

She drew in a sharp breath.

Tigernan appeared at her elbow. "We saved her," he said, hardly able to believe it. "Saved a burning ship at sea." He shook his head from side to side, smiling a dazed smile. "There's a lot of damage, some of it below water level, but Magnus and Ruari Oge are preparing to take her in tow with their galleys. There's no harm done that can't be fixed in the shipyard at Kinsale."

"Look, Tigernan," Grania said.

He followed her pointing finger, and the exhilaration drained from him. The bright summer morning was being invaded by a long line of black cloud, racing out of the west. One of the savage Atlantic gales all sailors dreaded was blowing straight toward them. Such a storm was impelled by a wind of irresistible force, capable of capsizing a topheavy galleon in good repair. A burned-out caravel would be swamped by the high seas the wind brought, if not overturned by the first assault of the storm itself.

"We can never outrun that," Grania said bleakly. "And we dare not even attach the tow lines; we would take the galleys down with us."

2

Tigernan swore an oath usually reserved for his dearest enemies. "We've lost her after all, then."

"Not yet, not while she's still above water," Grania contradicted him through clenched teeth.

"But . . ."

"But first we have to get my men off. I won't have their lives thrown away."

Putting word to deed, she ran to the nearest crewman and urged him overboard where the waiting galleys could pick him up. But he argued with her and refused to go as long as his captain was on board. Every member of the crew would respond the same way, she quickly realized. She had worked so hard to win them. . . .

✠

Many of the men of Iar Connaught had considered themselves impoverished when Gráinne Ni Mháille strode onto their beaches, mocking their neglected fishing boats, insulting their seamanship, making them so angry under the lash of a woman's tongue that they began caulking curraghs and mending lines. "The Black Oak of Umhall would scuttle wrecks like these and order new ones!" she had cried, knowing full well the men of Iar Connaught could not afford new vessels. But then she had pitched in beside them like a man, with tar on her hands and nails in her teeth to help repair their boats, and when a revitalized fleet left Bunowen harbor and came back with the best catch in years, Grania personally visited the fishermen's homes to be assured the rewards of their efforts were evenly apportioned.

She had sat by their heathfires and dandled their babies. Their own chieftain had never done as much. She had stood on their docks and talked knowledgeably of fishing grounds and boat tacklings. Their chieftain was not interested in the sea and had left them to their own devices for years, merely demanding they pay him the rents due on their cottages from whatever they could earn.

When she suggested repairing the rotting galleys left by earlier, more aggressive generations, the men of Iar Connaught had been dubious. But Grania insisted it could be done. "We can carry our wool abroad and get a good price for it. I have contacts in foreign ports who will give you more for it than you'll ever get selling it locally." She had laughed then, anticipating. "And if we encounter a smaller, weaker merchant at sea, we may relieve him of his cargo and sell that too! I learned the art at my father's knee, and it's a fine trade, a good way to augment a poor man's income."

She had such confidence, such vitality. She infected her followers with both. The spectacle of a woman holding her own in a man's profession was so remarkable that once they accepted that, they were prepared to accept almost anything. They repaired the galleys because she told them it could be done. They traded wool and fish and Gaelic craftsmanship and brought profits home because she told them it could be done. She seemed to think nothing impossible, and they believed her. They began to succeed and enjoy the first gloss of prosperity. They began to speak Grania's name in the same tone they used for a chieftain, with respect and reverence—these men who had been dispirited for years by a lack of caring leadership.

✠

The able-bodied would not now leave her on a burning ship. They knew her well enough to realize she would not desert her beloved caravel, and to a man—even the rawest apprentice—they meant to stay with her.

"Dar Dia, you fools, this is an *order!*" she bellowed at them. She spun on her heel and found herself facing a young man both shorter and lighter in weight than she, one of her best foremastmen. Without hesitation, she grabbed him by both shoulders and ran him toward the rail. "Throw down another ladder quickly!" she cried to the others. "This man is going overboard, and you're all going with him!"

From the nearest galley they could see Grania herself seize a second rope boarding-ladder from hands that hesitated and pitch it overboard. They watched her force a man onto it, and then shove another after him. She was making them abandon ship; she was making them abandon her.

The commander of the nearest boat urged his oarsmen closer.

Man after man she forced to save himself as the gale rose and the sea became more violent, great deep troughs of greenish water opening to swallow the hapless.

When only a few remained aboard, she glanced at Tigernan with a triumphant light in her eyes. "They're all going to make it!" she shouted over the roar of the wind and the groaning of the dying ship. "You and I will have to carry a couple of men off on our backs, but once they're clear, I can board again and . . ."

"Board again!" Tigernan echoed in horror. "She's going down within minutes, Grania!"

"So you say. I say she is not. I will not surrender my men to the sea, nor will I give up my ship. I've almost won the first battle and I intend to win the second as well. If I stay on board I can do some patching, hold her together somehow until this blows over. . . ."

Her mind was racing ahead, and he feared it might be unhinged; the shock of the fire and the desperate urgency of the struggle might have temporarily robbed her of her senses. She had already won a great victory, Tigernan thought—the majority of her crew was safe now on the galleys. The few still on board the caravel were probably beyond saving, under the circumstances: badly burned, unconscious. Dying. As Grania would die if she risked staying on board any longer. The ship was in imminent danger of going down, and he knew it. "You can't keep her afloat by yourself, Grania!"

She gave him a hard look from beneath the level line of her brows. "You're staying with me?"

At that moment the caravel shuddered beneath their feet, and he felt her settle in the water like a living animal accepting irresistible death. "There are still men on board that we have to get off," Grania gasped.

"There's no time left to save anyone but ourselves," Tigernan tried to tell her, though he had never persuaded her to take his counsel in any matter large or small.

"My men first," she insisted. "And you. Then my ship."

Her will was iron; he saw there was no breaking it and no reasoning with her. Gráinne Ni Mháille was always determined to win when she gambled.

Tigernan was Gaelic, with millennia of loyalty to a chosen leader bred into his soul. If Grania died he would go with her. He would go in the style of his warrior ancestors, fearless in the face of death;

the ancient, pagan Gaels had known death was only a brief incident in the ongoing flow of life, a transitory happening of little importance.

Reminded of Ireland's pagan past, Tigernan automatically made the sign of the cross on brow and chest. "We're all as good as dead now!" he yelled at her. Grania was the Black Oak's daughter; a man could at least yell at her with no fear she would dissolve in tears and whimpering.

They stood toe to toe and eye to eye on the tilting deck. Grania could judge the condition of her own skin from the blisters rising on Tigernan's. A lean man with the ropy sinews of a sailor, he had plaits of ginger-colored hair hanging on either side of a sharp-nosed face with a jutting, asymmetrical jaw. He wore a full and drooping mustache in the old Gaelic style, though otherwise he was clean-shaven. A man as tall as Grania herself, strongly built and doggedly stubborn. Homely, fierce, funny Tigernan.

A flood of fondness washed through her. "I won't let you die, you fool," she said, smiling through her soot. "I've never let you die before, have I?" Then she turned away and headed for the nearest injured man, meaning to carry him off the ship herself and come back for more—a physically impossible task she would probably accomplish, Tigernan thought ruefully.

The wind wailed, and he thought it was the sound of his own mourners he heard, keening for him. Surely he was but one step away from heaven. He would soon face his Maker and answer to judgment. And worse yet . . . if he survived and Grania did not, he would have to answer to a more fearsome judgment from Dubhdara Ui Mháille for letting the Black Oak's daughter die.

The thought of having to face Dubhdara gave Tigernan the strength of terror. He went running after Grania, though he knew she could no more be turned aside than the wind could. With a groan of despair, he seized a length of broken spar from the deck and managed to catch up with her in a few leaping strides. He tried to measure the degree of strength required to strike an incapacitating but not deadly blow and then, with a wordless prayer to the Madonna, he swung at Grania's head from behind.

She dropped without a sound.

The full force of the squall hit them like a broadside from a Spanish cannon. "Help us, someone!" Tigernan yelled uselessly, his voice lost in the crash of a raging sea flooding over the bulwarks. The oarsmen in the waiting boats suddenly had their hands full just trying to keep their own craft afloat and move clear of the stricken caravel, so that a few men were caught between vessels, the sea tearing them from the bottom of the boarding-ladders just as the rescue boats pulled away.

Tigernan crouched on the deck beside Grania, cradling her head in his arms. His fingers searched her skull within its mass of tangled hair and found no break, but she was definitely unconscious.

"May she stay asleep just long enough," he muttered. With a heave he raised her body enough to get his shoulder under her midsection and lifted her, then began climbing the tilting deck, bracing himself as best he could against the seawater pouring over the gunwales.

A huge wave broke over the side and washed his feet out from under him. He fell with a groan but was instantly up again, lifting Grania, grunting beneath her weight. The clan O Malley bred big bones into men and women alike.

Grania came out of darkness slowly. At first she was aware of only a black density, enveloping, cushioning. Then she heard a buzzing sound that gradually came closer. She struggled toward awareness, trying to identify the noise.

The hiss of fire?

No, not fire. She was lost in the dark, but she recognized the ringing in her own ears and was reassured. She felt a rocking motion—seawater in her mouth and nose!—a sense of weightlessness.

Easy to surrender. Let go, sink down.

No! Instinct flailed her arms and lifted her head, gulping for air. Then the darkness closed over her again.

Reality was hard-edged, hot and cold, bitter and demanding, and she fought to reach it. She knew she was alive when pain reassured her of it.

She was being carried across someone's shoulder, and the bony joint was digging into her rib cage with every jolting step. She squirmed, and a man swore.

"Tigernan?" she managed to whisper. "What . . . where . . . ?" Her head was hanging down, and she was nauseated. She gulped back the taste of bile. Then she was being lowered onto a hard surface and there were people crowding around her. She wanted to speak to them, but a dark vortex lay at the edge of awareness, spinning larger, welcoming her. . . .

Don't give up!

She started violently and opened her eyes. She saw the blurred outlines of a galley around her, and heard the rhythmic grunting of oarsmen stroking to the repetitive beat of the bodhran, the war drum.

"My ship!" she cried, sitting up. Her head swam and her vision was obscured by a gray mist.

"Dismasted by the gale," a voice told her. "And going down."

Grania shook her head to clear it and struggled to her feet, pushing away the hands outstretched to help her. She stumbled to the nearest bulwark and clung there, fighting off dizziness.

Attached to the galley's gunwales were the battle shields of the clan O Flaherty and its allies who had provided manpower for this venture. Below them, in near-perfect unison, the oars swept forward, thrust down, swung back, and lifted to stroke again. But Grania did not look down, did not appreciate the colorful shields or the skillful rowing. She saw only the caravel.

The abandoned flagship drifted some distance from the galley, a distance the oarsmen were increasing with every stroke. The caravel was heeled over at an impossible angle, fore and mizzen masts broken to stumps, charred decks awash in the pounding sea.

"The hull's burned through," Tigernan said, coming to Grania's side. "That ship could never have made it back, even under tow."

"She could have," the woman replied in a whisper. "I could have taken her home."

The burned ship shuddered throughout her length and almost instantly started to go down stern first, rolling over as she went. She slid into the dark waves as eagerly as she had once sped over them; it did not take very long.

Good sailing ships do not just sink. They die, leaving an awful emptiness behind them, a void in sky and sea. The strong vertical lines of the masts that divided the heavens into manageable segments are gone. The billowing sails that testified to mortal harnessing of invisible power are no more. The rolling lift and purposeful forward plunge of a valiant vessel are only a memory, leaving behind ceaseless waves, motion without meaning, and a bit of debris floating on the surface. Burned planking, sodden canvas, a hatch cover.

"It tears my heart to see her go," Tigernan said in a subdued voice.

Grania did not respond. Her eyes were fixed on the glassy pool

marking the site of the sinking, one briefly smooth pond in a turbulent sea. Strings of bubbles escaping from the submerged hull
rose to the surface like strings of jewels and burst there.

Gone.

Grania looked down at her hands as they clutched the gunwale
of the galley. Red, chapped hands with spatulate fingers, skilled at
annotating a ship's journal or capable of splicing a line with equal
dexterity. And now those hands had nothing to do.

Tigernan was saying to her, "When I realized the situation was
hopeless, I just had to take you off, Granuaile . . ."

Graunyuh Wale, Tigernan pronounced it as men from the western coast did.

✠

Granuaile: It stood for Grace of Umhall, but a trick of pronun-
ciation made it sound like Grace the Bald. Grania Mhaol. That
long-ago nickname summoned a lively, headstrong little girl with a
great goose-honk of a laugh out of all proportion to her size. Her
laugh had a life of its own, even then; it rang frequently across the
green hills of Umhall, where Grania grew up as wild as an unbroken pony, playing games of her own devising in the fields and
beside the bay. Usually beside the bay. The sea was her father's
special domain, and she loved everything that was his, because she
adored her father in those days.

In her eleventh summer, Grania's father, chieftain of Umhall,
planned an extended trading expedition to Spain and Portugal. The
weather during the last year had been good; the produce of his clan
was exceptional and would bring a high price abroad. For such a
journey across the bay of Biscay he would use the masted sailing
ships in his possession as well as an accompaniment of large galleys,
and for months his conversation had been larded with references
to sailing on open sea, to friends and sights he anticipated enjoying
once more on the coast of Spain.

His enthusiasm infected his daughter. Before the ships began
loading, Grania was already begging to go along. The Black Oak,
it seemed to her, sailed off to exotic otherworlds such as Scotland
or Wales or Portugal whenever he liked, and she was tired of being
left behind. Grania at eleven had been no farther from her birth-
place than Clare island and Achill, and the need to expand her
horizons was becoming imperative.

Sometimes Dubhdara looked at his daughter speculatively when her attention was elsewhere. Such a boisterous child, full of mischief, unlike her quiet mother. The two might have been totally unrelated. He thought of Mairgret's soft hands reaching for him, her mild voice saying, "If only you would stay with me this time, until the baby comes, I know it would live. But you'll go away, you always go away to sea, and they die. . . . I'm so afraid for you when I can't see you, and the fear kills the babies in me. . . ." The priests had taught Mairgret that guilt was a part of the human condition, and she in turn used it on him like a weapon—or tried to, but he would not let her. She was a perfect woman in every way save that.

Dubhdara's wife Mairgret had raised only one living child and meant that child to be a daughter, feminine and fine-grained.

"The ocean is no place for a girl," she admonished Grania. "The sailors say women don't belong on ships, and they are right. Your father should never have taken you into his galleys and let you pretend to handle oars and sails—he has put wrong ideas in your head. Your father . . ."

Grania grinned. Her father was amused by her interest in sea life, and boastful of her accomplishments. Her father made her feel seven feet tall when she stood beside him and helped haul a curragh up onto the strand like the other men.

"My father is going to *Spain*," Grania said. "Don't you ever want to go to someplace wonderful and different?"

Mairgret put her hands on her ample hips and faced the child with a resolute expression that got lost in the plump, gentle curves of her face. "I am where I want to be," she said. "No place could be better than this and no life better than mine, and it's foolish you are to try to be something you can never be, Grania. God has not fashioned you to be a sailor, and you should thank Him for that on your knees. The sea makes a hard life." Her eyes clouded; she wept for Dubhdara each time she waved him away onto the intemperate ocean, and she was always faintly surprised when he returned alive.

But Mairgret spoke the truth when she expressed her pleasure with her existence. A woman comfortable with woman's work, she reigned as uncontested matriarch of the clan O Malley, a stately and gracious woman attired in linen smocks and silk-embroidered overdresses, with a fine linen headcloth ruling her curls. Her sovereignty extended to spinning and weaving and butter-making, and with a sure hand she ruled the various households required by a powerful chieftain. So her mother had done before her and so her daughter must do, a world defined as rigidly by practicality as by tradition.

Young Grania, however, saw no appeal in such a life—not when her father's ships glided across Clew bay with their sails spread like wings and all the world waiting beyond.

Crouched down behind some casks in the buttery, she had chopped off her long black hair with the household shears, then scraped her skull with a knife until the skin bled. She slipped aboard Dubhdara's flagship with the other newly shorn apprentices. By the time she was missed at home—and her deception was discovered aboard ship—the fleet was already well on its way.

Surprisingly, the Black Oak was not angry. Her bold spirit seemed like an echo of his own, and he could not punish her for it. "You look as if you've been nibbled by a goat, my bald daughter," he chuckled when they brought her to him. "But why should I waste a good wind taking you back? If you have such a mind to see the world, you might as well come with me and we'll make a sailor of you. I'll take the rough edge of your mother's tongue when we get back to Umhall, but we'll bring her some pretties from Spain and she'll forgive us both."

Tigernan had been an apprentice himself on that voyage; had seen Dubhdara's child be violently seasick, had seen her learn to coil a rope the way the sun goes, had seen her scramble up a ratline with her face pale but her jaw set and determined. When the crew began teasing the little girl and calling her Grania Mhaol his voice had been as loud as the rest.

✠

Now her hair hung free to her waist and smelled of smoke and disaster.

But Tigernan had said "Grania Mhaol" as if by summoning the past he could win forgiveness for his crimes in the present, his unforgivable disregard of a commander's order. The woman at the rail slowly unclenched her fingers and turned to face him. Her eyes were like stones. He shifted his weight, bracing himself for the blow that was sure to come.

Then Grania laughed.

She hurt so much there was nothing else to do. Her head felt like an overripe Spanish melon split by the sun. Her face was burned, her body bruised, the ship built to her heart's design was lost. So she threw back her head and buffeted Tigernan with laughter.

"I beat the sea though, didn't I? I got my men off before you assaulted me, you rogue. And what am I going to do to you for that? Look at you, standing here proud as a dog who's rolled in a dungheap, expecting me to praise you.

"You robbed me, don't you know that? If I had stayed with the caravel I would have saved her as well—the sea's not strong enough to swallow me yet. As it is, she had to go to the bottom, and without even a guard of honor." Suddenly Grania's eyes danced. "Someone go find me a set of dice and we'll throw them, Tigernan and I. If he loses I'll pitch him overboard by the scruff of the neck myself and he can keep my seabird company."

Tigernan squared his shoulders. It was not always easy to tell when Grania was being serious, and instinct warned him she was angry now beneath the laughter. "And if you lose?" he asked.

"If I lose I'll still throw you overboard, but I'll jump after you to make certain you don't come crawling back up the other side of the galley and cheat me again."

"We'd do better to forget about the dice for once," Tigernan replied. "I haven't the strength left to save you from the sea a second time."

Grania shrugged, though the effort made stiffening muscles scream with protest. "And the water's colder than I like anyway," she commented. "So that may not be the best idea I ever had. Besides, I can hardly send my men back leaderless now that they are safe, can I?"

Then something on Tigernan's face alerted her. "We did get all the men off, didn't we?" she demanded, searching her own memory and finding little but smoke and storm and confusion.

He tried to talk around the answer he did not want to give. "It was a miracle you saved so many, Grania Mhaol. They fought you, many of them, but you got them over the side anyway and steadied the rope with your own hands. I did what I could to help, but it was mostly you. You gave orders as if it was any other day, and you were so steady they took heart from you. I've heard of men panicking in a situation like that and getting themselves all killed, but . . ."

Tigernan was talking too fast, running his words together, but he could not distract her. "What do you mean, 'saved so many'? Who did we not save—aside from my beautiful ship? Did you drag me away before I got all of my men off the caravel?"

"A few of them were lost in the water when the galleys had to pull clear," Tigernan told her in a sober voice. "And there were a few more on deck, not very many. We couldn't have gotten them anyway. There was no time left."

Her lips felt tight against her teeth. "What about the apprentice, the one called Fergal? I thought I saw him . . . I seem to remember heading toward him . . ."

Tigernan swallowed hard. "I don't think Fergal got off. I remember a lad hanging half overboard with his clothing caught on something," he told her. "He appeared too weak to free himself; I'm certain he never got clear. Unless I'm mistaken it was Fergal. And I'm sorry."

"Sorry," Grania echoed. "Sorry." Her voice was a whisper, softened by grief.

"I doubt if he could swim anyway."

"Neither can you," she reminded him. "But you got us here."

The captain of the galley came toward them from the stern, his head lowered and his massive shoulders rounded against the diminishing storm. Ruari Oge—Young Rory—had long since outlived his nickname, for his hair was grizzled and his face as lined as a fisherman's net. Yet his gray eyes were still young and keen; a warrior's eyes. Rainwater dripped from his hair and ran in a stream from the high bridge of his nose. "This is about to blow over," he told Grania. "I thought it hit us too hard to last very long. What shall we do now?"

Grania made an impatient gesture. "Do. Men dead and lost. The boy Fergal . . . I saved him once. He looked at me in such a way . . ."

Tigernan and Ruari Oge exchanged glances. "I await your order," Ruari said loudly.

She drew a deep breath and sleeked her wet hair back from her eyes with the palms of her hands, grateful for his insistence. A captain who had just lost a ship might feel adrift, but the commander of a small fleet had ongoing responsibilities, welcome distractions.

"If the wind changes you can set your sail and give your oarsmen a rest," she told Ruari Oge. "We're going back to Bunowen."

"Empty-handed?"

"Need I remind you we just lost our trading cargo with the caravel?"

Ruari's lips skinned back from his teeth. "We could pick up another cargo," he said, hinting broadly. "There are plenty of good fighting men on these two galleys, and the waters along this coast fairly roil with trading ships in this season." He had always preferred the bold dash of privateering to the tedious balancing act that was honest trade. And he knew perfectly well that the Black Oak's daughter had no aversion to acquiring a cost-free cargo from time to time.

But not today, her eyes told him. "Need I remind you that the caravel was not only our deep-sea cargo ship but our gunship, Ruari Oge? Your galleys are fine harrying hounds, but my caravel was a lion with bronze cannon to roar."

Scowl he might, but he could not deny the truth of her words. Shallow-draft galleys similar to the old Viking longships had been the traditional vessels of Gaelic trade and piracy in the seas around Ireland for centuries. High in prow and stern, they were fitted with a single square sail for good wind but relied primarily upon the strength and skill of their oarsmen. Such galleys were either imported from the Hebrides or built by Gaelic-speaking shipbuilders of European origins in the many harbors lining the Irish coast, from Galway to Kinsale to Drogheda. The ancient design was nimble and seaworthy, and though it could not carry a lot of cargo, it could easily overtake the clumsy European merchant vessels of the period and relieve them of their choicest merchandise.

But since the discovery of the New World, ships were being redesigned. Tall galleons with massive square sails were being launched to cross the Atlantic and bring back incredible treasure, and carracks and caravels were being refitted with cannon in response to the bitter competition spurring the maritime countries.

With a caravel of her own—and the tolerance of the Spaniards, who were more inclined to be generous to Catholic Ireland than to Protestant England—Grania had built a successful trading network in the past several years. True, she occasionally indulged in a little piracy, getting the most value from the guns on her caravel. But without that ship, and hampered by an injured, demoralized crew, she was reluctant to face one of the heavily armed galleons known to frequent these waters. From their towering decks such vessels could rain death down upon her galleys.

She shook her head at Ruari Oge. "We will seize no prey this day, my friend. Give the order to your helmsman to return me and my injured crewmen to Bunowen."

Ruari Oge stood unmoving. "I have a responsibility to my crew, too!" he argued. "They're not like the seagoing scum foreign captains drag onto their vessels in chains and use like slaves. These are clansmen and friends who came with me for a share of the profit, Grania. We have to go past Galway harbor anyway—with just the two galleys, we could still seize an unescorted cromster or a Dutch hulk inbound. Galway harbor owes it to us for locking your husband's clan out."

Grania's eyes sparkled with the temptation, but then common sense reasserted itself. "No," she said, making certain he understood the finality in her voice. "And don't glare at me. I give you my word every man who sailed with us will receive recompense, even if I have to pay with my own property."

Tigernan had been following this dialogue with interest, but at Grania's last words his bushy red eyebrows crawled up his forehead. "What will your lord husband say to that?" he could not resist asking. And then, because he also could not help twisting this particular knife, he added, "Or will Donal O Flaherty be so delighted to have you back home in his bed he'll forgive you anything?"

The face Grania turned to him had been swept clean of weariness; rage burned there instead. "At last you have gone too far!" she yelled, making startled heads turn in the nearest rows of oarsmen. "Mock me no more, Tigernan, or I vow to the Virgin I will see your impertinent carcass rotting in chains at Bunowen landing!"

Tigernan clenched his teeth and fell silent. Grania with all her sails set was too much for him. He realized he had made a bad mistake in referring to her peculiar relationship with her husband. He had been in the castle at Bunowen himself; he had seen with his own eyes that Grania's belongings were taken to one bedchamber, and Donal O Flaherty's were put in another. Many might speculate in private about the arrangement, but only a fool would have mentioned it to her face.

Yet he could not help himself. Tigernan was a man with an incurable itch, and the name of that itch was Grania.

"Ruari Oge, take this man from my sight," she ordered now. "Give him some job to do—let him empy slop buckets over the side for the oarsmen. And have him do it facing into the wind."

Ruari Oge looked pityingly at Tigernan. The voyage home did not promise to be a pleasant one.

The wind whistled; rain-spears pelted the sea. Then the gale blew past and was gone. In an azure sky, great clouds of polished silver sailed, and the coast of Ireland was radiant in summer sunlight.

The survivors from the caravel were sleeping in crumpled heaps, jammed into the crowded foot-space of the galley. Grania, exhausted but unable to close her eyes, sat with her back propped against the mast holding the vessel's big square sail. She had eaten nothing since coming aboard, though Ruari Oge had persuaded her to water her headache with some ale from a wineskin. She merely sat and watched the sea, thinking her own thoughts.

From a safe distance Tigernan watched her, and thought his.

Ruari Oge took up a station in the upcurved prow of his vessel and eyed the land as it glided by. "The last time we came this way, we were bringing back a treasure from that Flemish trader we captured," he remarked to one of his officers. "Wrought China silk and curled cypress, we had." The officer's eyes glowed. "Musk and civet and ambergris—I still have *that* smell in my nostrils. And pepper and cloves and camphor that brought a good price as I recall.

"We came out of the fog and were aboard before they knew what happened," Ruari Oge reminisced. "I took my wife some peach-colored silk from that haul, the first silk ever on her skin. She looked like ripe fruit; it would feed your eyes to see her. When she wore it I took her into the bed and we stayed there the better part of two days." He grinned, then the gray eyes beneath his hooded lids turned dark.

"It's a fine thing to see your own looking prosperous," he said, more to himself than to the other man. "I've not been able to give that woman what I once expected to give a wife. When I was a boy, my clan held a great stretch of land surrounded by forest so deep we were as safe as if we lived in God's pocket. Game was as abundant as timber; we wanted for nothing in those days. Like kings, we lived. I thought when I married things would be the same and I would dress my woman in pleated linen and always have grease on my knife.

"But those forests have disappeared in my own lifetime, though I haven't had the profit from them. Now I make a seaman's living on a ship I do not own. The trees that sheltered the deer and boar are gone, and the wind has scoured away the soil my clan once tilled and left it too thin for farming.

"I will not see those forests I knew again, except as the timbers in English ships or the staves of English barrels or the charcoal in English braziers." His voice rasped harsh with deep and smoldering anger. "The sacred oak of Ireland is burning in English stoves," Ruari Oge said bitterly, watching the land glide by.

His companion, who could tell a similar tale, merely shook his head.

3

A light rain began to fall as the galleys nosed into the secluded
bay of Bunowen, their home port. They would moor near the
landing at Bunowen castle, in sight of the narrow inlet which ran
below the walls of the stronghold. Without the caravel they could
enter the shallows—a fact that did not go unnoticed by the throngs
of people who noted their arrival and hurried to water's edge to
greet them.

Grania never made this approach by sea without imagining a
different approach to a different stronghold, Cuan Mó, the vast
Clew bay she had known as a child.

Closing her eyes for a moment, she let her heart leap across Iar
Connaught to Umhall of the rolling green hills, the rich mantle of
blanket bog, the white heather. Her inward eyes saw once more
the perfect cone of the holy mountain, Croagh Patrick, where the
pilgrims' path had been worn down to bare and sparkling quartzite
by the feet of the faithful over the centuries. She could almost hear
the cries of the colonies of kittiwakes and fulmars and razorbills on
Clare island, at the entrance to the bay. Heightened by memory,
the shimmering expanse of water mirrored the burning blue of the
sky and a fresh wind blew straight in off the Atlantic, riding the
slow swell of the rollers as they came in past Achill head.

Behind her closed eyes, Grania was briefly at home again.

Cuan Mó. The great bay.

As she landed, she was called back to the land of the O Flaherties
and the perpetually angry man who awaited her.

Clustered around the stone walls of Donal's stronghold were a
number of thatch-roofed stone cottages belonging to his servitors
and dependents, small round structures that looked surprisingly
primitive beside the sprawling, spacious castle built in the previous
century by Hugh Mór. Other cottages clung to the flank of Doon
hill and straggled down toward the white-sanded cove to the south,

where the fishermen kept their small boats moored. As the galleys entered the bay, men had hurried to put these boats in the water and help off-load the valuable cargo Grania would be bringing.

But there was no caravel to be off-loaded, and the galleys themselves rode too high in the water to be carrying anything but men.

Grania was the first to climb the stone steps to the narrow landing beside the castle, and a crowd gathered around her immediately, buzzing with questions. Some of them were women whose men were not returning, and she bit her lip and could not meet their eyes. "Not yet," she said aloud. "There is much to tell, but first I must tell it to my husband."

The formality was inarguable, and the crowd fell back to wait for the next person of any consequence who might be more forthcoming. This was Magnus, captain of the second galley, a bluff bearlike man with blue Viking eyes set in a broad-boned Gaelic face. He hurried to catch Grania before she left the landing.

"It's too bad about the caravel," he said to her, coming as close as his nature would allow him to offering sympathy. "I'll speak to these people, if you like. . . . What do you want me to say to them?"

She waved her hand dismissively. "I'll talk to them all myself, later. I'll want to be certain the survivors are doing well and their wounds are tended."

"It was a grand thing you did, saving so many. And almost saving the ship as well," he added on a rising note of admiration.

She hardly seemed to notice. "Magnus, you didn't happen to pick up a boy called Fergal, did you? From the Twelve Bens?"

"I did not. Was he special?"

"Just a country lad," Grania said, fighting back emotion. "No more or less special than any other, I suppose."

"Injured?"

"I think so—his lungs, perhaps more."

Magnus elbowed back some of the people who were crowding too close and filling the air with questions. "The only way you might have saved everyone is if you'd abandoned ship when the fire first broke out. I understand why you didn't, of course. I would have tried to save her myself. But still . . ."

"Still." Grania turned from him and walked with slow, almost blind steps to the narrow stone stairs that led up to the castle above. Fergal. Boy with a face and a name, she was thinking. Boy with his future in my keeping, my responsibility. And somehow I failed him.

The galleys were soon emptied of men. The injured from the caravel were gathered in by the strong arms and ample bosoms of the local women, who gave equal attention to their own menfolk and strangers from distant families. As the names of the missing were discovered, a thin high note of keening speared from the shoreline to Doon hill, a sound that had chilled the blood of generations of seafaring families before them.

Tigernan helped Ruari Oge secure his galley, then came ashore with him. "It's been an ill-omened voyage," Tigernan said to the galley captain. "Did you mark how Grania fled from the sight of the ships? She feels the weight of the dead men like stones on her own grave."

Ruari Oge scratched his wiry beard. "You think she's gone to grieve in private? I can't quite imagine her weeping and wailing over anything—her eyes have always been as dry as ship's biscuit. When we're at sea she's stout as a mainmast, that one."

"She's a woman, for all you say," Tigernan said, his jaw firm.

"Aye, and didn't she put her children out to fostering before they could stand? A woman's not usually that anxious to get away from her children that she takes to the sea to avoid them."

Scowling, Tigernan examined the blisters rising on his forearms and pinched one with a grimy finger. Clear fluid ran across his sooted skin, but he did not wince. "Grania's young ones aren't the bone sticking in her throat," he told Ruari Oge.

"You think she avoids Donal of the Battles, then?" The galley captain smiled to himself, and a light leaped in his hooded eyes. "A man would be a fool to drive a woman like Grania from his bed."

"I thought you found her unwomanly."

"Did I say that? I did not. I compared her to a mainmast, and more than once I've owed my life to the strength of my mast. My words were meant as a compliment. Though I do prefer a female who has a soft side to her nature, like my Evleen," he added.

When his galley was fully secured and all his men safely ashore, Ruari Oge availed himself of the hospitality of the region's one inn, a small stone bruighen with a thatched roof held in place against the western wind by ropes binding it from eave to eave. In Connaught many of the ancient Gaelic customs were still observed, and the bruighen, or free public hostel, was one of these, a testament to the importance of hospitality in Ireland.

The innkeeper, or brughaidh, was bound by Brehon law to keep open house at all times for the entertainment of wayfarers, and the man who kept this hostel—which must be financially supported by the nearest clan chief—had become increasingly busy since sea trade picked up in Bunowen bay. Now sailors appeared at all hours at one of the several doors in the oblong building, always left open by custom. A torch was kept burning night and day at the principal entrance, visible from a long distance and guiding the weary to safe haven.

This was a small bruighen, not to be compared with the gracious compounds of ancient days, but every effort had been made to make it comfortable. Two vats stood in the court, one for ale and one for milk; a tiny bakehouse, dairy, and butchery supplied the tables, and the brughaidh's wife and daughters daily cut fresh rushes to strew the floors.

When Ruari Oge arrived, a peat fire was burning merrily on the hearth and scenting the air with its pungent earth-and-smoke fragrance. The room was filled with conversation and the odor of cooked fish. Tired seamen had already curled into corners or rolled up in their cloaks beneath the wooden trestle tables. Ruari stepped over several of his crew on his way to find the innkeeper and request a bowl of barley ale. He found a bench close to the hearth with only one man on it, a fellow well slumped into sleep. Ruari Oge shoved him to the floor without malice and took his place, after spreading his mantle near the hearth to dry it on the mantle piece, a row of bronze pegs set into a wooden plank.

No sooner was he comfortably settled than he saw Tigernan enter.

Several of Grania's men shouted welcome, but Tigernan made his way to Ruari Oge. The galley chief moved over to make room on the bench for him.

"I thought you'd gone to the castle after Grania," Ruari said.

Tigernan hunched his shoulders and held his hands out to the blaze. "I avoid Bunowen when her husband's there. We get along like a dog and a badger. Besides, if I stay out of her sight for a day or two she may forgive me."

"She always does," his companion remarked dryly.

Tigernan stood up and turned his rump toward the hearth.

"This has not been the easiest voyage of my life, Ruari Oge. Didn't I warn herself she was asking for trouble when she sailed off without remembering the flask of holy water for the prow? But she was too distracted; I think that husband of hers had been crying poverty so loud and long he made her deaf to everything else." He leaned toward Ruari and added in a confidential tone, "Someday I may have to shut that man's mouth for him. He does nothing but cause her trouble."

Ruari Oge grinned. "You appoint yourself Grania's watchdog, my friend, but I tell you she needs none. It's more likely she looks after you most of the time."

"She does not!" the other replied, stung. "Didn't her own father put me into the first galley he gave her? Why do you think he did that, unless he expected me to look out for his daughter? She depends on me, Ruari Oge; she hardly makes a move without me."

"Let me tell you something about women, Tigernan," Ruari offered, stretching his legs and holding up his empty ale bowl to attract the innkeeper's attention. "I've given a bit of thought to them, having lived more years than you. Women are something a man requires, as necessary as air to breathe and ale to drink. I cannot boast of understanding them, mind you, but I suspect nature designed them for a specific purpose, and it would be a mistake to try to change them.

"Women render men an invaluable service that may not at first be apparent. They are born to be responsible, to caretake. It is in them to probe their men as they would examine an old cloak, looking for holes that could let the wind through. Women understand survival better than we do, I think. They will nag and probe and provoke until they find a lowered defense, even the smallest hole, then they poke their fingers through and shout, 'Aha!'

"In this way they force their men to keep their cloaks mended and their weapons in repair, and ultimately this helps them survive. With a woman treading on his heels a man must stay alert and in the proper frame of mind to go out and slay dragons. Never provoke a quarrel with a man who has just had his flaws pointed out to him by some woman."

Tigernan laughed aloud. "What would Evleen say if she heard you? Does she know you think such deep thoughts?"

"Evleen." Ruari's deep voice changed, became almost a whisper. "Evleen is my armor, though I can't expect an unmarried man like yourself to understand that. But I know what I'm talking about; I've had plenty of experience with women, some of them as full of fire as Grania."

"There's no one like Grania. And if you tried to get the best of her you'd do no better than Donal O Flaherty."

All his life Ruari Oge had thrilled to a challenge, and for one quick moment he imagined himself with Grania, his strength and her strength, her will and his will. His eyes grew smoky. Then he shrugged away the vision. "If I were a younger man and there were no Evleen, I might try that big strong woman and see if there is something yielding hidden inside her. I suspect she would give a man a measure for his manhood."

"Bold words. Don't forget she is married to the tanist of the O Flaherties."

"What is that to me? The O Flaherties are no clan of mine, Tigernan; I was born to clan O Donnell of Tirawley and we fear no man. If I wanted Grania I would take her. But as I said . . . another time, perhaps. For now my Evleen fills my bowl to the brim and empties it just the way I like. I can do without Grania."

✠

The large, rectangular hall of Bunowen castle, its walls gleaming with new whitewash, was enriched by numerous luxuries purchased—or pirated—by Grania herself. A massive stone hearth stood at the far end, and in front of this Donal lounged on a cushioned bench, an empty goblet dangling from his fingers. He rolled his eyes as his wife entered but did not straighten up. "Leave us," he ordered the rechtaire, or house steward. Then to Grania, "Why are you back here so soon? Did you have a failure, my skillful sailor?"

"That's a thin bone of greeting to offer me."

"Do you expect me to throw my arms around you?"

She slipped her fingers under her hair to knead the nape of her neck, trying to rub the tightness out of her muscles. "I do not expect that, Donal," she said. "Nor would I welcome it. I'm surprised I ever did."

✠

Their marriage had been a grand event, the joining of two of the most important Gaelic clans in Connaught, Ireland's ancient kingdom of the west. Ui Mháille and Ui Flaithbheartach were families of almost equal prominence in their separate territories. As chieftain of the O Malleys, Owen Dubhdara controlled the region of the two Umhalls and bordering Clew bay. To his south was the land of the Joyces and beyond that the O Flaherty country of West Connaught—Iar Connaught in Gaelic. The northeast shore of Clew bay was held by clan Burke, Anglo-Norman in ancestry but almost totally Gaelicized in habit, heirs to the title of The Mac-William and on amicable terms with clan O Malley.

Umhall included the rich plain of Murrisk, which supported immense herds of small black cattle, all of whose hides were claimed by Dubhdara O Malley as a prerogative of his chieftainship. But his principal livelihood was the sea. With curragh and coracle O Malley clansmen harvested rich catches of herring, pilchard, oysters, lobster, enough to support their families well and have adequate stocks left over for trade as far away as the Welsh ports or Spain. Dubhdara could also load his merchant vessels with leathers highly prized throughout Europe, and with the superfine linen referred to as Irish silk. In addition he exported magnificent Gaelic mantles that became heirlooms in Venice and Florence, and he sold with them such local produce as oats, rye, barley, beeswax, and tallow.

This far-reaching commerce was augmented by selling licenses to foreign captains to allow them to fish in O Malley waters, and was also enhanced by the age-old and semi-respectable trade of piracy. Dubhdara's thirty-oared galleys could dart swiftly from his shoreline's maze of sheltering islands, seize a rich prize, and vanish into the seamist before any retaliation was possible.

The O Flaherties were likewise a seagoing tribe, the major family in the peninsulated region known as Iar Connaught. They were, however, denied access to the area's principal port, Galway city.

Founded by Norman merchants on the site of an early O Flaherty fishing village, Galway city had prospered during the early years of English expansionism in Ireland. But the O Flaherties, furious at being dispossessed of their harbor, had waged unrelenting warfare against the Galwegians ever since. In time the city council had been forced to erect walls around the town to turn back "the fearsome O Flaherties," but the feud between Gael and foreigner continued unabated.

When Donal O Flaherty had come to Umhall to make inquiries

about Dubhdara's unmarried daughter, the Black Oak planned sumptuous hospitality for his guest. Grania watched the preparations with a dubious eye. "Am I going to be pinched and prodded like a cow at the market?" she wanted to know. "I warn you, I won't tolerate it."

"Of course not!" Dubhdara assured her. "You are a noble Irishwoman, you go to no man's bed unless you want to—but I ask you to remember what an advantageous match this would be for our clan. Besides, you are sixteen-summered and have grown up quite uncombed, I'm afraid. Your mother blames me. If some man is willing to take you anyway, you should be thankful. As I recall, the last unfortunate lad who spoke familiarly to you at berrying time got a fist in the belly for his pains." Dubhdara chuckled. "Or perhaps you hit him lower down, now that I think on it. But I hope you will be more courteous to Donal an Chogaidh when he arrives."

"Donal of the Battles?" Grania asked, brightening with interest.

"That's what he is called. He's a famous warrior, though young. In fact, the only thing I know against him is that he neglects the sea which is the O Flaherty heritage in favor of fighting on land. The O Flaherty septs fight continually among themselves, and he is usually in the middle of any good bashing, they say. But surely once he becomes chieftain of the entire clan he'll take his rightful place in the prow of a seagoing galley and resume the family trade, so I hope you'll be, ah, civil to him. You could strengthen the bonds between Umhall and Iar Connaught if you please him."

"Then he should be the one who worries about pleasing *me*," Grania said with a toss of her head. But she was already predisposed to like him. His nickname delighted her. Donal of the Battles. Grania had been raised on the epics her father's ollave poet recited of the warrior Cuchullain and the Red Branch knights; she had thrilled to the battle songs of Brian Boru as played by her father's harper.

When she first saw Donal an Chogaidh, however, she had been disappointed. He sailed into Clew bay with a fleet of shabby galleys, and when he stepped onto the jetty below Belclare he was short. Shorter than Cuchullain or Brian Boru, shorter than Grania. Furthermore, there was a thinness to the young man's lips that Grania definitely disliked.

Donal seemed no more charmed by her than she was by him.

His expectations had been higher than the reality. "She is as ordinary as a toad's toes," he muttered to his retainers. "It's a pity Owen Dubhdara doesn't have another, more beautiful daughter."

Grania's hearing was keen. Her temper flashed. "I was not warned you are so well acquainted with the nether parts of toads!" she snapped at her would-be suitor. "It's a pity you have no familiarity with women. You might like them better."

Donal stared at her in surprise, then let loose a rusty guffaw of laughter that astonished his retinue as much as it did himself. Grania hesitated a moment, then laughed with him, that great whooping laugh of hers that caught everyone up in it and swept them away. Merriment was a stranger to the young man, and for a while he was captivated by the novelty of it. Impressed by the prosperity he saw in Umhall and the numbers of armed men surrounding Dubhdara, he made an effort to appear jovial and at ease, like one of the family. He succeeded in convincing the inexperienced girl. In a few days she forgot to notice he was short, and she began to believe a grand big hero lurked within him.

"You will be twice-married, as your mother and I were," Dubhdara reminded her when it was obvious she was amenable to the match.

"Which bond will hold tightest?" she asked him, her eyes dancing with mischief.

The Black Oak could not help smiling, but he tried to keep his voice serious. "The Church ritual binds you for life, expecting the human soul to surmount all difficulties and remain faithful to its vows," he said. Then the smile broke through into his voice as well. "And the Brehon law protects you in case you prove to be less than saintly."

"I never wanted to be a saint. I'm not sure I want to be a wife, either," she told him. "Donal is charming and tells me we will have a wonderful life together, but . . . but how can I promise to be obedient to him forever? To be . . . just like Mother," she finished in a whisper, dropping her eyes against the sudden anger in Dubhdara's.

"Be careful what you say, girl. You can do no better than to model yourself on Mairgret. You have indeed run wild, but it can't go on forever any more than a good pony can be allowed to remain unbroken, and so wasted. If you want to please me now, you will be a fine and loyal wife to Donal an Chogaidh and raise a brood of healthy children."

If you want to please me, he said. And she had done everything all her life to please him, not out of a sense of obligation but out of love.

"I'll do my best," she promised.

"Your best is better than anyone else's," he replied happily, putting his hand on her shoulder. For a moment he had been afraid the girl would balk and the old occasional feud between O Malley and O Flaherty might renew itself, jeopardizing his freedom of the coastal waters. "The Church will be your guide," he added. "When you are in doubt, just adhere to your vows and put everything else out of your mind. That's what your mother always says."

Playfulness rose in Grania like a seal from the surf. "Which church?" she could not resist asking. "I heard you talking with that German sea captain about the religion of the Protesters the English king has embraced so he could have more than one wife. The German seemed to think that kind of church would replace ours someday. Mother was very upset by the suggestion, but I remember you questioned him about the Protesters' faith. You said. . ."

"I said many things," Dubhdara interrupted her, "but they weren't meant for your ears. I understand neither this thing they call Protestantism nor the English king either, though I tend to pity the man. I hear he is in poor health—perhaps he's being talked to death by all those wives—and fears imminent invasion from France or Scotland or both. But none of that has anything to do with Umhall, not while I live. So put the affairs of foreign princes out of your head and concentrate on your marriage. Your marriages," he had amended, pinching her cheek.

In a private ceremony to which the Catholic priesthood was not invited, Donal and Grania had first shared a plate of oatmeal and salt and heard the Gaelic brehons, or tribal lawyers, recite the conditions of a detailed pre-Christian marriage contract to which both parties had agreed. A harper played, and a poet with a voice like a bell recalled from perfect memory the genealogy of Grania's family to the twelfth generation. The season was Beltaine in the pagan calendar, the season of fertility, and the young men and women of the region cut down the tallest tree they could find and decorated it with ribbons and bells before setting it up outside Grania's door. Dances were held around this potent symbol—and when word came of Grania's first child being born nine months later, the old wives nodded at each other and smiled knowingly.

The Gaelic ritual concluded, Grania wed Donal again in the

chapel of the Augustinian abbey the O Malleys had built near Belclare in the previous century. A beautiful Gothic building with a window of stained glass that cast a rainbow glow upon the faces of the newlywed couple kneeling before the high altar, the abbey was the guardian of St. Patrick's Black Bell, as well as many other treasures. With his shoulder touching that of his bride, Donal an Chogaidh stole furtive looks at the silver candelabrum, the lace altar cloths, the obvious wealth and generosity of those who had endowed the abbey.

When they left the chapel he gripped his new wife's arm very hard, feeling pleased with the day's accomplishment. She whirled toward him instantly and twisted out of his grip with surprising strength; he felt her hard muscles under his hand. "Don't do that," she said.

His proprietary grip had startled her, somehow casting a shadow over the day. Everyone else looked so proud, so happy, she tried to disregard the feeling, yet as she entered Donal's galley and the wedding party on shore cheered and threw flowers, she had an almost irresistible desire to clamber overboard and splash through the shallows to her homeland again, never to leave. Never, never to leave.

Later, of course, she would wish she had.

4

Everyone knew the Black Oak's daughter never cried, but she had had to turn her face into the wind to keep her eyes dry when her new husband's galley cleared Clare island and headed south, for O Flaherty country.

The first sight of Iar Connaught, after pastoral Umhall, would have made a stone weep, Grania thought. Donal's territory was rough, broken land, with more rocks than soil. Lakes puddled everywhere among barren windswept hillocks. A million tiny fields were partitioned by walls built of a million million gray stones, shouting division among the O Flaherty families.

There was no softness to be found in Iar Connaught, and the people it bred were not soft, but as earthy as the brown peat and as enduring as the gray stones. Their land heaved and bucked, pushing the broken bones of its underlying rock through the soil as if crying out in angry protest against the very creation that shaped it.

God's hand had seized and squeezed and crumpled Iar Connaught in ancient time. Having survived such a cataclysm, it was peculiarly immortal.

"Welcome home," Donal an Chogaidh said to Grania.

Home.

Home was to be Donal's stronghold at Bunowen or another at Ballinahinch on the Owenmor river. Trips between the two were usually made by water, the boats following the coastline until they turned into the salmon-filled and pleasant river that meandered toward the sharp peak of Ben Lettery, a finger first glimpsed through trees, pointing at God. A seagull could fly from Bunowen to Ballinahinch in an afternoon, Grania estimated, but a journey overland through the wilderness between the two took many days.

Donal's O Flaherty sept in Iar Connaught was composed of hard-bitten folk who lacked the gift for laughter, Grania thought on first meeting them. They seemed to her both morose and excessively contentious even by Gaelic standards. She was upset to see her new husband revert to the same character once he was back within his own borders. All too soon she found she was living with a very different man from the one she thought she'd married.

She had been only a few weeks in Iar Connaught when the ollave poet in Donal's retinue died and he announced he would not support another. "My money will be better spent feeding and equipping some additional men-at-arms," he told Grania, who had already observed how he devoted his days to feuds and skirmishes.

"But chieftains have always kept poets, Donal. And harpers, and craftsmen . . ."

"Times have changed," he said impatiently. "Those are archaic luxuries, and luxury has worn thin here. Perhaps in Umhall there is still leisure for sitting around listening to bards, but it takes every resource I can command just to maintain my territory against those who constantly nibble at my borders."

Grania had brought a handsome marriage portion with her, her own property under the Brehon law, for a woman of her rank must be able to stand on equal footing with her husband. She had thought then of using her own purse to support a new poet for the sept, but instinct warned her against it. Donal might find a way to get rid of the man and add that money also to his military expenditures.

Then her children began to come, and she was distracted from her growing unhappiness with the marriage. The pleasures of motherhood had come as a revelation to her. When her first son was placed in her arms and his wrinkled, red little face nuzzled for her breast, an outpouring of emotion shook her to the depths of her soul. In a blink the last vestiges of the adventurous child from Umhall disappeared and a passionate, maternal being took her place. The helpless dependency of the new life for which she was responsible left her breathless, as if a great hand had crushed her womb and heart together. She had gazed in wonder at the child— his perfect ears and fingers, the miniature penis that would eventually become a mighty rod for transmitting further life.

Little person, she thought as he fixed his blank blue gaze fiercely on her breast.

This is a separate little person. A miracle!

From that moment her horizons narrowed to embrace her chil-

dren. Every thought and action was considered in light of its consequences to them. The full measure of Gaelic devotion to the next
generation brimmed in Grania, making her forget everything but
what really mattered . . . the children, the children.

Grania inserted the tip of her smallest finger into the baby's open
mouth and felt him bite down on it with surprising strength.
Through the ridge of gum she could feel the unborn teeth. He
tasted his mother's skin, then drew his features into a miniature
scowl and spat out the finger.

Grania laughed with delight. He already knew what he liked,
this one! He was not a part cut off her but someone different, who
must grow in a different direction, with different tastes and hopes
and fears. . . .

The weight of responsibility settled over her. What could she do
for her baby, her son? How could she guide him; how could she
teach him—or spare him—the lessons of life she had learned at
such painful cost?

To be brave. To stand alone. To hide your vulnerability and
follow your own path.

My son, she thought. My immortality.

Sex with Donal seemed to offer him pleasures that eluded her,
but from the first her babies had given her joy—for as long as she
had them, which was not very long.

✠

Now she stood in front of Donal in a castle emptied of children,
and there was nothing between himself and her but a chasm of
bitterness.

"You'd better explain why you're back so soon," he said coldly.
"You hardly had time to get a good cargo, and I was counting on
one. Explain, Grania."

She actually made herself smile at him, though it was a sarcastic
smile. "You know better than to command me to do anything—
and that includes giving you an explanation for my own business.
So I assume you just meant that to be a polite request?" She was
angry, with a cold, deep anger that was not entirely Donal's fault,
yet he must bear the brunt of it as she bore his. "You're always so
polite," she went on in the same sarcastic tone. "Even when you
snatched my children out of my arms you were so very polite about
it."

"Dar Dia!" Donal swore, rolling his eyes. "Are we back to sniffing that stick again? Once I thought you understood."

Grania's body ached; she could scarcely keep her eyes open. But she would not let him see her weakness. "I understood, all right," she told him through teeth clenched on an old wound. "Wasn't I raised in a Gaelic household in the west country myself? When I was no bigger than a tall goose I knew that the head of a noble family might send his children to be raised by other clansmen as foster children, strengthening the ties between clans. The custom knotted our people together long before we were Christian and endures still, and I have heard the brehons chanting the laws governing fosterage, describing every article of clothing that must be furnished a child and every detail of the training the child is to be given.

"I know the custom, Donal. But never did I hear of it being done against the will of the mother who bore the children—never till you insisted on taking my little ones before they were even weaned. You were anxious to form family ties with a warrior whose sword you needed, and you never gave a thought to what I needed. All that was important to you was your wars, your endless wars against this one and that one. . . ."

Donal was not listening at all. He had not listened when she originally protested all those years ago.

"The priests are right in giving husbands authority over their wives," he had shouted at her then, while she pleaded to be allowed to keep her babies with her longer. "The old Gaelic way gave women too much freedom altogether, and you are a fine example of the folly of that custom. I warn you, Grania—you will accede to me in this or I will send you back to Clew bay and denounce you throughout Connaught for a lack of womanly graces. Is that what you want, to be sent home rejected with your shortcomings shouted from the hills?"

"Who would believe such charges?" she had demanded to know, outraged at his unfairness.

Donal's thin lips had smiled a thin smile. He had her in a trap, and he knew it; he enjoyed closing it on her. "Everyone would believe the word of an O Flaherty chieftain over that of the Black Oak's half-wild daughter who never even learned to weave and sew. As you so frequently remind me, we were wed by your clan's request under that same Brehon law which controls fosterage, and by Brehon law our marriage contract can be broken if one side proves to be inadequate."

"You can't put honey on both the top and bottom of your bread, Donal. You can't extol the Christian style of marriage when it serves your purpose only to revert to the pagan traditions when they serve you better," Grania had argued.

But she was still very young, young enough to care what others thought of her. She did not want to be sent home to her parents, set aside and rejected. So Owen and then Murrough and at last tiny Margaret had been gathered into their mother's arms for the final caresses and sent away, each in turn, to capture politically expedient hearts. And having won one skirmish, Donal wanted to win them all, fighting Grania on even the most trivial matters.

She found herself resisting with increasing determination, because her nature would not allow him to whittle her down. In time she had become as wily as he was in finding a weak spot or pressing an advantage—or hiding her own vulnerability.

"I'm going to bed," she announced now in a toneless voice, wanting no further discussion until she had a chance to rest.

"You are not. I want to know what profit you made from your voyage, Grania, and I want to know now!"

"Profit. There isn't any profit. The carvel caught fire and sank in a storm."

Donal leaped to his feet with an expression of genuine shock on his face. "That cannot be! The ship was worth a fortune; it cannot be gone!" The mantle of quilted frieze he wore fell aside, revealing a square, short-statured man quivering with the passion of financial loss.

"Not your fortune," Grania reminded him. "I bought the caravel with my own marriage portion."

"You bought it behind my back, like a rat stealing grain in the dark," he said in the old, surly voice she knew too well. "And you have held out on me ever since, I know it. You've given profits you've made with your seafaring to the sailors who follow you instead of bringing every scrap of it home to your own husband, as a loyal woman would. You've cared more for that ship and the sailing of it then you ever did for me," he went on, "and now you've lost it and done me out of what little share you might have given me otherwise. And I was counting on it, Grania, you knew

I was. You knew I needed new weapons and supplies for my men-at-arms."

Her temper snapped like a burned line on the caravel. "You think I sank my own flagship just to deny you *money*? That act would be more in keeping with your character than mine, Donal O Flaherty! I've given you plenty, both your share and mine, over the years."

"You've left my bed cold and empty while you followed an unwomanly profession," he said, his voice skidding into a whine of self-pity.

"I've gone to sea to help *your* kinsmen," Grania reminded him. "Your cousins, your dependents, your tenants; those who look to you as chief of the sept and have supported you, expecting support in return. Iar Connaught is poor land; its best crop is rocks. If your people are to keep flesh on their bones they have to use the sea as generations of O Flaherties have done before them—but where were you, when you should be leading the fleet? On land fighting, that's where you always were, enjoying your grudges while your people grew more apathetic and poorer every year. You took their young men from them to fight your wars and gave them nothing in return, neither leadership nor hope for anything better."

His mouth flew open in protest, but she would not let him interrupt her now; things had gone too far. Her grief and anger—and a nagging sense of guilt over the fate of the men in the caravel (oh, Fergal!)—combined to spill out of her like boiling oil.

Summoning the power of command-toughened lungs, she shouted at Donal, "Don't you ever dare criticize me for sailing my ships! You and your clan should give thanks on your knees to God that I learned the sea trade from my father."

"Yes, your father," Donal sneered. "I've always known Owen Dubhdara could be blamed for all our troubles."

The skin around Grania's mouth went white, but her husband did not notice. "Dubhdara never tried to come between us," she said, "if that's what you're suggesting."

"You went running back to him!"

"I went to him after my mother died because his kinsman brought word my father was . . . was not himself. And it was true, he was in no condition to captain the fleet. I had little to do myself at the time, you will remember, with my children gone." Her voice was cold; she gave Donal a stony stare. "Was I to fill my days supervising your households when you were away fighting battles and your rechtaires were already perfectly competent at the job?

"So of course I stayed with Dubhdara until he was himself again, and during that time I managed his seafaring enterprises. In gratitude he gave me a galley and crew of my own to keep. And when we encountered that Portuguese carrack on the way to Iar Connaught and rowed into Bunowen bay loaded to the gunwales with pirated treasure, I didn't hear you object. Your men rallied around me then. They didn't care that I was a woman; what mattered was they needed a leader who was adept at using the sea. Once they saw that, they repaired their fishing curraghs and increased their catches, they began preparing wool for trade again, they took *heart*, Donal."

"They had plenty of heart for following me into battle," he said defiantly.

"They can't make a living out of border wars, Donal. Someone has to plant and harvest, whether it's the land or the sea that provides."

"You've turned my own people against me," he accused, not for the first time. "I've heard the whispers. In the bruighen they say, 'She's a better man than her husband.' And you've never understood what I was trying to do, how I was trying to defend my people as best I could, with enemies everywhere." He sank back onto the bench and put one hand over his eyes.

To her astonishment, Grania saw his fingers trembling.

In their years together they had come to blows more than once, and they usually kept a measured distance between themselves now by unspoken agreement. But she could not keep her heart totally hard, no matter what he had done to her. It was not in her nature to do so—a secret she carefully kept from everyone, a lesson learned the hard way. She would reach out even to a savage wolf, if it was in pain.

She stepped within the range of his fists. "What's the matter?"

The face he turned toward her contorted in anguish. "What's always the matter? The blight on our land, the sasanach, the English!"

The English. Again and ever increasingly. The native Gaels and the descendants of the Anglo-Norman feudal lords who had settled in Ireland in the twelfth century were agreed on one issue: their resentment of the heavy hand of the English monarchy. The new breed of English, Elizabeth's English. And now some blow from that quarter had knocked Donal to his knees. Grania had never seen his hands shake before.

Infuriating, heedless, and sometimes cruel, he was nevertheless her husband, bound to her by the real Church. Grania believed Donal to possess a lion's heart for all his faults; she would not deny him that credit. Occasionally his intentions were even good, though they fostered ignoble deeds.

She pulled up a low stool and sat down close to his bench, wishing she did not demand so much of herself.

"I curse the clan Tudor, root and branch!" Donal immediately burst out. "An excommunicated heretic born of an adulterous mating has been six years on the throne of England, styling herself ruler of both that land and this one. How can such a misbegotten person claim sovereignty? Devil's work, the priests whisper, because they no longer dare say it aloud. Elizabeth has set out to complete what her sire, that imp of hell, began—the Reformation of both England and Ireland. Reforming us, Grania!

"Within the protection of the Pale, in Dublin city, she has her Parliament making all sorts of rules they intend to try to force upon us with their governors and administrators. Governors and administrators; the Tudors love those titles. Elizabeth now calls herself the Supreme Governor of the Church of Ireland—can you believe such a joke? As if God reached down and put his hand on her head, anointing her? A *woman?*" He added this last with special emphasis, as if it were the worst crime charged to Elizabeth Tudor's name.

Grania raised her eyebrows. Her mother had never listened to talk of politics, claiming it made her head ache, but Grania was cut from different cloth and all her life had absorbed knowledge like a sponge . . . as Ireland had absorbed the first invaders from England, the Normans, subtly converting them to Gaelic ways. But the new foreigners, the Tudor English, had resisted the land's seductions. They brought over army after army to intimidate the natives, they made laws prohibiting Gaelic clothing and even the Gaelic tongue, and they had added to that the insult of the policy they called Surrender and Regrant, under which the English monarch offered to "give" the Irish their own lands back to them in return for submission by the Gaelic clan chiefs.

In recent years, the hated Surrender and Regrant was more often interpreted to mean the Irish surrendered their lands outright and the English planted colonists on them instead, regranting them to people with no Gaelic heritage. Dispossessed of the kingdoms they had held for two thousand years, the Gaels reacted with shock and often violence. And that violence was met with ruthless oppression in return.

Donal's face mirrored the plight of his people. He groaned like a man who has received a mortal wound as he said, "The English are determined to humble us, Grania. Elizabeth of the Tudors means to grind our faces so deeply into the mud that the Irish will get used to looking up at the English rather than seeing them as equals. They have some terrible need to humble us; I cannot understand it."

His wife's eyes were narrowed in thought. "The Augustinian monks of Umhall, who taught me history in my childhood, explained that when the Romans left England and that land sank into barbarism, it was missionaries from Ireland who took God's words to the British tribes and taught them to read and write.

"Perhaps they hate us, Donal, for being a more ancient and educated race. Perhaps they mean to drag us down by treating us as savages until we do not remember ever having been anything else. And along the way they can take our land from us with a clear conscience because we are only savages and deserve no better."

Donal did not have an analytical mind. He saw things only in terms of himself, rather than with the long range of one who must constantly scan the horizon. "Whatever the reason," he said now, pounding his fist on his thigh, "they are relentless. And now that Tudor woman has gone one step too far. She has dedicated herself to destroying *me!*"

His face was red and he sprayed spittle when he spoke, but there were trumpets of resistance in his voice. Donal O Flaherty might spurn such traditions as having a court poet, but Donal an Chogaidh Ui Flaithbheartach was of the ancient blood, and pride ran hot in his veins.

"Just today," he continued bitterly, "messengers brought me word that Murrough an d'Tuadh O Flaherty, Murrough of the Battle Axes, has been seduced into becoming a bootlicker for the heretic English! When she couldn't defeat him in battle, the Tudor woman found another way to get to him, Grania. He is not of the senior sept of clan O Flaherty and therefore not eligible to be elected to the chieftainship, but to win him to her feet Elizabeth has agreed to declare him *The* O Flaherty in return for his formal submission to her."

Grania gasped as his words pierced the fog of her exhaustion. The O Flaherty, the title designating the chieftain of the entire clan, was Donal Crone, as everyone knew, and upon his death that honor would have gone to the tanist, Grania's husband. The Brehon law that had structured Irish society for two thousand years had governed the election of those men—and with one willful blow the English queen had swept that law aside as if it meant nothing.

The stones themselves must be shuddering, Grania thought. "What will you do, Donal? Surely the clan as a whole will fight such a usurpation of authority."

Donal's expression was somber. "Some septs will fight and some will be bought, to put it plainly, in hopes of being allowed to keep the lands that are rightfully theirs anyway. And you haven't heard all of it. I have also learned that the heretic Elizabeth keeps a fat purse in Dublin for the sole purpose of buying off one clansman and setting him against another! That speaks louder than a pig's squeal about the policy the Tudors mean to pursue in Ireland."

"You will fight." It was not a question.

Donal nodded. "The first step will be to strengthen my defenses here and do whatever I can to consolidate the support of my allies. I'm going to hire all the mercenaries I can, Scottish gallowglasses and disaffected fighting men from other clans. I have always known it would come to this, me fighting to the death to protect my people's heritage." He was pleased with that aspect of it; he stood taller and his voice rang with anticipation. He saw himself as a hero, as Grania had once seen him—before she learned he took his pleasure from the fighting rather than the accomplishment.

"So you see there will be nothing to spare for getting you a replacement for the caravel you lost, in case you meant to ask me for it," Donal added.

"But with another caravel I could help you . . ."

"Do you think another fancy ship would pay back its cost within the year?" Donal interrupted. "Even if it would, I can't afford to have the money tied up. I need all I can get my hands on, for who knows what resources the English can mount against me? Money is power, Grania, and don't forget it. But you can always apply to your father's clan for another ship if you've a mind to; the O Malleys are in a much better position than I am." He hesitated; cunning peeped from his eyes. "Ah, yes, the prosperous O Malleys. . . ."

The weariness Grania had held at arm's length washed over her again, more demanding than ever. "Do what you have to, Donal," she murmured inaudibly, getting to her feet and heading for the doorway. She could absorb no more; she had to get to bed. If she was rested she would be able to find some answers; she always did.

She was almost out of the hall when Donal caught up with her. "Wait, Grania. I'm distraught tonight—this news about Murrough has fallen on me like a flock of ravens so that my eyes are blinded with my own blood. Come back and sit by the fire with me and let us talk of your concerns, as we once did."

She stared at him. Her ears were ringing; perhaps she had not heard him correctly. "When did we ever discuss my concerns?"

"Didn't we? When you first came to Bunowen seventeen years ago? Ah, then, the more reason for you to give me a chance to correct my omission." As he spoke he caught her by the wrist, his fingers pressing on blistered skin. Grania winced in spite of herself, and Donal looked down in surprise.

"You're hurt," he said, frowning as if the sight pained him. "That's a bad burn, but I have some excellent salve in my chamber. You must let me take care of this for you—your attendants have long since fallen asleep in their own beds. And then perhaps we can talk about buying another ship, after you're feeling better."

Grania's head was throbbing like a bodhran. She wanted to reach up and feel the lump on the back of her skull where Tigernan had hit her, but she dared not reveal a second injury to Donal. Yet his hands were gentle, supporting her, and his voice sounded wonderfully sincere as he promised her aid. She allowed him to lead her. Exhaustion and pain had at last broken down her defenses. A small voice warned her that giving Donal any kind of opening was always a mistake, but for the moment she was past caring.

Then they were in Donal's bedchamber, and with his own hands he turned down the linen sheets on the big carved bedstead. Grania lay down in a kind of dazed wonder, trying to remember when she had last lain on that bed and seen those heavy woolen curtains hanging around her, suspended from copper rods that connected the bed pillars.

Donal eased her clothes from her and hung them on the rack of bronze hooks by the foot of the bed. Then his hands were touching her bare skin, smoothing a fragrant salve onto her blisters.

How light his touch was.

She must have dozed, though her skin remained awake and aware, responding to the fingers that sought out and tended every injury. Donal had a talent for single-mindedness. When all his concentration was bent on something, nothing else existed, and so it was now with his care of Grania. He bent over her with the same intensity with which he had long pursued his own ambitions, treating her more solicitously than a trained physician might.

The application went on a long time, while Grania sank deeper into sleep.

The touch of his hands changed.

Donal's fingers cupped her breasts, and then the fingerpads butterflied across her nipples. She squirmed and half lifted one arm, but she did not push him away. Her body and mind were aware of two separate realities. Her body lay on Donal's bed, experiencing a mindless pleasure, and the thinking part of her had returned in a confused dream to the deck of the caravel, where she sought the missing apprentice Fergal. In her dream he had the face of her son Owen.

Donal's hands moved lower on her body, caressing her stomach and thighs, rubbing her flesh with a circular motion that fitted itself to the rhythms of her troubled sleep.

Grania muttered something and rolled onto her side, facing away from him. Donal's hands followed her. He explored her buttocks, patiently insinuating his fingers deeper and deeper into the private parts of her body. If she stirred or made a sound he stopped, but did not withdraw. When she was quiet he resumed again, touching, petting, caressing. He was on his knees on the bed by this time, and he very slowly eased one hand from her body long enough to pull his own clothing aside. Then he lowered himself to lie next to her, pressing against her.

It had been a long time since his body had felt the touch, throughout its length, of hers, and the unfamiliarity excited him. His hips began moving in the same rhythm his hands had established. He rubbed his groin against her and enjoyed the mounting heat, the good hot throbbing that echoed in his temples and pounded through his veins.

Now, *now* they would be joined again, they would be undeniably man and wife, tied with cords of honor and law, bound to aid and support one another. If she at last accepted him into her body again she could hardly refuse him a small request, the sort of request any husband should be able to make of his wife.

He plunged into, her, losing himself in mounting pleasure.

"Murderer," hissed Grania.

5

The unexpected word in the silent room shocked the man into immobility. The spasm of his pleasure drained away. For a moment he could only lie there clutching her; then he flung himself onto his back with one forearm across his eyes.

"What right have you to call me that? I was trying to be kind to you, Grania, to show the concern a husband should show to his wife."

Grania snorted. "You? Kind? That is a change in the wind not to be trusted. You just wanted something."

"Something I never get!" he flung at her.

"Come, Donal, it wasn't my body you desired. I've known you too long and much too well to believe that. You just wanted to be on the top with me on the bottom, the powerful lord and his submissive lady. I would wager the reason behind this sudden spate of affection is to make me feel so wifely I'd be willing to ask the Black Oak to support you in whatever new campaign you're planning. But I won't have my body used as your tool, and I won't draw my clan into your wars."

Donal drew himself into a short tower of offended dignity and got out of the bed, being careful not to touch any part of her flesh on the way. Pacing the chamber floor in agitation, he snarled over his shoulder, "I should have known better than to expect any support or loyalty from you."

"I've never been disloyal to you in any way. I just don't want to involve the O Malleys in your schemes; the Black Oak has tried too hard to remain neutral and keep from encouraging English armies into Umhall."

Donal did not want to talk about Dubhdara O Malley right now. His grievance was more immediate. "You've been disloyal for years!" he cried. "The very first time I left you alone at Ballinahinch while I went to defend our borders you moved into another bedchamber and had a bar put on the door to keep me out when I returned. Is that what loyal wives do?"

"I didn't want you then for the same reason I don't want you now," she told him in a voice chilled with revulsion.

"I should have broken that bar the same night and given you what you deserved," Donal went on, not listening to her. "But I thought it was just a woman's foolishness and you'd get over it. I never expected you would use every possible excuse in all the years since just to avoid my bed. You've always held it against me that I put the children out to fosterage, I know that. And I had every right to force you . . . but I had already learned that the less we were together, the better we got along, so I didn't. Yet I have the right, Grania." He swung toward her. There was a determined set to his jaw.

"The fosterage wasn't the reason," she told him with weary candor. "I never explained because I thought it would put too many rocks in a marriage already full of them, but . . . but I had no stomach, then or now, for being bedded by a deliberate murderer with a kinsman's blood on his hands."

Donal stopped as if his feet had grown roots to the flagstones. "Damn your soul!" he shouted. Red veins appeared in his eyes.

She faced him without flinching. "Deny it," she said in a level voice.

She could almost see the thoughts race across his face like the shadows of clouds scudding across a hillside. "I don't need to deny it, it's all lies," he said too quickly. "My enemies have put these notions in your head, haven't they? To rob me of the support of a good wife."

"Just deny it, Donal," Grania said. "Say the words. Swear to me on the Virgin that you had nothing to do with the murder of Walter Fada."

"I would do it in a blink if I thought you would believe me, but I can see already your mind is closed to me."

He could see no such thing. Grania actually wanted him to be able to deny it, to make something different of the dreary wasteland of their marriage. But she had chosen wisely; Donal would not vow on the Virgin. A thousand excuses, evasions, justifications were racing through his brain as she watched him, and at last in disgust Grania waved them aside with her hand.

"Your sister told me everything, Donal, and Finola is not your enemy. She is one of those who would love you if you would allow it."

"She is another traitor if she ever accused me of that killing!" He was all bluster now, unwilling to give an inch. But Grania bore in on him with the truth. It had been unsaid for too long.

"That first time you left me alone at Ballinahinch castle was shortly after little Margaret was born, you might recall, and Finola came to see her new niece and bring us presents. She kept me company for a while, and on a lonely night when the wind howled around the sharp peak of Ben Lettery your sister drank too much wine. It was then she told me how you had killed her husband's son by his first wife."

"I ought to break her lying neck. And yours too," Donal added, looking as if he meant to suit action to word. But when Grania got to her knees and started across the bed toward him she saw him deflate a little, sucked dry by a guilty conscience.

"Finola thought I already knew the whole story, Donal," she said aloud, "because I was long acquainted with her husband, David Burke, whose lands adjoin O Malley territory. I had known David's son Walter when we were children, before his mother died and his father wed your sister. So I knew that David Burke's title as The MacWilliam was expected to go to his oldest son someday. What I had not known was that Finola coveted the title, and the property, for her own son instead, Richard an Iarainn. So with promises of future MacWilliam support for your clan she bribed you to eliminate Walter Fada, Tall Walter, and the deed was done at Invernan when you and I were but three years married. Shall I go on?"

He was watching her with fascination. "Please do. I enjoy a fanciful tale." There was no enjoyment in his eyes.

Grania shivered a little, looking back into the dark past. "Finola spoke of the murder as if it were a matter of simple necessity, like the autumn butchering. She told me, 'You will understand such things when you have to fight for your own children's position in the world.' "

"Why didn't you say anything about this to me sooner?" Donal wanted to know. "Or have you gloated over your knowledge in secret, cherishing your hatreds? There is a saying, 'Beware the quiet man,' and it well applies to you, woman. If my own sister had kept her mouth well shut, things would have been different."

"She had kept her mouth shut as long as she could," Grania replied, "until the wine made her head swim and the fire of the hearth at Ballinahinch heated her chilled blood. Then, while the wind howled and the rain beat upon the roof tiles, Finola recounted every moment of the slow dying and terrible death of Tall Walter Burke.

"And from that night until this, every time you tried to touch me I could hear her voice describing you chasing a mortally wounded man up the staircase at Invernan, hacking at his legs with an ax and slipping in the poor man's blood. And you were *smiling*, Donal. She said that again and again, a horror even she could not accept. You *smiled*, and when all that was left of Tall Walter was a legless ruin shorter than yourself, he fainted from agony and you threw water on him to revive him so he would be awake for his own dying. You watched every moment of his torture. And you smiled."

The truth so bluntly told was mirrored on Donal's face. He could not deny it now, even if he dared. "You don't understand," he managed to say. "A chieftain . . . there are things that must be done . . . political alliances for the good of the whole that are more important than one man's life."

He spoke with the earnest passion of one who believes what he says, and this sickened Grania still more. She eased out of bed and pulled on her discarded clothes while he tried, too little and too late, to justify himself. Keeping her eyes fixed on Donal's face, she circled toward the door of the chamber.

"Where are you going?" Donal suddenly demanded. "Are you leaving me again just because my miserable sister is such a liar?"

"You are very quick to accuse others of lying, Donal. An insect knows another insect," Grania said wearily. "But our life together has become one long, angry shouting match, so I would have left you even if this were not between us. Let Richard an Iarainn have his title when his father dies—it was bought dearly enough. I don't care, I don't even know him. But I know you all too well, and I want nothing to do with you."

She turned and slipped out the door. Her exhausted brain was only mildly curious as to whether he would try to stop her. And what she would do if he did. One foot in front of the other, she made her way down the passage that seemed as long as a river, until at last she turned a corner and was out of sight of the chamber door. Then she paused to lean her back against the cool stone wall and gather her strength.

"No matter what you say, you'll never shame me into buying an expensive ship for you!" Donal suddenly yelled after her.

In spite of herself, Grania chuckled. Then she threw back her head and laughed. Oh, Donal. You never disappoint me.

She made her way to her own bedchamber, and when she was safe inside it she barred the door.

The strong walls of Bunowen should have comforted her, but they did not. This was not a home, but Donal's armed camp. His, not hers. She knew every pace of land at Bunowen. In the earliest years of her marriage she had stalked restlessly through chapel and chamber, climbed nearby Doon hill and wandered along the white sand beach in the harbor beyond. The only part of Bunowen she had thought of, for a time, as her special place was the thatch-roofed haggard where grain was stored. Donal kept his hunting hawks there, and when she first entered the storehouse she felt as if she had come into a private kingdom inhabited by kindred souls. In golden, dust-moted light, the hawks stood proud on their perches, ignoring the hoods that blinded them. Above their imprisonment. She talked to the birds and brought them bits of meat, and after little Margaret was taken from her she spent much of every day in their company. As a child she had enjoyed falconry with Dubhdara, but in time the company of Donal's birds began to depress her, and she visited them no more. She saw a calculated cruelty in the release of captive birds to soar, only to summon them back to be enslaved again by jesses and force of habit.

Her marriage to Donal was her cage, but it was bearable as long as she had the sea, the empty sky into which she soared whenever she could.

Grania climbed onto her bed without bothering to undress again. She lay with a blank mind, waiting for sleep, but her eyes refused to stay closed. At last she sat up groggily and began removing her clothing after all, thankful she was not laced into female apparel.

Every movement was an effort. Her fingers were numb; it seemed hard to breathe. If only she were out of this oppressive stone-walled box and on the deck of a ship once more!

At sea she felt invigorated and intensely alive. The keen sharp air melted through the walls of her lungs, filling her like new blood, salty and clean. A running tide and a freshening wind demanded her body be nimble. At sea Grania was eager and buoyant.

On land she felt heavier, slower. Her strong feet with their splayed toes were ideally shaped to give her stability on a rolling deck. When she thrust them into leather boots they became cramped and clumsy, like a duck's beautifully designed paddling foot transformed into awkwardness on land.

Feet, she thought. Sea legs. When you pass the last spit of land and commit to the ocean, you are taking a step into the infinite and might set your foot down anywhere.

She smiled at her own foolishness as she slipped beneath the embroidered coverlet and felt the featherbed form itself around her. Feet do not really take giant steps over the sea, she reminded herself, snuggling down. Only your heart can do that, like a dolphin leaping free.

Grania slept naked. She liked her skin to breathe as she slept, not encumbered with a gown that would twist and bind. She lay awake a few moments longer, letting her eyes roam unfocused around the bedchamber. She did not really see the narrow room, the glazed window in its embrasure, the Flemish tapestries brightening the walls . . . or the treasures she had claimed for herself from looted vessels, the Florentine goblets, the gold Portuguese casket for jewels she never wore.

Drifting at last into sleep, Grania saw other scenes looming from the shadows of memory and briefly took refuge in the past—in the free, archaic way of life that was dying throughout Ireland, beyond the walls of Bunowen.

✠

In summer Dubhdara's family and retinue had always left Dún Béal an Chláir, the Fort at the Mouth of the Plain, and headed for the uplands to graze their herds and live as one with the wind and weather. Summer was the booleying-time; time for breathing pollen-heavy air and listening to the contented lowing of the cattle, while the more musical members of the O Malley entourage serenaded them with pipe and harp. They built simple, seasonal shelters of wickerwork and slept on three-layered beds of branches, moss, and rushes, close to the earth, while stars wheeled in the night sky. During the day they took their meals whenever hunger seized them, using sweet green ferns for both table and napkin.

Everyone went barefoot. Even fastidious Mairgret bowed to the customs of the season and, dressed in a homespun kirtle dyed with saffron, searched the meadows for poppies and St. Daboec's heath.

Mairgret amused herself by weaving flowered garlands around the necks and horns of her husband's black cattle.

Her daughter, meanwhile, had run unchecked under the summer sky, skipping over broad brown cowpats that hid like crusting puddings amid the grass and daisies. Soft wind blew, rain misted the air. Thistles sprouted purple crowns.

Because the sea provided his principal livelihood, Dubhdara often returned to the shores of Clew bay to check on his fishing fleet and inspect the latest catch of herring before they were salted and packed in barrels to ship to Spain and Portugal, in exchange for wine and iron and European luxuries much desired by his fellow Gaelic chieftains. He also kept watch over his other strongholds throughout Umhall, and visited the island of Cliara, or Clare, in the mouth of the bay, where he had built a fortresslike tower house. As she grew older Grania accompanied him on these journeys, riding in the prow of the chieftain's galley with salt spray frosting her hair and her eyes shining.

Booleying-time was part of the cycle of the seasons, as old as the history of the Celtic Gaels themselves. Theirs was a culture intimately involved with the earth and its produce; cattle and crops and fishing had imprinted their rhythms onto the nature of the people, shaping a way of life that demanded hardiness but encouraged longevity. Many of Grania's kin lived to see ninety summers.

But there was another, less pastoral side to Irish life. Dubhdara and his peers were the noble descendants of a heroic Bronze Age warrior society defined and circumscribed by the requirements of honor. Men proved their manhood by defending and enlarging their clan's territory, and battle had been as integral an element of Irish society as cattle-raising for the last two thousand years. Even several centuries of Viking invasion, of rapine and pillage, had not disturbed that order, and after the Vikings suffered their ultimate defeat at the hands of the Irish High King, Brian Boru, those of their number remaining in Ireland had merely been woven into the cultural fabric.

So it had been and so the Irish thought it would always be— until the coming of the Norman mercenaries in the twelfth century, and the beginning of England's long struggle to dominate her neighbor.

There had been an English presence in Ireland for centuries before Owen Dubhdara was born, yet at that time much of the land was still only nominally under any form of foreign authority. In its far reaches Erin remained Gaelic and free. Various Anglo-Norman warlords had settled in and built their own feudal kingdoms throughout the island, at a safe distance from the taxing English monarchy that first sent them to Ireland. The land had become a patchwork held by native Gaelic princes or by Norman nobility who had eventually embraced both Gaelic customs and language. And the two sides were almost evenly matched in their struggle for dominance.

Now, in the year 1564, the Tudor ascendancy was forcing a dramatic change in this static situation. The absolutism of Henry VIII and then his daughter Elizabeth had combined with the vigor of the Renaissance, giving rise to a nationalistic fervor in England that would no longer tolerate the stalemate across the Irish sea. The intention to complete the conquest of Ireland, an idea that had become almost dormant while England was preoccupied with troubles elsewhere, sprang back to life. The Tudor monarchy set about tightening its grip throughout the island by appointing new administrators and adopting strict new policies intended to make Ireland the first colony of an empire—an empire to rival the holdings of Spain in the New World, in time.

As a child on the shores of Clew bay, Grania O Malley had been insulated from the winds of change beginning to sweep Ireland. She had grown to maturity in the old Gaelic world soon to be lost. It was a world she would remember, ever after, as having been suffused with a silvery glow like the sea light on Cliara.

✠

In her dreams she still retreated to that world. Lying in her bed at Bunowen, the taut, tough woman with the weathered face thought she heard the seabirds calling, far out over Clew bay.

She smiled a gentle smile in her sleep.

By the next morning Donal's temper had worsened. Grania awoke to the sound of him shouting in the passageway, "Never! Do you hear me?" and by the time she had dressed and reached the hall he had left the castle.

The rechtaire told her, "Your husband had worked himself into a fine lather before cockcrow this morning. His attendant says he did not sleep at all last night, but barred his door and could be heard swearing behind it. When I first entered the hall he was surrounded by men-at-arms and had already collected his weapons, saying he would never accept the authority of the Tudor she-king and threatening all sorts of attacks upon her agents." The man frowned in anxiety. "Do you suppose he will go so far as to attack The O Flaherty, the new one? He might try to persuade Donal Crone to go into it with him, though Donal Crone is well past his prime. At any rate, he gathered up all the fighting men he could and rushed out of here without even leaving me any instructions, so what am I to do?"

Poor Donnchad, Grania thought. How hard it was to uphold the dignity of his calling when his lord treated him with such neglect. "It will be all right," she assured the steward aloud. "This isn't the first time Donal has gone off at the gallop and left us to fend for ourselves. But I don't think even Donal, reckless as he may be, would attack Murrough of the Battle Axes without first taking time to rally all the support he could get. So he's probably gone to do just that, and he'll be back." She paused as an idea occurred to her. "In the meantime, Donnchad, I think you had better be certain we have a season's supplies within the castle walls, just in case some of Donal's enemies think it safe to attack him now that he's no longer the tanist."

The rechtaire hurried from the room to reassure the other members of the staff responsible for running Bunowen, "Things will be all right. *She's* in charge."

An air of relief pervaded the castle.

Late that afternoon Tigernan appeared at the entry gate. He came sauntering from the nearby cluster of stone cottages as if he were on the most casual of outings, and identified himself to the gatekeeper though that man had passed him through numerous times before.

Tigernan often put in an appearance when Donal O Flaherty was away.

Grania greeted her erstwhile first mate with a ferocious scowl. "What, you mean you're still alive? Didn't I throw you overboard as you deserved, you rascal?"

Tigernan grimaced. "You did, I remember it distinctly. I must have bobbed back up and floated in on the tide. So I came to see if you had any orders for me."

She surveyed him up and down, from his freshly braided hair to his reasonably clean tunic and trews. He had made an effort with his appearance for her sake, but neither of them acknowledged it. "You look as if the tide washed you up," Grania said. "But since you're here, you might as well come in. We're shorthanded at the moment, since Donal went off in a cloud of dust and took most of the guards with him. At least if I put you to work with a spear in your hand I can be confident you haven't gone aboard some other ship and deserted me."

"I thought of it," Tigernan replied, sucking his teeth.

"I wouldn't miss you," she answered amiably.

As the sun sank low in the western sky, Grania summoned Tigernan to share a bowl of buttermilk with her in the hall before finding sleeping accommodations for himself among her guardsmen. The day had been long and unusually hot, with summerlight glaring off the water and sumerheat lying heavy on the grass. Buttermilk was a favorite beverage among the Gaels in warm weather, and the Bunowen dairy provided an ample supply.

Tigernan could not help swaggering, just a little, when Donnchad came for him. He felt the eyes of the other guardsmen on him and took great pride in being singled out; in being so special Grania sought his company as she would seek the company of one of her own rank. They did belong to the same class, he thought. They were seafarers, a close brotherhood.

Yet otherwise the bar of status lay like cold iron between them, forcing Tigernan to keep his private dreams very private indeed. Sometimes he thought that was enough for him, for he was a simple man and easily contented.

Sometimes what he could never aspire to tortured him.

The buttermilk was served in olivewood bowls. "I thought this might taste good to you," Grania greeted him, holding out a bowl. The day had been long and lonely, her only companions the castle servitors and her female attendants—women with whom she had nothing in common. Tigernan seemed, at such times, like an extension of herself. They had shared so many experiences; she could talk to him in the truncated language of those who had been together a long time and spoke from fragments of common memory.

Grania laced her buttermilk with sea salt and peppercorns. From time to time Tigernan dipped chunks of black bread in his, afterward wiping his fingers on a hand napkin, a habit he had learned by watching Grania. Tigernan had not been raised in a chieftain's house; the few formal manners he possessed were painfully acquired through imitation. "This is a grand treat," he sighed appreciatively, blotting a thick white rim from his mustache. "We had no cows and so no buttermilk on Inishbofin when I was a lad, and I love the stuff. I think I could even drink it hot."

She grinned. "Then give me back your bowl and I'll have someone put it in the kettle for you. We spare no effort to please our guests."

He gripped the bowl firmly. "I'll thank you to leave my milk as it is."

They sat comfortably together as light faded in the hall. Attendants brought in candles and torches of bog pine while Grania and Tigernan talked of various schemes for financing a new caravel, of crewmen and sailmakers and fishing season—or occasionally fell silent together and just listened to the sounds of the sea coming in through the open windows.

A knot had begun to relax in Grania's stomach. At last she brought up the subject of the Tudor overthrow of chieftainly succession, and Tigernan admitted he had already heard rumors beyond the walls of the castle. "I cannot understand," Grania said, "how a foreign monarch can overthrow our own laws and customs and take a man's future away from him with one stroke. If the elected chieftain of a major clan like the O Flaherties can so easily be set aside, it means Donal an Chogaidh has lost the rank of tanist too . . . and then what power do the clans have left to determine their own course?"

"Donal must be wild with anger," Tigernan commented.

"There are no words to describe it. And for once, I have to agree with him. He sees this mainly in relation to himself, as a personal affront to him, but I see something much larger happening. If the English she-king can overthrow clan authority, she can also strip our children of any inheritance we might try to give them. How can we provide for our young in such a world? What is certain? It's like being blind when a storm is coming; you don't know how to trim your sails for it and you can't begin to estimate its force until you feel it hit you."

Tigernan squirmed uncomfortably on his bench. "Too many changes," he complained. "Every day we're being hit in the face with something new. I haven't even gotten used to the idea of there being another land on the other side of the ocean, though I've heard enough jabber about it in the harbors. But a New World? Can such a thing really exist?"

"I suspect it does," Grania told him. "And because it does, there will be more changes than we can even imagine. But this problem with the Tudor woman is more immediate. Oh, I'm not worried about Donal, even if he has lost his rank as tanist. He will continue the same as before, only angrier, lashing out at everyone. But what of my sons? What of Owen and Murrough, who are growing beards by now, and what of little Margaret, who will bear children of her own someday? I've worked harder than any foremastman to bring back a measure of prosperity to their sept so they would be assured of a good future. Now what will happen? Will the Tudors strip us of everything?"

This was the second time recently Tigernan had been reminded of Grania's children, and he had to stretch his imagination to picture her in a maternal role. He had never witnessed that aspect of her nature. To him she was first the Black Oak's daughter, Granuaile, and then a unique being who had set herself apart from the rest of her sex by virtue of her adventurous nature. In so doing she had enlarged Tigernan's ideas of womanhood far beyond cottage and children. The puzzle of Grania's personality seemed to defy unraveling, thus ensuring his fascination.

He found it very difficult to stay away from her.

Now he sat with her in Donal O Flaherty's hall letting her unburden herself to him as she did to no one else. When she began to yawn he excused himself and went off to find a bed on a straw-filled pallet between two snoring guardsmen.

Sometime in the darkest watch of the night he dreamed a disturbing dream about falling off the edge of the world.

The next day Grania summoned Tigernan and gave him the mission of finding her scattered crewmen. "Take this purse," she instructed him. "It contains all the money I have on hand, coins of fine honest Irish silver and a few coins of bastardized English copper. Divide them among my men and see that an extra share goes to the survivors from the caravel. Tell them all . . ."

"Tell them what?"

She was staring into space. "Tell them to be prepared to sail again soon. I don't know what Donal is likely to do. Anything might happen. They can go their homes for now, but ask them to wait for word from me."

✠

A period of waiting ensued for Grania as well. Donal did not return within a few days, nor did he bother to send back any word. She spent much of her time at the water's edge, inspecting her fleet or staring moodily at the bay. Waiting.

To Donnchad she remarked, "He's been gone long enough by now to have reached clan Ui Laidhigh and rallied the O Lees around him."

"That family has furnished physicians to the princes O Flaherty for centuries," the rechtaire replied, ever mindful of the social order.

"They have that—but they are good fighters, too. If Donal is waging war somewhere he will need allies. . . ." She fell silent.

The uncertainty of the situation oppressed her.

Sea and sky blurred together as if swept by a careless hand. Dark hummocks of land rose from the shallow bay at low tide like the backs of emerging sea monsters. And from the west came the wind, the prevailing wind that buffeted all of Connaught and taught even little children to walk leaning into it, forever setting themselves against an implacable force.

Days passed. Sometimes Grania sent for Tigernan to share a meal or engage in a conversation about commonplaces—to fill the void of waiting with a predictable voice.

Eventually Donal returned, followed by a band of travel-stained warriors with grimy faces but the light of triumph in their eyes.

"Did you strike a blow against the she-king's authority?" his wife asked him, looking over his shoulder and recognizing familiar faces from the clan O Lee among his followers. That surmise had been right, then, she thought with satisfaction.

Donal wore a heavy leather tunic scarred with sword cuts, and an iron helmet was still jammed down on his skull, insulating him from her questions. He worked off the helmet and rubbed the angry red line its weight had made on his forehead. Grania took a step back from him; like all his band, he bore the smell of a man who had marched long, fought hard, and not washed in many days.

"I couldn't find anyone who would admit to sympathies for Elizabeth," he told Grania as he unsheathed his sword, ran an appraising finger along its nicked blade, and put it back again. "But The O Lee told me of his suspicions about several septs of clan Joyce, those most close to his own borders. The Joyces like to claim descent from some Welshman who settled in Galway generations ago, but in truth they are just Anglo-Normans like the thieves who originally locked the gates of Galway against the O Flaherties. I would not be at all surprised to hear of them siding with the Tudor English; bones and offal come from the same carcass."

"You attacked the Joyces?" Grania asked in some surprise.

"Indeed we did!" Donal was positively cheerful. He had taken the edge off his anger by fighting; it did not really matter that he had not challenged an English army on the field of battle. He had fought; that was what was important to him.

"When we went after the Joyces, we learned that a band of them was trying to take over a stronghold well within O Flaherty territory, on an island in Lough Corrib. The thieving magpies! That was proof enough for me that they are in league with the Tudors; they're all grabbing Ireland by the handfuls now. So with my friend Dermot O Lee at my back I marched on Lough Corrib and reclaimed the fortress, and I myself placed the O Flaherty banner atop the roof. It was a fine victory. We beat those thieves into the earth. They at least will not challenge the authority of my clan for a while."

One of the O Lee warriors, a hollow-eyed, hard-muscled man, cried out, "We renamed the place Cock's Castle in honor of Donal an Chogaidh, who surely fought as fast and furiously as any fighting cock."

The flattery hit its mark. Donal beamed. He puffed up his chest and bobbed his head, and for a moment Grania thought he did indeed resemble a fighting cock: a proud, angry, tough little rooster, forever battling.

But he could make an enemy out of anyone, and so in the long run his battles accomplished nothing, no matter how just the original cause behind them. Like a loose cannon aboard a ship, he was not properly aimed.

Perhaps we do not dare take proper aim, Grania said to herself. How much power does the English she-king have? Is it already too late to shrug her off our shoulders?

✠

Flushed with success, Donal was soon filled with plans for new campaigns. If other O Flaherty septs accepted Murrough of the Battle Axes as clan chieftain, Donal would wage war on them as traitors, he declared. The line would be drawn; the Gaelic lords must fight for their patrimony.

Some of them would. As Donal had predicted, some of them would not, and messengers brought word of first one and then another who accepted the outstretched hand of England in what must surely be misplaced trust. Suspicion lay like dust in the hall of Bunowen, and an undercurrent of anger was building in the passageways.

The O Lees were very much in evidence. There was loud talk late into the night of deeds to be done on the battlefield, of this group or that which was not to be trusted and must be taught a lesson at sword's point. Men-at-arms slept among the weeds outside the castle walls and caused a great commotion in the cottages for several miles around. Arguments became more frequent among warlords and their followers alike about the question of leadership. Every man had a different idea about the best way to deal with the problem, and every Gaelic noble had his own coterie who were loyal to him but not eager to take orders from someone else.

All this, because a woman in a faraway land had signed her name to a piece of paper. Elizabeth R.

Grania felt a mounting anxiety. A fated inexorability seemed to characterize the advance of the English through Ireland, bringing out the worst in the Irish themselves as a plague brings out the worst in its victims.

The Tudor regime seemed determined not only to reform religion in Ireland but to rip the very soul out of the Irish people, overthrowing their laws and traditions, denying their very history. And the motive power behind this policy was a woman, a fact Grania found disturbing.

And interesting.

Elizabeth was not a queen acting as consort for her lord, but a female king with all the powers inherent in that station. This brought a new element of uncertainty to the one surety of Gaelic tradition, the patriarchal rule of a chieftain. Not since pagan times had Ireland seen women in positions of authority. In such a reversed world anything might happen.

Grania had only to consider her own situation to see how easily traditions were overthrown. When she remembered her contentedly domestic mother, she saw that a distance more vast than that between England and Ireland separated herself from Mairgret.

Grania had created a way of life her mother could never have understood. She had begun it as a result of circumstance and frustration, but she had succeeded through her own stubborn will.

That was the secret; that was how things were accomplished. Someone just went and did them, refusing to be deterred as Grania had refused to be deterred from the day she commanded her first galley. The sensation had been one she would never forget. When the vessel surged forward at her command, impelled by oars bent to her bidding, she had felt her soul in her body like wine brimming in a cup, full-flavored, translucent as rubies.

Was that what Elizabeth felt when she sent out orders to her officers in Ireland and bent the Irish people to her will?

The arguments over leadership were growing more heated, and Donal felt the clan O Lee turning away from him. He had no gift for winning hearts, but he knew what the O Lees loved: hunting. So he organized a party to take Dermot O Lee and his retinue into the mountainous region of Sléibhte Mhám, where wild boar and red deer would prove handsome trophies for their spears. Men who hunted together could be held together, for a while, he reasoned.

Once they had departed, Grania's thoughts returned to her own enterprise. Whatever happened, the sept would need sea trade. Commerce or piracy were the choices, and she opted first for commerce, if she could get her hands on another vessel like the caravel.

She sent for Tigernan. "While Donal is away hunting we will have a quiet time here, and I mean to make use of it by organizing a quick voyage to Clew bay. Dubhdara has caravels; perhaps I can make a business arrangement with him for the use of one."

"He's your father—won't he just give you one if you ask him?" Tigernan inquired.

Grania's eyes were suddenly cold. "I never ask the Black Oak for *anything*," she said in a strange voice.

Tigernan took the news to Ruari Oge straightaway. "It's time we got busy," the grizzled captain said. "Clew bay, is it? O Malley territory?"

"From the way you're grinning I would say you're pleased."

"And shouldn't I be? Men are cheerful in Umhall, and women flirt their saffron petticoats at sailors. There is always music being played somewhere on the shores of Clew bay, which is more than you can say for Iar Connaught these days."

Tigernan was amused. "Your smile when you mentioned the

saffron petticoats makes me think you need a visit to the confessional."

His friend did not take offense, but claimed, "My soul is as spotless as a new sail. I attend Mass just as faithfully as you do, Tigernan, and I'm as good a Christian."

"Yet you married an unbaptized woman," the other reminded him.

Something gentle and peaceful glowed for a moment from the old pirate's eyes. "Evleen," murmured Ruari Oge.

Tigernan left him and Magnus preparing for a voyage and returned to the castle just in time to encounter a somber party approaching with a cloaked body carried on linked shields.

6

Tigernan broke into a run, reaching the entry court in time to get a good look at the set, angry faces of the men who followed the body on its makeshift bier, and to recognize the cloak of the man they carried. The O Flaherty colors were sodden with blood.

"What happened? What happened?" Tigernan asked of each face in turn, but no one answered him. The castle door within the arched portal creaked open, and Donnchad emerged. One quick glance told the rechtaire all the story he needed to know, and he turned with self-conscious grace in this historic moment to summon his chieftain's widow.

Grania came to the hall at once. She did not seem to notice Tigernan there, though he had trailed in behind the entourage. She watched silently as the men carrying the body lowered it onto the trestle table in the center of the room. They stepped back then, and the O Lee chieftain, Dermot son of Lorcan, cleared his throat.

Grania waited. Dermot was an iron-gray man with lean, ascetic cheeks and a naturally grieving mouth. His tone was sepulchral.

"Murdered by his enemies," Dermot announced. "Slain by a foul hand, Donal O Flaherty; he that was by no means the worst son of a chieftain in Connaught. A man who never let a wrong go unavenged; he that made his allies' enemies his enemies. He will be missed in the meadhalls and bewailed on the battlefields."

Grania spoke for the first time. She had a pinched look around the nostrils, but was very much in control of herself. There would be no weeping and wailing from the Black Oak's daughter. "Name me the murderers, Dermot O Lee," she requested. "If the Tudor she-king herself put a spear in my husband's heart, I will pluck it out and drive it into hers." Grania knew the forms appropriate for a slain chieftain's widow.

Dermot plucked at the fringe of the cloak outlining the uninhabited hills and valleys of the dead man's body. For a moment it seemed he might twitch the cloth back and uncover Donal's face, but then he recovered himself and dropped his hand to his side. "The English did not do this," he said. "A Joyce javelin, thrown from cover, struck Donal down. We identified the weapon by its engraving, but the man who threw it has escaped—for now."

Grania took a step toward him. "You exonerate the English, do you? Did not you yourself hint of English sympathies on the part of the Joyces, encouraging Donal to march against them in the first place? Did you think he would run them from their lands and allow your clan some of it, perhaps?"

Dermot looked dismayed. "You can't charge his death to me! My clan and the O Flaherties are as close as the two fingers on your hand! I have already sworn a vow to track down his killer and slay the man myself."

Her smile was bitter, and the effort it required hurt her face. "Do that, Dermot. Then his people will come after yours, and your allies will attack his . . . and meanwhile the Tudor she-king sits like a spider at the center of her web, growing stronger as we weaken each other."

He does not understand, she thought, watching his face. Like Donal, he thinks in terms of regional wars and border squabbles, of titles and rank. He is a land man; he sees no farther than the next clump of woods. If he spent much time on the open sea he might learn to look to the far horizon.

She insisted on the full rites of a fallen warrior for her husband. The respect she had ceased to accord Donal in life she would at least give him in death. Funeral games were held in his honor, and a great feast was served in the halls of both Bunowen and Ballinahinch, one so sumptuous that the uneaten remnants fed Donal's nearest tenants for a week.

"How he would have yelled at that expense," Grania remarked to Donnchad. The rechtaire drew himself up in silence, shocked by levity during such a solemn time. Grania fought back a desire to say something more outrageous still and left him alone with his professional dignity.

She would not have Donal waked for twelvenights, as had been done for the great Brian Boru. She knew all too well the measure of her dead husband. But torches burned around him for three nights and three days while mourners keened, and the priests rang the death knell to mark the canonical hours. After Donal was put in his tomb, Grania ordered his bier burned according to Gaelic custom so the Little People, the sidhe, would not use it to carry off his corpse at night to frolic with them.

"Though the idea of Donal frolicking with anyone is beyond the reach of my imagination," Grania confided to Tigernan.

Lacking Donnchad's sense of the proprieties, Tigernan was free to laugh. Grania's lips twitched for a moment, and then she laughed with him, throwing back her head for a good hearty bellow.

"Dar Dia, that felt wonderful!" she said at last. "My belly aches and I'm getting hiccups, but it was worth it."

She should have felt guilty, she supposed—laughing while Donal was still cooling in his tomb. Perhaps she had become as hard as everyone thought. But no—she had only to think of her children to know the capacity for loving was still alive in her. Owen. Murrough. Little Margaret. Then briefly the Black Oak's face flitted through her mind with those other loved images.

Tigernan saw her stiffen as if from pain. Misinterpreting the cause, he tried to help. "You don't have to pretend to be more grief-stricken than you are about your husband," he said solicitously. "Not with me. I know how things were between you. And now he's gone off again, in a way, and left you defenseless one more time."

Her eyes flashed. "I'm never defenseless, Tigernan."

"Not as long as you have me."

"Not as long as I have myself." Her eyes saw through him, discounting him, and Tigernan suffered his own pain. But he stood his ground and stayed beside her, grateful for what he had, never really hoping for any more.

"You remind me that it's time to look ahead," Grania told him. "We have to make plans. When my oldest son reaches his seventeenth year his fosterage is formally over and he will be counted a man, expected to move into his father's stronghold and take up his father's responsibilities.

"A struggle for power in Iar Connaught is a certainty, now that Donal Crone is deposed and many septs are refusing to honor Murrough of the Battle Axes as chieftain of the clan since they did not elect him. My sons will be drawn into that fight, Tigernan—it's inevitable.

"They will need all the support I can give them . . . and so will

Donal's sept." She had borne her husband's burdens while he lived, and she was a chieftain's daughter; she would not set them aside now. But she would take something for herself, she could do that much. She would at least live where she liked.

"I've been thinking hard about this, Tigernan," she said, "And I've decided I could ply the sea trade more effectively out of Clew bay than I can here at Bunowen. I can continue to take O Flaherty men on my boats and to ship O Flaherty produce, but I will also have my base farther away from English eyes. If my sons pit themselves against English authority in Iar Connaught, that could be a blessing."

Tigernan was pleased. "You never fitted among the O Flaherties," he told her frankly.

"And who are you to judge, you bandy-legged scoundrel who belongs nowhere and so contents himself with walking on my heels?"

Picking his teeth with a sliver of wood, Tigernan replied amiably, "I have nothing better to do."

Donal's kinsmen and dependents, the cousins and nephews, the warriors and craftsmen and farmers and tenants on the sept's land, were shocked by the news that Grania was leaving. A chieftain's widow should stay soberly in place, waiting for a relative of the dead man to marry her. But Grania had no intention of doing that, for by such an action she would be introducing a rival to her sons' claims to Bunowen and Ballinahinch, to the small measure of prosperity she had managed to preserve in the southern tip of Connaught, in the land of the late Donal an Chogaidh.

As quickly as possible, she removed her belongings from the castle beside Bunowen bay and made ready to sail northward. O Flaherty men who had shipped with her before flocked around her, assuring her they wanted to continue in her service. They could send money back to the stone cottages and the stony fields, but they had to go where a man could make a living. Donal, uninterested in the sea himself, had made no arrangements to have his sons trained for it. "The sea will be used only for fishing when you are gone," Donnchad told Grania. "There are no great traders among the O Flaherties in this generation."

As her galleys were being loaded, Grania turned her back on the sea and took one long look at the land of Iar Connaught. I could have loved it here, she thought. It might even have seemed beautiful if everything had been different.

If Donal had been different.

If I had been different.

At low tide the galleys swung in lazy indifference on their hawsers. Grania noticed that their red-and-black paint was peeling.

"Inactivity is no better for them than it is for me," she remarked to Magnus and Ruari Oge. "We'll all rot if we don't take to the sea again quickly."

"We were just waiting for your summons to come running back," Magnus told her. "After you sent my men home with a coin in every purse they've been listening eagerly for your whistle on the wind."

Ruari Oge, sporting a new mantle dyed Bristol red, balanced his sea chest on his shoulder as he remarked, "All seafarers listen to the wind. And my Evleen says that once a woman has men away at sea she never sleeps the same again, because she lies with one ear awake, dreading the sound of the storm."

Grania held her arms wide, as if she would embrace the boats and the bay and whatever lay beyond. "I'd rather be the one who goes and dares than the one who stays behind and worries," she said, ending with a shout of laughter that startled the seagulls bobbing on the water. Screaming their own derisive reply, the gulls leaped into the gray sky.

Accompanied by a flotilla of fishing curraghs, the galleys rounded Slyne head and turned north, soon leaving the fishermen behind. Grania rode in the prow of Ruari Oge's ship. She wanted to be the first to leave O Flaherty waters, the first to enter the territory of the O Malleys. When her ships swept past the mouth of the fjordlike Caol Saile Ruadh—which the English pronounced Killary—she ordered the O Flaherty banners taken down and replaced with the red boar of O Malley.

Donal's clansmen raised their eyebrows but prudently said nothing.

"What am I to do with your husband's flags?" asked the man holding the folded banners.

"Put them away in a chest," she told him. "In the very bottom of a chest."

When the solitary merchantman appeared from behind a headland, Grania saw it before her lookout could yell. The vessel was a three-masted carrack, wide-beamed and innocent of gunports. It was an old ship long past its prime, relegated to the dregs of the sea trade and currently carrying a cargo of tar and salted herring out of Trondheim, bound for Portugal. Originally part of a small fleet, the carrack had fallen behind in the rough sea off the Orkneys, for she was slow in her stays and topheavy. Now she was beating south unescorted, manned by a mixed and sullen crew who were aware of the danger of pirates in these waters and were hugging the coast.

Ruari Oge shouted an order for his men to ship oars and wait for instructions. Magnus did likewise, and the two galleys hovered in the sea, watching the approaching vessel. "Do we board her?" Ruari asked Grania.

His commander shaded her eyes with her hand. "Do you think she carries anything worth taking? We've just the two galleys."

"Sixty men apiece, counting thirty on the oars," Ruari replied. "And that ship's riding very low and appears to have no guns to speak of. I think I've seen her before, in fact—off Donegal, flying Flemish flags. She was in better condition then, and better handled, too, by a helmsman who knew enough to keep her clear of the rocks. Look at that, will you? It would be a mercy to board her and relieve her of that load before she founders herself."

"Then let's do it," Grania ordered. Pointing toward the carrack, she sighted along her arm as a bowman would aim his arrow. "Take them!"

When the captain of the carrack had catted his anchor in the harbor at Trondheim, he was already unhappy about this voyage. He did not know the ship, and her owners had hired him for one trip only with no promise of a better vessel if he made a good profit. He hated the old carrack on sight. She ran with rats and reeked of bilge.

He had brought aboard a crew to match the vessel, mostly drunkards and layabouts known in many ports under many names, including several ruptured foremastmen and a light-fingered quartermaster. Some of them came to him one step ahead of the law, or direct from prison. Some would die of illness or in fights and be of no more expense than the hard bread and rotten meat they had eaten. The captain did not expect to make much profit from tar, and he did not intend to contract first-class seamen from his own purse.

When the carrack was separated from her companions in the merchant fleet, opportunity had presented itself. The captain went ashore on the northern coast of Ireland to resupply his vessel with fresh water and happened to meet two merchants from London, come to Ireland to bid on pirate loot. The captain was a practical Dutch Anabaptist from Deventer, a man embittered by a long run of ill fortune who felt no loyalty to those who had hired him for donkey's wages. He struck a deal to meet the Londoners' agents at Sligo bay on his return voyage from Portugal and sell them the merchandise he would be carrying. Then he would sail on to Trondheim, claiming he had been robbed by Irish pirates. With the proceeds from the Portuguese cargo he could buy a ship of his own at last instead of sailing on other men's derelicts.

Musing over this fortuitous arrangement as he followed the west coast of Ireland, he had his dreams rudely interrupted by a shout from the lookout in the foretop. The Dutchman ran to the rail and fixed his horrified attention on a pair of Irish galleys lying sleek in the water, waiting for him with menacing stillness.

He swallowed hard and began shouting orders. His ship was a square-rigger, totally dependent on sailpower, and whatever small maneuverability she could muster lay with the skill of her crew and the generosity of the wind. But even as he realized his precarious situation the wind, which had been blowing all afternoon, began to drop off.

"Get your tacks close aboard!" the Dutchman cried urgently.

The carrack was cumbersome and slow to respond, and the galleys were suddenly racing toward him, their oars having slashed down into the water in one smooth swoop at Grania's command. The carrack's sails collapsed to hang limp from their yards as the cursing foremastmen scrambled aloft, but before they could be clewed up, the galleys were on either side and someone was shouting, "Strike your flags to us or prepare for boarding and battle!"

The Dutchman could hardly believe his eyes. The voice, though deep, was unmistakably female and belonged to a tall figure in the prow of the galley on his port side. "I'll not give over to any *woman!*" he roared.

"Won't you, now," said Ruari Oge in a deceptively gentle voice. "Then it will be battle."

At his signal, twenty bowmen launched a barrage of arrows toward the open decks of the carrack. Simultaneously Magnus fired his artillery, which amounted to no more than a few robinets and sakers, all a galley could carry. It caused more noise and smoke than damage, but that was sufficient to unnerve the carrack's crew.

There were many cowards aboard; the captain had not paid for gallant men.

The galleys moved closer. The Dutchman yelled an order for his men to tack evasively, but most of them just looked at him. It was no use anyway; the wind had deserted them.

"Prepare to board amidships!" cried Grania.

Ruari Oge's galley moved in under the carrack's port side, and grappling hooks were thrown up, clawing like a raptor's talons at the gunwales. Deckhands tried to dislodge them, but the Irishmen were already hand-over-handing up the lines. The first man over the side had a knife in his teeth and a shortsword in his belt, and the sight of him so alarmed the ship's cook, who had just come on deck, that the poor fellow shrieked like a virgin being raped, as Tigernan related afterward.

While attention was focused on Ruari Oge's assault party, Magnus maneuvered his galley closer to the carrack's starboard side and soon was putting men aboard as well. The merchant ship was so old and poorly maintained that she lacked not only guns but nets to shield her decks from attackers. Grania's men shouted at the ease of capture as they boiled over the sides and dropped into the waist.

A few of the carrack's crew offered to fight. Press-gang veterans who had faced every imaginable danger in every known port, they refused to be intimidated by Irish pirates. They all carried knives, and the quartermaster had a Saxon wheel-lock pistol. Unfortunately, he was not well practiced with a handgun. He gave himself a bad powder burn and completely missed his target, a man with braided red hair and a ferocious mustache. This intended victim promptly snatched the pistol out of the quartermaster's hand, thrust it through his own belt, then knocked its erstwhile owner to the deck with one blow.

The rest of the Dutchman's crew broke and scattered. Some threw back the gratings and dropped into darkness; others scrambled up the ratlines, impelled by the atavistic human urge to climb out of danger even when there is nowhere to go.

One of the pirates threw down the carrack's boarding-ladder. Moments later a woman was climbing over the rail with practiced ease, followed by more of her men. She strode purposefully across the deck, though sporadic fighting was still going on around her as one man, then another, was cornered and forced to surrender at the point of a blade.

A brown-haired foremastman noticed the woman aboard and

stopped in his tracks. When she came straight toward him, instinct prompted him to throw out his arms and prevent her from going farther into danger.

"Where is your captain and what is your cargo?" Grania demanded of him.

He continued to bar her way but did not answer. A man of her own age, he had a brooding, penetrating look about him, and there was elegance in the line of his shoulders and the flatness of his wrists. Grania wondered briefly what he was doing aboard such a vessel.

"Do you speak Gaelic?" she yelled at him above the noise around them, the shouting and cursing, the thuds, the running feet.

He was gazing at her in disbelief and still did not reply.

"Spanish, English . . . Latin?" she cried in exasperation. When he still said nothing, she shoved against his arm and was past him. Though he was both taller and heavier, he could not stop her. In her determination the woman was like a force of nature; her expression told him she would walk through a wall if it stood in her way.

The battle was soon decided, and the chagrined Dutchman stepped forward to surrender his cargo to the victors. His clothing identified him—a doublet of blue changeable camlet and padded breeches, the tailored clothes of a captain set apart from the common seamen. Aside from his garments, however, he was no more impressive than his motley crew, but the tradition of a meeting between chieftains must be observed. Grania strode up to confront him.

"I am Gráinne Ni Mháille," she announced in Gaelic.

Nothing in his background had prepared the Dutchman for negotiating with a woman pirate. The level gaze the creature fixed upon him was that of a person not easily dissuaded, so he tried to stall for time. "I do not understand your language," he said in the pidgin German of the northern seaways.

Grania spoke no Germanic dialect, but she had grown up among traders and knew what languages were common to them all. In heavily accented but serviceable English she replied, "My men are setting fire to your ship."

He betrayed himself by an anxious glance around his decks, and Grania laughed. "So you do understand English."

"Yes," he muttered, looking at her body rather than her face, refusing her any dignity.

"Let's go to your cabin," Grania ordered briskly. She would not

allow this sweating, nervous man to insult her; she had been insulted by better than he. "I will order my men to do no pillaging
until we have come to an agreement," she promised.

The captain's cabin was as shabby as his ship. The woodwork
smelled of rot, and the filthy quilt on the narrow bed stank of
mildew. Grania wrinkled her nose and declined to sit. "Let us talk
of cargo. What are you carrying?"

He slumped against the bulkhead and eyed her sourly. "Nothing
you want. Barrels of tar and casks of salted herring. I suppose you
might sell the tar in Galway city, but I doubt there's any market
for imported herring on an Irish coast famed for its fishing."

"I could not sell your tar in Galway," Grania informed him.
"My husband . . . my dead husband was an O Flaherty; his clan
is barred from any trading there."

"So you prey on ships inbound to Galway to get even?" the man
guessed.

He was shrewd; she would give him that much. "Sometimes,"
she replied evenly. "I prefer to buy and sell like any other merchant, but the English do everything possible to hinder us. They've
outlawed the export of wool from Galway, and wool was a staple
of commerce for my husband's clan. So now . . . we do what we
can." She waved her hand negligently. "We do what we can."

The captain gnawed his heavy underlip. "What do you mean to
do with me?"

"Since your cargo is of little value to me, I might let you go
unmolested . . . for a fee, of course."

"Look around," he said with a snort of derision. "If you find any
caskets filled with money, you can keep it all. Until my cargo sells
I have almost nothing."

"You were paid for making this voyage?"

He shuffled his feet. "Half the fee. I left the money for safekeeping."

She could not be certain he was lying. Instantly she was searching the cabin, ripping up the bed and rummaging through the
chests and small built-in cupboard. When everything the Dutchman owned had been thoroughly examined, she turned back to
him. "You *are* poor," she said pityingly.

"I said so."

"The only thing you have of any use to me is this ship."

He clapped one hand to his forehead. "If you take the ship I am
ruined!"

"You appear to be one step from ruin anyway," Grania pointed out. "You can go the rest of the way and then turn around, if you have the spirit for it. But I am not without mercy. I'll put you and your men ashore, and if you get to a town you can tell them you were attacked by pirates or you can even say you were shipwrecked, if you would prefer that to admitting the truth to the ship's owners. I doubt they will pay you the other half if they know you surrendered their carrack."

A few hours earlier the Dutchman had anticipated a windfall. He took his loss with bad grace. "I will not let a woman do this to me," he cried, lunging toward her.

She took a catlike step backward, and a knife materialized in her hand. Too late his mind registered the fact that in addition to wearing man's clothing, she carried a man's weapon in her belt.

"Hit me," she invited, crouching. Weaving the knife back and forth in front of his eyes. Beckoning with her other hand. "Indeed, do try to hit me."

He paused, flaring his nostrils and puffing like a winded horse. He did not like the look on her face at all. With a ponderous shrug, he straightened and backed out of her reach.

Grania continued to hold the knife, but her eyes danced. "Your luck is dreadful. I can't blame you for wanting to strike back. But . . . all luck turns, does it not? Perhaps the tide of yours is due for a turn now. Shall we try it and see? I'll make you a proposition, my impoverished sea captain. We will throw the dice together, you and I, and if you win you can keep your ship and your tar and take them wherever you like. Buf if I win, I get the carrack and you have to start thinking of a good story to tell to explain its loss. You won't want to say a woman took it away from you, will you?"

"You are laughing!" he exlaimed with relief. "So you are not serious."

"On the contrary," she assured him, "I am never more serious than when I laugh. Bring out your dice."

"I have none."

The look she gave him was more pitying than ever. "What sort of man are you? When I first went to Iar Connaught I could not make friends among my husband's followers—until they discovered I shared their taste for gambling. I won often and lost graciously, which pleased the men, and I was a match for them at dice or chess or brandubh. Then I showed them I knew something of boats and the sea . . . which is more than I can say for you, judging by the way you keep this vessel. What can you do well, if anything?" she asked mockingly. Her knife darted out again, threatening his lower belly. He took another step backward and dropped his hands to cover his groin, fearful she meant to castrate him from contempt. Grania flung back her head and laughed.

Within half an hour the carrack's boat was lowered and the captain and his men were put ashore, angry castaways on a foreign coast. Grania stood at the rail, still rolling her winning dice in her fingers. "Foreigners seem to do well in Ireland," she called out as the boat pulled away. "You might find you prefer to stay here and live on fat salmon rather than salted herring."

The Dutchman swore at her. But the brown-haired foremast-man caught and held her eye for a long moment, then touched his fingers to his forehead in a kind of salute.

✠

Grania appointed Tigernan to captain the pirated carrack, and he took for his crew the men on the two galleys who had had previous sailing experience aboard the caravel. Grania stayed with her newly acquired vessel. They were barely underway again before Tigernan began complaining about the ship.

"In a beam wind she'll sail like a haystack. When I used the sea with the Black Oak, none of his masted ships were as clumsy as this one. What did you want to burden yourself with her for?

"Ruari Oge says she was a decent enough ship once. A gallant lady's life need not be over just because she suffers from neglect and weathering, Tigernan. This one can be overhauled at Kinsale and fitted with guns, and she'll give us good service on the sea routes."

"You planned all that before we even boarded her," Tigernan guessed accurately. "You're a thinker, like Ruari Oge."

"I had a better head on me before you hit it with a plank."

"The plank split," he claimed, "but your skull didn't."

"Next time you'll need to hit harder then."

They passed the holy island of Caher off their port bow, and sails were briefly lowered in reverence. Cliara itself rose before them from the sea, Sphinxlike guardian of the vast mouth of Clew bay, with the peak of Cnoc Mór forming the leonine head that had gazed across the ocean for millennia.

Did that mountain peak see the New World? Grania wondered.

She could believe anything of Cnoc Mór. Like giant, conical Croagh Patrick off to starboard on the mainland, the mountain of Cnóc Mor was a presence.

Numerous fishermen in their black-hulled curraghs stood up to wave to Grania's fleet as it swept by. Grania cast a longing look at Cliara, for the island known as Clare was her favorite place in all the world and a welcome sight after years in Iar Connaught. Then she turned her face resolutely toward the distant, mountain-embraced head of the bay and the many humpbacked islands guarding the seaward approach to Umhall.

"You'll be glad to see Owen Dubhdara again, I'm thinking," Tigernan commented.

Some inexplicable undertone of anger could be heard in her voice as she replied, "I'm not returning to see Dubhdara. I'm going to make Clew bay my base because it will give me more freedom than any harbor in Iar Connaught. The English don't breathe down our necks so heavily here."

"But surely you'll be happy to be with your father again." Tigernan wanted to believe he understood her better than anyone else. Sometimes Grania was amused at the way he interpreted her words and actions to fit his own ideas.

Someone was always trying to make her fit his own ideas, she thought. Someone else always needed something of her; someone else always had to be taken care of. This move to Umhall was necessitated as much as anything else by the need to put herself in a strong position for her sons' sake.

She gave Tigernan a sidelong glance. "Happy to be with him? Frankly, I hadn't thought of it."

Her voice when she spoke of the Black Oak was more than cold, it was indifferent. She seemed to withdraw into a hidden core where no one could reach her.

Tigernan added this discovery to the other pieces of what seemed an unconnectable puzzle. He remembered the radiant sunshine on Grania's wedding day and the way Owen Dubhdara had smiled. He remembered the closeness he had once seen between father and daughter, and he scratched his head and wondered what had happened.

Not that she would ever tell him.

Owen Dubhdara himself did not know, for he was not aware of the change in his daughter's attitude toward him; the incident that caused her separation from him belonged to a time mercifully blotted out of his memory. When word was brought to him of O Malley flags sailing down Clew bay, he hurried joyfully to the strand to welcome his daughter.

The galleys were pulled into the shallows; the carrack swung on her hawser like an overweight dowager, winded and worn. O Malleys of every age and description—most of them dark-haired, all of them strong and red-cheeked and vital—came running to welcome the Black Oak's daughter home.

In the years since Grania had last seen him, Dubhdara had bowed to the weight of time's passage. He was still tall and imposing, but his skin had the texture of a badly cured hide and was splotched with broken veins. When he held out his hands to his daughter she could see the knotting of the joints. Hair once raven-black was silver-touched and thinning now, and the Gaelic fringe cut straight across his forehead did not hide his whitened eyebrows.

He still cut a chieftainly figure, however, dressed in his most noble attire. The traditional long flowing cloak of the chieftain was fastened over his chest by a massive gold brooch set with a cabochon ruby. Against his skin was a shirt of Irish silk, full-sleeved, beneath a jerkin lavishly trimmed in marten's fur. Dubhdara's lower body was encased in the archaic one-piece trews many Gaels still wore in regions sufficiently distant from English influence. It was a tight-fitting woolen garment that served as both trousers and stockings and clung so closely to the legs the play of the muscles beneath was visible.

Grania wore a similar pair of trews, Dubhdara saw as he opened his arms to envelop her in an O Malley hug.

Standing a little part, Tigernan could not help noticing the way Grania turned her cheek sideways against her father's shoulder. Her face was controlled and expressionless.

When Dubhdara opened his arms and pushed her back to arm's length to take a closer look at her, Grania told him, "Donal an Chogaidh is dead."

"By the paps of Danu! It's true, then—we'd already heard some rumor it it, running like brushfire through the tall grass. What did he die of?"

"An excess of suspicion," Grania said.

Dubhdara turned his head slightly so he could look at her out of his stronger eye. "You'll have to explain that. But there's time, there's time. You'll be wanting to get yourself on the outside of a good meal—and the same for your men too, of course."

Over a hearty meal of roasted ox and oysters, Grania told Dubhdara the story of Donal's death. Her sentences were clipped, straightforward; this was not a tale to be told with hysterics. The Black Oak listened quietly, only nodding from time to time as he recognized the old story of attack and counterattack, reprisal and revenge. They were in the hall of Belclare, a fortress that was little more than a stone tower house with a commanding view of Clew bay, but Grania's mother had made its interior comfortable during her lifetime with the many luxuries her husband imported. Some fine tapestries glowed on the walls, their bright colors more enduring than those of the faded battle shields hanging beside the stone fireplace.

Cut deep into the mantle piece of that fireplace was the O Malley motto: *Terra Marique Potens*, Powerful by Land and Sea. Above the motto, in bas-relief, was the figure of a raging boar and Dubhdara's personal device, a galley with its sail set.

When Grania finished speaking, her father gazed into the fire for a long time. Logs burned on his hearth; Umhall was not yet reduced to using peat for fuel, because the English had not timbered here. At last he commented, "You bear your loss well, daughter."

"I mourned my husband as was appropriate. I gave him the honors due a fallen chieftain."

"But what of the grief due a slain husband, a *man?*" Dubhdara asked, puzzled by the restraint in her voice.

She looked him in the eye. "I know of no man worth crying over." Then she laughed.

Dubhdara blinked, hesitating before he laughed with her. "You have an odd way of joking," he said. "But you always were a tough piece of leather; I should have expected as much."

"Yes," Grania agreed, gazing past him into the shadows in the corners, and the faded battle shields on the walls, "I always was a tough piece of leather."

part two

---

huw

7

The Black Oak summoned neighboring chieftains to a feast in his daughter's honor. He took it for granted that her visit was only temporary. She had not yet told him otherwise, so he expected her to make her permanent home in Iar Connaught with clan O Flaherty. But in the meantime he wanted to show the widow of an elected tanist the honor due her, and in a subtle way demonstrate his personal support for Donal an Chogaidh's resistance to English domination.

A diplomatic gesture would carry weight with with the other Irish. A shouted defiance might bring down disaster.

Though fishing rivals of the O Malleys, representatives of clan Donnell from Tyrconnell made the long trip to Clew bay to show their respect for Owen Dubhdara. Likewise members of clans Seonin, O Hara, Maoilir, O Conor, and O Kelly were present, and Richard an Iarainn arrived from the northeast shore of the bay to speak for the Burke family.

Iron Richard, Finola's son, for whom murder had once been committed.

The weather had turned dirty, with a driving rain off the sea that transformed roads into sticky puddings and filled Dubhdara's hall with the stench of wet wool as one guest after another entered and edged quickly toward the hearth. Rain played a somber rattle on the roof. The music of pipes and tympan endeavored to drown out the sound, accompanied by a clatter of dishes, a buzz of conversation, and the bellow of laughter.

Grania had set the tone for the occasion. Attired in a gown of soft cameline from Flanders, a cashmerelike fabric of woven goat hair, she was obviously not in heavy mourning. A gilded girdle flattered her figure; her uncovered hair had been brushed until it shone.

When Iron Richard first glimpsed her across the room, he thought the O Flaherty widow was a handsome woman.

She heard his name announced as he entered, but at first it did not register. Grania's thoughts were very much elsewhere. Dubhdara's allies had offered her their formal condolences, but then upon realizing—thankfully—that she was not going to grieve and weep and make the day wetter than it already was, they had gotten down to discussing the really important matters of fishing and trade. The way they included Grania in these conversations and the deference they showed her assured her the name Grania O Malley was already well respected in the sea-lanes.

She had accomplished that for herself; Donal had given her nothing of importance but the children he then took away. Their childhood was irrevocably lost to her, but the chainless sea was still hers. As florid chieftains and their white-skinned women swirled around her she held her head high and thought of her private kingdom, the domain where she was sovereign.

Kingdom. Sovereign. There was a real female sovereign across the Irish sea, a woman with the power to disrupt lives and change the future, and as they often had recently, Grania's thoughts returned to Elizabeth of clan Tudor, wondering about her.

What are you doing this day, Elizabeth? Are you warmer in your hall than we are here? Would you envy us our laughter; would you join in our feast if we invited you?

Are you so very different from me, Elizabeth?

A late-arriving piper took his instrument from its otter-skin case and lovingly assembled it while the usual collection of children circled around him to watch. The venerated harper of the O Malleys, occupying the place of honor on the stone bench built into the wall beside the hearth, ran his fingers across the harp strings, and the hall fell silent in respect. Smiling as if he saw, behind his sightless eyes, the very shape and color of the notes he played, the harper filled the room with music. Then Phelim, Dubhdara's ollave, fulfilled the function of poet/historian by reciting from memory the names and lineage of his chieftain's guests.

"Richard an Iarainn, oldest surviving son of David Burke, once The MacWilliam Iochtar," he proclaimed toward the end of his recital, thus identifying Iron Richard as one of the Mayo branch of the Burke line, rather than the family headed by The MacWilliam Uachtar in the Galway region. Both lines were descended from Sir William Liath de Burgh, the Norman lord whose name would be afterward commemorated in Gaelic fashion by the titles of the two

MacWilliams. The family de Burgh had been a strong influence throughout Connaught since the beginning of the thirteenth century. Since, as Phelim pointed out proudly while reciting the history, "A de Burgh married the daughter of Donal Mór O Brien, King of Thomond."

Subsequent centuries of intermarriage with the Gaels had not removed the Norman stamp from Iron Richard's face, Grania noticed, now that her attention was drawn to him. For all he was the son of Donal's sister, there was nothing of the O Flaherty clan in his features. A long-headed man with iron-gray eyes that might have been responsible for his nickname, Richard possessed a heavy jaw that widened into sloping shoulders without any perceptible neck. He tended to shift his glance from one direction to another without moving his head. Grania got an impression of a man whose passions moved sluggishly within him until roused, like water seeping through a blanket bog until it poured into a freshet.

Sensing her gaze, he turned toward her. "My mother asked me to inquire as to the details of her brother's death," he said, his voice a low rumble in his chest. "She shares your grief."

"Does she?" Grania lifted an eyebrow. "And did you weep and keen with her when you heard the news?"

The sarcasm in her voice surprised him. "Why should I? Donal an Chogaidh was nothing to me. I hardly knew the man."

Now she raised both brows. "Really? I had the notion the two of you had something in common—particularly after the death of your stepbrother."

"Walter the Tall? That was a long time ago. He was murdered by thieves and his mutilated body tossed into a marsh. What has that to do with myself and my uncle?"

Grania restrained a cynical smile. Perhaps he really did not know; it would have been like crafty Finola to keep the secret. "Murdered by thieves," she said aloud. "What an apt way to put it."

He set himself in front of her like a man with a mission. "You are to tell me of your husband's death," he repeated, and Grania fancied she could hear Finola's commanding voice.

"Very well." Even before she could begin, a crowd gathered around them, eager to hear every detail.

She told the whole story through and had hardly finished speaking before some of the men in the hall began calling for a general slaughter of the Joyces. "The loyalty of the clans must be upheld! If we stand with O Malley we stand with O Flaherty."

Such unity was not universal, however. "The O Flahertys don't even stand with each other," an O Hara pointed out. "That clan is bitterly divided. I've heard that some follow the new chieftain appointed by the Tudor she-king and others still adhere to Donal Crone."

"And Donal Crone is too ill to lead anything, " said one of the Silmurray men. "He's losing his eyesight."

"Clan Joyce may attack him too, then."

"You can expect it. They're Normans, aren't they? Foreigners?" The old resentments were very close under the skin.

"Now's the time to raise a hosting against the foreigners, before they get any stronger," yelled a mighty O Donnell voice.

"I'll lead it myself," said another.

"In that case I won't go," stated a third. "I'd follow an O Malley, but I have no ties to you. One of your clansmen killed one of mine only three generations ago, in a dispute over twin heifers, and I . . ."

"Kill the foreigners!" screamed someone from the rear of the hall. "Kill them all!"

"What foreigners?" asked a deep, cold voice. Iron Richard, when he put wind into his lungs, could speak with such resonance it rang through the bones. Even Phelim was impressed. "Do you really think Ireland is Gaelic land now?" Richard went on. "What about my family? Or clan Rickard and The MacWilliam Uachtar? Or the mighty clan Fitzgerald"—he curled his lip as he spoke this name; the Geraldines had long been in opposition to the de Burgh line— "or any of dozens of other famillies I could name you? Or you over there with your Norse-white hair and your Viking eyes . . . your ancestors were foreigners to this land in Brian Boru's time, but you are here still, like Welshmen and Flemings and Scots and Saxons too. Are you all to be driven out? And how?"

A stunned silence gripped the hall. Then Phelim roused himself from admiration—and envy—of Richard Burke's voice, and spoke up. His was the tradition of the arbiter, the bard who stood outside the argument, like the brehon judge, who had made the scales weigh even. "Ireland is full of foreign tribes," he said, "and there has always been room for them. Most of this land has been wilderness, forest land and bog land and wild mountains. Ireland has been able to absorb the foreigners and make them Irish. Look at yourself, Richard an Iarainn. You wear Gaelic clothing, you speak the Gaelic tongue as does your father and his father before him. We cannot call you foreign."

But he is not one of us, Grania thought, stealing a glance at Richard's profile. When it is all over, will his be the winning side?

"The Normans came from England," she said aloud.

"They did," Phelim agreed. "But at the specific request of a prince of the Gael."

"And let that be a warning to us against inviting the armed stranger into our midst!" roared Dubhdara O Malley.

Phelim shook his head. He was a lean old man, straight as a pikestaff. Advancing age had given him as bald a scalp as the tonsured pate of the abbot of the nearby Augustinian abbey where Grania had married Donal O Flaherty. The current head of that abbey—and newly appointed to the position—was one Calvagh of Bregia, who sat at Dubhdara's side as an honored guest. When Phelim spoke, the new abbot leaned forward to listen.

His slight movement drew Grania's eye to the man who would be expected to keep a Catholic foothold in Umhall in spite of the rising tide of English-enforced Protestantism. Calvagh was fair-haired and narrow-headed, with a very long nose.

He looks like a blond wolf, she thought. What ever happened to the jolly, jowly friars I remember from my childhood?

Then she saw Calvagh's hand reach out and surreptitiously caress the passing buttocks of a young page, even though he kept his gaze fixed on Phelim with every indication of interest.

The boy flinched and glanced back, startled, but Calvagh seemed totally unaware of him.

Grania frowned.

The little page scurried across the hall, out of reach.

Phelim, in full bardic voice now, was saying, "The truth remains, the Anglo-Normans came here originally at the behest of a prince of the Gael, Dermot of Leinster, who had been thrown out of Ireland for the kidnapping of another man's wife, and who fought his way back to power with mercenaries he begged from the English king."

"Strongbow," someone muttered darkly, and the shadows in the smoky hall spread across the walls like a stain.

"Strongbow," Phelim agreed. Looking with a bard's eyeless vision back through time, he recited:

> *Dark Dermot of Leinster brought two hundred*
> *knights in their armor*
> *And a thousand mercenaries into the heart of the*
> *land that bore him.*
> *Their leader, Strongbow of cruel memory, Dark*
> *Dermot made his ally,*
> *And held out his hand to welcome the Norman to*
> *Ireland.*
> *Strongbow seized that hand, and seized that land,*
> *and*
> *Though blood broke like snowflakes from the noses*
> *of the Gael,*
> *He has never let Erin go.*

The voices in the hall were raised to a sullen roar, as happened each time the story of the Leinster prince and the Norman knight was retold. It had the familiar horror of a nightmare from which there was no waking, a nightmare in which the sacred land was raped and betrayed by one of her own children in return for a few years' worth of holding a title and wielding power.

Listening, Grania mused—not for the first time—that perhaps even Dermot of Leinster might have thought he had some justification for introducing Norman adventurers into Ireland and thus opening the door for the English monarch to follow. But no Gael was willing to hear Dermot's side of the story. The man was thoroughly dead and thoroughly hated—and the foreigner was, indeed, here to stay.

Everyone seemed to be shouting now; every eye gleamed, every cheek blazed. The room was overheated with old history and fresh passions. The rushes on the floor were bunched and trampled by feet ready to march again in a rising, a rebellion, any sort of battle. The great hounds who lazed by Dubhdara's hearth in anticipation of bones from the feast got to their feet and whined, sensing tension.

Old Ireland, Gaelic Ireland, was coming alive in the room as the words of the bard summoned it from smoke and music and blood. The assembled chieftains were ready to refight fabled wars. On their arms and around their necks were rings of precious metal five hundred years old; thrust through their belts were daggers and shortswords carried by their grandsires' grandsires. If just the right note was strummed on the brass harpstrings—if just the right beat was sounded on the goatskin head of the bodhran—the lot of them would march from the hall straight into battle and glory.

Richard Burke snorted and turned his back on them, taking a deep drink of ale from the flagon he held. To Grania, who happened to be standing next to him, he said, "Of course the Normans stayed. This was a rich land. Timber, gold in the streams, fat cattle. And handsome women to marry." He cut his eyes toward her, but she did not meet his glance.

Phelim did not call for a rising against the English. Instead, he changed the mood by singing a different song about a fair maiden combing her hair, and a red stag watching from a thicket. At last the hall calmed down and the explosive moment had passed . . . for a time.

Dubhdara's guests, ignoring the incessant voice of the rain outside, gave themselves over fully to their feasting. Quiet with her own thoughts, Grania watched them. Watched Richard an Iarainn reach across the table and cut a dripping slab of meat from a roasted haunch of venison, then plunge it into a silver bowl filled with honey. He ate in great gulps, letting the juices run down his chin, but he showed the Norman in his blood by not wiping his face with one of the linen napkins every noble Gaelic household provided.

Grania turned her back on him and paid no attention to the Burke man for the rest of the evening. She dismissed him as an unattractive man with a reputation for being irritable. He might wear Gaelic clothing and speak with an accent almost identical to her own, but she felt no kinship with Richard nor any interest in him. He was associated with too unpleasant a memory in her mind.

Coldblooded Norman, she thought to herself.

Iron Richard Burke took note of the way she avoided him for the rest of the occasion, but he was not offended. Indeed, her coolness intrigued him. And it had been quite a while since any woman had attracted him; women usually reminded him too much of his mother.

Richard's mother of the red-gold hair had once been famed for her beauty—her son had heard whispers that she lured her own brother Donal into her bed on more than one occasion—but Finola's charms had raddled and shrunken in recent years as her health began to fail. Yet she had made a weapon of her weakness; with frail voice and bony hands she bound her son to her. *I haven't long to live, Richard. Your poor mother needs you, Richard.*

By comparison his uncle's widow, Grania, looked substantial, healthy, and vibrant. Richard noted the high color in her cheeks, and saw how her nipples stood out strongly under the soft fabric of her gown. She had been much younger than Donal an Chogaidh when they married, he remembered having heard. How old was she now, in her thirties? Some women were old in their thirties, but Grania was not old. Seafaring had ruined her complexion yet lent her a curious agelessness, because the suntanned, windburned skin with its network of fine lines disguised her years. She could be anywhere from thirty to fifty.

Not fifty, Richard Burke amended to himself, watching the way she moved. *Nor forty either. She is as lithe as an eel, that woman.*

He found nothing in her gestures of that birdlike quality so characteristic of the mother he had grown to hate.

Iron Richard watched Grania over the rims of countless goblets until his scrutiny made her uncomfortable and she left the hall early.

✠

Even before the seagulls were flying next morning, Grania slipped out of Belclare and made her way down the hill to the beach. She was barefoot, but her feet had always known how to pick their way over the rocky shores of Clew bay.

She stood at water's edge and drew a deep breath. Her galleys waited for her in the shallows; her new carrack was farther out, anchored off one of the numerous small islands studding the head of the bay. Grania squinted in the dawn light and made out the figure of a man moving around the decks of the carrack, probably trimming the fore-and-aft lanterns. The rain was over; the sun would be out today.

Tigernan, she smiled to herself. *Already at work, trying to do everything, as usual.*

She started to raise her arm and wave to him, then thought better of it. She relished this quiet time alone. Belclare had been built near a small river because a fortress must possess a convenient fresh-water supply, and where the river met the bay the beach pebbles were particularly beautiful. Grania hunkered down, bunching her skirt between her legs, and began examining various ones, turning them over in her hands and finding some beauty in each. A rounded shape that exactly fit her palm, or a mysterious hole drilled by a long-dead sea animal . . . red sandstone and green marble among darker stones, and an occasional nugget of pink quartz like those she collected on Clare island in her childhood's summers.

Unknown to Donal, she had had an O Flaherty stonemason place a big chunk of pink quartz in the wall of Bunowen, just for her to touch from time to time in passing.

The bay waters surrendered their phosphorescent predawn shimmer to a pearly glow. The sun lifted into the sky; the seabirds darted and screamed.

Absorbed, Grania wandered up and down the beach, letting herself think about rocks and nothing painful at all. She did not hear Dubhdara come up behind her until he spoke.

"You always did like to play in the water."

She dropped the apron she had made of her skirt and let her treasures fall back to the beach. "I didn't know you were up."

"I don't sleep as well as I used to. I thought I might as well start preparing for the day's fishing . . ." A harsh cry in the clear air caught his attention, and Dubhdara glanced up. Following his gaze, Grania saw a white-tailed eagle come winging inland from the direction of Achill island. "Reminds me of the eagle you had for a while when you were a little girl," the Black Oak said with a reminiscent chuckle. "Odd pet for a girl, but that bird loved you, I think. Followed you everywhere."

The two watched in silence as the eagle glided above them on invisible currents. "When I was a boy," Dubhdara remarked, "I once dreamed of shape-changing, like the Druids of old, and becoming an eagle. I was that certain I could fly if I just tried hard enough."

"Did you ever try it?" his daughter asked him. "Flying?"

His laughter rumbled. "Once, from a mountain ledge when no one was around to laugh if I failed."

"Did you fail?" Her voice was cool. He could not understand why she endeavored to keep distance between them. Her behavior seemed so different from that of the child he remembered.

"Me, fail? I flew!" he shouted. "I am Owen Ui Mháille, and I could fly for you this very day if I had a mind to. If we were on a high headland I could leap off and soar halfway to the New World."

The child Grania had been would have loved such boasting, would have laughed with him and entered into the game. But the grown woman shifted her gaze from the circling eagle to the western horizon, gravely regarding the blue peak of Clare island and the Atlantic Ocean beyond. "Can a new world be so very different from this one?" she mused. "Hispania. Mexico."

Dubhdara thought for a moment. "The old bards told of voyages to the Islands of the Blest, did they not? Maybe the Gaels have been there before. Maybe we'll go again. It would be a grand thing to see, this new world."

"Only if you were sure you could get home again," Grania replied very softly.

"And you—when are you going home?"

Her mind skipped, and she had no quick answer. She thought of herself as being at home here. "To Iar Connaught, you mean?"

"Of course, girl, what did you think? I expect you'll be leaving us soon, though I'm not pushing you out the gate. But that's why I was looking for you. After you deserted us in the hall last evening a messenger straggled in from your husband's clan, wanting a meal and some dry straw to sleep on. He brought word that clan Joyce has reoccupied some O Flaherty castle on Lough Corrib. Donal's sept thinks it's a deliberate insult to his memory and summons you to do something about it."

Grania closed her eyes. "They expect me to carry on his feuds?"

"You're the mother of his sons," Dubhdara pointed out. "It is their portion that needs defending."

"There are plenty of male O Flaherties capable of falling on Donal's enemies in his name. His sept doesn't even have any real claim to that castle; some other O Flaherty family built it."

"But your husband's clansmen sent for you," Dubhdara insisted.

"Should it be a wife's business to carry on her husband's wars even when the moss grows over his tomb?"

"Such is the tradition of our people," the Black Oak reminded her.

"Times have changed," Grania said, hearing in herself the echo of Donal an Chogaidh.

"But you have not. You're a woman of the old style, and I'm proud of you for it." Dubhdara draped an approving arm across his daughter's shoulders.

"Yes," Grania replied in a flat voice. "I'm a woman of the old style. So I will raise an army and go to recapture the castle my husband captured. And so it goes on. . . . Is that what you want for me, Dubhdara?"

"What a creature you are. What kind of question is that?"

"Is that what you want for me?"

The Black Oak frowned. "What else is there to do? Shall I put that poor lad back in his boat and send the word south that you're on your way?"

Grania stared up into the sky. The eagle had disappeared. "He came in a boat?"

"A big curragh, with a crew. It's pulled up there on the beach."

"Then hold him here and I'll take him and his men with me," she decided. "I'll have need of them."

"What a creature you are," Dubhdara repeated proudly. "You."

He did not notice the look she gave him. The look of agony frozen into ice; icy shards of an old and terrible pain still lancing through her. Pain she had learned to survive.

✠

Years earlier, when news of her mother's death had reached Grania, she had hurried to Umhall to show her respect for Mairgret and add coins from her own purse to the aprons of the mourners. She had asked no one's permission to make the trip. Donal was away on a campaign at the borders of Ros Comáin, so she simply went to the fishermen in the cove and asked them to take her north. One shabby, neglected galley with faded paint lay overturned on the beach like a giant turtle, but there were holes in its bottom. The fishing curraghs were safer, the fishermen glad enough to transport the chieftain's wife.

Following the coast in an open curragh held no fears for Dubhdara O Malley's daughter.

She had been unprepared for the scene that greeted her in Umhall. Leaving Belclare, scene of Mairgret's death, open and deserted like a sacked city, her husband had withdrawn to his older stronghold at Cathair na Mart. This was cattle land, with a river winding like a roadway down to the bay, but the emphasis was on the beeves. The fortress at Cathair na Mart was built of rough stones with a dungeon underneath, a grim place Mairgret had tried throughout her lifetime to improve. Now refuse littered the chambers and cattle roamed unchecked across the ornamental lawn Mairgret had painstakingly established, the traditional Gealic aurla.

The Black Oak was in worse condition than his stronghold. His clothing was filthy and torn, his blue eyes were on the verge of drowning in watery reddened sclera. Great hunks of hair were missing from his scalp where he had torn them out with his hands.

Seeing her father in such condition tore Grania's heart. She ran to him where he sat slumped on a bench outside the portal. When she tried to put her arms around him he shrugged them off and did not even look at her. "The sun is gone from the sky," he said in a voice she hardly recognized. "Mairgret Ni Moher is gone from me."

Grania bent over him, desperate to comfort him. Her coarse black hair, so like his and so unlike her mother's auburn ringlets, fell in a veil around his face. When her hand attempted to stroke his cheek he slapped it away. "Your skin is rough. Where is the silken touch of Mairgret Ni Moher?"

"It is your own Grania," she whispered urgently, "come to take care of you."

"I want no one but Mairgret," he insisted. Cocking his head to one side, he looked up at her with such an expression of scorn she drew back. "I need a *female* woman!" Dubhdara cried. "Don't you understand about such things? The brehons urge maidens to prize the six womanly gifts: beauty of form, beauty of voice, sweet speech, skill with a needle, chastity, and female wisdom. My Mairgret had all those in full measure. And look at you!"

The rejection was brutal and total. Grania shrank from him, her mouth an open wound.

"I am what you made me," she tried to tell him. "I was always in your pocket, I copied everything you did . . ."

"You should have copied your mother. What made you think you could turn into a boy and be a son to me?"

"You don't know what you're saying," she told him. She leaned toward him again because she could not help herself, and this time he stood up and stepped out of her reach. "Go away and let me alone. I don't want you pawing me," he growled, glancing at her irritably. "Trews. You're wearing trews."

"I came up from Iar Connaught in a curragh. I wore trews at sea with you and you laughed . . ."

"It doesn't amuse me anymore," he said. "How could you be a son to me? I sired sons." He heard her startled gasp and smiled a bitter smile. "Oh, I have living sons this very day if I want a man's company in my grief. I kept them and their mothers at a distance so as not to hurt my Mairgret who could give me no boys . . . no boys but you." He whirled and looked her full in the face, seeing nothing of Mairgret there at all.

The terrible disappointment was like lead in his voice. *"You,"* he said again, condemning.

Daily for a fortnight Dubhdara paced the precincts of Cathair na Mart, crying aloud for his dead wife. Grania in her chamber could hear him, even when she pulled the heavy old-fashioned wooden shutters across the arrow slits. When she could bear it no more she went to him, past his hushed and nervous attendants, past his concerned clansmen who milled as uncertainly as their cattle. She went to her father again and again, and each time he pushed her away.

The taste of rejection was as bitter as bile in her mouth. She had adored Dubhdara always, sharing his mead horn as openly as she shared the dangers of the sea with him. She had given her heart to his way of life while Mairgret limited her horizons to embroidery frame and prayer stool. But it was Mairgret he admired; Mairgret who embodied love and womanhood for him!

And all the decisions were irrevocably made. Grania could not go back, now, and recast herself in a different mold.

Grief has deranged him, she tried to convince herself. He does not know what he says. But the weight of his words piled up. Grania could not see that he caused her pain to relieve his own, blaming her for still being alive when Mairgret was dead. For his beloved wife's sake, Dubhdara was jealous of the life still flowing through his daughter's veins.

Mairgret, Mairgret. Mairgret was perfect and precious and lost, and he tormented himself—and Grania—with her memory.

The young woman listened, writhing inwardly, as the Black Oak catalogued her mother's virtues, speaking of Mairgret as no one had ever spoken of Grania. "She had perfect fingernails the very shape of almonds," Dubhdara would muse suddenly. "And such white, round arms. And ah, the arch of her foot! There was beauty for you. I used to come home from the boats in a rush, just to take the shoe off her foot and press my cheek to it."

Grania listened in astonishment as her father said these revealing things. She had never guessed the depth of the bond her parents enjoyed in private; she had never even thought about it. Shy Mairgret, quiet, deferential, standing with folded hands in her husband's shadow . . .

Dubhdara wrung out all his grief and fell silent. He went outside bareheaded in sun or rain, but he did nothing. His galleys rode idly at anchor, his fishing boats ventured out leaderless. The clan was numbed by his dereliction, and when they sought guidance Grania found herself answering questions and giving orders as she had learned to do during Donal's absences. Hides and dried beef and salted fish were piling up and customers awaited them, so in time Grania stepped into one of Dubhdara's galleys and picked up the dropped thread of sea trade herself.

Dubhdara was aware but did not comment. She was nothing to him; she was not Mairgret.

But even grief wears out, slipping from the surface into the connective tissue of the soul. The day came when the Black Oak ate with a real show of appetite, and a fortnight later he came down to the docks and ranted about barrels of lard for export that had been stacked in the sun.

A messenger arrived from Iar Connaught. Donal was back at Bunowen and angry at having returned to a wifeless house; people would suspect Grania preferred her father's clan to his.

"If you no longer need me I will leave," she informed Dubhdara. He was surprised by her formal tone. Taking a close look at her for the first time in weeks, he noticed she appeared withdrawn and remote. Perhaps her mother's death still pained her, he thought, tardily realizing how preoccupied he had been with his own grief. At least he could make amends, cheer her with some reward, he decided.

The last weeks were a blur to him. No shred of his conversation with Grania on the day of her arrival remained in his memory, no matter how deeply it was carved in hers.

"Go, if you feel you have to," he said. "Or stay here and continue leading my fleet until the end of the summer trading season.

I don't have the heart for it yet. When the weather turns I'll send you to Donal an Chogaidh with a fine share of the proceeds and . . . and a galley of your own, with your choice of crew from among those who will volunteer."

The offer was meant with the greatest goodwill. Not bolts of fine fabric, or her mother's jewels, or fancies to delight a womanly heart—Dubhdara rewarded his daughter with command and a vessel, and he was honestly puzzled by the look he glimpsed in her eyes before she carefully wiped them blank.

She thought of Donal and she thought of the sea. In the end she chose the sea. When at last she went back to Iar Connaught, Tigernan and Ruari Oge were among her crew, and when they encountered a Portuguese merchantman heading north from Galway bay they boarded and looted it at Ruari Oge's suggestion.

Ruari liked action. He had volunteered to sail with the Black Oak's daughter because he saw a spirit in her eyes that was dimming in her father's. "She looks angry, and I like that," he told the others. "Angry people make things happen."

A more observant man than Donal O Flaherty might have noticed that Grania rarely spoke of the Black Oak after her return. But all he saw was his wife sailing into Bunowen bay in command of her own galley, a vessel packed from prow to stern with treasure.

8

Now Donal was dead and Grania was once again summoned back to Iar Connaught.

Others expect it of me, she said to herself. Others *need*.

My sons need.

She found Tigernan sitting on the flagged courtyard beside the stables, out of the wind. An assortment of metal pieces was arranged before him on a square of homespun. From time to time he dabbed at one of these pieces with an oily rag, or fitted it to another piece and then took it apart again to continue his scrutiny of the entire collection.

Grania stopped short and watched him. "This goes here," he was muttering to himself, making some small adjustment. "And this should go . . ."

"In God's name, Tigernan, what are you doing?"

He gave a start and looked up to see her stride toward him. "This is a Saxon handgun," he explained. "I took it from one of the sailors on the carrack we captured, and I've dismantled it myself to better understand how it works."

"Can't you fire a pistol without knowing how it works?"

He thrust his crooked jaw forward and caught his upper lip briefly with his lower row of teeth in a characteristic gesture. "I suppose I could," he said at last, after thinking about it. "But I always want to see the inside of things, see how the pieces fit together. Look, now; this bit here, for example . . ." He held up a small spring for her inspection and went rhapsodizing on, elated at being able to demonstrate how it functioned in relation to the whole and certain she would find the explanation equally fascinating.

Grania waited with a smile in her eyes until his momentum ran down. "I need a band of warriors for Iar Connaught," she said then.

Tigernan forgot the Saxon pistol. "Warriors?"

After she explained, he insisted, "You'd better include Ruari Oge. He's that fond of a good fight he'd never forgive you for leaving him behind."

Ruari was indeed pleased to be included. "These gray hairs don't make me any less a warrior," he assured Grania.

"I never think of you as graybeard."

"No more do I. The spirit within me is eighteen years old and as strong as a bull." He towered over tall Grania, did Ruari Oge. Brawny forearms were crossed over his chest beneath a short cloak dyed olive green, and no padded clothing was needed to augment the width of his shoulders. "If you need a champion I'm your man," he boasted.

"Tigernan reminded me how much you love a fight."

"I do. Although . . ."

"What?"

Something about her level gaze prompted him to reveal a secret he would not have shared with anyone else. "When I was a lad I had the most terrible dreams about warfare, about some sort of battle going on all around me in a dark forest. I could hear battle-axes hewing down the trees as men struck at one another; I heard cries of agony and other sounds that sickened me even though a child could not understand them."

"The timberlands of Ireland are being cut down so they cannot conceal warriors who could attack the English," Grania reminded him. "You told me so yourself. Maybe that's why you had that dream."

His gray eyes mirrored doubt. "Maybe. It's true enough we've seen our woodlands butchered—that was one of the reasons I went to my cousins on the coast and learned from them to fish and use the sea. We of clan O Donnell are resourceful. But I'm not sure that's the source of my dream. Whatever it is, the nightmare still returns to me sometimes."

Grania nodded. "I used to have nightmares about fire at sea after I saw a ship burning in Clew bay."

"Yet you stayed on the caravel and fought the fire."

"I did."

He gave her a long look. "Warrior," said Ruari Oge.

✠

Raising a band of fighting men proved easy. O Flaherties who sailed on Grania's ships volunteered to a man, as did the crewmen from other clans who had learned to respect her leadership. In addition, more O Malleys presented themselves for battle than would have been needed to lay siege to a town. And she could still lay claim to the services of Donal's Scots mercenaries in Iar Connaught—men who had been paid by money she brought into the sept.

But the Black Oak's daughter did not plan to attack Lough Corrib by way of Iar Connaught.

"That's what the Joyces might expect," she explained to her captains. "And if I could sail ships into Galway harbor it would be the most straightforward approach to Lough Corrib; we could be there very quickly. Since that isn't possible, I think the best thing to do is the unexpected. We will march inland to Lough Mask and down its eastern shore to Lough Corrib. There we will, I hope, find some O Flaherty allies who will be willing to supply us with boats to reach the Cock's Castle. I doubt that its defenders expect attack from such a direction."

It was a singularly merry war party. They sang as they marched, shouldering their weapons; they joked and teased and scuffled in mock battles that sharpened their edges for the real thing. And Grania's big contagious laugh ran back along the line, shortening the miles they had to travel.

On the shores of Lough Corrib they obtained enough boats to carry them to the island of the Cock's Castle. Grania waited until the dark of the moon before setting out, with muffled oars. They made their way cautiously down the long lake, taking whatever cover was offered by the forested and irregular shoreline, until the walls of the O Flaherty stronghold rose before them from darkly glimmering water.

"I see no watchman on this side," Ruari Oge whispered. "If I wanted to hold this position, I would have a watch at every wall."

"When we win this castle, you'll be in charge of strengthening the fortifications so it won't be taken from us again," Grania promised him.

She said "when," Ruari Oge noted. Not "if."

The skiffs eased into the shallows. Men slipped over the side, fumbling for footing in the water. Grania started to go with the others, but Tigernan grabbed her arm. "What are you doing?"

She tried to pull free. "I led this army, I mean to lead the attack."

"You can't!"

Her spine stiffened. "Don't ever say that to me!"

"I did not mean . . . what I'm trying to say is, you could be captured. The Joyces would sooner grab you than beat all the rest of us, and if they seized you and held you as hostage we would be helpless. Stay with the boats for all our sakes!"

"That's good advice," Ruari Oge's gruff voice commented on her other side.

She made herself stop and think. If she had learned nothing else from Donal an Chogaidh, she had learned the danger of rash actions. "Go, then," she said.

But as they moved away from her into the gloom, her soul leaped out of her body and went with them. She had sailed with these men and boarded captured vessels during the thick of the fighting; battle held no terrors for her. She had marched with this little army and slept on the ground wrapped in her cloak while forty men slept around her. Part of her gift for leadership lay in the fact she had made herself one of them, and it was hard to stay behind now, to be forced to surrender to her sex and station.

It was very hard.

Bending low, the assault party eased through the weeds at water's edge and up onto the land. In a single line they softfooted their way along the castle walls, each man no more than an arm's length behind the man in front of him. When they reached the castle's one portal they encountered a single guard, dozing at this post, and Tigernan had slit his throat from behind before the astonished man could make a sound.

Grania's troop poured past him and slammed against the wooden door. It was not stout enough; under the repeated assault of brawny shoulders one of the staples pulled loose on the inside and the bar gave way. The door opened, spilling warriors inward.

As was customary in Gaelic tower houses like Cock's Castle, the lowest floor of the stone building served as armory and sleeping apartment for the stronghold's defenders. A lone torch of bog pine lit the room with gloomy gold. The smells of sleeping men were thick on the smoky air. Grania's band fell on the men of clan Joyce with wild yells, swinging their weapons and inflicting as much terror as they did wounds. Tigernan had just grabbed a groggy giant of a fellow by the hair and was about to pummel his face when he saw Grania come through the open doorway and froze in mid-blow. His opponent took advantage of the opening to grab him by the testicles with a savage squeeze. Tigernan howled, incapacitated by pain. His eyes filled with tears . . . and through them he saw Grania charge into the center of the room.

The warriors of clan Joyce saw her too. They had already thrown off their shock at being attacked in the middle of the night, and were on their feet as they had been since the first thud against the door. Their captain recognized the face above the leather jerkin and trews; someone had pointed out Donal an Chogaidh's wife to him years before, at a festival attended by both O Flaherties and Joyces.

"The dead cock reaches out of the tomb to send his scrawny hen to attack us!" the captain yelled as, sword in hand, he leaped for her.

9

In the chambers and on the stair lay a quiet more arresting than the din of battle. The stone walls echoed with it. Silence had an oppressive weight, sucking every sound into itself like a bog that gives nothing back. The moans of the dying, the final convulsive thrashings, the harsh panting of the survivors—all were absorbed into an eerie hush now filling the castle.

Silence was the ultimate victor.

On the ground floor, a huddle of men slumped amid a scattering of weapons. Stiffening bodies had been pulled to the sides of the room, or dragged out through the open doorway. A dim sense of approaching daylight filtered through that portal but had little power against the gloom inside.

A man groaned, stretched his arms, and got slowly to his feet. With a toe he nudged the warrior who had been crouched unmoving beside him. "That was a battle," he remarked hoarsely.

"It was," agreed the second man in a strangely choked voice. He did not seem inclined to speak much.

"The problem was too many men trying to crowd in here at once," said his companion. "There wasn't enough room to swing a weapon and make a clean kill. That's why there was so much gouging and choking."

"Are you wounded?" came a question from the man still on the floor.

"Just a couple of lost teeth and a bit of unpleasantness where someone clubbed me in the ribs. Nothing much."

"I wish I was that lucky," said Tigernan, trying to get up. He made a noise in his throat and folded down from the waist, cradling his groin. "I think I've lost my manhood, Ruari," he whispered.

Ruari Oge stooped over him. "No, you haven't. I've had the same thing happen to me, and the effects pass."

"This doesn't feel like it will ever get better," Tigernan said, rolling over on his side and drawing his knees toward his chin.

Ruari Oge shook his head. "It will. But since I never see you with a woman anyway, there's no reason for you to worry."

Tigernan managed to struggle up onto one elbow and glare at his friend. "If I felt better I'd hit you."

"Didn't you two get enough fighting?" Grania asked, striding into the chamber. Her living warriors greeted her with weary cheers. Grania went first to a blond young man who leaned heavily against the wall, bracing his feet against the body of a dead Joyce. "Kieran O Flaherty, you took the blow that was meant for me and I won't forget it," Grania told him. "Put your arm across my shoulder and let's get you out to the light where we can take a look at that wound."

Tigernan watched them go through bleary eyes. "That should have been me," he muttered. "I would have taken the sword wound for her."

Ruari Oge caught him by the shoulders and pulled him to his feet, ignoring the other man's gasp of pain. "Lean on me and we'll go out into the morning too," he said, not unkindly. "I'm not herself, but she can't help everybody."

Ruari helped his friend find a place where he could sit in the sun, with his back propped against a wall and his knees drawn up to his chest. To help pass the time until someone could see to his injury, Ruari chatted at Tigernan about the battle and war in general.

"I much prefer seafaring and boarding ships as a pirate to being a land warrior," he admitted. "The long march here reminded me. You walk until you're exhausted and then there's always a little bit farther to go. You sleep in a muddy ditch with cold rain running down your neck while the lice squirm around in your groin . . ."

"You can pick nits on shipboard too," Tigernan said with a moan. He did not like talking about discomforts in the groin area.

"You can," the other agreed. "But at least there's a tub to wash yourself in and usually a wind to blow your stench away. Before I took to the sea I fought in clan wars when my neck was caked with mud so it hurt to turn my head, and the dried salt sweat rotted my clothes until they parted and fell off my body. Those who think battle is all glory have never been in one."

"Nonsense," said Tigernan faintly, closing his eyes and cradling his hurt parts. "This is grand fun. Just grand."

The wounded were tended in the clear dawn light, and Grania made a point of talking with every one, her own men and those of clan Joyce alike. The castle's defenders had taken a savage battering. The chieftain of the sept that had occupied the Cock's Castle after Donal's death had fled from the attack to the upper chambers of the building, pulling up the wooden ladder that gave access from the ground floor. But some of Grania's men had boosted others up to the second story, where a stone stair was fixed to the wall. They had trapped the Joyce chieftain in the bedchamber and swarmed over him, clubbing the man senseless before they dragged him down again. Now he lay on the dew-damp earth among his wounded men, his hands and feet bound with leather thongs.

He returned to consciousness to find a tall, lean woman standing over him with her hands on her hips. She was dressed like her warriors, but he knew that face. "Gráinne Ni Mháille," he acknowledged.

"This castle is an O Flaherty stronghold and shall remain so," she told him sternly. "You will agree here and now, or I will have my men kill you where you lie."

"You would slaughter a helpless man?"

"Your men killed my husband from ambush. I will be exactly as honorable as you are, in dealing with you—and no more. It is up to you to determine what relations will be like between O Flaherty and Joyce in the future."

Standing above him, she seemed even taller than she was, and more powerful. "How many of my men are left alive?" he wanted to know.

"Half. Counting you. A just exchange for the tanist's life."

The chieftain closed his eyes, but the bad dream did not go away. When he opened them again she was standing exactly as she had before, feet spread, hands on hips. She seemed prepared to stand like that through all eternity if necessary.

"The castle is yours," he said at last, low and sullen.

"I demand your word of honor that it will not be attacked again by your clansmen. In return, you will have my word that no further reprisals will be carried out by my dead husband's sept against you."

He squinted up at her. "No further reprisals?" he asked in surprise. The pattern of revenge, attack and counterattack, was as old as Ireland; as old as man's concept of honor, perhaps. And this woman was proposing to set it aside.

"Listen to her," murmured the badly wounded captain of his guard who lay near him.

The Joyce chieftain thought for another long moment while Grania waited. "You have my word," he said at last. "I can speak only for my own sept, my own blood-kin, but I will do what I can to influence the rest of my clan as well." His bloodless lips curled in a bitter smile. "I will tell them this is no longer the Cock's Castle, but the Hen's."

A member of clan O Lee who served as physician to Grania and her sailors cleaned and bound the wounds of the Joyce survivors, and with her own hands Grania gave food and drink to those too injured to feed themselves.

Perhaps it stops here, she thought to herself, wincing inwardly at the sight of each bloody, gaping wound, but keeping her face impassive. Perhaps I can at least assure my sons will have nothing to fear from their neighbors.

When she found Tigernan curled up in his cloak, his face very pale, she crouched down beside him. "Are you all right?"

"I'm surprised you got around to me," he said without opening his eyes.

"Ruari Oge told me you were not badly hurt; I had to see to the others."

"Easy for him to say," Tigernan groaned.

"Where is your wound?"

"He didn't tell you?"

"No."

The ginger-haired man turned his face away from her. "I was hit on the hip with a club," he said.

The Joyces left the island in abject defeat, dragging their belongings with them. "They'll be back," Magnus predicted. "You can't trust them to honor their word. They're not really Gaels."

"They are Irishmen," Grania said, "and I'm going to trust them to honor their word. You have Norse ancestors, don't you? And you consider yourself Irish. And your honor is beyond question."

"That's different," Magnus said huffily. "But I'm warning you, watch out for the Joyces."

They stayed at the castle until the quality of light on Lough Corrib began to change, signaling the onset of autumn. Grania was determined to so fortify the place that it could be held against any further assaults.

"This fortress was built to provide security when all else failed," Ruari Oge had observed on the day after the battle. "It has water around it like a Norman keep, but instead of a dug moat the water is a lake. Our people used to build dwellings on man-made islands for the same reason—you've seen crannogs, Grania."

"I have."

"So the water should have proved a defense, but it didn't. We use water as land men use roads. There should have been . . . ah . . . a tunnel built, connecting this island with the mainland and offering an escape route once they realized they were outnumbered."

Her eyes lit up. "Of course! Where did you get such a clever idea, Ruari Oge?"

The big man shrugged. "I have a head for strategy, I suppose."

"We'll have to make more use of your head. And I have another idea, one suggested by your tunnel. If even one man had gotten away through that tunnel and to the mainland, he could have signaled others and summoned support. If a set of beacons was set up, something stretching from hill to hill over a great distance, it could reach the sea, even."

"It could," he agreed, looking at her with admiration. "Where did you get such an idea?"

"History, I find, is full of usable lessons," Grania told him. "Celtic signal fires from the high ground are a very old idea, a way of communicating more swiftly than any human messenger could travel."

"Sometimes the old ideas are best," said Ruari Oge. "There are too many new ones I don't like." He was thinking of the butchered forests.

"I agree," said Grania. She was thinking of Elizabeth and her policies.

During the period it took to fortify the island according to Grania's specifications, representatives from various O Flaherty septs began arriving to call upon Donal an Chogaidh's widow—and see for themselves if she had actually recaptured a castle as rumor claimed.

They found a resolute woman very much in command of a tightly knit company of confident men. Not only was Grania's band victorious, but there seemed to be a special camaraderie among them. Perhaps it was the shared brotherhood of the sea; perhaps it was a spark she herself lent them. She did not burden her vitality with self-doubt, and her confidence was contagious.

Some of the O Flaherties who came to see her had not been allies of her dead husband. "Donal an Chogaidh never made a friend nor lost an enemy," she heard more than once. But they found his widow to be a different sort of person. She welcomed them with typical O Malley warmth and hospitality, and old quarrels were never brought up.

Not all of the clansmen returned home.

"I am making friends for my sons," Grania told her captains. "Friends are allies, but allies are not always friends. And in times like this they will need all the friends they can get."

To the southern chieftains she offered a message of hope. "I will enlarge my fleet," she promised, "and carry more than the products of my husband's sept to foreign ports. I will take yours as well; wool from Iar Connaught can command a high price in Spain. Murrough of the Battle Axes can't do that for you because he must adhere to English policy now, and the Tudor she-king means to destroy Ireland's foreign trade and keep all our produce for her own people."

"Her men will never let you set sail from Galway port," Grania was told.

"I have no intention of trying to use Galway. I'm going to make my base in Umhall, on Clew bay. The long arm of the English does not quite reach that far. But I won't forget clan O Flaherty; you have my word that I will be your friend and ally and do what I can for all my sons' clansmen."

So she bound the O Flaherties to her sons—with the strength of the sea.

The nights were brittle with frost. "If you mean to go back to Clew bay we had better go soon, before the weather gets too bad for an overland march," Ruari Oge advised.

Ruari Oge had become Grania's principal adviser, Tigernan noted with resentment he could not quite conceal. It put a certain strain on their friendship. Ruari Oge was the younger son of a chieftain in an O Donnell sept. He was of Grania's rank; she listened to him. And Tigernan, for all his striving, was only the son of an unimportant fisherman from Inishbofin.

Every evening, when the day's work was done, Grania crowded

the chambers and hall of the Hen's Castle with her followers and they shared whatever the day's hunting party had provided—goose and venison and fat fish from the lake. Whole deer were roasted in a pit beyond the walls, a large hole dug in the earth and layered with heated rocks. The meat was wrapped in wet sedge to keep the flesh from burning, and the fragrant smoke hung like sweet fog over the little island. Late into the night, Grania's band feasted and chanted battle songs and swapped tales of land and sea, and every day it seemed there were more men than the day before. Soon there were over two hundred of them, with faces from every O Flaherty sept in Iar Connaught.

Two hundred men determined to follow her back to Clew bay and share the prosperity she was determined to wrest from the future.

She picked a core of reliable warriors to stay on at the Hen's Castle and prepared to leave for the journey northward, but before she could depart, one final band of visitors arrived. A young man was brought forward to meet her, a tall young man wearing a fine linen tunic instead of country clothes, and a golden fillet on his head.

At first she did not recognize him. Then something about the thinness of his lips spoke to her, and she said, "Owen? Is it really you?"

"Owen, son of Donal of the Battles," he replied, bowing his head to his mother.

She had seen so little of the children. Fosterage was intended to weave them inextricably into another family, and their parents visited them only on special occasions. Busy with her ships, Grania had not seen her eldest son since the year before Donal's death, and in that time he had become a man.

He was a handsome man, big as an O Malley, and her first impression was one of maternal pride. But because she was Grania, she could not help looking at him through narrowed eyes as she would survey a boat, and she recognized a certain softness in the lower part of his face, an indecisiveness in the shape of his mouth that troubled her. He was of man's years, yet in his expression there lurked something of the child still waiting for direction from outside itself.

He needs seasoning, Grania thought. Aloud she said, "If I put the maintenance and defense of this fortress into your hands, will you take full responsibility for it and hold it safe for your clansmen when they are in need of a refuge?"

Pride leaped in his eyes, but she saw a flicker of hesitation as well.

"Can't you handle it?" she asked, challenging him. He was her son; he should rise to a challenge.

"I'll try," Owen replied.

Grania felt a blaze of anger. " 'Try' is a word to excuse failure. Just tell me you'll *do* it." He was too old for gentle handling, she thought; too old for patience and mothering. The world was a demanding place, and if he was to make his way in it successfully he must have a firm backbone. No one had coddled Grania; she would teach her sons not to expect coddling either.

The young man looked at his mother's face and drew a deep breath. "I will maintain and defend this island," he said as if by rote. "And Bunowen and Ballinahinch as well. Murrough will soon join me, and between us we will collect our father's rents and protect his holdings."

"See to it," Grania replied. She wanted to smile at him then, but she thought he needed the firmness more, and so her expression remained that of a stern commander.

Owen looked at his mother in puzzlement. He had been raised in the old traditions. This image of a mother as warrior and provider was unsettling to him. He wanted to see her in a more familiar role. "It was you who sent me those presents, wasn't it?" he asked suddenly. "Every month or so, for as long as I can remember. They told me they were only gifts from my father's sept, but . . ."

"I sent them. Donal was too, ah, occupied elsewhere to think of such things. Did you . . . did you like them?" she asked almost shyly.

"That fine Flemish blade, it's one of my treasures. And the ermine mantle. But sometimes I could not understand what the presents were supposed to mean. There was a lock of black hair in a little casket, for example, just hair, nothing I could *use*. What was I supposed to do with that?"

"Do you still have it?"

"I don't know. I don't think so—I suppose it was thrown on the midden-heap long ago. Was it important?"

"No," said raven-haired Grania, lifting her chin. "It was nothing."

Grania explained the newly dug tunnel and other fortifications of the island to Owen. "I've made friends among various clans from here to the coast. Similar beacons are being set up that will reach from Iar Connaught to Umhall. If you need help you have only to light the first fire. But you won't need help," she added, willing it to be so. "You're going to do just fine."

"Just fine," Owen echoed.

"We have to get back to the sea," Grania announced to her men.

Because they were victorious, the return trip to Clew bay did not seem nearly as long as the journey to Lough Corrib had been. Some of the O Flaherties played the pipes, and other men carried bodhrans; there was even a battle harp, light in weight and easily slung over the shoulder. Music accompanied Grania's troops, and in camp at night they sat around the fires and drank ale or threw the dice like people at a festival.

"She's nothing like Donal an Chogaidh," one O Flaherty warrior remarked to another.

"That proves God is not as unkind and stern as the Protesters would have us believe," replied his companion.

One evening when the stars were very close and the wind off Lough Mask was cold, Grania approached Tigernan. "Where's that pistol you were carrying?"

"In my pack. Why?"

"Did you use it at the castle?"

"When we all came boiling through the portal together it was too dark and too crowded; I never got the chance. To aim the thing takes time and room."

"If I'd had it in my belt I could have used it," Grania told him. "As it was, I arrived at the scene of battle practically defenseless."

"You wouldn't have been in any danger if you'd stayed with the boats."

She dug an elbow in his ribs. "I'm surprised you didn't hit me over the head to be certain I did."

"Someone should have," Tigernan told her. He would never let her know how badly he'd been frightened when he saw her enter that doorway.

"I don't mean to go unarmed again," Grania decided. "A knife is something, but I want to learn how to use that pistol of yours. It's like a miniature cannon; even if you don't hit anything you can frighten someone—and it has a longer reach than any blade."

Tigernan was appalled. "You'll shoot off your own toes!"

[117]

She raised an eyebrow. "Did you?"

"That's different."

"Why?" She dared him to say it, to claim some expertise for his sex that would not apply to hers. But Tigernan just gave her a long look, then surrendered the Saxon pistol. "You'd better do some practicing with it," he advised. "And . . . I'll show you, you don't need to bother Ruari Oge."

"I hadn't thought of asking Ruari Oge," she told him honestly.

✠

They were victors, and word of their victory preceded them. Clan chiefs along their route were watching for them and sent messengers to greet them, to invite the Black Oak's remarkable daughter to share their meat and salt. The army stopped at first one stronghold and then another, accepting some of the age-old tribute due champions. At each place, Grania was careful to mention the names of Owen and Murrough O Flaherty and urge that whatever friendship was shown her be extended to them as well, if the occasion ever arose.

Her men followed her into Gaelic tower houses and unfamiliar Norman keeps. There were a few awkward moments, the uncertainty which always surrounds the meeting of strangers. But then the rituals of hospitality caught up hosts and guests alike in patterns they knew, so the unfamiliar became familiar. Basins of scented water were furnished for washing hands and feet; honey-milk was proffered to sweeten parched throats; an exchange of the names of septs and kin uncovered distant relationships and friends in common.

The elaborate meshing of clan loyalties followed Grania from Lough Corrib to Clew bay.

When they arrived, Dubhdara greeted them and saw at once that his daughter was not as hawser-lean as she had been, and there was considerable color in her cheeks. "I've come home," she told him.

"You mean to *stay* here?"

"I do."

"But . . . where will you live?"

"Where do your sons live?" she asked him.

The bluntness of the unexpected question briefly shattered Dubhdara's composure. "How did you . . . I mean . . . ah, there's one who occupies his mother's cottage north of Cathair na Mart."

"And where's the mother?"

"Dead, three years ago Samhain. We had a union of the fourth degree under Brehon law, that of a man with a loved woman who was not his avowed wife."

Grania digested the information, seeing through Dubhdara to horizons he could not imagine. "I assume the boy is not in line for the tanistry of clan O Malley?"

"He is not. That rank sits secure on my nephew Cormac's shoulders. But I want him to have something."

"Then install him in the fortress of Cathair na Mart," Grania said, the words sounding almost like an order rather than a suggestion. "You prefer Belclare anyway, closer to the bay. And there's no reason why a son of yours should not take charge of your herds on the Murrisk plain. If he is content with that he will have no reason to object to my occupation of Clare island."

Astonishment piled upon astonishment for the Black Oak. "You want to live in the tower house there?"

"And fill the harbor with my ships. From there it is an easy enough run down the coast to Bunowen. I can carry O Flaherty exports as well as handling . . . enterprise of my own. And I need a house to bring my daughter to, for Margaret is almost fourteen and of marrying age. Her fosterage is ending, and I mean to find her a good husband." The slightest stress accompanied the word "good," but Grania did not look at her father as she said it.

"You have this all planned," Dubhdara commented, scowling. "What if I refuse?"

"Then I'll go north to clan O Donnell," his daughter told him without hesitation. "They will welcome my ships and trade."

"You're welcome to Cliara," Dubhdara decided. "You didn't have to hold a knife to my neck." He looked at her closely, trying to see through vision webbed by age. "What's happened to you, girl? When did you turn so cold? Was it the doing of Donal an Chogaidh? I seem to remember you as such a merry little body."

"I still laugh," Grania told him. "I laugh all the time."

She laughed when Tigernan set up a target and reminded her to practice with the handgun. At first she was so determined to prove she could fire the weapon that her shots went wild and her powder was wasted. When Tigernan tried to correct her she lost her temper with him and refused to give the pistol to him so he could demonstrate.

A thin, rare sprinkling of snow glittered as white as the quartz on Croagh Patrick, and the snap in the air was rivaled by the snapping eyes of the black-haired woman clutching the pistol. Her mouth was red; it seemed to taunt him.

Something snapped in Tigernan. He grabbed both Grania's wrists with his two strong hands, giving her such a shake she dropped the gun. "That isn't a toy!" he shouted at her. "Have some respect for it."

"And you're going to be the one to teach me respect?" She tossed her head, the heavy hair whipping like a horse's mane.

"It's time somebody did," Tigernan told her. He stooped and seized a handful of ice crystals and hurled them in her face as he had once thrown salt water in her face many years ago, teasing her on an O Malley ship bound for Spain.

"You mangy hound!" She returned his fire, throwing hard. A wad of ice struck his cheek, and he lunged for her. They fell together onto frozen earth and he lay on top of her for a moment, breathing heavily, unable to believe he was feeling her body beneath his.

She opened her eyes and looked up at him but said nothing.

Tigernan did not move. He did not trust himself to move.

Then Grania laughed. Her ribs rose up, lifting him, and she pushed him away good-naturedly. "You're crushing me, you great hulk," she accused, grinning at him. She rolled over and scrambled to her feet. "But you win. If you're that determined to teach me, I'll at least listen." She folded her hands and made a doomed effort to appear demure and obedient, looking so unlike herself that Tigernan laughed too. He laughed until he hurt—or until whatever was hurting had stopped—and she was as merry as he.

Just so had they played together when they were still little more than children, on that first and long-ago voyage to Spain. He would always remember. He wondered if she ever did.

Grania transported all her belongings to Clare island, which was so far out in the mouth of Clew bay that Croagh Patrick appeared more hill than mountain, and Belclare was quite invisible. The O Malley stronghold there was a Gaelic tower house owing much less to Norman influence than such sprawling keeps as Bunowen. It was built beside a small harbor on the eastern side of the island, offering an excellent view of Clew bay and its approaches but not visible to ships passing on the open sea. The sturdy shoulders of Cnoc Mór rose to a windy peak on the western side of the island, effectively cutting much of the Atlantic wind and concealing the harbor and stronghold.

The tower house had never been more than a summer residence for the O Malleys, and in recent years its use had diminished until its wooden floors were rotting and piles of rubbish furnished its chambers. Originally built as a watchtower, the structure perched on a black cliff eroded by caves where small boats could be hidden, and from the exterior the rectangular fort appeared to be a bleak, inhospitable stone block with only arrow slits to light its lower stories. Yet beside the castle was a tiny cove, hidden by the black cliffs; a cove of pure white sand and peacock-green water as transparent as the sky.

Though naturally treeless, Clare island was not without its beauties. And in the crevices of her soul, Grania hungered for beauty.

The islanders included among their numbers enough carpenters and woodworkers to repair the castle to suit her needs. Throughout the darkest days of winter, when no ships took to the sea, Grania kept busy making her new stronghold habitable. It was a fortress when seen from outside, but beyond its tiny entry court and the portal of oak carried from the mainland, a blaze of color shouted welcome.

There would be no soldiers garrisoned on the ground floor, because many of Grania's men would be living just beyond the walls. So she made the entry level her public hall, plastering the walls and painting them a vivid apricot color. A turf fire was kept blazing on the hearth facing the entryway. In the center of the side walls, deep window embrasures were let into the stone, allowing an amplification of light, and Grania had these alcoves plastered white to further brighten the room, then filled them with down cushions to make comfortable seating. Bare floors of multicolored flagstone added to the cheerful effect. Hers was not a feminine hall replete with trinkets, but a boldly handsome room where a man might sit at ease and take his boots off . . . or a tired woman could lean her elbows on the table and down one tankard of ale after another while she watched the fire.

The two floors above were reached by a wooden ladder and stone stairs, and contained sleeping chambers and a privy room, as well as a pair of defensive perches sheathed in slates from which men-at-arms could shower arrows and stones upon invaders if it ever proved necessary. A separate kitchen was built adjacent to the stone wall surrounding the castle, and a woman whose husband served as gatekeeper and sentry supplied Grania with butter and bread and cooked indifferent meals for her that first winter. Grania encouraged no other attendants. The serenity of her own hall, where no voice but her own carried weight, was a pleasure she wanted to savor.

On a blustery December morning, Ruari Oge came up from the harbor to find his commander struggling alone to drag her feather bed outside for an airing. "You should have a serving woman to do that for you," he said. "It's no job for a . . . for you."

"I had serving women in Iar Connaught, and my ears are still beaten flat from their gossip. I can care for myself; my needs are simple."

"I can bring you a woman who won't gossip," Ruari offered. "Since you've provided your crewmen homes on Clare, I've sent for my wife to join us. The weather's improving; she should reach Clew bay soon. She can sew grass into silk and cook nettles to taste like a king's dinner. No man has a better wife than my Evleen."

Grania chuckled. "A good wife is just what *I* need." She arched her back and massaged the area over her kidneys with splayed fingers. "Why haven't I met this paragon of yours sooner? Surely you've had her close by before."

"I have . . . but Evleen is not a great one for meeting people. She has quiet ways."

"Sounds better and better," commented Grania. "If she's willing to attend me here, she could be a great help in getting this place ready for my daughter to join me when the time comes. It would ease my mind to know there was someone I could depend on in the castle while we're at sea."

The old pirate's eyes gleamed. "We're sailing soon, then?"

"Very soon. I mean to make myself welcome in more ports than Owen Dubhdara."

He hitched his thumbs through his belt. "You've a rare ambition for a woman."

"Life is short," Grania replied. "And I'm thirty-four years old. About the same age as the Tudor woman," she added as an afterthought.

She glanced east, beyond Umhall and Ros Comáin and even the Irish sea, as if she could see all the way to England if she stared sharply enough. She felt out with her mind, groping for Elizabeth of clan Tudor, an ambitious woman, husbandless, powerful. A female king.

What do you think in your secret thoughts? Grania asked that unknown woman silently.

As was the custom, the festival of Christmas was celebrated on the mainland from Advent to Epiphany. Grania returned to Belclare for the climax of the holy season, more for the sake of appearances than because she felt either reverent or festive. Attending Mass on Christmas Day in the Augustinian chapel, she obediently opened her mouth for Christ's body and blood and consumed both, yet felt empty afterward, though faces all around her appeared exalted.

Something, she thought, fumbling unsuccessfully in her mind for an image to match the need. I want *something*. For myself. If even the body and blood of God does not take away that hunger, what can I hope for?

From beside the altar, the abbot Calvagh watched her. Owen O Malley was growing old and his tight grip on Umhall was loosening, even as the English relentlessly destroyed the Gaelic system of chieftainly elections and tanistry. What would be the new power in Umhall? Looking at the resolute face of the dark, windburned woman in the O Malley pew, Calvagh determined to get to know Gráinne Ni Mháille better. Politics, he thought to himself, smiling inwardly. All the political struggles are not in Rome.

I want something for myself, Grania was thinking, staring at her folded and clenched hands.

10

Calvagh of Bregia had a friend. Not the sort of companion from his days of theological study who might now sit by the fire and reminisce over golden hours in Roman courtyards—but an ashen-faced man in dark clothing who arrived with an armed retinue and tapped for admittance at a rarely used doorway in the abbey's tower. A dour man with a nose and chin that yearned toward one another, guarding a mouth collapsed inward on secrets. A man as stern as the unusual battlemented walls of the Augustinian abbey, his only grace note the massive ring of the archbishop of Armagh.

Adam Loftus did not, however, travel with the panoply to be expected of a Catholic archbishop. He was not Catholic, but a dedicated Protestant of English birth who had come to Ireland with a reformer's zeal and been rewarded for his services by an archbishopric in the newly designated state religion.

The previous year, a Court of High Commission had been set up to enforce conformity to the new religion and to administer an Oath of Supremacy which was to be taken by all bishops, mayors, and other officeholders in Ireland. The commission had not been strict enough in enforcing this mandate, however; the forests and bogs and roads that turned into muddy tracks at the touch of rain all mitigated against overriding authority. The people themselves were stubborn and resistant, even when their ecclesiastical leaders were more reasonable. The bishops of Meath and Kildare had been dismissed for refusing to take the oath and preach the new religion, but other good Catholic men, like the bishops of Tuam and Limerick, were permitted to remain after taking the oath though everyone knew they allowed Mass to be said and protected Catholic missionaries.

But men like Adam Loftus were not content with outward conformity; they had a message and heard God's command to spread it. Adam also had eighteen children, and his stipend as archbishop of Armagh yielded only twenty pounds a year. As an Englishman, he had little hope of converting the Irish personally, but he was convinced that if he could convert enough of the Catholic clergy they would do it for him, and his success would thus move him into a more prosperous situation—such as Dublin, safely within the Pale.

To this end, he made quiet calls on bishops, priests, and abbots in outlying Gaelic areas, using whatever persuasive means came to hand to guide them to the true faith and catch their followers in the same net. Had he not already known Calvagh of Bregia, however, he would never have ventured so far west as Clew bay. He felt he was truly in alien land here, and his men waited nervously in the abbey's refectory, half expecting to be attacked by Papists and dragged out into the bitter night.

Scorning the padded couch his host offered him, Adam Loftus seated himself on a wooden bench and clasped his hands in his lap. "It has been a long time since we met on the ship returning from the Continent," he began. "You are looking well, Calvagh."

"I do as well as one can under the circumstances," the abbot replied carefully.

"You have a sufficient living here? This seems a wild and primitive place, surely not suited to the tastes of a man who has spent years in Rome."

"I was pleased to be sent here," Calvagh told him. "We are far away from the rest of the world, that is true, but this is a fine abbey and well endowed by the clan O Malley. I want for nothing."

"Ah, yes. The clan O Malley." The archbishop of Armagh nodded to himself. "Practically the last of the old Gaelic clans which has not had at least some members submit to the Crown."

"Nor to your religion," Calvagh added, framing the words gently so they would not sound defiant. He knew perfectly well what Adam Loftus had come for; he had come to buy souls. Perhaps Calvagh's own. The question was, what was the going market price?

The abbot of Murrisk was an educated, traveled man, and he knew the days of the old order were numbered. Whatever came he meant to survive it. Surely God wished him to survive, or He would not have brought him so far.

"We have heard something of the O Malleys," Adam said. "I

was in Cong recently and heard of a female O Malley who is commanding a fleet of ships, in fact. There is great consternation about her activities in Galway, where the merchants' guild accuses her of illegally exporting and selling wool. They also accuse her of piracy." His mouth folded sternly down on this last word.

"You speak of Grania," Calvagh told him. "She is . . . a most unusual woman. Only recently she—"

"—Attacked and captured a castle and returned to this region with an army at her back," Adam interrupted. "Yes, we heard that too. Furthermore she is the widow of a defiant O Flaherty chieftain who refused to acknowledge his queen, and whose sons look fair to follow in their sire's path. Like all her sex, the woman is a fountainhead of problems," said Adam, the father of eighteen children, "and she appears even more troublesome than most. Are you by any good fortune her confessor, Calvagh?"

"I am not. There is a friar on Clare Island whose job it is to guide her devotions."

"She is a pious woman, then?"

Calvagh hesitated, thinking back on what he had heard of Grania. "Not as pious as some. And if I am any judge of character she is most headstrong and willful. Her late mother is still celebrated for her good works, but the daughter has other interests."

"So it seems." The archbishop stroked his nose thoughtfully, tugging at it as if he meant to make it still longer. "In Galway it is believed she could spark Gaelic resistance throughout the entire province of Connaught, not just in West Connaught. May I confide in you, Calvagh? The Queen's Council is deeply troubled by the constant rebellions of the Catholic chieftains in Ulster. They have been tolerant, even lenient, about religious issues, believing the Irish are basically ignorant but will embrace the new religion once they are properly educated to it. But the council's patience is wearing thin. There will soon be more forcible church closures throughout Ireland, and the abbey of Murrisk might well be among them. Because you and I are personally acquainted I have come all this way to talk to you as one reasonable man to another, Calvagh. I can say a few words into the proper ears and life will go on here undisturbed—provided the abbey itself does not become a voice for rebellion and sedition, as has unfortunately happened elsewhere."

"What do you want in return?" Calvagh asked bluntly. Adam

was not the first Protestant he had met. The nature of such men seemed to lend itself to plain speaking, rather than the elaborate and often artistic circumlocutions beloved by the Gaels and many of Calvagh's own faith.

"I? I want nothing—except that you spend some time reading the new Book of Common Prayer we have provided for the education of the people. See if you do not find it a reasonable, indeed a beautiful, ecclesiastical tool. Keep your mind and your soul open, Calvagh. You have been entrusted with caring for a flock, have you not? Then care for this one. Change with the times. Grow spiritually, and guide others."

"You attempt to convert me?"

Adam made a deprecating gesture. "I attempt nothing, I only suggest. We became friends on shipboard and had long discussions as to the true nature of God, do you remember? A God who, from time to time, sends prophets to enlighten His people and lead them back onto the paths of righteousness. Rome has become a fat and greedy whore sunk in debauchery, Calvagh. You know that. Everything is for sale in Rome—to Spain, to France, even to England if they were willing to pay the price. But there is a new voice now, a new hope! Think about it.

"And think, too, about the clan O Malley and the territory the Gaels call Umhall. I tell you privately that sometime later in this year, very likely in the autumn, the Queen's Council will appoint a new governor for Ireland. That man will probably be Sir Henry Sidney. He will in no way be as lenient as his predecessors have been. The council has already convinced the queen that the policies of her man Sussex in governing Ireland have been nothing but an expensive failure. Sidney is a good administrator; he is now lord president of Wales, which has problems similar to those here."

"Do you know Sidney?" Calvagh asked.

"Not personally. But I know enough about the man to predict what he will do. The O Neills and O Donnells in Ulster continue to resist the queen's authority, endlessly plotting with foreign powers against England. They might be able to enlist the military aid of Catholic Spain or France or both, eventually. The new governor will take steps to break their power before it gets out of hand. And that brings me back to Connaught, Calvagh. Through the O Malley woman the clans of O Flaherty and O Malley unite, and both clans count the Burkes among their allies as well. The Burkes were one of the first great Norman families to disassociate themselves from the English Crown and claim autonomy in Ireland. A confederation of these three families could conceivably put its weight behind the Ulster chieftains and set all Ireland aflame with war.

"So you see, Grace O Malley is a very dangerous woman. The fact that she was able to unite various O Flaherty septs behind her bodes ill for the future. Her bizarre actions seem to exert a powerful appeal upon the uncivilized Irish.

"So there is a second favor you can do for me, Calvagh. You are in a good position here, having the trust and support of the O Malley clan. You can keep watch over the activities of this woman of theirs, Grace, or whatever her name is, and report on her actions. Write directly to me and I will see that your information reaches the appropriate authorities."

Calvagh's throat went dry. He was being asked to be an informer, a Judas—if one chose to see the situation in such bald terms. But an educated and realistic man, such as he believed himself to be, might view the situation from a historical perspective and make a wisely pragmatic decision to safeguard Church property.

Land and property had always been the bedrock issue in Ireland, since Pope Adrian titled Henry II of England as "Lord of Ireland" in the twelfth century, giving him permission to overrun the island with his own troops in an effort to force Strongbow's Normans to be obedient to the letter of their English fealty. Descendants of those Normans like the Gaelicized Burkes and the great earls of Kildare and Desmond still held their private feudal kingdoms as best they could against Tudor authority—and the Catholic Church would be well advised to try to hold on to its own property against Tudor Protestantism.

By any means it could, Calvagh thought.

The abbot of Murrisk remembered, all too vividly, seeing one friary after another stripped, looted, desecrated, its fields partitioned into tiny farms, its buildings left to fall into decay with the Crown's seal barring the doors. Crucifix, bell, censer—gone. Nuns raped, friars beaten. Human feces upon the high altar. Priests who resisted dragged to the nearest crossroads to be martyred with a zeal equal to that of the Spanish Inquisitors.

Blood sacrifice in the name of God.

Calvagh had no taste for martyrdom; not for himself. He had campaigned shrewdly for his position as abbot of a peaceful monastery in an untroubled and overlooked backwater. Let others be sacrificed. If necessary, he would do the job himself, seeing it as historically inevitable. And were there not considerable justifications? Even Protestantism had its good qualities; the new order seemed to be more successful in eradicating the old pagan Brehon law than Rome had ever been.

Calvagh was willing to be persuaded. "I will study your prayer book," he told the archbishop of Armagh, "and I will also observe the actions of Gráinne Ni Mháille insofar as I am able, and let you know what she does. Her father is aging and exerts less influence in the region than he once did, while her power seems to grow. She may well be a dangerous troublemaker. For the sake of these people, I would not want to see war come here—nor see this monastery dissolved, either. Give us a little time, that's all I ask. Just a little time."

"I knew you were a reasonable man," replied Adam Loftus.

When he was gone, the abbot went alone to the chapel to pray. Give me a sign, he asked his God. If this is what You really wish, give me a sign that Grania is unworthy of the Church's protection. When I go to bless her ships, perhaps, before she returns to Clare island. . . .

Calvagh had great faith in his ability to interpret signs to his own benefit.

✠

In the night, in her chamber at Belclare, Grania awoke from a troubled sleep and wild dreams to find her flesh burning with the remembered imprint of Tigernan's body lying atop hers, as vivid as if he had just gotten up after their fight in the snow. She sat upright in bed, her heart racing.

The room was echoingly empty.

She swung her feet over the edge of the bed and buried her face in her hands. "Tigernan," she murmured to herself. "What a preposterous dream. You are a foolish woman, Grania. Men are nothing but burdens. *Tigernan*, of all people. . . ." Punching her pillow with her fist, she twisted back onto the bed and laughed at herself as she pulled up the covers.

But sleep took a long time coming.

✠

Just as Grania was making preparations to return to Clare island, Ruari Oge's wife arrived at Belclare. She rode down to the quay on horseback, like a princess, and laborers who had been hard at work moving hogsheads and stacking salted hides stopped and stared as they would at passing nobility.

Yet Evleen was not a prepossessing figure. She was small for a Gaelic woman, and pale, a tiny wraithlike creature who exuded a contradictory air of resilient strength. Her clothing consisted of an unfitted gown of homespun and a shaggy mantle, and her feet dangled bare against the horse's sides, in spite of the weather. Unlike other Irish women, she wore no crucifix around her neck. Her only ornament was a triskele of silver in an ancient pattern, suspended upon her flat bosom by a leather thong. She was, perhaps, as old as her husband, but the years were dealing kindly with her and her wrinkles seemed no more than the veining on a leaf.

In a voice rich with pride, Ruari Oge introduced her formally to his commander. "Evleen Ni Brien, of clan Dal Cais," he said. "I once encountered her on the bank of the Shannon river and she has possessed me ever since."

Evleen made the briefest of bows to Grania, polite but not deferential, just as the abbot of Murrisk approached to discuss the blessing of the fleet. He took in the tableau with one piercing glance and stopped in his tracks, gripping his walking staff.

The O Malley's daughter was accepting homage from a . . . he could hardly believe what he was seeing, and yet there was no mistake . . . from a wild pagan. He had only heard whispers of such people, but enough tales still abounded concerning them to make them readily identifiable—even if this one did claim the noble name O Brien.

More than her clothes gave her away. The horse she rode was equipped with an embroidered dillat, a thick cloth used instead of the hard leather saddle the English had introduced. On its head was an archaic single-rein bridle, with the rein attached at the top of the noseband instead of the side and coming to the rider's hand over the animal's forehead, passing between eyes and ears and held in place by a ring on the browband.

Grania was looking with surprise at Evleen's horse fittings. The little woman smiled. "I ride in the old way," she admitted in a

whisper-soft voice. With the gentlest touch on the rein she commanded the horse to stand still, and leaning down over its neck she
showed Grania a yew-wood rod she carried. "This is for turning.
Touched to the shoulder here . . . or here . . . it directs my friend
to go this direction or that, and the pressure of the touch tells her
how fast to move, though we scarcely need it, the mare and I. We
have better ways of talking to each other."

Pagan! Calvagh thought, repelled and intrigued. I am looking at
a heathen who arrogantly displays a Druid emblem on her breast.

Evleen's horse was chestnut in color, with a light gold mane
artfully dyed in stripes of green, providing a brilliant contrast to
her shaggy red hide. Seeing Grania looking at it, Evleen explained,
"Dyeing the mane is another old custom. Beauty for its own sake,
and to please the spirits." She made a gesture with her hand almost
like a Christian signing the cross, but subtly different.

I have my sign, thought Calvagh with relief. More easily than he
had anticipated, Grania had revealed herself, welcoming this savage to her retinue. Though his position and perhaps his very life
depended on the tolerance of the Protestant Adam Loftus and his
peers, the new abbot of Murrisk was a man of rigidly inflexible
spirit himself, and the otherness of Evleen branded her as a born
enemy to him.

Grania liked her at once, though there was something discon-
certing about the woman. Evleen quickly agreed to help in the
tower house on Clare island, and was most gracious in thanking
Grania for the house and field being given to her and Ruari Oge on
the island. But when she spoke, her words seemed to angle off
from the subject at hand; she always appeared to be talking about
something else, on another level.

Grania told her, "I'll entrust you to find people among the islanders to help you, if you need more assistance managing the
household. I doubt you'll locate a man to serve as steward, for they
are a rough lot on Cliara, but if we need one I can bring one from
the mainland eventually."

To which Evleen replied, "A rechtaire can wait. Following is
harder than leading. A leader can go where he will, but a follower
must pay attention and not get left behind."

Grania glanced toward Ruari Oge and saw him taking in this
conversation with considerable amusement. Behind her hand, she
whispered to him, "Are you certain your wife is able to do this?"

"Evleen's able to do anything she wants to," he assured her.

Grania's vessels were blessed by the abbot himself—which pleased Tigernan, she noted. Her thoughts were filled with returning to Cliara and getting various seafaring enterprises underway, so she did not notice the keen eyes of Calvagh raking every line of her ships, making mental record of their size and oar-power and possible armament.

That night, by the light of a bronze lamp, Calvagh recorded all he had seen. "She has only one possible gunship capable of cannon," he wrote, "but that is an old carrack in poor condition. Yet from the enthusiasm shown her by The O Malley's followers, I suspect she will soon include many of her father's vessels among her own and substantially increase the threat she represents to commercial shipping. Besides, she is a woman of questionable faith, having enlarged her retinue to include an obvious heathen person from somewhere in the forests of the interior. She must be closely observed from now on; Gráinne Ni Mháille is indeed dangerous."

Grania was not a consistent churchgoer, but on the occasions when she did appear in the chapel built by her forefathers she began to notice Calvagh soon made his own appearance. Watching her covertly, he placed himself in the confessional so that it was he to whom she must reveal her secrets, crowding her emotionally though he stayed at arm's length from her physically. Grania experienced an atavistic reaction to the man. When he was around, she wanted to bare her teeth and raise her hackles. It was not just because she suspected him to be a sodomite; Grania had never been judgmental in that respect. She understood that people must seek comfort where they could, each in his own way—except for Dubhdara, of course. He was her father and therefore her standards were different for him.

But Calvagh seemed to emanate an invisible cloud of nastiness like a fish gone bad. Grania sensed a corruption in the man that sickened her and made her long for the clean air of the sea.

She went less and less to chapel, and soon she went to confession not at all. She told herself she was too busy with other things.

✠

No sooner was Evleen installed on Clare island than the tower house seemed to bloom, even on the sleety gray days of January.

She took over the cooking and provided excellent meals seasoned with a variety of unfamiliar herbs. Grania's clothes were kept clean and mended, and even the pathway around the castle was swept smooth daily and lined with shells.

"Your Evleen's a wonder," Grania told Ruari Oge. "When my daughter comes to me I will have a real, comfortable home to offer her, thanks to your wife's energy. But . . . I hardly understand why she seems so eager to do it."

"I suspect she's keeping an eye on me," Ruari Oge said ruefully, though he was flattered by such possessiveness at his age. "Evleen's had the devil's own curiosity about the woman whose flag I followed."

"Did she think . . . you and I . . . ?" Grania laughed and Ruari laughed with her, but both were self-conscious, for different reasons. Ruari's admiration of the woman was one he would take to his grave, and Grania was startled to find in herself a new-blooming physical response to men that she had never suspected while she was still the wife of Donal of the Battles.

Whenever weather allowed, Grania's ships left the harbor at Clare, carrying merchandise—or occasional passengers, for a price —and taking prizes when the opportunity presented itself. The carrack was sent to Kinsale for refitting, but more vessels joined the fleet with Dubhdara's compliments. His strength was not what it had been, and he hated seeing ships he had loved riding idle at anchor while someone might be getting use out of them, adding luster to the name O Malley.

He did not think of that someone as his daughter, but as his strong right arm who held the fortress on Cliara and guarded the entrance to Clew bay for him.

St. Brigid's Day approached, and Tigernan made an issue about Grania's joining the annual pilgrimage the Carmelite sisters of Cliara led to the saint's holy well on the island. He had noticed the peculiar interest the Augustinian abbot was showing in Grania's affairs. "Let no one question your piety," he cautioned his commander.

"Piety and religious belief have become matters of considerable argument in Ireland," she reminded him. "It seems to me one can operate more freely if religious affiliations are not, ah, flaunted."

Tigernan was shocked. "Would you ignore your faith?"

"Of course not. But neither can I forget that it was the strictures of that faith which kept me bound in marriage to a man I learned to despise. Tigernan, there were actually moments when I could understand the English king, and his willingness to embrace a religion that would free him from an untenable situation. If I were ever to marry again—which seems highly unlikely—I think I would not do it before a Catholic altar."

He stared at her in alarm.

Grania laughed. "Don't look so astonished, my friend; I'm not going to start wearing Evleen's triskele and lighting fires on the four Celtic feast days. I just have other things on my mind than prayer stools and confessionals. But if it will make you feel better for my sake, we will join the pilgrimage tomorrow—though I smell a storm on the wind."

The storm came during the night, leaving the island brittle with cold, a rime of frost on the beaches. Before dawn a line of pilgrims, praying aloud and carrying torches, was snaking its way over the wintry land to a small, stone-encircled well curb, as unpretentious a shrine as even a saint could wish. The site seemed a lonely place for worship, but on the west coast of Ireland the Gaels understood that God is best encountered in lonely places where a man can hear the quiet voice speaking in the depths of his own soul. Even Grania, who had rejected her mother's obsessive religious devotion, felt the pull of the place.

With a roar similar to that of the ocean sounding in the caves below the tower house, the wind rose and swept over Clare island once more. Though wrapped in warm woolens and hides, the devout shivered as they waited their turn to sip from the well supposedly purified by the saint's visit. Toddlers clung to their mother's hands; toothless oldsters leaned on their walking sticks. Exalted by the hardship, the nuns were radiant.

As she turned away and handed the olivewood cup to the next in line, Grania caught a glimpse of a spot of light in the far distance. Stepping forward, she recognized it as a fire burning on one of the signal points she had set up along this section of coast. As she watched, a second spark flared into existence close to it, and then a third.

Grania grinned and looked around for Tigernan. "There's a tall-ship in trouble off Achill island," she told him. "The islanders have lighted the signals. Do you think our galleys are up to this gale? There may be survivors in need of rescue . . . and undoubtedly there's a cargo just waiting to be taken!"

The gale might have been sufficient to run a tallship aground, but rowed galleys with their sails lowered were a match for it. Hurriedly dispatched, with Grania herself in the prow of the lead vessel, they beat their way toward Achill island. But by the time they arrived the wreck had already broken up and the sea had claimed the salvage.

"We've wasted the day," Ruari Oge complained. He was about to order his men to turn back when Grania caught sight of a dark shape clinging to a rock in the boiling surf. One man out of the doomed crew still survived.

"You can't leave him there!" Grania screamed above the wind and the waves. "Get in as close as you can, Ruari Oge, and put men overboard with ropes around their waists. I won't surrender that man to the sea if I can help it!"

It did not matter who he was, or what flag had flown on his ship. The sea was at once Grania's strongest ally and her implacable enemy. It had taken her men and her caravel; now she meant to rob it of at least one of its victims, and she felt a deep fierce joy. This time she would win.

When the shipwreck victim was at last hauled over the gunwales and carried into the relatively dry prow of the galley he looked drowned. His brown hair was plastered across his waxen face like strands of seaweed. Bending over him, Grania exclaimed, "I know this fellow!"

Tigernan peered at their catch. "Who is he? Or rather, who was he?"

"He's alive—can't you see him breathing? Rub his hands and his feet, quickly, get warmth back into him—and turn him over and pound the sea out of him, will you? All at once, hurry." Over her shoulder she added, for Tigernan's benefit, "This was one of the crewmen on the carrack when we seized her. I remember him because he saluted me when we put them ashore."

It appeared no one else remembered but the man himself, for as consciousness returned and he opened his eyes to see Grania's face above him, he gave her an unmistakable look of recognition. Then the world blurred around him again and he drifted away into a nightmare of storm and shipwreck.

She took him back to Clare island and ordered him carried to her chamber, where the waiting fire on the hearth would warm him. Dismissing her crewmen, she told Evleen, "He is uninjured, aside from being very cold and half drowned. You and I can care for him together; there is no need to send for a physician. I've seen men pulled from the sea before, and I know what to do."

The two women removed his sodden clothing, peeling it from him like skin from a boiled onion as he lay sprawled across Grania's own bed. Grania could not help noticing how straight his limbs were, how elegantly modeled the articulation of wrist and ankle. This was no rude sailor born near one noisome dockside and destined to die upon another.

She found herself being gentle with him, though Evleen tugged him this way and that as they pulled his clothes from him and dried his body with cloths. Once the man's eyes fluttered open and appeared to look directly at Grania—deep, dark, fathomless eyes, as lustrous as if he had fever.

"Bring some coarse sand to rub his arms and legs," Grania ordered. "And materials to make a pallet for him right by the fire. He can stay here tonight and I'll watch over him; I'm not sleepy anyway."

Evleen hurried off, and Grania continued chafing the chilled body, watching eagerly for the first sign of returning color. Coverlets had been piled upon him, and she bared first one portion of his anatomy and then another, stroking his flesh with strong, sure hands as she summonded life back into it. When she pushed the covering off his shoulders and upper arms she saw that the column of his throat was cleanly carved and the skin over his collarbones possessed an ivory sheen.

He is beautiful, she thought. She believed she was using the same dispassionate appraisal she might venture upon examining a looted tray of hammered silver shaped by a Florentine artisan.

Beautiful.

Something for myself, a voice murmured within her.

She rearranged the covers over his upper body and pushed them away from the arch of his ribs, studying their rise and fall as he breathed. Then her gaze shifted to the mat of brown hair that lay, fine-textured as silk, upon his chest and continued down in a narrow line across his belly until it formed a nest of ringlets to cradle the somnolent penis.

Grania watched with a sense of surprise as her hand reached out like that of a separate entity compelled by its own brain. The sentient hand hovered over the man, then fitted itself smoothly to the contour of his belly, open palm on bare flesh.

The sailor was chilled, yet his skin felt warm. When Grania's fingers moved lower, close to the swelling, muscular thighs, she felt heat . . . or perhaps the heat was in her own blind fingertips.

Evleen had piled rectangular bricks of peat upon the hearth and drawn the woolen hangings tightly closed over the window apertures. Walls six feet thick shut out the cold wind and held in the rising heat.

Heat. Grania straightened and pushed her damp hair back from her face, but she could feel her heart hammering. The room had grown too hot, too airless. Her lungs lifted and labored. The chamber had become a blacksmith's furnace, melting and reshaping her. The temperature was too intense to be tolerated; in such a furnace anything might be forged. Grania's brain roved in the oven of her skull, seeing strange crimson visions. Sensual visions of flesh and heat and touch. And smell: skinsmell so strong in the room it seemed as solid as the walls. Heat and fire and the naked man lying like ivory beneath her hands. . . .

A wave of cool air jolted her as Evleen opened the door and slipped into the chamber.

At a glance she saw it all: Grania's flushed face and fever-bright eyes, and the color seeping back into the cheeks of the man who lay on her bed.

Saying nothing, Evleen brushed past the younger woman and knelt by the hearth to prepare a pallet. She stoked the fire with an iron poker; she put the bag of sand she had brought close to the flame to heat it. Tucked into the foot of the bed it would at least keep a chilled man's feet warm.

Evleen stood up and smoothed her skirt. Her eyes met Grania's with ancient wisdom, a wisdom that acknowledged neither sin nor shame, but understood need. She put her fingers against the man's throat and felt the strong, steady beating of his blood. She saw the flicker of his eyes behind the lids and knew they would soon open with returning consciousness. He was strong, this sailor, and healthy, a man near Grania's age with a good constitution. By the morning he would be well and hungry.

Or perhaps he might be hungry before.

Evleen smiled a small, wise smile. "There is beef broth in the kettle in the hall," she said, "and I brought in fresh water and a keg of red wine. I could help you move him onto the pallet now . . . but it seems a shame to disturb him when he looks so comfortable." Her gaze held Grania's.

"It would be cruel," the other woman agreed.

Evleen's smile grew imperceptibly wider. "The fire may be getting very low on Ruari Oge's hearth," she said.

"You had better go home and poke it up for him, then," Grania replied, smiling herself now.

"I had."

They regarded each other across the man on the bed. Grania suddenly realized she had never had a woman friend before. She had scorned feminine chatter and been disinterested in domestic detail . . . that was her mother's world, not hers. Yet in the small, hot chamber she found herself gazing into the kind and humorous eyes of a woman who understood and approved her deepest female self.

"I can take very good care of him tonight," she said aloud to Evleen, "All by myself."

"Of course you can. Two guards stand watch at the gate; if you need anything you have only to shout down to them, and myself will be not a hundred paces away in Ruari's house. I shall wait there until you send for me. Tomorrow." Putting one small hand briefly on Grania's shoulder, she slipped past her and out the door.

11

Though Evleen was gone, some hint of her presence seemed to remain in the room like a trace of musk on the air. An ebony crucifix hung on the wall over Grania's bedstead, but there would be no familiar prayer mouthed out of habit before the woman fell asleep this night.

Grania had never felt less sleepy.

The sailor was breathing normally now, and when she touched him his skin was neither clammy nor dry with fever. He looked like a man asleep, a healthy man lying at ease in his own bed but capable of waking up at any moment.

One by one, Grania pinched out the candles in their holders. Watching the sailor on her bed, she removed her clothes very slowly. When the room was dark except for the glow from the fire, and she was naked, she turned back the coverlet and slipped into bed beside him.

He murmured something and turned over, but his breathing stayed quiet.

Perhaps he is dreaming, she thought.

When she felt sure he had not awakened, Grania moved closer. He was lying with his back to her; in the dim room she could just make out the bulk of his shoulder. How strange it felt to be in bed with a man again! Like a magnet, his body drew her. She could not remember the last time she had longed for Donal's physical presence, though she remembered all too clearly a similar night when her husband had tried to take advantage of her as she slept.

This isn't the same at all, she told herself. There is nothing I want or need of this man and nothing I can force him to do. He is just a stranger.

A stranger.

She closed her eyes and willed herself to sleep.

She opened her eyes, and the dark shoulder still loomed beside her, like Achill head rising against the Atlantic horizon.

The peat on the hearth had burned down, and the room was beginning to cool. Grania felt her heart beating, listened to the man beside her breathing, occasionally pulled the covers higher as the night wore on.

Behind closed eyelids, she saw his naked body again. Looking the length of it, she memorized every detail. Donal an Chogaidh had never, even in their first days together, seemed a thing of beauty to her, and she could not recall having studied his body in the same way. She did not remember ever having reached out in the night to place her hand on his naked hip. . . .

The sailor moved under her touch and turned toward her.

The rhythm of his breathing quickened.

Grania lay still, but she left her hand where it was.

Then she felt his placed over it, his fingers tightening. He pressed her hand against himself, then moved his own up her arm, feeling the firm muscle beneath her skin until he reached her shoulder. He cupped its roundness briefly before continuing his exploration, sliding his fingertips along her body until they encountered the swell of her breast.

He said something then, in a liquid language she did not recognize. The bed shifted beneath his weight. His breath was warm on her face, then on her breast, the hot mouth seeking, the parted lips gentle but insistent.

The woman groaned.

Her hands gripped the curls of his hair and pressed his face against her body. He was not a stranger. He was a necessary element, like the air she had to breathe, and she could not get enough of him, could not get close enough to him. He crushed her breasts together so he could tongue both nipples at once. His hands were not soft; salt water and tarred rope had made them as rough as hers. But they were as gentle as they were strong, and when they moved down her body, imitating her earlier exploration of his, they seemed to point out unsuspected beauties. His hands told her her waist was lean and graceful; her hips were round as a woman's should be, deep through the pelvis but tight in the buttock. His hands praised her.

When he parted her thighs and lifted himself over her she opened to him as if she had done so a thousand times before. When he drove deeply into her she felt as if some part of herself that had been amputated long ago had at last been returned, making her complete again.

He lay still upon her body, surprised to discover his ears were ringing. He could not tell if this was a dream or reality. His last clear memory was of the shipwreck and the panic, and the bitter cold salt water flooding into his mouth and nose. How long ago? Where? Where was he now? Could this be some form of heaven no priest had ever promised?

If he dared to move, would it all vanish?

His body insisted. He thrust once and felt her shudder. He clutched at reality, but it was slipping farther and farther away until nothing was left but lust and need and this one tenuous connection with a life he thought already lost.

He plunged into her again with all his strength.

One stroke, two . . . and she felt a quick, hot climax flooding through him. Her body struggled to keep up. The heavy ache of unbearably sweet sensation concentrated itself between her legs, and she moved against him in her own desperate rhythm, her fingers clawing his back.

His penis, which had begun to soften, stiffened again.

"Please," she whispered to him.

And in Gaelic he responded, "Hold me."

She did. With all the strength in her arms, Grania gripped the man who rode her in the night, holding him fast in the real world, holding him with a passion to match his own.

The last residue of shock from his ordeal faded and his body reasserted its life force with a vengeance, demanding he celebrate his continued existence in the most primeval of ways. Life bound him to the woman who lay beneath him.

He thrust again, and again, and again.

Because she had come to this moment with no expectations, he could not disappoint her; she was launched on a voyage of exploration, thinking herself fully prepared for whatever might happen, some small satisfaction or even scorn and rejection.

She was unprepared for the shock of joy.

He filled her to the utmost; if he had been any larger their coupling would have been painful. If he had been smaller some vital part of her would have been left untouched. He moved with exactly the same rhythm she found natural, a deep, slow rocking like the sea, rolling up from one sunlit peak down into a deep trough and then up again, up, up . . .

She was gasping for breath. A sound—a scream, a song?—rose in her like a bubble from the bottom of the sea. She had to do *something;* there must be some release from the incredible pressure building within her. He gave one final plunge and they were past flesh and bone and solid land, they were very far out at sea, and the great sails were billowing with the white wind and nothing would ever be the same again.

"*Yes!*" cried the woman, exultant.

✠

When she awoke in the morning he was still in her bed, his arms around her, her head pillowed on his shoulder. He seemed to know she was awake, for he opened his eyes almost at once and drew back a little to look at her.

His eyes were very dark, and he was smiling.

"Who are you?" she heard her voice asking. As if it mattered. He was part of her; giving him a separate name would almost seem like an act of betrayal.

The man frowned slightly. "I am . . . I am called . . ." He spoke in Gaelic but with an accent. Perhaps the language was giving him trouble. He shook his head and tried again. "My name is . . ." The dark eyes opened wider. "I do not remember!" he said in alarm. "Who are you?"

"Gráinne Ni Mháille. You are in my fortress; my men plucked you from the sea after your ship went down."

He struggled up onto one elbow to look around the room. His eyes examined every inch of the walls, the carved wooden chests, the mantle pegs by the hearth. Then he looked at Grania's face with that same searching gaze. "Pirate," he said.

"So you do know me. Your memory is coming back, then. It can be shocked out of a person for a brief while if he has a bad accident, as you did. You'll remember the rest soon. I'm relieved that you speak Gaelic—the last time we met I thought you might be mute. But you're not an Irishman."

He frowned, trying to remember. "Not an Irishman," he repeated. "And I think I did not speak to you before because . . . because I was so surprised by you. As I am now," he added. He had just realized he was naked, and the woman lying beside him in the bed was as bare as he. "How did I get here, again?"

She told him in detail, and he listened like a child hearing a marvelous new story. "I recall none of that," he said at length.

"Just what do you remember?"

"You. And being put ashore. Some of us made our way to the port at Galway eventually, and I was in that city for a time. Then I signed aboard a Portuguese ship en route to Scotland. That is all I know."

"You signed aboard," Grania pounced on his words. "And you speak like an educated man, so I think you know your letters. What name did you sign? Can you see it in your mind?"

He frowned. The appalling gaps in his memory were frightening him more than he wanted to admit. He had a confused recollection of holding this woman in his arms, and of passionate lovemaking that surely must be only a dream. But they were both naked! How could he concentrate on anything else when that overwhelming fact kept pushing to the forefront of his mind?

His frown deepened with a mighty effort at concentration. "I signed. A name. I can see the letters, almost. It was . . . I think it was . . . Yes. Yes! Huw! I am certain. I signed Huw!"

Hugh, and he pronounced it in the Welsh way. Grania nodded. He was as dark as a Welshman, and the singing of that language seemed to underlie the Irish Gaelic he was struggling with for her sake. "Was there any more to your name?" she wanted to know. "Or was it just Huw?"

He concentrated again, and she saw the light of recollection flare in his eyes—and be quickly stifled. "Just Huw," he told her firmly.

Grania startled him by throwing back her head and laughing, a good big hearty laugh, like a man's. The situation was absurd and life was absurd and she had never felt better. "Very well, Huw-from-the-sea," she told him, "if that's all the name you admit that's all the name you shall have. Is your belly empty? I'll summon someone to feed us; I think I could eat a whole roast ox myself this morning."

He lay back on the bed and watched as she dressed. She did not seem self-conscious, as any other woman would in the same situation. She made no feminine pretense of covering her breasts or turning her hip to keep him from seeing her pubis. She simply got dressed, letting him look at whatever he liked and silently demanding he accept what he saw.

For Grania, the chamber had become a separate world. If the man it held chose to have no name and no past, so much the better.

She was sorry he knew anything about her; it would be better if they were total strangers, she thought, and he had no image of her already formed in his mind.

Pirate.

But at least he knew nothing else. Here she could be, with him, whatever she chose, for as long as the enchantment might last.

Instead of a shirt and trews, she took a gown with a fitted blue bodice and slashed sleeves from one of her wooden chests, and added an embroidered overskirt to the costume. She had no female attendant to dress her, but Huw slipped out of bed and tied her laces himself, pulling them snug at her waist. She let herself look again at his naked body, and he took pleasure from the enjoyment on her face.

He swayed a little unsteadily, and at once she had her arm around him, guiding him back toward the bed. "You're not as strong as you think you are," she told him. "You must rest here and stay quiet. I'll bring you some hot food."

"I am strong," he argued. "Last night . . ." Then he hesitated. He could not be certain last night had happened as he remembered.

"Last night," Grania echoed softly. Then he knew. "All the more reason for you to rest and get your strength back. And I will take care of you. When we are certain you have fully recovered, we can talk about sending you home." She did not miss the quick flicker of refusal in his eyes. "Or find another ship for you," she added smoothly. "But nothing need be decided now. Lie down, I'll be back soon."

His eyes followed her until she pulled the door closed and her footsteps sounded on the stone stair.

Halfway down, Grania stopped and just stood, feeling the walls of the tower house around her. Her walls. Embracing her. The early morning was as quiet as sunlight, radiant and gilded with happiness.

Happiness, Grania said to herself. Joy. This is what it feels like. I must never let myself forget this moment, this feeling. As long as I have such memories I am a wealthy woman with a treasure no one can take away from me.

Joy, joy, joy!

She skipped down the rest of the stair like a little girl, and the cheerful greeting she called to the guard at the entry gate as she opened the heavy oak door elicited a gap-toothed grin in response.

"A grand day it is, Liam!"

"A grand day," he agreed. "Cold, though, for February."

Grania lifted her eyebrows. "Do you think so? I find it uncommonly warm."

✠

The abbot of Murrisk wrote to the archbishop of Armagh, "Rumors reach us of a man living with O Malley's daughter on Clare island. No one seems to know anything about him, other than that he is a foreigner she rescued from a shipwreck. But it is said he sleeps in her bedchamber. This may be attributed to the influence of the heathen she has taken into her household, but it shows how far from God's grace the woman has fallen.

"You may be right, my friend. The vigor of a fresh new interpretation of religion may be what the Irish most desperately need. Signed, Calvagh of Bregia."

He dropped a blot of blood-red sealing wax upon the message and imprinted it with his ring, smiling to himself.

Huw's strength had returned quickly, but he seemed in no hurry to return to his former life. Indeed, on faraway Cliara it was hard to remember any other life. The ocean surrounded them; Ireland was just a jagged mountainous line on the eastern horizon. Time had stopped and old indiscretions were forgotten.

He and Grania lounged on benches on either side of the fireplace in her hall, their bellies comfortably rounded with one of Evleen's excellent meals. The room was warm. Unless one looked out the window, it was possible to forget that winter lay just beyond the walls.

"I know a poem about February," Huw remarked, smiling lazily at Grania.

"You have a poem for everything," she answered. "How can you recall so much poetry and remember nothing else?"

By now he knew what she wanted to hear. "There is not anything else," he said. "Just you and me, and this place."

"And February. Tell me the poem."

Huw swiveled around on his bench so he could prop himself against the wall—Grania's apricot-colored wall, its plaster embedded with tiny fossils from the beach sand of Cliara. He raised his arms and laced his fingers behind his neck while she waited, then he recited in a resonant, sonorous voice:

*White flour, earth flesh, a cold fleece on the
mountain,*
Small snow of the chill black day.
*Snow like a platter, bitter cold plumage, a
softness sent to carry me away.*

"It sounds like February," Grania commented. "Is that the entire poem?"

"No, there is some more, then the last lines are:

*White snow on the cold hill above has blinded me
and soaked my clothes.*
*By the blessed God! I had no hope I should ever
get to my house.*

He unlaced his fingers and sat up, leaning across the space between them to put his hand on her knee. "But here I am after all," he said. "Safe and warm, owing my life to a remarkable woman."

She did not know how to accept such compliments from him. "Who wrote that poem?" she asked.

"A Welshman."

"Are you the poet?"

His hand moved up her leg, burrowing between her thighs like a small warm animal hurrying home. "I am just Huw," he told her.

✠

Tigernan was in a terrible mood. He had a little oval cottage of mud and stone, with a thatched roof and limewash on its walls; he had oatcakes and beer in his larder, and from time to time Ruari Oge's wife brought him one of the blood puddings she made. He had work to do preparing for the oncoming fishing season, when Clare islanders would be kept busy catching, salting, and barreling fish and preparing Grania's fleet to set sail.

But he took no satisfaction from any of this. He stamped along the white sand beach encircling the harbor and glowered up at the tower house which dominated the scene. Light seeped through the arrow slits—firelight, lamplight, candlelight. Sometimes the only light came from Grania's bedchamber.

When she emerged to tend to her businesses she seemed unaware of the talk rippling around the island. Grania had never cared what people thought, Tigernan reminded himself. But to openly take a common sailor to her bed . . .

An *ordinary* man, that was what Tigernan found unbearable. Not a chieftain in crimson velvet coat with golden aglets and a feather in his bonnet, but a foremastman!

"Tigernan thinks Grania's lost her mind," Ruari Oge told his wife.

"There's nothing at all wrong with her," Evleen said. "The first time I set eyes on the woman I thought she looked like someone carrying too much weight on her shoulders, but she's much improved now. There's nothing like a brisk rod to give spirit to the mare."

Ruari Oge rewarded his wife with an affectionate slap on the buttocks. "You're pleased for her sake, are you? Dar Dia, woman, sometimes I think you want to see every living thing mating right in front of your eyes."

"Not all at once." Evleen smiled demurely. "I could hardly decide what to watch."

Ruari gave his wife a piercing look. He had lived with her a long time. "Did you somehow arrange this because you pitied Grania for being alone?"

The little woman laughed. "I wish I could claim the credit! But no, this goes to poor Tigernan; in a way he's responsible."

"He's the last person who'd have thrown a man in her bed. Unless the man was himself. He's got as bad a case of the burning balls as I've ever seen, and he'll die with it."

"But he's also a devout Christian," Evleen explained, "and he insisted on her making a pilgrimage to the well they call St. Brigid's now."

"What do you mean . . . now?"

Evleen's eyes shimmered with mysteries. "Ireland's holy places were sacred long before the Christians tried to claim them. Whatever spirit lurks in Brigid's well has powers neither monk nor priest can claim, and it was once whispered that the well on Cliara could fulfill a person's deepest need, if visited at just the right moment, when the stars formed a certain pattern in the sky."

In spite of himself, Ruari Oge signed the cross on his breast, though he knew his wife was watching with vast and timeless amusement.

✠

Besotted with Huw, Grania was still realist enough to know she was allowing herself an emotional indulgence to compensate for the long lean years with Donal an Chogaidh. In one night with a stranger, she had discovered an undreamed-of freedom to enjoy and explore her own sensuality. In the dark, with a man who did not know her except as a responsive female body, she had been unhampered by old grudges and smoldering resentments and the need to erect barriers and guard against vulnerabilities. Rapture came to her for the first time, brought by a man with no name and no past.

She sought to keep the enchantment intact for as long as possible by preserving that lack of history which would make them known and familiar to each other. She so pointedly avoided any personal references predating their time together that he soon realized this was an unspoken rule which must be observed, and he was willing to abide by it—for a while.

She was nothing like any woman he had known. She spoke bluntly and lacked the practiced arts of femininity, yet in her strength and health she was wonderfully female. And intelligent, he discovered with pleasure. The friars had educated her well; books in several languages were scattered about her chamber, and she could talk knowledgeably about seafaring and politics and even some history.

He countered with colorful tales of his own remembered from his childhood, spun out at length in Welsh-accented Gaelic. She loved stories that made her laugh, and he knew them and repeated them for her by the score as they strolled together along the cliffs or beside the sea.

She never let him see her in her role as sea captain, ordering men, and he understood that this, too, was one of the rules. Yet he could not avoid meeting some of them from time to time, and he sensed their curiosity and occasional resentment. If one of them had questioned him he would not have known what to answer. Grania was a sea captain who had taken a bedmate as sea captains had done since time immemorial. That was the only answer he could have made, but he suspected it would not suffice. Better to leave everything unspoken and unexplored. While the enchantment lasted.

One morning after Grania had left for the harbor he fell asleep again, to be awakened when Evleen peered round the door. "Are you going to stay in bed all day?" she asked. "I need to air the linen."

"I will get up," he assured her. "But first—will you answer a question for me?" He beckoned to her.

"Isn't one woman enough for you?" she said, eyes brimming with mischief. But she entered the chamber and perched on the bench beside the bed. He had thought her an old woman, but now that he saw her so close he was no longer sure.

"Tell me something, Evleen. Has your mistress known many men?"

"You should ask her."

"I cannot. But I think I should know—for her sake."

"She had a husband," Evleen replied. "From what I hear he wasn't one to make the rose bloom, though."

Huw smiled. "Do you think I make her bloom?"

"Do you think she's a rose?" Evleen parried. "Is that how you see her with those brown eyes of yours? Nice for her if you do, I think."

"You are fond of Grania, aren't you?"

"I am. I was jealous of her, at first, because I had never met another woman whom men admired as they admire Grania. But as soon as I met her I liked her. Some people cherish the weak; I cherish the strong. Strong folk who know how to endure give hope to us all."

Huw observed Evleen with interest. "Have you had so much to endure?"

"Haven't we all? Even a big strong man like you?" She was unmistakably flirting with him now, her eyes dancing. She shifted her body on the bench so he could hear her bottom slide along the wood.

A spatter of rain beat against the window shutter. The room seemed very small and cozy, and Evleen was within easy reach of his hand. Huw had never hesitated to reach for a woman in similar circumstances, and this one looked strangely young as he studied her. He had a vivid image of sunwarmed brown earth waiting for the plow.

"Your private parts are making tents of the bedclothes," Evleen laughed, slipping off her bench abruptly and opening the chamber door.

He glanced down and felt his ears redden, but he would not let her embarrass him. "Are you so far beyond temptation?" he asked before she could leave the room.

"I'm never beyond temptation," she replied. Then she was out the door and gone.

Huw rose and dressed, bemused. He must have undergone a sea change, he thought. The man he had always been would have already tumbled the serving woman into the bed. But he was not the man he had always been. He was some different person here.

From time to time, as he waited for Grania to return, he knelt on one of the cushions in the deep window embrasures and looked out at the gray day and the lowering sky, forcing himself to summon up images from his past. There were still great gaps in his memory, but every day he recalled more about himself . . . and was thankful Grania knew none of it.

He was a man to whom the lure beyond the horizon had always seemed more inviting than whatever lay close to hand. He had been born to the Welsh aristocracy struggling to adapt itself to the domination of England, and under English law he, as a younger son, had been unable to inherit either his father's land or his honors. As a young man he had been bored by the political intrigues with which his family endeavored to maintain its position under the conquerors, and he had no interest in the life of a mercenary soldier, which drew many in his position. He had two passions, poetry and gambling. Beauty and risk. Whatever definition he might find for life seemed to lie between those two borders.

When he gambled away property that was not his to lose, his family threw him out, and the last words he ever heard from his father were curses.

The shock had spurred Huw to attempt to change his ways, but shock wears off; it cannot provide lasting motivation. He wandered on the Continent for a time, feeling sorry for himself and accepting the hospitality of friends and strangers equally, repaying them with the coin of his charm and his companionship over a gaming board. Why not?

After one particularly long debauch he awoke, however, to find himself an unwilling captive aboard a cromster bound for Jutland. Sea captains often filled their crews with drunks dredged from the floors of certain disreputable inns, men who woke in irons to find their acquaintances had sold them for the price of a bottle.

The ship was already at sea. He had no hope of escape until they reached the next port, and because he was tall and well built he was singled out from the press gang to be forced to serve aloft, for the captain had a shortage of foremastmen.

Huw was appalled when he realized what was expected of him. There would be no period of apprenticeship; the shortage was too grave. He must crawl out on a slippery yardarm in any kind of weather, risking death every moment while he struggled to master the intricacies of sails and rigging. Meanwhile he was subjected to a constant stream of orders and curses, abuse both verbal and physical.

But he felt he had nothing to lose. He was gambling for his life, his last and only possession, so he flung himself headlong into this greatest gamble of all and began, agonizingly and step by step, to win. He endured all the agony of strains and sprains and salt sores, he felt his muscles harden and his sinews toughen. He dared death daily and won, and a certain arrogance came into his step and his voice that had never been there before.

At sea, he could not fall back on the charity and sympathy of friends, for neither emotion existed there. Only life and death and profit and loss, and the latter two were more important than the former aboard a merchantman.

"Seafaring is trade, that is its heart and soul," he remarked to Grania one day. "What happens on the ocean only has importance as it relates to the land. Commerce is a long arm reaching out from the land, an arm that really has nothing to do with what the sea is or what the sea demands. But the ships that other men think of as tools have a beauty, Grania. An unintentional beauty but no less real for all of that. When I see a mainsail bellying with the wind it is like hearing music to me, or like poetry. A man with enough talent could write a great poem about the curve of a sail."

They were in the little cove just west of the tower house. Huw had accompanied Grania ostensibly to search for shellfish, which they rarely found there. But the cove with its spotless apron of white sand sloping straight down into turquoise water was a place of such perfect loveliness they spent much of their time there, even on stormy days. Then the surrounding arms of the black cliffs sheltered them and they could almost believe they were the only two people in the world.

The day was cold, but the high yellow sun was a spring sun, shedding radiance that promised greening fields and herring in the nets. Creation was in the air. "Write a poem, here, now," Grania urged Huw. "About the curve of a sail."

She had hoisted her skirt and waded into the water, though it immediately turned her legs bright red with cold. But she did not flinch; she laughed, and he applauded her daring. He caught her arm and guided her back to the beach, then rubbed her icy feet with his warm hands. "I cannot think about sails today," he told her. "The only curve that seems to interest me is the way your lips curve when you smile. The smile disappears right"—he bent forward and kissed the edge of her mouth—"here. And then the curve goes on down your throat, to your breast . . ." His hands molded the lines he admired as he spoke.

No one could see them, unless they came past Grania's guard and stood at the edge of the cliff, or clambered down the worn, steep path that led through brambles from the rear of the tower house. When Huw's hands found their way through Grania's clothing to bare flesh, no one but the seagulls heard her gasp of pleasure.

Beyond the hidden cove on Clare island, the vast reaches of Clew bay sparkled in the sun, alive with curragh and canoe and caravel, seething with fish, forested with seaweed, vital and vibrant as the woman Huw held in his arms.

"I never met a woman like you," he told her honestly.

"And what sort of woman am I?" She did not ask the question coquettishly, but out of a genuine desire to know. She could not imagine how he envisioned her.

"You are beautiful," he said, and laughed at the disbelief in her eyes. "Really. Not the sort of beauty that comes with paint and powder and tuftaffeta gowns, but something strong and clean."

"Strong and clean," Grania mused.

Suddenly he knew what she wanted, needed. "Ravenhaired and whitebreasted," he said. "Fair Grania—do you not know how you look?"

She shrugged, still disbelieving.

Huw made a whispered suggestion to Evleen, and one day Evleen brought Grania a present. "This was all the property my mother possessed," she said, offering a packet tied with twine. Grania unwrapped the package and tucked the twine through her belt for later use. Everything practical eventually found a use at sea.

When the wrappings fell aside, they revealed a copper-backed mirror enameled in green and crimson and engraved with Celtic knotwork.

Grania was surprised by the lump in her throat. She could not remember when another woman had given her a present for friendship's sake. "Are you certain you want me to have this, if it was your mother's?"

Evleen nodded. "I do what my mother would have done," she said. "Sometimes I hear myself speak with my mother's voice."

Grania turned the mirror over in her hands and found herself staring into its polished surface at a face she did not know. Her black hair was windblown and her skin was as lined as ever. But her eyes seemed larger than she remembered them, set in violet shadows that spoke of wonderfully sleepless nights. Her lips were no longer chapped but full and soft, bruised by other lips.

As she watched, Evleen caught Grania's wild mane with both hands and began shaping it into wings that curved down over her temples and then lifted to swirl around her head like a crown.

"That isn't me," Grania said.

"Yes, it is," Evleen contradicted her.

Grania gazed for a long time at the face in the mirror.

12

Memory had come back to Huw in snippets and segments until the whole history of his life lay open in his mind, and he was utterly dissatisfied with it. He saw that he had let fate blow him in whatever direction it chose while he played at being first one person and then another—a nobleman's son, a tragic dispossessed minstrel, a daring foremastman.

Which was truly Huw? He had neither known nor cared.

Then he found himself with Grania, a woman of large honesty and few pretensions. What he had been meant less than nothing to her. Confronted by her forthright spirit, he would have to find his own real, inner self to match it, for she deserved nothing less.

If he could create poetry he could create a man, one worthy of the extraordinary woman who ruled Clare island.

"I cannot live here indefinitely on your generosity," he made himself say to Grania. "I must go back to the sea; it is the only trade I have."

"You weren't born to it," she said with certainty.

"I was not," he agreed. "And it was not even a life I chose for myself. For the past several years I have drifted from ship to ship, none of them very fine vessels, and when I drew my pay I gambled it away in the nearest port until I had an empty purse and stomach and had to sign aboard another disreputable ship."

He was breaking their rule about personal histories. She laid her fingers across his lips to silence him, but he pulled her hand away.

"It embarrasses me to admit I was wasting my life until I met you, Grania," Huw insisted on telling her. "I was a wastrel; there is no kinder word. I grew up knowing my eldest brother would inherit everything, and somehow that robbed life of any meaning for me. I felt robbed from the start, and it made me reckless.

"You don't have to tell me any of this."

"The sort of man I had become would never have told you. But here, with you . . . I feel as if I've just been born. A new start with all the past wiped away. The only thing I want to keep from that past is my connection with the sea."

She looked at him quizzically. "A seaman's life is not easy," she said.

"But you obviously love it."

"I am a captain." Said with pride.

He nodded. "An ordinary sailor knows a different existence. Disease, rupture, alcoholism, or amputation end most mariners' careers. But I learned to love the life anyway, Grania. A man does not know his limits until he lies out on a yardarm with darkness howling around him and tries to gather in yards of frozen canvas weighing more than the earth itself. There is no hand to spare for holding yourself on—the Lord takes care of you if He chooses, and if He does not you have a long deadly fall and few captains will bother to pluck your carcass out of the water.

"It is a hard school but one I think I needed. I learned just how much I can survive, and that is a valuable lesson."

"Oh, yes," she said softly. "Oh, yes."

"I *need* to go back to sea, Grania. For a while it was enough to idle here, thinking myself lucky to have escaped such a brutal existence. But then I discovered another new thing about myself— I am no spaniel to sit on a woman's warm lap. I come from a line of men who have always owned their own souls because they could take care of themselves. Only someone who can do that is free. I thought I found freedom in running away, in tempting fate, not being responsible even for myself . . . but I was wrong.

"Now I want the freedom of taking my life into my own two hands and shaping it to suit my will. I want what other men have, a permanent home. A wife. Children. It just happens I want that home to be here and that wife to be you."

She was looking at him incredulously. She who had been hammering her own freedom and independence together plank by plank had rewarded herself with this man of mystery, this seafaring poet with no past and no home.

"You recited a poem the other day," she reminded him, "that I understood so well I memorized it. Do you remember? I thought you were speaking of yourself and I was certain you were speaking of me."

Locking his eyes with hers, she quoted:

[155]

Happy the wild birds soaring
To sea and mountain freely roaming;
Wing where they will, and what is more,
No awkward questions after homing.

He put his hands on her shoulders. "Was your marriage so bad, Grania, that you have turned your back on your own womanhood forever?"

Her eyes were fierce and sad; they pierced his heart. "You speak of freedom, Huw. When I first heard that poem, I remembered a fledgling sea eagle I found injured on the shore of Achill island when I was a child. I took it home with me and tended it until it was strong enough to fly, and then I set it free."

"I have thought of you as . . . as that sea eagle. Wild and free, to be enjoyed for a brief time but never bound."

"And that is how you want to see yourself, too," he guessed shrewdly. "But there is more to you than that. I saw your eyes flicker when I mentioned children, and Evleen has told me you have sons and a daughter who were sent away from you to foster-age.

"If a sea eagle came to you freely and wanted to stay, would you not be willing to share a nest? And raise some new fledglings, perhaps?" He was smiling, trying to keep it light in case she refused him, but she heard a longing in his voice that struck a responsive chord in her.

"You say you want to go back to sea," she reminded him.

"I need to be my own man."

"I understand that. But I have ships. . . ."

Pride he had once thought dead stirred in him. "I do not want to serve under someone else's banner . . . particularly yours. The time has come to fly my own flag."

That, too, she understood. "You're a gambler," she said thoughtfully. "And I have a carrack you know well, a vessel I won by gambling and now being refitted at Kinsale. Prove your skill; wager me for it. If you have a ship of your own you can be independent, you can fly any flag you like. You can go or . . . or stay." Her eyes danced. "Though I warn you, I would charge you an anchorage fee for using my harbor."

"And I would gladly pay it," he answered. "But I have nothing to put up against the carrack, Grania. I own nothing I can wager."

She was a brave woman; she had won and she had lost, she knew the costs of both. Looking in his eyes, she knew full well that much of the beauty of the gamble lay in the risk.

"Wager your freedom," she suggested. "If you lose, you will serve in any capacity I name on any vessel under my command, for seven years. And you will be no different from any other crewman; you will have a cottage and a small field here on Cliara.

"But you will have no bed in this tower house," she added. She had to make the wager fair. They must both have something to lose, as well as something to win.

He bowed his head and considered the offer. With another woman—any of the lace-ruffed noblewomen he had once known, or the flea-pocked and rotten-mouthed whores he had also known—the game would have been only a game, a flirtatious pretense.

But this was Gráinne Ni Mháille, and she was serious.

She gave him his choice of contests. He scorned the dice—she had originally won the carrack with dice, he knew. And he was not familiar with the peculiarly Irish game of bandubh, a board game with pegs representing warriors besieging a stronghold.

Chess he knew; surely knew better than a woman from the wild west coast of Ireland.

Not by the flicker of an eyelash did she reveal pleasure or displeasure at his choice.

They set up the chessboard in front of the fireplace, and the game lasted for a long day and well into the night. Grania fought ferociously; she had never played better nor with more skill. She had her own clever strategy involving the queen and both knights, and the moves she forced Huw to make told him soon enough that he would be given nothing. Each time he thought he saw an opening she closed it; twice he achieved check, only to have her break free and cost him first a rook and then a bishop.

He could tell how desperately she wanted him to win by the degree of desperation with which she struggled to beat him.

"Checkmate," he said at last, sweating, exhausted. Triumphant.

She stared at the board in surprise; she had honestly not seen the danger until it was too late.

"I won," Huw told her, smiling. And loved her for the quick anger at herself he saw on her face.

"I should have foreseen that and blocked you," she grumbled. "Next time I'll know better."

"Come here," he said, opening his arms.

He took her in the full flood of triumph, as an aggressor, as a winner. And she lay back and let him. Her body became a city he had laid siege to and conquered, and Grania found herself enjoying surrender to an honorable opponent. She lay smiling in his arms, occasionally making some small and feminine sound to contrast with the hoarse panting of the aroused male, and she thought . . . how pretty it all was. How easy, how undemanding.

Assuming the dominant role, gentle Huw became strong and sure and Grania felt fragile in his grasp. Yet . . .

Yet she was not fragile. When he had spent himself in her and lay holding her close in the subsiding aftermath, she felt her own body's demands reassert themselves. The lovemaking had been sweet. Now it must have spice; nature demanded balance.

With a powerful wriggle she rolled from beneath him and reversed their positions. Huw opened his eyes in surprise, staring up at the woman astride him. Her muscles were polished with sweat, but they were undeniably muscles; there was no flaccid dimpled plumpness on Grania's body. Her thighs clamped Huw's hips with surprising power, challenging him to try to buck her off.

"Grania, I can't . . ." he started to protest, but then he saw the way her eyes changed, like sealight changing before a storm, and he felt a powerful throb in that hot and private part of her that was pressed against himself.

"Don't say you can't," Grania whispered huskily. "You never know what you can do until you make the attempt."

✠

When they awoke in the morning the imprint of her ear was pressed into the flesh of his shoulder.

The carrack would not be ready for weeks, and there was much to be done in the meantime. Fishing season was upon them, and the traffic of merchantment along the coast was growing daily. Grania was also becoming aware of an increasing number of vessels bearing Tudor green-and-white; according to her lookouts on the western side of the island, there were now more English ships to be seen than any other nationality. It was as if the English were deliberately peering over her shoulder.

She had not yet told her men of the change in the carrack's

ownership; there would be time enough for that. First, let them get used to Huw as a permanent fixture on Cliara, as a person of authority. When she went out with her fleet to transport some goods from Iar Connaught to Ulster for her son Owen, she announced that she was leaving Huw in charge of the harbor in her absence.

Tigernan was the most vocal in his resentment. "Who is that man?" he asked repeatedly—though he did not ask Grania face to face. "What right does he have to be in command of anything? He's no better than the rest of us!"

"Calm yourself," Ruari Oge advised him. "It's none of our business."

"It is! He's wriggled his way into her confidence, that . . . that foreigner! Who knows what harm he means to do her? Do you suppose he's a spy? English ships crowd ever closer to Clare island; could that Huw be calling them in? She's supporting her sons' resistance of English authority in Iar Connaught, and she's sure to draw some form of reprisal. I tell you plainly, Ruari: when we get back from this voyage to Ulster I'm going to catch that Huw by the ears when Grania isn't looking and find out the truth of him. All this mystery, never telling anyone who his family is or where he comes from . . . I'll get it all out of him. If he intends to do her any damage I'll leave him floating face down in the tide. I'm as big as he is and just as strong.

"And meaner," he added, his blue eyes blazing.

As the galleys departed from Clare island, Tigernan looked back to see Huw standing on the beach, waving goodbye. And Grania rode not in the prow but in the stern, staying close to him as long as she could.

"Next time she'll probably want to bring him with us," Tigernan said bitterly to Ruari Oge.

Watching the departure, Huw was suddenly overcome by a wave of melancholy. Grania would have understood. She was Irish, he was Welsh, both were Celts, and for them the sun always cast shadows.

He could not simply wait for her return. There must be a gesture he could make, something grand and unique that would thank her for giving him back himself. When she returned, he would insist that they marry. She was a chieftain's daughter and as a mere foremastman he had no right to reach so high, but he was not just a sailor anymore. He was a nobleman's son again, proud, responsible. With a future. All this she had made possible.

He would stand beside her in front of a priest and they would exchange unbreakable vows. They would. . .

He sought out Evleen. "Is Grania past childbearing?" he asked bluntly.

Ruari Oge's wife rewarded him with a startled smile. "She is not."

His mind was churning, presenting him with a flashing succession of ideas. The gesture he had sought occurred to him. "Evleen, is it true eagles nest on Achill island?"

She cocked her head. "I think so. Why?"

"And Grania left me in charge of the harbor. That means I can ask the fishermen to take me in one of their curraghs, can I not?"

She heard the eagerness in his voice, but her ear gave it a different quality, that of a dark thread. For Evleen, reality existed in layers, one overlapping another and sometimes submerging it. When Huw spoke of Achill island the atmosphere of tragedy rose around them like morning mist from the bogs.

"Don't go back there," she whispered, laying a hand on his arm.

He looked down at her from the heights of confidence. "But I have to get a sea eagle for Grania," he said. "A wild, living bird that we will feed and raise here, and teach to make its home here. She is going to have an eagle that does not fly away."

"Don't," Eveleen said again, urgently.

But he would not listen. The gesture was too perfect.

✠

He found a boat and a crew to carry him to Achill. The sun was warm, though the long rollers coming in off the Atlantic would never surrender to summer heat. Clew bay was choppy, white-crested, and the oarsmen bent to their task, for the wind was against them; there was no point in raising a mast and sail.

They left Clare's harbor and headed toward the rising point of the mountain known as Curraun, on the northern shore of the bay, then swung west toward the ocean and the great couchant form of Achill island. The curragh was a small, open boat, but it cut through the sea rather than bobbing atop the waves like a skiff. Huw marveled at its construction. Only planks and a leather skin separated him from the water, yet the boat was like a marine animal, perfectly at home in its element. In Huw's experience with boats he had encountered nothing to equal the security he felt aboard an Irish curragh.

Achill was a large island, with scattered communities of fisherfolk and farmers. It took a while, but eventually Huw found a guide willing to take him to the north side of the island, where eagles built their nests along the craggy, inaccessible cliffs facing Blacksod bay. The peak of Slieve Mór dominated the scene as Cnoc Mór dominated Cliara. But Achill was not Clare, not small and known and well trampled by familiar feet. Most of Achill was empty and savage, a suitable home for eagles.

"I will go no farther with you," Huw's guide told him. "The clan MacMahon of Blacksod bay claims this region as their hunting land and I have no rights here. Nor do you," he added pointedly, though he had not refused Huw's request to guide him this far. The man from Achill was not one to deny a nobleman's request, and nobility was implicit in every line and gesture of the strange Welshman who came seeking an eagle's nest.

"I will not be hunting anything another man claims," Huw replied. "What is the game here, deer? I have no need of venison. I only want a feathered fledgling not quite ready to fly."

"You want a lot," he was told. "See that tangle of sticks under the ledge up there? It's a dangerous climb, but there you have an eagle's nest. If you watch until both birds are away, you may find what you want there—or the eagles may seize you. They are jealous parents, I've been told; they can tear off a man's face."

"Will you go with me?"

The other man barked a harsh laugh. "I haven't been to confession this week. I'll wait for you at the foot of the trail."

To reach the eagle's nest, Huw would have to crawl, spider-fashion, along the vertical face of the cliff, seeking minute finger and toe holds in the fissured stone. The task was daunting, even for a foremastman, but it was worthy of Grania, he thought. And worthy of the man he meant to be for her sake.

His toe dug into a mossy pocket where, protected from the wind, a tiny sea-campion was struggling to survive. The little bit of earth it had found for itself was not sufficient to support the man's weight and crumbled away, and Huw felt his foothold collapse. He scrambled forward, clutching at air for a moment. Then his seeking fingers and toes found new surfaces and he regained his balance, thankful for the sea training that had given his bare feet agility. A man who could not go without boots could not hope to hunt sea eagles' nests on Achill.

From the area where he clung to the cliff's face, the nest was not visible. He had no way of knowing if the adult birds were there, or fishing the bountiful sea. He needed to get above the nest and find a vantage point where he could watch from cover until the fledglings—if there were any—were unguarded.

The ledge his guide had pointed out looked reachable, if a man was strong enough. Hugh began hoisting himself hand over hand toward it, relieved to see that it stretched back to a small plateau of level land encircled by rock outcroppings. A faint trail marked the strip as grazing, for goats perhaps, or agile mountain deer.

Huw reached the ledge and thankfully swung his body onto a horizontal surface just as a hunting party made its way along the trail from above, pursuing a stag rumored to live here.

The men stared in astonishment at the solitary figure just clearing the edge of the cliff. The climber's face was unfamiliar; the colors he wore were not McMahon colors, nor the coarse homespun of native islanders. He was a stranger and an interloper, no doubt here to steal a stag that did not belong to him.

They had not yet seen the stag, of course, but the chase was hot in them and they were eager for a kill.

The man who led the hunting party hurled his spear straight at Huw, with an outraged cry of "Poacher!"

Huw ducked instinctively, hearing the whistle of the javelin as it sailed past him and arced out into space, then dropped to the sea. He tried to get back over the edge of the cliff, out of their immediate range, but going down was harder than coming up. He had no time to pick and choose holds for himself, because the yelling, angry men were right above him now, leaning down and grabbing at him. One held another by the legs, and they succeeded in catching the hair atop Huw's head, giving it an agonizing yank. In another instant he felt hands around his neck, tugging upward as if they would rip his head off. He could not hold on to the cliff face and fight them off as well, and they managed to pry him loose and pull him back onto the ledge.

The shock of the moment drove his knowledge of Gaelic from his mind, and he protested in his native tongue, "I am no poacher, I don't want your game. I . . ."

But the foreign language only succeeded in maddening them.

Huw's guide, waiting beside the trail leading back to his own village, heard the angry shouts quite clearly as they echoed from cliff face and resonant sea. The assault on Huw was out of his line of vision, but those cries told him all he needed to know. He was brave, but he was one man alone and the noble MacMahons always came to this region in a large party, well fortified with both drink and weapons.

The guide turned and ran for help.

The man being battered on the cliff above the eagle's nest was fighting as he had never fought for anything before. Life had become very sweet to him, and he would not surrender it easily.

✠

Grania's ships returned to Cliara well laden. The voyage had been a success from every point of view, with good prices being received for O Flaherty wools as well as O Malley leathers and fish. The galleys brought back salt which had been purchased in Sligo, damask, canvas, frieze, English alum and Egyptian cottons brought by way of the Continent. Boxes and tins of spices were crowded into the sea chests the galley oarsmen used for benches. As they swept in past Achill and curved toward Clare harbor, Grania stood in the prow of the lead galley like a conquering queen.

People dotted the shore, watching the ships approach, but the crowd seemed strangely subdued. Men spying their womenfolk shouted and waved and were greeted in return, yet there was something about the atmosphere on shore that Grania found disquieting, even before they reached the shallows.

She was almost the first person off the ship—and Evleen came to meet her, a hooded mantle covering her hair, and her eyes were red-rimmed.

"Where's Huw?" Grania asked at once.

"Gone," Ruari Oge's wife told her. "Gone to Achill island to get you a sea eagle."

Grania caught Evleen's chin with her hand and lifted it so she could study the other woman's face. "What do you mean, 'gone'? Hasn't he come back?"

Ruari Oge, hurrying forward to greet his wife, stopped short. "What's all this about? Why these long faces? I'm home, woman!"

Evleen glanced at him and then away. "Not everyone will be coming home," she said.

"Tell me, Evleen," Grania commanded.

"Two curraghs came from Achill with the news. Huw was caught and killed by the MacMahons of Doona. They accused him of poaching."

"What was the man doing as far north as Blacksod bay?" Ruari Oge demanded to know.

"Getting me a sea eagle," Grania replied in a toneless voice.

Tigernan came up to them. Something in Grania's posture warned him, and by the time he reached the knot of people he had a sword in his hand, just in case. A crowd had gathered around Grania and Evleen, and from their whispered comments Tigernan pieced together the story. Then he fell silent as everyone else had, watching Grania and waiting.

She stood as if she were alone, her eyes gazing into some inward space. Finally she said, "What about his body? Did they bring it to us?"

Evleen could hardly bring herself to relate this last news. "There is no body. The MacMahons threw him into the sea after they killed him."

One of the old men of Cliara, a fisherman who exchanged words with other fishermen on the bay almost every fairweather day of his life, said, "There are rumors of the clan MacMahon boasting of the deed in the bruighens around Blacksod bay. They say it is a warning to keep other clans off their territory."

Grania's face was as white as the beach sand. Looking at her terrible eyes, Tigernan thought of the lightless caverns under Cliara's back cliffs, where the sea boomed hollowly. "While we were striking a hard bargain at Port Rois he was dying," she said. "But we made a profit. Commerce is a long arm, reaching out. . . ." Her voice trailed away.

"Get her inside before she shatters," Tigernan whispered urgently to Evleen.

"I'm all right!" Grania said, quick and hard. She would not let any of them touch her. She turned back to the galleys and began shouting orders for the unloading, shouting orders that ran together and were not always intelligible but were loud and strong and frantic in their intensity.

Tigernan had never felt so helpless.

"Damn him," he muttered to himself. "Damn him, damn him."

Grania would not leave the harbor and make the short hilly climb to the tower house until long after the sun set and the work on the quay was completed by torchlight. She had driven herself past the point of exhaustion; she had carried boxes and bales like the lowest porter; she had insisted on supervising every detail of storing the cargo and securing the ships.

But nothing could make her stop thinking. And the worst thoughts were the memories of her exultation at sea, when the sharp wind curled around her and foam hissed beneath the prow of her galley. She had not thought often of Huw then, or marriage, or babies. All the small domestic joys she had once attempted for Donal's sake, in the earliest days of her marriage, seemed trivial by comparison when she felt the bold lift and forward plunge of her own ship beneath her, and knew that whatever she could wrest from the sea with her physical strength and mental acuity was hers to take. She needed no man's permission or approval.

And all that while Huw had been going to get her a sea eagle. And dying.

She wanted to howl at the world and tear it apart with her two hands.

At last she made her way to the tower house. Her belly was empty and her throat dry with thirst, and she did not want to satisfy either of them. She took an obscure pleasure from her discomfort.

Evleen met her at the entry court and waved the guard back. Grief was a woman's domain.

"Now," she said, patting Grania's shoulder, reaching up to stroke the coarse, wild hair. "Now you can keen and grieve, child. It will do you good, and no one beyond these walls will know you're not as strong as the hardest man."

Grania pushed her away. "I never cry," she said. "Crying wouldn't bring him back anyway, would it?"

"Nothing brings them back but time," Evleen said cryptically.

Grania wandered around the hall, trailing her fingers along the thick solid walls. Her voice was distant, higher-pitched than Evleen had ever heard it.

"Huw never came close to me without touching me," she mused. "Just a hand on my shoulder, or the back of his fingers laid against my cheek in passing. But . . . he touched me."

Evleen's heart contracted with pain. "That's the way it is with men," she said. "They touch us. For the feel of strong arms around her and a solid chest to lean her head upon, a woman will put up with a lot of misery. It's the curse of our skin to be hungry for the feel of a man's skin."

Grania whirled suddenly, her eyes huge. "Maybe he isn't dead, Evleen! You said there was no body. They thought they killed him and they threw him in the sea, but he was in the sea before and almost everyone thought him dead. Except me. Yet he lived. He could do it again. We have to send out the boats, we have to start searching . . ."

"Child, child," the other woman murmured. "Hopeless hope will eat your heart away. Don't do this."

She might as well have spoken to the stones in the walls.

✠

Every ship and boat under Grania's command headed for Achill island the next day. They searched the stony cliffs and the countless bays and inlets from Dooega to Achill head to Doogort and found nothing—not even a stray member of the clan MacMahon, which seemed to have returned to the family stronghold at Doona.

Toward the end, when everyone but Grania admitted the search was hopeless, only Tigernan continued to drive himself and his comrades to keep looking. He was the last to give up, but finally he had to tell Grania the man was gone for good. Much of the summer had already been lost; the boats had to get back to their livelihood.

"We've searched for weeks," he said, "until I know Achill better than the island where I was born. All you can do for . . . for your friend now is pray for him. We'll go back to Cliara and you can light candles at the altar in the church."

"Light candles? What good would that do, Tigernan? My mother was always on her knees. When I was a child I saw one after another of her babies born dead, and the priests anointed the little bodies and prayed with Mairgret all through the night. With candles burning. But it never made any difference; none of those prayers changed a thing. In time she conceived again and bore the Black Oak yet another dead son and we had to see the disappointment in his face all over again. She believed in God with all her heart, but He never responded to either her entreaties or her tears."

"Of course He did," Tigernan replied. "God told her no, for His own reasons. Often that's the only answer any of us get, and we have to be content with it."

The eyes that burned from lack of tears turned their full heat on him. "If God isn't answerable to us, Tigernan, then why should we be answerable to Him? God the benevolent patriarch promises us rewards in the next world if we're willing to sacrifice in this one. But maybe I don't believe in patriarchs anymore. Maybe I want my rewards now, in this life, and I'll let my soul take its own chances after I die."

Tigernan's eyes opened very wide. "What are you saying?"

"I'm saying I mean to take a very un-Christian revenge on Huw's murderers," Grania told him. "I dealt a measured response to the Joyces for Donal's death, and afterward I sent a message to their chieftain that I wished the feud ended, so my children would have fewer enemies they needed to fear in Iar Connaught. I did what was expected of me in attacking the castle and then I tried to make an honorable peace.

"But this is different. This once I am going to do something just for myself, because I can't stay in my skin any longer if I don't. And I'm asking you—will you go with me again?"

Her eyes challenged him.

Tigernan took a deep breath, trying not to imagine what he might have to tell later in the confessional. "There was never any doubt of it," he said.

Anger was the anodyne that could consume even pain in its flame. For as long as Grania could sustain her rage she could survive the loss of a possible future she only fully appreciated after it was taken from her.

When she told her followers of her plans they were alarmed by the ferocity of her face and voice—except for Ruari Oge. "I always knew she had it in her," he said.

13

Energy is the concomitant of anger, at once its fuel and its expression—and energy must have a source. Grania drew on all the angers and disappointments and injustices of her past, the large and small bitternesses that had once been swallowed in silence but could now be piled up stone by stone to build a great fury. She cemented them together with half-forgotten lines from warrior epics she had loved as a child, searching within herself to find the battle frenzy of a Cuchullain, the joyous savagery of warriors turned to dust centuries ago. The old poems helped, for any poetry summoned back Huw, full-fleshed in her memory.

She constructed rage and hugged it to her heart.

Her energy was contagious. Huw had meant nothing to her followers, but when Grania stood before them with set jaw and slitted eyes and cried for vengeance, the warrior blood surged in them too.

"Yes!" they shouted with one voice. "Abu! To the victory!"

Yes! thundered the bodhrans. Yes! skirled the war-pipes.

Yes. And the woman who signaled battle felt that music in her bones.

She would not let them beat her—whoever they were. "They" had become, to Grania, an amorphous entity embodied by neither Gaels nor foreigners, but by dark fates that meant to drain every drop of sweetness from life, to make living nothing but a tragic tangle of roads all bound toward the tomb.

Every instinct in Grania rejected such a destiny. Not the dying; she had no fear of dying. But she was desperately afraid of a life that might prove to have been not worth the living. She would not allow "them" to distort her existence into such a shape. If one satisfaction was snatched from her she would find another; if she lost love she would embrace hate, and glory in it.

Her ships were fitted out for war. The carrack was not yet ready, but when she requested one of Dubhdara's caravels complete with cannon he could think of no reason to refuse it to her. She did not tell him the reason; she no longer explained anything to anyone.

She intended to sail north to Blacksod bay and attack the clan MacMahon in its stronghold, and to this end she successfully recruited many of her father's mariners, who proved as eager for a good fight as her own men. But even as she was making final preparations for departure—and promising full looting rights to any who accompanied her—word came from her sentries on the oceanside of Clare island that vessels flying the MacMahon banner had just passed on their way southward, obviously headed for the holy island of Caher to make a pilgrimage there.

Tigernan was not happy at this turn of events and tried to talk Grania into waiting until the pilgrimage was completed, but she would not listen.

"When did she ever listen?" Ruari Oge reminded him.

"It is a great sin to attack men on a holy mission," Tigernan said.

"Are you so upset you'll refuse to go?"

"I wish I could," Tigernan replied. "But I can't because she needs me. She's been buying weapons—pistols. And I'm the only one who understands them."

"As you think you are the only one who understands our commander," Ruari Oge commented.

Caher island was a tiny lift of land south of Cliara, a goodly journey from MacMahon territory. But sacred. A saint's foot had trod upon it, and according to Evleen, who knew such things, a pagan god had breathed upon it much earlier than that. A man's soul was strengthened by visiting such places, and no holy sight in Ireland, no matter how remote, was exempt from the attention of the faithful.

So the MacMahons made their dutiful pilgrimage to Caher, and Grania sailed in behind their ships at the anchorage and cut their vessels to ribbons, dismasting boats, ripping sails, setting fire to every galley and curragh so there was no escape from Caher.

Then she led her men onto the holy island and the slaughter began.

In her belt, Grania carried Tigernan's Saxon handgun. She liked the weight of it, the long solid barrel pressing against her thigh. The warriors she took with her were also supplied with pistols, swords, daggers, staffs, spears, axes . . . each man carrying the weapons traditionally favored by his clan, and boasting to his comrades of their particular efficacy.

The noblemen of the clan MacMahon were utterly unprepared for such an attack. But as soon as they saw their ships afire they knew they were at war; why and with whom hardly mattered. Good Gaels, they did not venture out on even a religious pilgrimage without their swords and other ceremonial armament, but they had not come to Caher in a martial frame of mind. Their thoughts were still numbed by reaching for God; they needed several minutes to become soldiers comfortable with killing.

Grania did not give them those minutes. They had not given Huw the gift of time. She surprised herself with her rapacity. She could not wait to get to the first man she saw and point her pistol at him. The weapon was longer than her forearm and heavy, requiring both her hands to hold it steady. But her finger slipped onto the trigger as if made for it, and when she fired and the wheel rotated she let out a glad cry almost equal to the report from the gun.

Tigernan, trying to stay close to her, saw her fire and stagger back from the recoil of the weapon. He saw the man she had shot, too—with a face blooming blood like a rose bursting into flower. The fellow waved his arms frantically and then fell backward without a sound.

Grania slowly lowered the pistol. She stared at the corpse twitching at her feet, and wondered if Huw had convulsed like that as life left him.

Then she wondered if this was one of the men who killed him.

At that moment, a MacMahon with the high cheekbones and small mouth common to the western islands ran toward Grania with an oath on his lips and a Scots claymore in his hands. Recognizing the banner of the red boar one of her men was holding aloft, he cried, "Beware, Ui Mháille!" in a carrying voice as he lifted his double-edged broadsword. "Beware, Umhall!"

Two things happened at once. Tigernan plunged forward to interpose his body between Grania and the claymore—and the MacMahon realized the person he was about to cleave in two was not a man, but a woman in trews. He twisted the sword in midair and slashed it down Tigernan's arm, and in almost the same breath yelled at Grania, "I won't war on a helpless woman! What kind of trick is this?"

He said the wrong words. The pistol was not ready to fire again, but Grania had a dagger in her belt and with one thrust of her strong right arm hurled the weapon straight at his throat.

Her aim was deadly. The man's face turned ashen and he sank to his knees, clawing at the knife hilt. When he dislodged it a great gout of blood came with it, followed by a pulsing fountain that swiftly drained him.

Tigernan, holding the torn edges of his arm together, bent over the man and saw that he was dying.

"Are you badly hurt?" Grania asked.

"I don't think so. I can bind it. He didn't even cut the muscle."

"Good," she said almost absently. As Tigernan watched she reclaimed her dagger from the grass and wiped it on her tunic with the neat efficiency of a cottage wife cleaning her butter knife.

She had already killed two men, and Tigernan had yet to wound his first. He was frightened for her. She seemed at the far edge of control; if he had been a fanciful man he would have thought dark wings hovered around her. She strode right into the heart of the fray, killing rather than wounding, fighting as strongly as the strongest man among them and asking no quarter for her sex.

Fighting in her wake, Magnus, who was also watching her, had the disquieting suspicion that she might turn on her own men if any of them tried to stop her.

Driven by such passion, Grania's forces soon won an easy victory. Too easy, she thought, as the dead and dying lay tumbled together. Like a meal of butterless bread, the killing she had done gave her no satisfaction. Nothing was solved; nothing was improved. If scales were balanced at all they existed in some other-world she could not see and touch. With Huw.

But her rage was not dead. It had been built too carefully, too lovingly; it possessed its own momentum now and would not pass until utterly exhausted. She could not bear to go unsatisfied. Someway, somehow, her losses—all her losses—must be made up to her. And she would do it herself. Must do it herself.

"We only got a small number of the clansmen who made up that hunting party to Achill," she told her captains after questioning the survivors. "We will go north to Blacksod bay and get the rest of them. For killing a guest of mine they have forfeited any right to friendship with the O Malleys. We will show them what it means to make such enemies."

North, up the coast, and the whole way Grania kept the bodhrans sounding. The low vicious rattle of war marked the beat of the oars. There was blood on her clothing, but she did not bother to wash it away. It was not her blood but a tribute exacted, a debt only partially paid.

Sentries and fishermen along the coast watched the fleet pass and heard the specific threat of the war drums. Runners were sent, signal fires ignited. By the time Grania sailed into Blacksod bay, Doona castle, on its eastern shore, lay abandoned to her. The MacMahons had prudently fled their stronghold to escape her wrath. Too late they learned the value placed upon the stranger they had casually killed. They wanted no part of the woman who came storming after them.

A resurrected figure from pagan Erin, the figure of the war goddess could still strike fear into the hearts of sixteenth-century Gaels, for all they thought themselves brave Christian men. The immortal soul remembers what flesh and blood deny.

Leaving a picked force of men to hold Doona in her name, Grania returned to Clew bay and reported to the Black Oak that O Malley territory had been expanded. "You went to war against a clan with whom I am at peace, and seized their stronghold?" Dubhdara asked incredulously.

"The first act of aggression was theirs," his daughter replied in a cold voice.

Owen Dubhdara had shrunk in the past few months, becoming gnarled and gaunt. He peered out at Grania from beneath a tangled thicket of white eyebrows. "O Malleys at Doona," he muttered. "Isn't that almost Burke territory? Are you not making dangerous enemies for our clan?"

"Are you worried about that watered-milk son of yours who hides behind the walls of Cathair na Mart and spends all his time playing the pipes?" Grania asked with a snort of contempt. "Poor weak stick of a thing, you must have sired him while you and his mother were both standing up. Your seed ran down out of her too fast to build you a strong son. But don't concern yourself; *I* can protect him if clan war comes to Cuan Mó."

✠

Flushed with victory, she felt invincible. It was now obvious to everyone that the Black Oak was too old for action, and though the vessels that sailed Clew bay were still nominally his, their captains followed Grania's banner. The twin magnets of her energy and her ambition were irresistible.

That energy drove her relentlessly. When there was no merchandise to transport she prowled the coast, seeking merchantmen to rob. She claimed a place in open fishing curraghs, hauling at the nets while salt spray coated her face and silvered her hair.

Anything to avoid returning to the empty tower house where Huw was not.

Occasionally, from the deck of a ship, she saw a wink of light burning late in the abbey at Murrisk. But Grania gave little thought to the Church. She had not received the Sacraments since Huw's death; she knew the good friars were angry with her for the attack on Caher during a holy pilgrimage. Even the gentle nuns who occupied the tiny convent on Cliara had gone out of their way to tell her so, but their disapproval meant nothing to her.

She and God had turned their backs on one another by mutual consent, she thought.

Calvagh of Bregia wrote, "Gráinne Ni Mháille has committed a blasphemous and unprovoked attack on innocent pilgrims which she justifies by claiming they murdered a guest under her protection—a male guest with whom she had a highly irregular relationship unsanctioned by the Church, may I add. The woman is a canker of corruption and is drawing an unconscionable number of men-at-arms to her, for what purpose one can only guess. With such an army, we do not expect her to limit herself to plunder and piracy forever."

Only a few weeks after he posted this report, Calvagh received word that the fine abbey of Burrishoole on the north shore of the bay had been seized and looted, its Dominican friars abused by soldiers loyal to the Tudor queen. But Murrisk remained inviolate, Calvagh noted with satisfaction.

Yet nothing was forever. A man had to look out for himself. He developed a habit of wandering through the abbey with an appraising eye, lifting a jeweled goblet and feeling its weight, considering the smelter value of a candlestick or the price some scholar might pay for certain dusty manuscripts hidden away in the scriptorium. These things should be preserved for God, Calvagh said to himself. They should be protected where they will be less obvious; some secret place only I know.

Yes.

For God.

One by one, he began secreting things away. In case the Protestants came, in case there was a war, in case . . . in case Calvagh of Bregia had need of them.

✠

Grania's men defiantly held Doona against several attempts on the part of clan MacMahon to recapture their stronghold. Expecting further reprisals elsewhere, Grania put Ruari Oge in charge of strengthening her sentry system up and down the coast, as far south as Iar Connaught. When she let herself slow down enough to think about it, she realized she was actually ruling a territory large enough to make any chieftain swell with pride. Much of the ancient kingdom of Connaught now sought alliance with her.

Grania welcomed to her stronghold men of pride and power, leaders of western clans that had become increasingly desperate to find ways of exporting their own commodities independent of the English-controlled ports. As long ago as 1518 the merchants of Galway city had enacted a typically repressive bylaw intended to deny the Gaels freedom of trade, and stating in part that "neither O nor Mac shall strutte nor swagger through the streets of Galway."

Men who bore the title of O or Mac now came before Gráinne Ni Mháille almost as petitioners, for she had shown that markets in Europe awaited their goods, and she was, for a price, apparently able to ship almost anything in or out of Ireland. She had the ships; she had the men. She had the knowledge of coastal waters that allowed her successfully to elude pursuit.

Grania savored the taste of power. She had not expected it, and she had certainly not expected to enjoy it so much. When a handsome blond chieftain from the banks of the Cromlin came to her and bowed his head before her, seeking her aid, she could not resist wondering aloud to Evleen afterward, "Do you think Eamon of the Bronze Shoulders has ever bowed his head to a woman before?"

Evleen grinned. "Not while he was standing up."

"You're wicked."

"I have a good imagination. And I hate to see an empty cup."

"What does that mean?"

Evleen made an explicit gesture, forming a bowl with one hand

and plunging the forefinger of the other hand into it. "It means you're a healthy woman who's gotten used to enjoying your body, and there's that golden-headed Eamon all aquiver with desire to please you."

"I'm still in mourning for Huw!" Grania snapped, annoyed to discover how avidly her imagination had galloped off, spurred by Evleen's words.

But there would be time, she knew. Time in the future, when the pain had faded and she could allow herself a sensual reward her body obviously craved. She was riding the exhilarating crest of a wave, and all things seemed possible.

Perhaps she was a little too arrogant—her own sons were beginning to say that of her. Perhaps she was a little too certain that success once achieved would be a permanent condition. But it was good while it lasted.

In October of 1565, Sir Henry Sidney arrived to serve as lord deputy. Sidney had served in Ireland before; he believed he understood the country. Old Celtic tribalism at its worst was keeping the Irish divided and therefore weakened, a situation that could be exploited to the Crown's benefit. Sidney therefore thought it imperative that no strong leader be allowed to emerge from the pack and unite the Irish in all their diverse factions. He brought with him men who shared his political philosophies, some of whom were well-intentioned bureaucrats, and others who were unscrupulous adventurers, useful weapons for the continuing struggle to subdue Ireland.

One of these, a lower-echelon aide just beginning to fight for his own place in the Elizabethan power struggle, was a volatile and bitter man named Richard Bingham.

Among Bingham's other assignments was the assimilation of information about the various Gaelic chieftains who could pose a threat to English control. Bingham was a seaman, and it was easy enough for him to slip around the Irish coast, picking up bits of information to carry back to Sidney. Not surprisingly, Bingham eventually learned of the activities of an abbot known as Calvagh, a cleric of repute in Murrisk. A new and secret visitor to Calvagh's apartments became the English seafarer with the hard eyes and a mouth stamped by the repeated disappointments of an unsuccessful career.

Gráinne Ni Mháille was frequently mentioned.

Sidney was thus aware of Grania before she ever heard his name. Ruari Oge first mentioned him to her, upon returning from a mission up the coast to check on Doona.

✠

"We're still in possession of the MacMahon stronghold," Ruari reported, "but it's hard to say how much longer they will wait before trying to recapture it. It's a terrible insult to The MacMahon to have a woman keep him from his home."

"He still has his life," Grania said, "which is more than some possess. He should be grateful for what he has."

"I doubt if he sees it that way," Ruari replied.

"I'm through with giving things up," Grania said with a determined jut to her jaw. "We'll hold Doona as long as it suits me; with Dubhdara's men behind me we have strength enough to do it."

"But the MacMahons may call upon the Burkes to stand with them," Ruari Oge reminded her. "They live on the edge of Burke territory."

"Iron Richard is an ally of my father's. I expect no trouble from that quarter."

"We're not talking about Iron Richard's territory, but that of another Richard Burke, the one they call the Devil's Hook."

Grania and Ruari Oge were standing just outside the entry court of the tower house as they spoke together, and Grania had only to look directly ahead to see Curraun mountain rise on the north shore of the bay, dominating the landward approach to Achill island. "The Devil's Hook," she mused aloud. "Ruler of Curraun."

"The same. And a clever man, as are all those Burkes. Now that the new lord deputy is planning to name a president officer to rule Connaught in the name of the English she-king, the Devil's Hook may be scrambling for some new alliances. Like all his family, he has no love for foreign control. He . . ."

"New lord deputy?" Grania interrupted in surprise. "President officer for Connaught? Where did you hear all this, Ruari Oge?"

The big man could not resist boasting, just a little. "Did you forget that I am of clan O Donnell?" he asked. "When I go north, I usually find time to visit my kin. They're very impressed with what they hear of you . . ."

"I don't want flattery," she interrupted him. "I want news. If you've been roasting your rump at an O Donnell hearth you must be well informed; the princes of the north have a talent for sniffing the wind."

"I heard that a man named Sir Henry Sidney, only just arrived in Ireland, is the new lord deputy and was giving orders before he had his boots off," Ruari told her. "It seems to be true about the presidents—Munster and Connaught are both to have them, and . . ."

"Munster and Connaught are Irish *kingdoms!*" Grania cried in outrage.

"Not to the English," Ruari Oge reminded her, his own voice bitter. "They have already crushed and destroyed our kings; now this Sidney means to inflict a new kind of government on us, with presidents ruling the provinces of Ireland assisted by a council of the principal landowners and a small army."

"Principal landowners," Grania snorted. "New colonists loyal to England are already becoming the principal landowners. What voice will the Irish have?"

"The idea seems to be that they have none. Even the tenants on the lands of the Norman earls are being urged to pay their rents directly to the Crown instead. The earls are in a great fury about it—and the princes of Ulster are equally angry, of course. They feel Sidney will greatly increase the plantation of foreign colonists on Irish soil, and they mean to resist it in Ulster, where Elizabeth wants Saxons who profess loyalty to her."

"Shane O Neill will fight such plantation," said Grania, nodding.

"Clan O Donnell too!" Ruari added hotly. "My people do not kneel to foreigners . . . though whether all the O Donnell septs will unite with the O Neills against English policy is another matter. There are ancient rivalries there."

"There are ancient rivalries everywhere in Ireland," Grania reminded him. "It was our way of life and at least we understood it; the English do not. But they understand well enough how to use our own divisiveness against us. Surely I learned that lesson from watching my husband. If I now continue my feud with clan MacMahon, and they draw in the Devil's Hook, and I draw in my father's allies . . . we will be so busy flailing away at each other we will not notice what is happening until English colonists are plowing the plains of Murrisk.

"President of Connaught indeed," she added in a voice steely with anger. "If there is any strong voice right now in Connaught, it is mine—who else is providing a living for so many people?"

"You're a woman," Ruari Oge reminded her. He was a brave man, Ruari Oge. "Under Irish law you cannot claim the title of chieftain."

"Titles don't matter," she told him. "Deeds matter. I told you I was through giving things up. If Shane O Neill means to hold the kingdom of Ulster against the foreigners, then I will hold my kingdom against them as well."

"All Umhall?" he asked, taken aback by the size of her defiance.

"All of Clew bay," she replied. "From Cathair na Mart to Cliara to Achill head and wherever I choose to sail my ships in between."

"Most of the north shore of the bay is in the hands of Burke septs," he reminded her.

"The *bay* is *mine*," she emphasized through gritted teeth. "And I will defend it by whatever means necessary against anyone who tries to crowd me out."

Later he would remember that phrase—"by whatever means necessary"—but now Ruari Oge whooped, "Glory be to God, we're going to war against the English!"

Grania put her hands on her hips and laughed, shaking her head at him. "I didn't say that! I'm not such a great fool I think I can take on the Tudor woman and the armies she has scattered all over Ireland. No, I'm not going to declare open war against her." She paused then, the laugh fading, the level brows drawing together like a dark cloud on her forehead. "But if she tries to reach for what is mine, I will cut off her hand."

14

Clew bay roiled. With fish, with boats, with Grania and her men consolidating support, winning allies, buying and selling and shipping and promising. To the astonishment of the MacMahons of Doona, she offered to return their castle to them upon receiving a pledge of allegiance to her banner—a pledge she would doubly reward by including Blacksod bay and environs in her commercial network. With Dubhdara's ships at her command she had become the most powerful and far-reaching sea power on the west coast of Ireland.

Grania never looked in Evleen's mirror anymore.

Only in the dark of night did she think of Huw, and then she lay rigid in bed with clenched fists. His hands, his mouth, his voice rumbling in his chest as his body pressed against hers . . . brief flashing days when she was beautiful . . .

She would be more than beautiful. She would be strong, she would be invulnerable. And if she had enough strength she could extend it to protect her children, for she saw them now as the only future she had. Elizabeth of the Tudors had no children, it was said.

To teach Owen and Murrough that life was never easy, she insisted they pay her a high premium for the shipping she did on behalf of Iar Connaught. Every time an O Flaherty ship anchored in Clew bay its captain had to pay Grania what many considered an exorbitant fee, and her son Owen complained bitterly that his mother had no maternal feeling for him, or she would make special allowances for his sake.

Both young men made the trip up the coast to see her, though they came separately and returned separately. Studying them, Grania realized their only real connection was one of birth. Otherwise they were totally dissimilar.

Owen had fulfilled his early promise by being handsome and

pleasant of demeanor, but he seemed too anxious to please. He could listen to the arguments in the hall which were such a fixture of Gaelic social life and take first one side, then the other, bowing to whichever was the prevailing wind. "Think for *yourself*, Owen!" Grania ordered him more than once.

Later, in private, she said to Evleen, "I'm too hard on Owen, and I know it. I begin to see that I only turn him against me, I don't give him the strength he needs to be his own man. But I know from my own experience what it takes to succeed, and I am frustrated by my inability to transmit that wisdom to him. I'm afraid for him; these are not times for an uncertain nature."

Murrough was his brother's opposite. His thoughts seemed carved in stone, and once he had made his mind up nothing could shake his convictions. He was passionate and hot-tempered and charming, drawing people to him effortlessly while his older brother sought with puppy-dog eagerness to win them. Murrough did not seem to care if anyone liked him or not, so almost everyone did, Grania included. But she fought with him, often and angrily. "He will rush headfirst into the fire and let no one tell him it will burn," she commented to Evleen.

"Every child is different, Grania. Have you ever looked at a field of flowers—really looked at them, one at a time? They appear the same and yet when you examine them one has a tougher stem, another is taller, a third sheds its petals too easily. Each thing that lives is unique, and none fits a pattern you or I might design. But we are not in charge of forming the pattern."

"I am responsible for what my children become," Grania told her.

"No. You are the seed from which they came, you give them their color and form. But wind and sun and rain will shape each differently, Grania. You cannot be blamed for it all. Besides, a messenger just brought word that your third flower is on its way to you, so now you can think of her for a change."

"Margaret?" Grania's face went blank. She had been thinking of other children, of sons . . . and now the image of a girl intruded, wrenching the course of her emotions in a different direction entirely. Margaret. "Coming to Cliara?"

"So it seems. Her foster parents are providing her with an escort to you, and as soon as I heard I began cleaning and airing the small chamber for her. There's a new featherbed and I took the liberty of asking the Carmelite sisters to sew some shifts for her, some new warm garments to shield her from the sea wind. If she's been raised inland, she might not realize how cold it can get out here."

Grania could not help smiling. "I would like to have seen you going to the convent to ask a favor."

Evleen sniffed. "Oh, I didn't go in person. I sent the wife of one of my husband's crewmen."

"Would it shrivel your skin to pass beneath a Christian cross?"

The other woman did not answer.

Excitement bubbled up in Grania like springwater. Her daugher, her own child, with her at last. She would not be such a mother as her own had been, pious and weepy. She would laugh and be young for Margaret; together they would giggle over whatever it was girls always seemed to giggle about. In her daughter, Grania would reclaim her own youth for a time and make up in some measure for all the years she had not held her children in her arms.

Then she looked in Evleen's mirror and felt a chill. What would Margaret make of a mother who was a sea captain in trews, preoccupied with trade and protecting the borders of her kingdom?

Donal fought to protect the borders of his kingdom, a deep and innate honesty forced Grania to remember. And I condemned him for it. Then. Nor did I understand the pleasure he took in battle, the joy of victory as he knew it. Then.

So life is learning, and I am not the woman I was. Not even the mother I was, perhaps. I have made mistakes with my sons that I will not repeat with Margaret. We will have more time together before she is grown and flown away, we will be friends. . . .

Friends . . . as Evleen had come to be a friend, particularly since Huw's death. Grania, who had never been close to another woman, had learned to value Evleen's innate understanding and wisdom during the dreadful period when the loss of Huw had seemed an insurmountable wall, separating her forever from life.

But Evleen had taught Grania to observe the way time flowed over and past that wall, eroding it, until the worst pain faded and light showed through the cracks. Evleen had explained to her mistress, "Death is a black-winged raven, shadowing the lives of the survivors, but it is really only one of Life's faces, a natural and inevitable part of the whole. In the Old Religion there was no acknowledgment of death. It was just considered a change in the direction Life takes. The life that you loved in your Huw has gone off in another direction for now—and so must you, Grania."

Yes, Evleen had become a friend. And having learned much of womanly wisdom from her, Grania was eager to pass that gift on to her own daughter, to be Margaret's friend.

Not long before the girl was expected to arrive, Grania went down to the cove she had visited so often with Huw. Went alone, at sunset. In this place her memories of him were most vivid, and until recently, most painful. Now they were growing soft and warm.

The tall woman spread a cloak on the sand and lay down on her belly, propping herself on her elbows to watch the water. She had survived Huw's death because she had no choice; she would go on living because life demanded it. And she would laugh again because Huw had enjoyed hearing her laugh; wherever he was, she wanted him to hear her laughter still.

The thought hurt. What was that Evleen said? "All births hurt. Remember every time something powerful forced you forward into a new kind of life. Did it not hurt? Did you not want to cry out in protest at each violent change? That is how we are made, Grania."

Grania remembered. She felt tears burning deep inside her that had been there for a very long time, like an ulcer in her belly. They predated Huw, or the loss of her babies, or Donal. They dated back to the first trauma of personal birth she could remember, the day she had learned life's dark face and begun to change into the woman she now was. Since then the tears had waited, denied their natural expression. But they had not dried up though many years had passed. They were all stored and waiting.

✠

The little girl was only seven, and thin, for her bones were outgrowing her ability to keep meat on them. She would be tall someday. But she looked fragile as she stood at the water's edge, watching her father's fleet pull away.

Grania had reached an age when a child takes notice of its parents' activities, and her father's frequent absences had begun to upset her. Her mother seemed to have little time for her, spending too many of her hours in the chapel or with her confessor—or weeping and worrying about her absent husband. Mairgret looked pale and melancholy to her child, while Dubhdara was robust and full of life, so Grania turned to him as a flower to the sun. But he was always going away! To which parent, then, could a small girl cling in those inevitable moments when she needed comfort?

On this occasion Mairgret seemed more distraught by her husband's departure than usual. She had had a bad dream, or seen bad omens, and had tried to dissuade him from sailing. When that failed she had burned candles and paid for masses and assailed the gates of heaven, begging mercy. So preoccupied was she she never noticed that her daughter had caught the contagion of tears and wandered away by herself to squat, sniffling, at the water's edge.

Mairgret did not notice, but some of the rougher boys sired by the Black Oak's clansmen did. With the sniggering malice of their kind, they gathered around the crying child and began to tease her. As the chieftain's daughter she was fair game; the jackal's kits must always spit at the lion's cub.

The harder Grania cried the more cruel their jibes became. When they saw they were frightening her they exchanged winks over her head and pretended they meant to drown her. "The O Malley girl is scared of water!" they yelled, ducking her repeatedly until she choked. They let her up long enough to take in one gasp of air and flail, bug-eyed, at the surface. Then they shoved her under again.

The desperate child tried to scream and attract the attention of some nearby adult, but without success. She thought her lungs would burst as the icy black water poured down her throat. Fighting with all her strength, she managed to get free of her tormenters and cry out her mother's name, only to see Mairgret turn and walk away from the shore, heading back toward the fortress.

Mairgret had not heard Grania's cry, but even if she had it might have gone unnoticed. All her thoughts were on Dubhdara and the urgent prayers for his safety she was mouthing over and over. She assumed her attendants would look after her daughter; they always did.

But her serving women were dutifully following her, because she acted so upset they were concerned about her. For a few minutes, no one at all was thinking of Grania.

The little girl was alone in a lightless universe that meant to destroy her with a total, irresistible malignity of purpose. In that moment of revelation all childish innocence left her. Death—which she had never personally seen, much less considered—became very probable. Fear overcame her.

To the casual observer the incident appeared to be only the play of children in the shallows, ducking one another and splashing and yelling. No one took it seriously.

No one realized a little girl thought she was being murdered, and had just seen her mother walk away to leave her to her fate.

The boys were enjoying the game, but when Grania's eyes rolled back in her head and she went limp they pulled her onto the shore and pummeled her until she recovered consciousness. They were badly scared by then; if they had actually harmed Dubhdara's daughter no power on earth could have saved them from the consequences.

When Grania opened her eyes and struggled to sit up, they ran away, lest she remember their faces and names.

She did not remember their identities, as it happened; the whole incident was cloaked for her forever with a fog of fear. But she never forgot the taunting words that accused her of being afraid of the water. She never forgot the way they had laughed at her for crying, and been encouraged by her weakness to torment her still more.

The story was too good to keep, so one group of children told another that the chieftain's daughter was afraid of the water and could be a grand source of fun. The next time she wandered away from adult supervision she was seized again and ducked again and threatened again, but this time it took a lot longer to make her cry. In her father's halls, Grania had seen the cowering hound draw the bully's kick.

The third time she was assaulted in this fashion she clenched her hands into tight little fists and bit her lower lip until it bled, but she did not cry. Instead she made herself laugh at her attackers as if she were having fun too. Disarmed, they decided the game had lost its savor and went seeking other amusements.

But the memory of the fear remained. Grania could awaken in the night in a cold sweat, thinking the water was about to close over her head again.

Dubhdara wasn't afraid of the sea. He challenged it constantly, and the rewards of his courage piled on the docks and filled the storehouses of Umhall. Tears such as Mairgret's, however, seemed to be rewarded only by pain.

The little girl resolved in her small bruised soul to find a better model than her mother—and that meant overcoming her fear of water, for the Black Oak's child must be as brave as he.

The walls of Belclare rose beside a pleasant little river, the stronghold's fresh-water supply. Dubhdara's hounds often frolicked in the river, as they did in the shallows of the bay, running in water deep enough to drown them but seemingly unafraid.

The trick, Grania decided after watching them closely, was to keep moving: to move legs or arms-and-legs in a running fashion. If you could swim you need not be afraid of the water.

She knew no one who could really swim, except the dogs, and so there was no one to teach her but herself.

When the opportunity arose, she slipped away from the stronghold and down to the river, seeking a bend in its course that formed a quiet little backwater pond fringed by reeds and frequented by ducks and an occasional heron.

I won't be afraid anymore, she said to herself, eyeing the water nervously. Being afraid hurts worse than anything.

Holding her small store of courage like a cup she feared to spill, Grania waded into the water. When it reached her knees she stopped in panic, but the thudding of her heart angered her, and suddenly she ran forward, straight into the main channel of the river.

Her fisted hands opened instinctively and beat at the water. She went under at once, but her legs kicked and she surfaced, to her vast surprise. The sun was shining! She had time to realize that much and clutch at the thought before she felt herself starting to go down again. Desperately, she made running motions with arms and legs, thrusting her head from the water and gulping air. But she did not sink. She moved erratically through the water, propelled as much by her own actions as the sluggish current.

At last she crawled up on the far bank, sodden and chilled and triumphant. As soon as she got her breath she plunged in again and beat her way across once more with a great deal of splashing. This time when she gained the riverbank she stood up and filled her lungs with a great deep breath.

Then she threw back her head and laughed.

A few days later she noticed a group of older children playing a game down on the beach, and among them she thought she saw some of those who might have tormented her earlier. The bay water was very cold, but she did not let herself think about that. With great calculation she circled around until she was out of their sight, then slipped into the water and waded out far enough to swim. Following the shoreline, and occasionally touching the bottom with one extended toe just to be certain she could, Grania swam parallel to the shore until she reached the beach where the children played. Then she shouted at them. "Come and join me!" she yelled. "Are you afraid of the water?"

They stared at her, their mouths making startled circles. The cold western waters of Ireland did not encourage much swimming, and none of them had ever tried. They could only watch as the chieftain's daughter defied the elements and splashed smugly past them.

When the Black Oak's galleys returned from their latest voyage a red-eyed Mairgret waved ecstatically from shore . . . but little Grania slipped into the water and swam out to meet her father's ship.

"Dar Dia, here's a child for you! Sire one like this if you can!" Dubhdara challenged his men laughingly as he pulled his daughter over the side.

✠

Violet surrendered to purple; the vault of the sky above Clew bay cracked open, spilling stars. Evleen, leaving the tower house, almost bumped into a dark, solitary figure before she saw him.

"What are you doing here at this hour, Tigernan?"

"She's still down in the cove." He did not bother to identify her by name; they both knew there was only one *she* in Tigernan's awareness.

"She'll be all right. Liam is standing watch."

"She shouldn't be be sitting down there on damp sand."

"She'd not thank you for disturbing her, Tigernan," Evleen told him. "Come home with me now; have a meal and a cup with us. There's plenty."

"There's always plenty. Grania sees to it. But we can't do anything for her."

"You're certainly not helping her by skulking around watching her when she obviously wants to be alone. Come, now."

He shrugged her away. "I'll be along," he promised. "I'll be along . . . soon. Go to Ruari and throw an extra fish on the coals for me."

She left him; there was nothing else to be done. As she bustled around her own cottage, feeling Ruari Oge's fond glance like firelight on her back, Evleen commented aloud, "Tigernan is a great pain to himself. It's unnatural, the way he lives, trying to draw the breath she breathes. And him just another captain to her."

"He's the sort of man who must have something to worship," her husband replied.

"I suppose his Christian religion doesn't offer him enough," Evleen remarked with a smug sniff and an energetic flap of her apron to feed air to the hearthfire.

"There's no need to speak against the Faith," Ruari Oge told her in a mild tone. "It does a lot of good. The crucifix hanging around my neck was put there by the hands of a saintly old priest who told me it would protect me at sea, and so far it has."

Evleen glanced over her shoulder at him. "You think that's what preserves you in storm and battle, do you? What about the other charm I gave you, the one you wear on a longer thong so it doesn't show in the neck of your tunic?"

Ruari Oge busied himself removing his boots.

"And as for priests being saints," Evleen went on, "isn't it a fact they take bribes and get drunk on their sacramental wine and occasionally hoist one another's robes in the back hall of some friary? And everyone knows it."

"They do all those things, I suppose," Ruari agreed. "At least some of them do. And those same men travel long distances in every kind of dirty weather to spend sleepless nights at the bedside of the dying, or thankless days instructing some chieftain's stony-skulled children who make their life a torment."

"So priests are a mixture of cattle dung and sunbeams just like the rest of Creation," Evleen said.

"When men talk of priests in the bruighen after too much ale, they say that very thing, though not quite that way," Ruari told his wife. His eyes twinkled with an ironic and very Gaelic amusement, understanding full well that cattle dung and sunbeams are part of the same world.

"And when a priest tells you something," Evleen went on, feeling combative, "don't fool yourself into thinking you are hearing sacred voices. Priests are human like the rest of us, and like the rest of us they are just one part of the Creator—the Mother, the Father, the God by whatever name. The God who is also in sun and stars and stags and salmon, in all things that burn with life and leap toward ecstasy.

"Your Christian priests burn, just as our friend Tigernan burns, but your Church tells them all ecstasy should be limited to its own pale rituals." She tossed her head. "I don't think much of any religion that claims authority over the fire of life the Creator set alight in us."

"Now Evleen . . ." Ruari attempted to admonish her, but it was already too late, and he knew it. Her hands were on him, kneading the tired muscles in his shoulders, sliding down his torso to caress, to kindle. Her warm breath blew in his ear and fanned his graying beard. "The power that created me would not have given me such a capacity for feeling pleasure if I weren't meant to use it," Evleen whispered to the man who sat rapt beneath her touch. "Your religion wants dominion over our bodies because sex is the one ecstasy they can't control, and they are threatened by any rapture other than that they offer. But what they have to offer isn't enough, or friars wouldn't sneak over convent walls and pious Tigernan wouldn't visit chapel as regularly as the sun rising and then haunt cold headlands, yearning for a woman."

Ruari could not think clearly when her hands were doing such delicious, magical things.

"Do you know what draws Tigernan to Grania?" Evleen asked, her voice soft as bog-cotton in his ear. "She's totally alive, Grania is. All by herself she's more of a celebration than anything he ever experienced kneeling in a damp chapel.

"What Tigernan feels for her he won't admit, because the Christmen have denounced that kind of passion until they've almost driven the joy and juice out of it. They want men to see women as nothing but brood mares, so they will have to seek comfort and happiness in the religion the priests teach. Christ-men—whether Papists or Protesters, I doubt there's a leaf's difference between them—try to convince you that life is barren and bitter and you can only be happy in the heaven they want to sell you. Don't look so affronted, Ruari," she laughed at him, moving her hands in marvelous ways. Stroking here, fondling there. Celebrating her man's body. "I'm telling you a truth. I doubt the lord Christ meant his followers to be so cold-blooded; from what I've heard of him he was a man who loved life and knew how to drain a cup to the bottom.

"But the priesthoods that build themselves kingdoms using his name function like the English administrators you hate, Ruari; they pile up great walls of restrictions and prohibitions to convince everyone theirs is the ultimate authority. I tell you, the self-anointed priests are as busy defending their territories as any Gaelic warlord.

"But Grania . . . ah, she is indifferent to restrictions and prohibitions. Tigernan can't help responding to that, to her. He comes from a bare-rock island where the people had little but religion to sustain them, and he's deep in the habit of it, even when his every instinct urges him to reach out and grab that woman. He'll never do it. His rank is so much lower than hers she can't be expected to marry him, and the priests tell him he can't have her any other way. Those nights when she was enjoying her foremastman, Tigernan was pacing the beach and wringing his hands, certain she'd doomed her immortal soul." Suddenly Evleen chuckled, just as Ruari Oge abandoned any attempt at control and pulled her down into his lap. "I wonder if Tigernan thinks you and I are damned," she asked her husband. "We were wed in no chapel."

"We were wed in sun and rain," Ruari repeated from a litany older than Catholic priesthood. "Worship the God with me, Evleen. . . ." His voice was hoarse; demanding.

Pressed together in the firelight, striving to share one skin, for a long moment they did not hear the rapping at the door. Then Evleen jumped up with a little squeak of dismay. "I forgot completely that I asked him to come down and eat with us."

Ruari Oge shook his head, his features still gathered in passion. "Him who?"

"Tigernan. He looked that cold and miserable, I thought he could share your good salmon. I didn't know we'd be . . ." She held out her hands and shrugged, smiling.

"That smells too much of Christian charity," Ruari Oge complained. "But go let the man in. The damage is already done."

"Every country woman knows how to firm up a melted candle," Evleen comforted him as she headed for the door.

Tigernan was soon seated at the one small trestle table the cottage boasted, and a heaped trencher was in front of him. Ruari Oge gave him the best portion of the salmon and smiled as he did so—though he would say in private to Evleen later that the fish had died a needless death, since Tigernan only picked at it with little show of appetite.

The other two ate their own meal with considerably more enjoyment, their eyes meeting from time to time and carrying on a conversation having nothing to do with fish or friends. When the aleskin was half empty, Tigernan leaned back and wiped his mouth.

"There is a worry on me," he said.

"We know," Evleen answered, and Ruari Oge shot her a sharp look, requesting she not embarrass a guest under his roof. Fortunately Tigernan was lost in his own thoughts and scarcely heard her.

"Do you remember, Ruari," he said, "a conversation you and I had some time back about that foremastman? I said then I suspected him of being a spy."

"You suspected him of every sort of crime. You would have blamed him for calling the Normans into Ireland if you could."

Tigernan bristled. "I am not an unfair man! But there are too many English ships too close to Clare island, you have to admit that."

"I do. I just don't think he had anything to do with it. Our Grania is shaking her fist at the world, Tigernan. Someone is bound to respond."

"Tigernan, are you in there?" cried a familiar voice.

"It's herself!" Tigernan sat bolt upright.

"Let her in, wife," said Ruari Oge.

Grania swept into the cottage, bringing the sharp sweet smell of winter night caught in the folds of her cloak. Without formality she pulled a bench close to the table and reached past Ruari Oge to help herself to a morsel of bread and cheese.

"Ah, that's good," she sighed with approval. "I didn't realize how late it was—or how hungry I was."

This was not the first time Grania had casually visited the cottage. Though commander of the fleet, she did not keep herself isolated from her men—except for the period of her idyll with Huw—and any of her captains might expect her to appear at the door for a chat or a flagon of ale.

She grinned at Ruari Oge. "Liam at my gate told me this scoundrel you're feeding had been lurking around the tower house, so I thought I would come after him and see if he'd stolen my salt or my candlesticks."

"Why don't you search him?" Evleen asked innocently.

Ruari Oge gave his wife a second, even more severe look.

The aleskin was passed around again, and Evleen hunted in her cupboard until she found a battered silver tankard of Ruari Oge's, a pirate's prize. Buffing it on her apron, she filled it to the rim for Grania.

The four lounged comfortably around the trestle table. In order to be more at ease, Grania took her pistol from her belt and laid it beside the silver tankard.

"You carry that all the time now?" Ruari Oge asked.

She nodded. "Haven't you noticed how the English cruise closer and closer to our shores?"

"We were just talking about that very thing," Tigernan said eagerly, "and I think a spy . . ."

Ruari Oge's strong voice overrode his. "Actually, before you and Tigernan arrived the wife and I were arguing religion," he said to change the subject before Tigernan succeeded in angering Grania to no purpose.

Grania laughed. "You two, arguing religion? Who wins?"

"Evleen, always. You can't debate her. She's twice too wise for an unlettered country woman; you would think she'd been educated in a king's household. You should hear her when she gets started."

"Is this true, Evleen?" Grania asked with interest, turning a penetrating gaze upon her attendant. "Where were you educated? I always assumed you grew up in a tenant family in Thomond."

"And I did, thislife," Evleen replied. "But I carry a very old soul."

Ruari Oge shook his head. The conversation was not easy to direct into safe channels tonight, and all he wanted was a little friendly banter and then for everyone to go home and leave him alone with his woman. A protracted discussion of old souls and pagan belief, with Tigernan in attendance, would make for an argumentative evening that could last until morning and was definitely not to his taste tonight.

He looked across the table at the figure of his commander with the glow of the firelight behind her. Grania's unbound black hair streamed over her shoulders; her eyes were direct and keen beneath her level brows. She wore a simple homespun tunic, open at the throat, and on one arm a pair of gold bracelets such as a Gaelic chieftain might wear. Tankard and pistol were on the table in front of her. She appeared simultaneously at ease and very much in control of herself. He had the impression that if they heard an untoward noise outside, Grania would be on her feet with a pistol in her hand before any of the rest of them could respond.

Yes, indeed, the old warrior said to himself, if I didn't have Evleen . . .

His wife's hand reached under the table and gripped his thigh, hard. "Your daughter is arriving very soon," Evleen said aloud to Grania at the same time. "I will come to you by sunrise to be certain everything is in readiness for her." Then she yawned, very widely and plainly.

Grania chuckled. "I'm leaving as fast as I can, Evleen." She turned her tankard upside down on the table to show she had enjoyed every drop of her host's hospitality. "Come on, Tigernan. This wise woman with the old soul thinks everyone should be in bed."

Ruari Oge could not help snorting with laughter, and this time it was Evleen's turn to give him a warning glance.

Outside the cottage, Tigernan hesitated before turning down the path to his own home. "Will you be all right?" he could not resist asking Grania.

The night was cold, the moon full, and the reflected light off the sea lent an eerie brightness to the quiet island. Grania could see, quite clearly, the familiar worried frown on Tigernan's face. "What do I have to fear on my own Cliara, with a pistol in my belt?" she asked him. "You worry too much, my friend. Remind me to talk with you about that sometime."

"You're not going to go back to the cove and sit out all night, are you?"

She took a deep breath before answering. "Why in Mary's name would I want to do that?"

"You're still mourning that foremastman, aren't you?"

"Me? Mourning?" He could not be certain if her laughter was forced, Grania wore bravado well.

"I saw you, down there in the cove."

"That just shows how little you know. I was making plans for the future, not making myself needlessly sick with grief for something that can't be undone. Death is inevitable, Tigernan. For you, me, Huw. . . . Since it can't be avoided, we should forget about it and spend our energies constructively while we live. Eat, drink, laugh, feel the sun. That's what's important.

"I'm a big healthy woman from a long-lived clan. I may draw breath for eighty years or more. That means I have time to live several lives, now that I think of it; all my existence doesn't have to be crowded into one short space. I had one life with Donal an Chogaidh and that's over. I had a season with Huw, and we dreamed some dreams that were no more than clouds piled up over the bay, blown away by a strong wind. So now it's time to get ready for my next life, and that takes planning."

"Your next life . . . you mean heaven?"

Her laughter was genuine this time. "Fool! I mean right here on Clew bay. That's what I was thinking about, no doubt, when you were busy spying on me and imagining all sorts of melancholy thoughts. I was sitting down there tonight thinking about holding and making the most of the bay, about building a new life here in a shape of my own choosing. In a place I prefer to heaven.

"I am virtually a ban-rion here, Tigernan; a she-king, as the Tudor woman is a she-king. That is my new life, and kings have to learn new skills. If I'm going to keep this territory for my own I will have to be smart and learn fast."

Suddenly she flung her arms wide, crying out in a strident voice that resonated across the night sea, "Hear me, out there! Clew bay is mine! I will make any wager, play any game to keep it, but this is mine until I die!"

Then she turned to Tigernan and laughed at the expression on his face. "You think I dare God? Perhaps I do. Or the sasanach, or the clans . . . why not? If you're going to gamble, you should play for the highest possible stakes, for what is all of life but a gamble? Perhaps that's why I love it."

He could not understand her. He had thought she grieved alone on the beach, yet here she was merry and defiant.

Perhaps it was not necessary that he understand her. He did not know what the sun was, either, but it kept him warm.

Yet she is a woman, a small voice inside him insisted. She is just an Irishwoman, and they will strike her down, those she dares.

He set his jaw and walked back to his cottage alone, listening for the crunch of her feet as she climbed the pebbled path to the tower house.

part three

IRON RICHARD

15

Anticipating her daughter's arrival, Grania paced along the cliff and gazed toward Iar Connaught, squinting as if she could shrink sea and land with the power of her eyes and actually see young Margaret hastening toward her. But this was Ireland, bound by its own natural laws. Sea faded into land, into haze, into mist, and even a skilled mariner could not always tell where one left off and the next began.

She saw the ships, though—the English ships, flying Tudor flags, patrolling Irish waters. The new lord deputy was keeping an eye on the west coast of Ireland.

On board one of those patrolling vessels, Richard Bingham adjusted the spyglass to his eye and sent a long, raking look across the lifted shape of the island known as Clare. "That's the island that savage Irishwoman makes her headquarters," he commented to an aide. "She takes far too much shipping in and out of Ireland to my taste, merchandise going to foreign ports when it should be fattening English coffers. She is like some sort of rodent, stealing grain and goods that do not rightly belong to her. And I hate rodents. Almost as much as I am repelled by the idea of a woman working at a man's trade."

Bingham's lips drew back from his teeth in a grimace of distaste. Fine-featured, with a domed forehead and clear olive complexion, Lieutenant Richard Bingham might have been considered a handsome man had it not been for his thin, bitter mouth and hard eyes. He trusted no one and nothing, and his dislike for all things Irish had become an obsession. The country seemed to be bad luck for him, yet he could never win his way high enough in the ranks to get reassigned to some more idyllic post—to a fine new ship on the Continental run, for instance. Or better yet, the New World.

He glared at Clare island, seeing it as a foggy, dreary embodiment of everything he hated. "Nest of vermin," he muttered.

"They should all be cleaned out so England has undisputed access to the North Atlantic. Then we'd see some action! Then we'd be underway for the New World ourselves, perhaps, and return laden with more gold than the Spaniards have even thought of taking out of it so far!"

While Richard Bingham fingered the coins of his ambition, Grania waited for her daughter; waited longer than she had expected, and began to worry. Could an English ship have intercepted Margaret and her party? Were they coming by land or by sea? The message had been unclear. . . .

She felt chilled. They called Elizabeth of England the Virgin Queen, and she had no daughters. Could she have reached with greedy fingers for Grania's girl?

The dark-haired woman shook her head and laughed at herself. Foolish, wild imagination, she thought. You are too old and too wise to scare yourself with such suppositions. Just because the English hover does not mean you need to crouch quivering on the earth like a rabbit under the shadow of the hawk's wing, Grania Mhaol!

The steel crept back into her spine, and her head came up.

Late the next day, an open curragh set out from the nearest spit of land to the south to cross the open water toward Clare island. Grania did not see its approach; the light was already fading and a rising winter wind had driven her inside, hungry for a hot meal and a fire to prop her feet up beside.

The wind turned the surface of Cuan Mó into a chop of foam-streaked waves that washed dismally over the sides of the open boat. The party huddled on the splintery plank seating pressed together and drew their cloaks over their heads, but nothing could keep out the wetness, or the cold.

By the time young Margaret and her escort landed in the harbor at Clare island, the sun had set and the entire group wore the greenish pallor of seasickness. Even the O Malley fishermen who had ferried them over were shivering. Sodden and miserable, the group did not resemble visitors of high rank, and they received little welcome from the few men still tending to their boats at water's edge. These were island people, inheld and watchful. They gave directions to Grania's fortress—though directions were scarcely needed, the squat square tower dominated the landscape. Then they went back to their work, only watching out of the corners of their eyes as men wearing O Flaherty colors formed a hollow square around a small figure and walked away with her.

Liam, guarding the tower gate, was startled by the appearance of a band of men carrying swords in their hands and looking very irritable indeed. In a moment his own weapon was drawn and he was shouting for assistance, even before the new arrivals could identify themselves. Pikemen came at the run to stand beside him, and several firearms were waved about.

The captain of the O Flaherty escort was immediately defensive, and hostile as men are inclined to be in strange territory at nightfall. "We bring Mairgret Ni Flaithbheartach to her mother's protection," he said in broad Gaelic, "but we expected a welcome, not a band of robbers setting upon us with weapons."

"And who's to say you're not the robbers?" Liam challenged him. "How do I know you're who you say? We expected the girl you name long before this. You may have kidnapped her for all I know, and be trying to gain access here through a trick."

The girl, who was all but invisible within a soaked velvet mantle too thin for the bitter Atlantic weather, thrust through her guardsmen with a wail of mingled anger and outrage. Fumbling at her throat, she managed to break a gold chain that hung there and thrust the bauble toward Liam. "Take this to your mistress and ask her if she recognizes it," the girl said in a high, furious voice. "She once sent it to me, but I return it to her now with no thanks for her poor welcome!"

That flare of spirit identified Margaret as Grania's daughter more clearly than her jewelry could. Liam quickly turned and hurried inside with the gold chain and the pendant that adorned it. He found Grania and Evleen together in the upper chamber, where they were moving chests across the floor and had heard nothing of the commotion outside. When Liam held out the chain and pendant, Grania gasped.

"She's here, Evleen! Margaret's here!" Dropping the jewel in her excitement, she pushed past Liam and ran down the stairs.

Evleen bent to pick up the forgotten treasure. The pendant was an exquisite Spanish piece of gold worked in the shape of a dolphin, ridden by a tiny human figure and studded with rubies and emeralds. It was typical of the gifts Grania had sent her children always, gifts increasing in value as her own prosperity increased. It was also typical of Grania that the valuable piece meant so little to her personally that she dropped and forgot it in her excitement.

At the portal, Grania stopped short. She saw two bands of men, her own guard and a group of strangers, facing one another with snarls on their faces and battle at their fingertips. The captain of the escort, seeing Grania, shouted, "This is an outrage! We're being kept in the rain as a deliberate insult, O Malley to O Flaherty!"

He did not really believe this, but he was exhausted and cold, and a wound was festering on his hand where the girl had bitten him during the journey, when he attempted to fondle her in a private place.

"Don't yell at Gráinne Ni Mháille," Liam warned him, hurrying to stand at Grania's shoulder.

"I'm an O Flaherty and I can yell at anyone!" the captain retorted hotly. "Stand aside and let us in, or I'll skewer you like Sunday's roast pig."

"And who will help you?" Liam inquired. "Do you mean to attack us with that collection of drowned chickens I see huddled around you?" This was Grania's daughter and her escort, all right, and tradition dictated hospitality, but anger had flared first and could not be easily overridden.

Some of the drowned chickens snarled and stepped forward as if to offer serious battle. "Stop this at once!" Grania commanded, flinging open the iron gate herself and hurrying to her daughter. Her relief at seeing the girl arrive safely was so great it briefly expressed itself in anger, an anger easily summoned by the hot tempers around it. "What kept you so long, girl?" she demanded to know. "Why did you worry me so? Didn't you think I had better things to do than pace the cliffs and watch for you?"

Margaret drew back from her mother. Her face was very white, but her eyes were aflame. In a peevish voice, she said, "You didn't have to watch for me at all. I don't even want to be here, and now that I've seen you and this place I'm going to leave."

"Oh no you aren't!" the captain of her escort said quickly. "I would as soon deliver you personally to the gates of hell as take you all the way back to Iar Connaught." Controlling himself with an effort, he turned to Liam as one man to another and said, "This is not the least difficult female in Ireland. In Mary's name, take her in and get her off my hands."

Grania tried to put her arms around the girl, unwilling to believe the situation could have gone so sour so quickly. But Margaret drew her wet mantle around herself like a cocoon and tilted her head back so she could look along her nose at the taller woman. "*Are* you my mother?" she asked. "You look more like a servant to me. If that's all you are, then pick up my things and carry them for me, and speak to me no more. I'm not in the habit of talking to servants."

Grania stared at the girl. "Pick them up yourself!"

They faced each other, the air tingling between them. Feeling the heat of their confrontation, the men stepped back.

"I hate you," Margaret said with no hesitation. "And I hate islands and open water and strangers." She said the words defiantly, daring Grania to challenge any of them.

"Do you? That's unfortunate," her mother remarked. "Now pick up that parcel of yours—I suppose that is it, over there?—and carry it inside. These men have brought you a long way, and I'm sure they are much too tired to haul your baggage any farther."

She turned on her heel and showed Margaret her broad back. Without even glancing around, Grania led the way into her tower, allowing the others to follow her or not.

The girl stood in the dark and the rain and bit her lip. Her whole body quivered with fury. So commanding was Grania's demeanor that even those who had escorted Margaret dared not disobey and pick up the heavy woolen bag carrying her clothing, so at last she struggled forward herself, dragging it after her.

When the party had entered the hall and the cold water from their clothes was dripping onto the flagstone floor, Grania gestured to Liam. "When they have recovered themselves, take these men down to the bruighen and see that they receive the best hospitality the island has to offer. Send them home tomorrow with full bellies and purses, will you see to it?"

"And with me!" Margaret cried, overhearing.

"No," her mother said. "Not with you."

"You can't keep me here as a prisoner!"

"I can't send you back to Iar Connaught, either. Don't you understand? Your period of fosterage is over—you are of marrying age now and it is time to begin your life." She tried, tardily, to soften her voice and let Margaret hear the sounds of a mother's love, but all Margaret heard was refusal.

"You're trying to tell me they don't want me, the very people who raised me. And you don't really want me either. That's obvious from the way I've been treated from the moment I set foot on this hateful island. And I don't care, do you hear me? *I don't care!* I don't need you, I don't need any of you!"

The child was on the verge of hysterics. Her fists were clenched, her voice spiraling upward into a shriek. Grania had never had to deal with such an outburst on the part of one of her own offspring, and she was genuinely baffled. She had meant to give Margaret so much love, to make up for so much with her . . . her own disappointment was scarcely less than the girl's.

Grania knew the bone-deep pain of feeling rejected by one's own parents. Now she saw Margaret turning into a thorn hedge before her eyes, all angry prickles and wild defiances. You could not put your arms around a thorn hedge. You could not explain anything to a girl too tired and hostile to listen.

Perhaps it will be better in the morning, Grania thought. When we're all rested, when there's been time to forget. "You at least need someone to show you to your chamber for the night," she said aloud. "Evleen will do that; she has the candles."

Grania found herself unwilling even to look at her daughter anymore that evening; the pain was too keen. And the girl's beauty, revealed in the torch- and firelight of the hall, only made the pain worse, for Margaret was everything Grania might once have wished to be herself. She was lovely, smaller than her mother and finer-boned, with clear-cut O Flaherty features and a round, charming chin. Her brown hair clung to her temples and neck in ringlets. She was a child to love, but she did not promise to be very lovable.

In the morning she was still sullen. Her escort had departed early, making it obvious she could not leave the island, but she was not making the best of the situation. She complained from the moment she arose. "This building is too small and there are too few rooms," she said. "My chamber is dark. And where are my personal servants?"

"On Cliara we take care of ourselves as much as we can," Grania told her. "Evleen is adequate for me and will help you, too."

Margaret replied with a snort of derision. "Is that the best you can do? The great Gráinne Ni Mháille?"

In less than a day even Evleen was complaining. "That girl is spoiled milk."

Grania sighed. "At least we could throw out spoiled milk."

At dinner, Margaret pointed an indignant finger at the food served her. "What is this?"

"Mussel broth," Grania replied. "Roasted eggs, dulsc, white pudding, eels, Spanish oranges . . . what are you referring to?"

"This." The disdainful finger stabbed downward.

"Ah, that's sea trout pickled last summer. We . . ."

"Fish." Margaret heaped the word with scorn. "I hate fish. At home they always gave me venison or pork. And I got the marrow bones. Where are your marrow bones?"

Grania gripped the table edge. "You are home," she said firmly. "And this is an island. We eat the produce of the island and of the sea, primarily. Marrow bones are a rare treat out here. We have sheep, but there is not the sort of grass for cattle."

"Bring cattle in your boats then," Margaret told her.

"My boats have other things to carry."

"Why do you live on an island, anyway? This is right out on the ocean, and it's terribly damp, isn't it? And stormy. I simply hate storms."

Grania looked her daughter in the eye. "I love storms," she said.

She left the tower house before dawn the next morning and stayed busy at the harbor until well after dark. She knew she was running away from a problem she would have to face sooner or later, but this was another indulgence she would allow herself, just for a day or so.

She only mentioned Margaret briefly, and that to Tigernan. "It will be nice to have a member of my family here on Clare with me," she said. "As soon as Margaret gets used to the place."

Then she found Ruari Oge and settled down to discuss the problems of fortification and defense.

"There's only so much we can do here," he told her. "Your stronghold is hidden from the eyes of ships passing in the ocean, but Clare is located so far out in the mouth of the bay that almost any ship that wants to could find a way to make landfall here. There are places all around the island where an invasion party could come ashore, and though sentries can warn of them, unless the whole fleet is in at one time we hardly have enough men to defend against an attack from several sides at once. If I wanted to attack you here, that's how I'd do it—from several sides at once."

"Do you think we will be attacked eventually?"

"Anyone who has anything worth keeping is attacked eventually."

Grania returned to the tower house deep in thought, aware of every islander and every cottage, of every man, woman, and child dependent upon her for protection.

"Your daughter's asleep," Evleen told her at once.

"Did she eat anything today?"

"I finally persuaded her to take some lobster and a little port with honey stirred into it. She likes sweets. She's very affronted that we have no cream; she couldn't seem to understand butter is easily brought from the mainland but cream is not."

Grania threw off her cloak and dropped onto a bench to pull her winter boots from her feet. "I realize now my mother and father could no more deal with me than I can with my child. It is surely a punishment on me, and one I justly deserve."

"Margaret grew bored by midday and talked to me, a bit," Evleen said. "She told grand stories of the splendor she was accustomed to, exaggerated stories, I'm certain, for I know as well as you that petty chieftains do not live like Norman lords. But there's no doubt she was raised with much petting and praise because she was the daughter of the Flaherty tanist. Her foster parents went without things themselves so they could give her the very best—until the English robbed Donal Crone and your husband of their status. Then your daughter appeared in a new light. Her foster parents had favored her over their own children and now began trying to balance the scales, which meant neglecting her to make a fuss over those she had long considered her inferiors. Margaret thought she was being robbed of something that was hers by rights. Then she was shipped here like a bale of flax, and she is striking out in blind fury."

"All of life is a matter of adjusting to the unexpected," Grania remarked. "If that's all that ails her, I would change places with Margaret in a blink. She doesn't know what trouble really is."

"If you had never seen Croagh Patrick," Evleen said, "you might mistake a midden heap for a mountain." As she talked, she was assembling packets of dried herbs to add to her formidable collection of medicinals, sage and hyssop and clear-eye, betony and dill and borage and boneset. For whatever indisposition one might name, Evleen could offer a remedy, and Grania reached past her to pick up one brown, brittle leaf and sniff it.

"Can you brew a tea that will give my daughter a sunny disposition?"

"She will not be so easily gentled. She has been building up an anger for a long time, and it will take a long time to go down. Until it does, you are its natural target, I'm afraid—that's what mothers are for."

"Wonderful news," Grania said. "Just wonderful. I tell you this, Evleen—I am growing angry myself. I wanted a child to love, but I too am being robbed."

"No one can force parent and child to love each other," Evleen commented. "More often than anyone wants to admit, they do not."

"Yet blood is the strongest bond."

"Is it? Ruari Oge and I are not related," Evleen said simply, "but even death can never cut the bond between us. And fosterage works because the child and the foster parents often grow at least as close as blood kin. Relatives are accidents that happen to us, Grania; some good and some bad. If you had not given birth to Margaret, I think you would have already shown her the backside of your hand and the outside of your door."

"I would indeed," Grania agreed ruefully. "But I feel guilty for not loving her as I expected."

"Guilty!" Evleen gave a contemptuous snort. "The Christ-men peddle guilt like fish at the wharf, and only priests profit from it. If you want the opinion of an old country woman, the only part of any person we are obliged to love is the immortal spirit in them that we all share. The rest is merely meat.

"I tell you this: if you are as patient with Margaret as with a new-met and unrelated stranger, in time you may find something in her you like. Or you may not." She shrugged and smiled.

"Ruari Oge is right," Grania said. "You are too wise. I thought you had no children, yet you understand so much. . . ."

Evleen's hands described a circle. "The stars and the stones are my children," she said. "And every leaf in Ireland."

Trying to follow her advice, Grania gritted her teeth and endured endless weeks of Margaret's unceasing complaints. If anything, they grew worse as she found new things about Clare to dislike. At last her mother confided to Tigernan, "I've never seen anyone so determined to wring the last drop of misery out of existence. She positively revels in it. The more I give the more she demands and the less she is pleased, and when I can hold my temper no longer she makes me feel guilty. There has to be a likable person inside her somewhere, but I can't find it, and if we continue to share the same space much longer I'm going to hit her on the head with a blackthorn stick. My own daughter."

"You could send her to live somewhere else."

"Discard her? I'm not that cruel. She *has* been hurt, I understand that, but how can I make it up to her when she . . ."

"She's marrying age, and the lord of Curraun is looking for a wife."

Grania raised her eyebrows. "Curraun . . . are you speaking of the Devil's Hook?"

"The same," Tigernan replied. "Ruari Oge mentioned he thought it would be an advantageous alliance. Or there is another male Burke currently wifeless and of even higher rank, Iron Richard of Carrigahowley."

"I know Iron Richard and his stronghold too," Grania said. "It's on a private harbor in a wonderfully defensible location. . . . If I could count on the support of both Burkes I would control the entire shoreline of Clew bay." She nodded, suddenly decisive. "Tigernan, take a boat to Curraun tomorrow. Request a meeting in my name with the Devil's Hook. Remind him of the number of ships I command and tell him how pretty Margaret is. . . . You can do that in all honesty, can't you?"

"I can. She is pretty."

"She's beautiful as long as she doesn't open her mouth."

"But what's that you're saying about Iron Richard?" Tigernan wondered. "You can't marry your daughter to both men. What if neither of them suits her?"

"I think she'll be delighted by any man who will take her off this island and install her in a household with plenty of servants, which I suspect the Devil's Hook possesses. He claims high rents from tenants all around Curraun and onto Achill, and I heard somewhere he lives like a Norman lord."

"Will Margaret make a good wife for such a man?"

"Who can say? I wouldn't put her to minding mice, myself, but we'll leave it to him to decide after you tell him how lovely she is and emphasize how much wealth I have in my storehouses. If he's like the rest of his breed he'll go for the coin, and to avoid risking the loss of it he'll treat the girl better than I'm inclined to treat her."

Tigernan was aware of a string hanging loose in the conversation. "What about Iron Richard and Carrigahowley?"

Grania smiled. "Carrigahowley. Rock of the Fleet, so named in the old days because it was an ideal site for . . .

"I think I'll see to that myself, Tigernan."

16

When Grania and her followers sailed north to attend the wedding of Margaret to the young Burke warlord known as the Devil's Hook, Richard Bingham boldly ordered his ship into Clew bay and anchored in the shallows west of Belclare. From there he went to pay a call on the local Roman cleric, the abbot known as Calvagh.

Bingham, a devout Protestant, considered this yet another onerous duty forced upon him by an unkind fate. Bad enough to be in Ireland; worse yet to serve as go-between for some informing Papist. But there were authorities waiting in Dublin castle for the latest word from the west, and Calvagh's reports must be delivered.

Bingham found the abbot of Murrisk in a dark mood. The passage of time was making Calvagh's lupine resemblance more apparent, his face leaner and his muzzle more protruding. Bingham was disconcerted to discover the abbot liked to clutch and stroke the arm of anyone within his range.

"Gráinne Ni Mháille is accursed of God," Calvagh assured his visitor. "Men on a holy pilgrimage have died at her hand, and she no longer attends Mass at all, at least not to my knowledge."

Nor would I go to church, if I had to do it in your presence, thought Bingham to himself, successfully maneuvering so that a table separated them. He did not think the abbot would be so foolish as to attempt an insult on his person, but he had seen men of this kind before, and preferred to avoid them.

"I was not asked to officiate at the marriage of her daughter to Burke of Curraun," Calvagh was complaining, "though Murrisk has provided spiritual guidance to the O Malley clan for centuries. Grania ignored me in favor of giving the honor to some northern priest, and it is a deliberate insult, one I will not quickly forget. It shows how she overthrows the traditions. I suspect such a person will soon be plotting with her new Burke kin against the English throughout Ireland," he added spitefully.

"Have you proof of that?" Bingham asked.

Calvagh hugged his elbows in their scarlet silk robe. "It's a safe assumption. I know that woman. Her sire is the last great Gaelic chieftain alive who has never formally submitted to the Crown authority. His daughter is spreading her wings and exulting in her unfeminine powers; she turns her back on God, and anything can be expected of her. For all I know she might even make an alliance against your people with the northern O Neill clan; I understand they are ever rebellious in spite of the fact that Shane O Neill, the chieftain of Tyrone, has been an honored guest in Elizabeth Tudor's court."

Bingham scowled; he disliked being reminded of Elizabeth's interest in colorful but unworthy individuals. A savage like The O Neill being entertained at court, while a hardworking man like Richard Bingham sailed leaky old tubs in hostile waters with never a nod from the queen or her henchmen!

Richard Bingham ground his teeth together and drummed his fingers on the abbot's table. But then an idea occurred to him. The O Malley woman was a minor figure at best in Ireland's parade of dangerous chieftains, as he, Bingham, was still a minor figure on the stage of power. But perhaps she could be made to work in his behalf. If he played up the danger of an alliance between her and other warlords—and made himself the definitive expert on her affairs, her ships and armed strength—he would surely become a figure of importance in his own right, mentioned in the dispatches from Dublin castle to the queen and her secretary, Cecil.

"If Grace O Malley is such a threat," he said aloud, "I must commend you for calling our attention to her. Now help me further. I've never met the woman, and I believe in taking the measure of one's enemies. Can you arrange for me to see her without alerting her to the fact that I am an agent of the lord deputy?"

"Of course," Calvagh agreed. "As soon as this wedding of her daughter's is concluded, we can expect at least *one* of the traditions of the region will be followed. The wedding party, in flower-bedecked galleys, will circle Clew bay so the adherents of both families can see them and wish them well. They will put in at many harborages, including this one, to receive gifts. You can disguise yourself easily enough as one of my friars and go down to the shore with the others; thus you can observe Grania yourself as much as you like, and she will have no idea who or what you are."

✠

Margaret's first impression upon meeting her future husband had not seemed favorable—"I hate him," she had said. But by that time Grania had learned this was Margaret's immediate and purely defensive reaction to everything. She had warned Burke of it in private, and he had laughed. "How refreshing!"

The Devil's Hook, a name that referred as much to his land of Curraun as to the man himself, was a stocky fellow with merry blue eyes and a cleft chin. He did not much resemble the other Richard Burke, Iron Richard, for which Grania was thankful. A dour husband would only have ruined her child's disposition further. But the Devil's Hook was gay and charming and soon had Margaret captivated.

He seemed as pleased with her. Instead of whining and affectation, he saw aristocracy and elegance in her mannerisms and decided she would provide a polished jewel for the rough setting of Curraun. Once the terms of the marriage were agreed upon, and Margaret knew she would not spend a continued indefinite time in a bleak fortress on Clare island, her whole attitude improved.

"I'll almost be sorry to see her go," Grania confided to Evleen.

"Wind blows and snow melts," the other woman said, "and nothing ever changes."

The wedding party was brilliant, the voyage of celebration spectacular. When the galleys put in near Belclare a huge crowd came out to welcome them, including even the most retiring monks from the nearby abbey. Also attending were both Owen and Murrough O Flaherty, who had come up from Connaught to honor their sister. For the first time since their infancy, Grania saw her three children together.

Margaret was not much impressed with her brothers. "Their gifts are rather shabby, don't you agree?" she remarked to her mother. "Even you were more generous to me than that."

"I'm in a better position to be generous," Grania said. I will like this child; I will, I will, she said stubbornly to herself. It's my daughter's marriage feast; I will love her and be happy for her.

Row upon row of trestle tables had been set up, both within the hall of Belclare and spilling out onto the lawns. Bright banners waved from poles, and musicians from throughout O Malley country vied with one another to provide festive music. Many a cask of

Iberian wine was rolled out onto the grass and broken open, drawing an eager crowd of friends, relatives, clerics, and bees.

In the midst of this gaiety, Margaret looked down her pretty
nose at the family she was marrying out of and found them lacking.
Her elder brother, Owen, did not cut a dashing figure, as did her
new husband. Owen was quiet, almost secretive, and too quick to
let others interrupt him. And Murrough had a tendency to start
quarrels, threatening to spoil the mood of the occasion.

Grania saw her children differently, now that she had them
together for comparison. They were all comely; she was proud of
that. And they were all strangers. Margaret was a married woman
already and launched on a new life, while Owen and Murrough
were two men she wanted to love but did not know.

I was robbed of my children, Grania thought. Her eyes were
briefly sad, though all around her people were laughing and raising
their cups in a toast to the newlywed couple.

And of my father, she added, catching sight of Dubhdara chatting happily with the young man known as Donal of the Pipes. All
the clan was in attendance . . . but the bonds between them were
thinner than an outside observer might guess.

There was an outside observer. Richard Bingham, sweltering in
a hooded monk's robe, mingled with the other guests and avoided
revealing himself with his English accent by making the sign of the
deaf-mute across his lips whenever someone spoke to him.

He was particularly interested in The O Malley and his notorious daughter, and kept edging his way through the crowd to be
closer to them. Obviously, Dubhdara O Malley was an aging man
who might not offer any resistance to English control of the region
for much longer. But his daughter was a strapping big woman with
undeniable force of character. . . .

His eyes on Grania, Bingham unintentionally collided with a
young Gaelic princeling and almost knocked the man off his
feet.

In an instant Murrough O Flaherty had both fists doubled and
was threatening to strike the friar in retaliation.

Concealed inside his monk's robe Richard Bingham carried a
knife. Forgetting his disguise, he grabbed for the weapon and
lunged at his Irish attacker. He was not about to stand still and let
himself be mauled by a foreign savage!

Grania was a half-dozen paces from the scene and took it all in in one startled glance. Murrough, hot-tempered as ever, about to fight with a friar, a man of God. And Owen standing nearby but hesitating to interfere on either side, as if he needed some silent permission before he could step forward and act. Margaret's angry shriek rang out over the assemblage: "Don't you dare ruin my celebration, Murrough O Flaherty!" As if a fight would ruin any Irish festival, for none was complete without one.

Yet Grania saw this was more than a merry quarrel, this was her son attacking a cleric, an unforgivable act in Catholic Ireland. Grania threw herself forward to intervene before Murrough went too far, and in so doing she found herself at exactly the right angle to see what no one else saw. A knife had appeared in the monk's hand, partially concealed by the folds of his sleeve but aimed at Murrough's heart.

In Margaret's honor Grania had dressed as a noblewoman, forsaking her comfortable trews. There was no place for a pistol in the girdle that bound her blue linen dress over a long silk shift. With her sleeves trimmed in gold lace and her braided hair intertwined with bright ribbons, she looked like any other gentlewoman, weaponless and defenseless.

But Grania always had weapons. Her agile mind and swift reflexes would serve her when no other came to hand. Without hesitation she lifted her skirt in both hands and aimed a powerful kick at the monk's groin.

The embossed toe of her stiff leather shoe thudded home, and the man doubled up with an agonized grunt. The knife flew out of his hand; she marked its path. Then, even in his pain, he looked up long enough to meet the eyes of his assailant—and Grania saw an implacable hatred in his face.

It was not an Irish face, but the eyes were unforgettable.

Realizing the danger of his position if his imposture was discovered, Bingham somehow fought back the pain long enough to turn away and stumble toward the nearest cluster of monks, submerging himself in their anonymity before anyone raised a hand to stop him.

Meanwhile, Grania bent and picked up the knife. It was no modest dirk for cutting meat, but a killer's weapon. An Augustinian friar had no business carrying such a piece. She raked the crowd with her eyes, searching for the man who had dropped it, but he had already successfully melted into the press of people. He must be in great pain, she thought. Yet he is brave enough, or frightened enough, to conceal that pain and walk and look like any other man in order to escape my notice.

There is more in these waters than fish. Something is going on here, she warned herself, something I was unaware of in my pre-occupation with my children and my ships and the marriage. If there is a foreign monk at Murrisk carrying a concealed wea-pon . . . or a foreigner pretending to be a monk, to get close to me or my sons . . .

She slipped the knife into concealment in her own clothing. For some reason it had been hidden, and it was better that it remain so. No one seemed aware that more had happened than a quick flaring of tempers. Turning to Murrough, Grania said, "You fool, what possessed you to strike a holy man?"

Murrough scowled. "He almost knocked me down without apol-ogy. I couldn't let him get away with that, could I? I'm tired of being pushed and shoved in too many ways by too many people. In Iar Connaught the English first bring political pressure and then armed forces and bribery and every sort of weapon to use against us; they treat us as if we are dung to be wiped from their boots. I thought if I came to my mother's kingdom at least I would be treated with a little respect, but even an Irish monk now thinks he can run over Murrough O Flaherty!"

The young man's face was bright red, the blue eyes burning from it in long-simmered rage. Angry mutterings sprang up around him, for many of his party had grievances and were only waiting for the right moment to voice them. Owen stepped forward, will-ing to add his own thoughts at last by saying, "Donal Crone's partisans are trying to get us to stand with them, and Murrough of the Battle Axes insists he is the true O Flaherty and wants our pledge of loyalty. We are being harassed from every side; what are we to do?"

Margaret pushed into the midst of the group with doubled fists planted on angry hips. She wore a scowl of her own, though her clothing was festive: a bright yellow gown fitted to her slender waist with whalebone, its bodice laced in front and the ends of a silk scarf slotted through the laces. Her elbow-length sleeves ended in cuffs embroidered with green ribbon, and she wore a petticoat of scarlet frieze, also embroidered with green. She was vivid and pretty and furious at any incident that marred her triumphal day.

She screamed at each member of her family in turn, berating them impartially.

Her tantrum proved a distraction, relaxing the general tension so that even Murrough calmed down a little, enjoying with the other men the spectacle of an Irishwoman in full sail. The party resumed; few there realized anything untoward had happened.

But Grania knew. When the Devil's Hook at last carried his new wife off to Curraun and the party died in a litter of gnawed bones and empty bottles and fading flowers, Grania still carried the incident in the forefront of her mind. When she returned to Cliara she told Evleen, "There is something very wrong at the abbey. I don't know what it is, but a friar was hiding a knife beneath his clothing and was very ready to kill my son with it."

She produced the weapon, and the two women bent over it in the candlelight. "This is English steel," Grania said softly.

Evleen looked up and met her eyes.

"England again," Grania said. "The she-king is using both chieftains and clerics in her game, it seems. I play chess myself, and I know enough to get my own pieces grouped into a more defensive position."

If she was newly wary, Richard Bingham had never been more angry. His bitterness and frustration had always been directed, in a general way, toward Ireland and the Irish. But in that moment when Grania kicked him in the genitals, a lifetime of random anger narrowed into an intense, obsessive focus. She would pay. She would suffer if it took years to achieve it. If it took a lifetime.

As men fall in love, so did Richard Bingham fall in hate with Gráinne Ni Mháille.

✠

Tigernan received a shock when a few weeks later Grania returned from paying a call upon the Burkes at Carrigahowley to announce she was considering a marriage to Iron Richard. She said it as casually as she would announce the new price of barrel staves, astonishing Ruari Oge and rendering Tigernan all but speechless.

"Iron Richard," he muttered, shaking his head as they stood together on the quay on Clare island.

"You disapprove of my choice?" she asked him as she threw back the hood of her crimson cloak. "I am not answerable to any man living for what I do, Tigernan; I thought you of all people understood that."

"There are rumors he gained his inheritance by murder, and it is said outright that he and his mother between them drove his first wife into her grave."

Grania shrugged. "I'm not so easily hounded to death. Besides, no matter how he came to his inheritance he stands in line to be The MacWilliam Iochtar, and that's a powerful position. The MacWilliam Uachtar of Galway has already submitted to the new lord deputy of the Tudors, but if we hold the MacWilliamship up here we can deny the English any part of Clew bay."

"You don't have to marry Richard an Iarainn to secure his loyalty!"

Grania threw her head back and clapped her hands. "Tigernan, you great fool, I'm not marrying the man for his loyalty. I'm marrying him for Carrigahowley!"

Then she laughed all the harder at the expressions on the faces of her two captains.

Ruari Oge recovered first. "Rock of the Fleet is a splendid stronghold; women have married for a lot less. If you're serious."

Grania was still chuckling. "As serious as I ever am. The longer I live, the more trouble I see, the less inclined I am to take anything too seriously. As Evleen says, it's all temporary anyway. So you might as well laugh at the bad times and at least have that much pleasure out of them. But I mean it about marrying Iron Richard to get Carrigahowley. Rockfleet is a most defensible enclosed harbor where I may beach small boats at the very walls of the fortress and no man will be able to take me by surprise.

"I even told Richard that was the only reason I would marry him —to have that fortress," she added, her eyes twinkling mischievously.

"You did?" Ruari Oge asked, unable to restrain a guffaw. "And did he believe you?"

"Of course not. I learned with Donal an Chogaidh that people only hear what they choose to believe. Richard Burke thought I was jesting."

She appeared as radiantly self-satisfied as a woman who has been with her lover. Tigernan could not bear it and turned away, pretending to fix his attention on a beached curragh nearby that needed no attention at all.

But Grania was not thinking of a lover. The dreams Tigernan thought he glimpsed in her eyes were of a different sort of beauty, one she found more enduring.

Dark upon dark stones, the fortress of Rockfleet stood sharp and clear in her memory.

Four stories high the square stone tower rose, innocent of windows but well equipped with arrow slits and two rectangular corner turrets rising above the parapet on opposite sides. Seen against a background of blue water and wooded hills, Rockfleet stood at the head of a small bay, and its lawn at low tide was a kelp bed draped upon a shelf of stone. The portal, which faced inland, had no tiny courtyard to hold a guard such as the one at Grania's residence on Clare island, but it did boast a massive oaken door topped by a finely chiseled Gothic archway.

By comparison to the Clare island tower, Rockfleet was both taller and more graceful, its dark grimness mitigated by a certain elegance of proportion, a simplicity of line. A pleasant freshwater stream meandered past the portal on its way to the sheltered and private bay, which in turn opened onto vast Clew. Enough small crabs, fish, and edible seaweed could be gathered within an arm's reach of the fortress to make a meal for the men-at-arms camped within on the ground floor. In the reverse of the arrangement at Clare island, the hall at Rockfleet was on the top floor, with broad, deep window embrasures lighted by the arrow slits, a timbered peaked ceiling, and a huge fireplace. The floors were multicolored flagstones, cheerful against the unplastered walls. Just off the curving stone stair was a tiny round privy room, complete with a tiny window through which one could watch the harbor while seated. The end product of eating fell down a channel inside the walls to an opening at the base, where it was flushed away with every turn of the tide.

Rolling green countryside, less wind-scoured than that of Clare island, gave evidence of good pasturage in the area, and an all but impenetrable forest guarded the landward approaches to the fortress.

Not everyone would think Rockfleet beautiful, but Grania found it so.

Rockfleet was . . . safe. A safe place from which to spread a defensive circle, where no Englishman could sneak up and take her by surprise.

If I am safe I can keep those who depend upon me safe, Grania thought. And there are so many who depend on me.

She had resented that; she had not sought it. Yet leadership had come to her unbidden, and when she had stood on the sloping hillside below Belclare for Margaret's marriage celebration and watched her children in the Irish spring sunshine, she had thought of *their* children . . . the young ones yet unborn, who could never be taken from her. And something began building in her, the idea of a net of security that could reach far out, across generations, giving infants that would not be born for decades a sure foothold here in Clew bay.

That much she could give them. To that extent she could provide as a parent should.

These ideas, half formed, amorphous, had somehow blended with the image of that Catholic monk hiding his English knife, and from the two a plan had grown of necessity.

✠

Richard Burke made no pretense of hiding his surprise at seeing her at Rockfleet. "If an O Malley deputation was coming to me, I would have expected Dubhdara to lead it," he said.

"The Black Oak rarely leaves Belclare any more," Grania told him. "The infirmities of age . . ."

"Yes," said Iron Richard, who had seen enough of the infirmities of age in these last years with his mother.

"I was sorry to hear of the death of your mother. I bring condolences," Grania began formally after they were seated in the handsome hall on the top floor of the tower. Richard signaled his servants to bring wine, and his rechtaire ordered a new log for the fire. They still have timber to burn here, Grania thought to herself. She missed the pungent smell of peat.

"That's a grand fire," she commented aloud. "Trees have never grown on Clare Island. We've always burned turf."

"Every Irishman will come to it eventually," Iron Richard predicted.

"I hardly imagine you with a spade, working in some drained bog to open a turf bank and struggling to keep a straight face."

"A straight face?"

"A turf cutter's term. The cutting bank must be vertical and clean or it makes the work harder for everyone."

Iron Richard's light gray eyes studied her. "A chieftain's daughter lectures me on turf cutting? Where did you acquire such a skill?"

"I know how to do a lot of things," Grania told him. "I've made it my business to learn. I don't necessarily live the life of a chieftain's daughter, but I assure you I'm very good at taking care of myself and surviving."

"So I've heard," he replied. His voice was deep and rich. Huw had made her sensitive to the timbre of a man's voice.

They drank their wine, a harper played music in the corner, a long-limbed shaggy wolfhound came up the winding stone stairway with a great scrabbling of claws and settled itself before the fire. Grania noticed how in the hall of Rockfleet one could not hear the sea.

They spoke of the events of the season, making the polite conversation of people who were observing the forms but had little to say to each other. "It's been a year for deaths and marriages," Grania remarked. "You know my daughter was recently wed to your western neighbor and kinsman, and I hear from Iar Connaught that one of my sons plans to marry a Galway woman."

"And what of you?" he asked her.

"I have neither died nor married," she told him with a laugh.

"Do you plan to do either?"

She stopped laughing and gave him a long look. There was admiration on his face, and the way he watched her was disturbing. The last time they met his scrutiny had made her uncomfortable, but since then Grania had known Huw. Appetites had been awakened unexpectedly, and skills discovered. She found herself smiling at Iron Richard in a totally new way and enjoying the response she got.

Her condolence call lasted three days, three days she spent in Richard Burke's company, covertly measuring both the man and his fortress with a speculative eye. Her guards slept with his on the ground floor of Rockfleet, and Grania herself slept alone in a tiny walled guest chamber above, but she was aware of Richard sleeping in the same house. A strong man, sleeping naked in a bed. . . .

How people change, she thought to herself with amusement. This is definitely not the same Grania whom Donal an Chogaidh knew.

When Richard Burke reminded her he was a widower and mentioned an interest in marrying again, Grania was not coy. They were standing at the foot of his tower, where he had come to bid his guest goodbye as she stepped into her curragh. Her oarsmen were ready, the interlude was surely over. But Grania looked past him at the secluded and seemingly impregnable strength of Rockfleet and said boldly, "If I were to consider marrying again you would not be my last choice, Richard Burke. I have a mighty desire to claim your castle among my holdings."

He was taken aback for a moment—then he decided she was joking. Richard Burke had little sense of humor, but he thought he would enjoy a light touch in a woman. Hid dead wife had always been a weeper, and his dead mother had never been one to laugh.

Gráinne Ni Mháille was obviously no weeper.

"Marry me for Rockfleet then," he told her heartily, "and I'll marry you for Clare island. We'll be great landholders together, you and I. There are countless castles in Burke hands throughout Connaught, but nothing to equal the possession of Clew bay."

If he had known Grania, he would have recognized the danger in that momentary flicker he glimpsed in her eyes. But he misinterpreted the expression; he thought he saw the usual female cunning of a woman who just wants to get a husband for herself.

"Come to me on Cliara," Grania said, "and we will talk more of this. If you like."

The idea did, indeed, please him, and in the following weeks Richard Burke made a number of visits to Clare island, sailing across the great bay in boats loaded with gifts. Each time he made the journey he thought to himself what a clever fellow he was, winning such a rich territory for himself through his own abilities. Finola had not done this for him. He would court and win the she-king and share her kingdom, and he would do it all on his own.

He began to take a great interest in commerce, which had never been of much interest to him before. He was a landman at heart, but when he began to spend more time on the bay he realized that the sea was turbulent with trade. Men spoke among themselves at every anchorage about the boom in shipbuilding since the discovery of the New World, and when Richard went to call upon kinsmen at Ardnaree he heard that the forests of Germany were going to the ax as surely as the forests of Ireland. The Old World was abustle. The Genoese financiers who had their fingers on Spanish pursestrings were investing in every sort of cargo from cognac to cereal grains to cork; all of Europe was buying, selling, trading, stealing . . . prosperity floated on the seas, and much of it sailed past the west coast of Ireland and into the hands of Gráinne Ni Mháille.

His courting grew very serious.

Tigernan was furious.

"I won't watch this," he told Ruari Oge. "I've been her mate and captain in fair sea and foul weather, but I won't stand idly by while she settles down as that man's wife and turns her back on all we've built. Remember how it was when she had that Huw here? We hardly saw her in the harbor.

"I tell you, Ruari, when I went to Curraun to meet with the Devil's Hook, I found a nice little bit of beach no one was using with a fine shelf for beaching a boat and the mountain at its back to turn the north wind. If Grania marries, I'll take me there and build me a cottage and spend my life fishing."

"You don't mean anything you're saying," Ruari Oge told him. "You won't do any such thing. You have yourself convinced Grania can't manage without you."

Tigernan took a deep breath and said, in the voice of a strong man being forced to look to the bottom of his soul, "Perhaps she can't. But I can survive without her, and if I must I will."

Grania had one more surprise for Iron Richard. Marriage would give her desired access to a fine fortress and protected anchorage, but she meant to have marriage without fetters.

"If you want me as wife," she told Richard Burke, "we marry only under the Brehon law. I will not kneel in a Christian chapel and be tied to you forever in God's sight."

Once again, Iron Richard was taken aback by the woman. "You aren't willing to be married by a priest?"

"No. I've done that and I wasn't happy with the outcome." If Richard took her at all, he must take her under the old Gaelic concept of "marriage for one year certain" to see if they suited one another. If not, by Brehon law either party could divorce the other simply by declaring his or her wish to dissolve the marriage at the end of that term.

According to pagan custom—which still lived in uneasy truce with Christianity in many parts of Ireland—there were ten degrees of marriage, all the way from a union between propertied partners of equal rank to union by abduction or the mating of the mad. From any of the ten a child could result, and the brehons therefore had allowed for every child's rights to be recognized by the social order. No human containing an immortal spirit could be illegitimate.

Richard was also thinking of children. "If you conceive and we were not married in the Church, what of our offspring, Grania?"

Grania laughed unself-consciously. "You're marrying a sea-worn woman who has been barren for almost fifteen years. If I were going to conceive again I would have with . . ." She caught herself. "I would have in my later years with Donal O Flaherty. But my womb is empty now, and empty will surely stay. So if you still want me with those stipulations . . . then you're surely mad enough to deserve me!"

He did want her. He wanted the health and strength and gloss of her, the long stride and easy slouch and proud way she held her head, the deep voice yelling orders to her men and the way she stalked into a room as if she owned it.

Iron Richard was a Burke, and the Burkes had their own long history of battles and rebellions. Their relationship with the English was as tangled and fractious as that of the Gaels, and like other men who were drawn to Grania for various reasons he was attracted to her apparent fearlessness in a land where and time when everyone had something to fear.

Besides, she held Clew bay.

"We'll marry as you wish," he agreed. "But at the end of the year you'll agree I have pleased you, and then we will renew our agreement."

"If you have pleased me," Grania said.

The news of the proposed wedding spread throughout Umhall, eliciting various reactions. Calvagh of Bregia was shocked for many reasons, as much by Grania's defiances of the Church as by the unwelcome news of yet another O Malley–Burke alliance. Dublin would not be pleased, and since the woman chose to grant the Church no power over her life he had little way of preventing her from doing as she chose.

Dubhdara, failing and almost blind in his bed at Belclare, was formally invited to a ceremony he could not possibly hope to attend, and could only shake his head in wonder at the news. Whispers of his daughter's entanglement with some common seaman had reached him, and now Iron Richard . . . yet he had never thought of Grania as a creature of allure.

The Black Oak had no sooner been informed of the upcoming

marriage than Grania's half brother Donal arrived at Belclare, having made the short trip from his residence at Cathair na Mart to ask his father anxiously, "What do such actions mean? Grania keeps extending her power—she already sails your ships and commands your men. Will she want Cathair na Mart and my herds next?"

"I've never known what Grania wanted," Dubhdara replied. "But I doubt if she has any sinister designs on you. From the day I first told her of your existence she has been remarkably indifferent to you, and I suspect she will continue to be so. If she were a man I would say she is enjoying the exercise of power, but . . . what can I tell you? She is a female I cannot explain in any way; she defies my understanding."

At Grania's request the wedding was to take place at Rockfleet, with brehons representing both the O Malley and Burke clans in attendance. The Burkes were, indeed, Norman-descended, but had for many generations adopted Gaelic dress and custom and law, married Gaelic women, subscribed to the Brehon order of succession. Thus Finola's long-ago conspiracy to have her stepson, Tall Walter, murdered had not automatically made Richard heir to his father's title of The MacWilliam. The brehons had ordered a new election for the tanistry, and to the surprise of many, a young kinsman named Shane son of Oliverus was chosen instead to be David Burke's successor to the chieftainship. Finola had watched in angry frustration but could do nothing; a second untimely death would have drawn dangerous attention. When her husband finally died and Shane became The MacWilliam, the election to name his tanist had indeed gone to Iron Richard, but Shane was a healthy man and it could be many years before Finola's son claimed the rank a murder had attempted to buy.

So Richard Burke paced like a hungry bear around the perimeter of a lordship, but did not yet have it within his grasp.

Like the Gaels they had almost become, Anglo-Norman lords such as the Burkes, the Butlers, the Fitzgeralds, controlled vast tracts of land by right of chieftainship, and in turn allowed collateral branches of their families to farm these lands. Other, less powerful clans also held tenantry, paying rents and taxes to the elected chieftain or lord in return for military protection. For the defense of the territory his family controlled around Rockfleet and several smaller demesnes in the region, Richard Burke was obligated to maintain a small private army at his own expense, men-at-arms he augmented with the Scots mercenaries who were currently a fashionable adjunct to Irish warfare. Richard had some land, some tenants, some soldiers—but Shane Oliverus claimed the rents from a domain several times larger than O Malley territory.

Throughout Ireland the English were overthrowing the old Gaelic order of succession, attempting to wrest control of the land from Gael and Anglo-Norman alike. As this was accomplished they claimed rents and taxes for the Crown of England instead, but in the domain of The MacWilliam Iochtar there was still a degree of autonomy—held firmly within the hand of Shane Oliverus.

As Owen Dubhdara O Malley had avoided unnecessary confrontation with the English in order to be left in peace, and thus had so far avoided pressure to submit to the Crown, so The MacWilliam Iochtar had managed to give little more than lip service to the English fealty inherited from his Norman ancestors, while retaining the wealth and control of his realm. The queen's administrators had their hands full, for the time being, with the rebellion of the Gaelic chieftains in Ulster and the simultaneously burgeoning rebellion of the Anglo-Norman lords in Munster. The Burkes of Galway, under the leadership of The MacWilliam Uachtar, had already submitted, but Shane Oliverus was playing the increasingly common game of appeasing the English verbally while taking part in various resistances and rebellions on a less visible level.

Iron Richard was obligated to assist his lord militarily in these ventures when called upon, but in the spring of 1566 there was a temporary lull in the ceaseless upheaval rippling across Ireland. It was a good season for a man to marry—particularly if he was marrying a woman of impressive property in her own right. Richard, a Catholic like all the Anglo-Normans, was not happy about Grania's determination to formalize their relationship only outside the Church, but she had made it plain he must accept or lose her altogether.

He had no intention of letting her slip away once he had determined to call her wife. When he set himself on a course, Iron Richard had no ability to turn aside; he would pursue a goal to the end with a stubborn determination that could be frightening. There were younger, prettier women than Grania in Connaught, women who did not flaunt convention and stride through life followed by shocked whispers and wild stories, but Richard Burke had set his mind on this one and nothing would deter him.

He sensed a similar tenacity in her, which added to the excitement. She was strong; it would be undeniable proof of his own strength, his freedom from his mother's shadow, if he could break Gráinne Ni Mháille to saddle and spur.

17

As Grania was taking a husband only under Gaelic law, she waited until the traditional Gaelic season for marrying. On the calends of May she prepared to go to Rockfleet and Richard Burke.

A new life, she thought. One of my several lives. But this one I will arrange to suit myself.

Before leaving Cliara, she went out once more in the spring sun to lie on her belly on the grass east of the tower house, peering over the edge of the cliff at the cove below. White sand and peacock-colored water and . . .

. . . and Huw.

She rolled over on her back and stared up into the sky, where a sea eagle floated high above her in lazy spirals.

Huw.

Flying off in some other direction, for now, as she would sail tomorrow to Richard of Rockfleet. . . .

She turned again and looked out across the broad shimmer of the bay; her bay.

This is freedom, she thought.

Next morning at sunrise she would leave Clare island behind and not look back.

The wedding was to be simple, with neither Christian nor Gaelic festivity. Grania wanted only the brehons and necessary attendants: his bodyguards, her captains, Evleen. But when her party gathered on Cliara's beach to set sail, Tigernan was conspicuously absent.

"Where is he, Ruari Oge?" Grania demanded to know.

The big man ducked his head and would not meet her eyes. "He's left his cottage door ajar and taken all his belongings in his fishing curragh."

"But I meant for him to captain my galley! Surely he knew that."

Ruari Oge scuffed the sand with his toe and watched the pattern intently. "He did. But he's gone off to a little piece of beach the Devil's Hook gave him on Curraun, and he said he wouldn't be back."

Grania felt as if she had just seen the sun set in the east. "You're not telling me this," she said flatly.

"I am telling you."

"But why? He's always been such a fool . . . yet I never thought he would desert me . . . anyone but Tigernan . . ."

"He did not desert you," Ruari Oge said in a low voice. "He just did not want to serve Richard Burke's wife. Are you going to send someone to bring him back?"

Two red spots flared in her cheeks. "I am not. Do you think I would hold him or anyone else by force? Let him go if he's no longer happy; I have boats full of O Malleys and O Flaherties and Conroys and MacAnallys, loyal followers who are better than a shipful of gold. What would I want with one more broken-jawed fisherman from Inishbofin?"

She was very angry and very hurt, so she laughed. "That fool. He probably won't catch enough fish to fill his belly, and he'll come back to me soon enough when the life gets too quiet for him. You'll be my captain instead, Ruari Oge, and I think I am better served."

Her eyes flashed and her voice was harsh. She stepped boldly into her flagship, saying nothing more about Tigernan. But as her fleet angled northeast across the bay, she cut her eyes toward the distant peak of Curraun and the expression on her face was such that no one dared speak to her.

In honor of the occasion, Richard Burke had decked Rockfleet for festival. Garlands and swags of greenery softened the stone walls, and baskets of spring flowers depended from the parapet. A crowd of brightly dressed retainers poured from the wattle-and-thatch cottages clustered near the fortress, pushing and shoving one another in their eagerness to get a look at Rockfleet's new mistress. When Grania arrived, the air was already filled with the sound of singing and the smell of roasted meat.

Rockfleet's small harbor was too shallow for deep-drafted vessels, but Irish galleys could be pulled onto the rocky beach.

Iron Richard was standing at water's edge, waiting for her. But she was not ready to look at him. Instead she stared down into the clear water, measuring her approach to shore by the changing seaweeds: long fronds like horses' tails in deep water giving way to growths resembling sheets of tanned leather, then to branching plants like deers' antlers and feathery green plumes that waved in an aqueous wind. The boat grated on stone, and she looked up to see Iron Richard holding out his hand to her.

She did not take it. She lifted her skirts with her two hands and jumped out unaided, splashing through the shallows and onto the shelf of beach at the very foot of the castle.

"I bid you welcome to Rockfleet," Richard Burke said, drawing back his hand and hoping no one noticed. "Your new home."

"One of my homes," she replied. "We are too exposed on Clare island. There might come a time when I need to bring my people inland to protect them, and this is an ideal place. No one can approach by water without being seen, and I doubt anyone can get to you unnoticed from the landward side."

Richard dropped his deep voice even lower, so that no one but Grania could hear him. "I hope I mean more to you than just a place to shelter your followers in times of trouble."

She smiled at him then, but something was missing from her smile, and Richard Burke knew it. He could not see what Grania was seeing in the landscape of her mind: a black curragh beached on a lonely strand, and a red-haired man all alone, mending his fishing nets.

She pushed the image away. "How much you mean to me remains to be seen, doesn't it?" Grania said to Richard Burke.

The ceremony was brief; none of the friars from nearby Burrishoole were in attendance, and Calvagh and his friars were not invited. The contract—"for one year certain"—was read aloud, and both parties agreed to it. Richard gave Grania a massive chain of gold links, and she presented him with one of the new banners she had recently had made, adding a personal device for herself, a white seahorse above the red boar of O Malley.

Food and drink were served afterward on trestle tables beside the castle walls, and Richard's followers crowded around to offer the couple congratulations and fill themselves with bread and fish and beef, with noble port and sack and mead and strong grain whiskey provided by the farmers as their contribution.

Then at last they went away, leaving Grania alone with her new husband and the retinue who served him in his tower.

The rechtaire, a portly man tonsured like a monk by natural

baldness, led his lord and new lady past the guardroom on the ground floor and up the customary tower stair, a defensive arrangement whereby the second floor was reached by a wooden ladder that could be hauled up after one. Beyond the second floor, the fixed stone stairs curved upward to Richard's private bedchamber below the hall.

Iron Richard did not possess an ollave poet—though Shane Oliverus did. But Rockfleet boasted a resident harper who came each day from his cottage on the hill beyond the bawn, the stone enclosure where Burke's horses and cattle were sheltered at night. For his marriage night, Richard had requested the harper to stay in the castle and play until sunrise, the plangent notes resounding sweetly, sadly, throughout the building.

"Does he play no merry airs?" Grania asked.

"I did not think you would want to hear some boisterous country melody on our wedding night."

"Now you know. I dislike sad music."

"I like it the best," said Richard Burke.

She turned to face him. "Then have it played when I am away."

They stared at one another. The rechtaire cleared his throat. Candlelight wavered on the walls, a guardsman swore somewhere below.

"Leave us alone," Richard ordered the servants.

Grania had brought only Evleen as an attendant, and Evleen followed no orders but hers. Burke's rechtaire and bodyservant left the room, but Evleen stayed, standing quietly with her hands at her sides. "I said go!" Richard roared at her, but she was as unmoved as a stone in the wind.

"Is your servant deaf, Grania?"

"She's not my servant."

"Bondwoman, slave, vassal . . . whatever she is, I want her out of my bedchamber."

"This is our bedchamber now," Grania reminded him.

"Only under Brehon law."

"And only under Brehon law do you have a right to take me into that bed over there. If you still wish to do so, you will treat my . . . my friend, Evleen, with the same respect you show me."

Iron Richard was startled. Never in his life had he heard anyone refer to a servant as a friend. He started to say something, then stopped himself. I must humor her a little longer, he told himself. Women. Even this one, mad one week out of every month, no doubt. Worse luck if this is the week. I'll have a bed as bloody as if I'd brought a virgin to it.

His eyes flickered toward the bed and back again. "Ask your friend to leave yourself, then," he said to Grania.

"You may go, Evleen. It's all right."

Evleen nodded. "But I'll wait outside the door," she added. "I'll be sitting on the stairs if you need me."

"God's death!" cried Richard Burke. "Do you think I'm going to rape your unwilling mistress and rip her limb from limb?"

None of Evleen's sympathies were with Iron Richard—not after Tigernan's self-exile. "If you take one hair from her head," Evleen told him as she left, "I can summon enough of her men with a whistle to cut you into pieces for me to cook in one of your own pots."

Then she was gone and the door pulled shut behind her.

"You keep a savage crew," Richard observed.

"They're loyal," Grania told him. Yet a picture of Tigernan welled up behind her eyes, and she had to turn her head away for a moment. This is my wedding night, she reminded herself. My husband has a reputation for virility, and I have learned to enjoy a man; I should be enjoying this. I *will* enjoy it, I won't let Tigernan ruin it for me.

Then, sharp as knives, the question: Why did he leave me without a word of explanation? How can I be Grania if there is no Tigernan at my shoulder?

Richard saw how pale she was, how vulnerable she suddenly appeared. So her strength and confidence were superficial after all, and she was like any other woman. He reached for her and pulled her body against his.

The iron of Richard's nickname described more than his stubbornness, or the color of his eyes. His shoulders and arms were like iron, too, as he clamped them around Grania to impress her with his power. His movements were abrupt and independent of any response from her. From the beginning, Richard Burke meant to be in charge of every aspect of his relationship to this woman.

Grania tried to relax in his embrace. She had accepted the union with every intention of living up to her half of the contract—and extracting the most possible pleasure from it as well. But the planes and angles of Richard's body felt wrong. Not in any specific way, yet in every way, he did not fit her.

He tried to lift her and carry her to the bed, but he grappled with her awkwardly, surprised by her weight. She slipped from his grasp and went to the bed on her own feet. "No one carries me," she said. "Not while I can walk."

Tigernan carried me, she thought suddenly. Across his shoulder.

Burke was beside her, fumbling with her clothes. She had dressed as a noblewoman for the occasion, in Continental fashion, with a gown and petticoat of heavy silk, a funnel-shaped Spanish farthingale (awkward on board ship), and puffed sleeves.

Evleen had fussed and sworn while getting her into it, and Grania had already promised herself to restrict her wardrobe thereafter to more comfortable clothing, whether she was the wife of a lord or not. But Evleen was no longer present to undress her, and Richard Burke had no skill as a ladies' maid.

"God's eyes," he cursed mildly, but soon the tangle of fabric resulted in stronger invective. Grania was lying in a tumble on his bed, watching with amusement but offering no help.

"Do you want me to call Evleen back?" she asked when it became obvious her costume was defeating him.

"I can solve this problem for myself," he replied. He did not seem amused; his mouth was set in a grim line and there were beads of sweat on his forehead. He rolled to the edge of the bed and reached for his discarded belt and the Italian dirk he carried in his knife sheath.

Grania saw the flash of steel and reacted without thinking. It did not occur to her he meant to cut off her clothing. She had been in battle; a naked blade had only one meaning for her.

Doubling up, she rolled the other way and grabbed a heavy silver candlestick from the table near the bed. She whirled and slammed it down across Richard's wrist in one swift movement. They both heard the snap of the wristbone. With a gasp, he dropped the knife.

Iron Richard stared appalled at his new wife. "What did you do that for?"

"Was I to lie here and let you attack me?"

"I wasn't going to hurt you! You're as savage as your heathen followers, woman! I've heard the rumors about you, but I was willing to overlook them. Now I see I should have paid more attention—any woman who would attack and murder pilgrims might be expected to attack her lawful husband in his own bed." He bent forward, cradling his injured wrist. His face was pale.

"Evleen!" Grania yelled. "Get in here and help this man!"

Evleen was in the room in a moment—she must have been leaning against the door. She took in the situation with one quick glance. The candlestick was still in Grania's hand, and Iron Richard was obviously wounded. She tried to pry his fingers away and look at the wrist, but he would not let her.

"I want my own people," he said angrily. "Who knows what more harm you mean to do me?"

He strode to the door and shouted for his rechtaire. Soon the chamber was full of people examining Richard's broken wrist, clucking over the incident, sneaking slyly salacious glances at Grania as she sat with the sheets pulled up to her shoulders and a look of mingled embarrassment and amusement on her face. She did not dare meet Evleen's eyes. If she did, she knew she would laugh out loud.

Richard Burke's physician was soon summoned and the injured wrist bound, the servitors dismissed. Half the night was gone by then. The wedding night.

Grania dismissed Evleen, though she felt as if she were sending away her only ally. The atmosphere in the room was as cold as the top of Ben Lettery in winter. When Iron Richard and his new wife were at last alone again, he got into bed in silent dignity and turned his back to her, to lie sleepless throughout the night cradling his throbbing wrist and silently cursing the female sex.

"I've made another terrible beginning with someone," Grania told Evleen next morning. "He kept a guard stationed just outside the bedchamber door all night . . ."

"I know—he wouldn't let me come near."

". . . and I gather that will be the custom from now on. A guard not needed to turn invaders away, but to defend Richard from his wife. Have you ever heard of such a thing, Evleen? He is furious with me, but he won't talk about it, he won't talk at all. What kind of a marriage is this going to be?"

Evleen smiled. "At least it isn't fettered with Christian chains," she said. "You were wise."

Grania shook her head. "Nevertheless, I made the marriage contract honorably and with every intention of fulfilling my part of it. I play the game fairly; I cheat no man. I'll have to find some way to mend the breach between us."

"There are aphrodisiacs . . ." Evleen suggested with an expressive roll of her eyes. "When lust takes hold of a man he can forgive and forget almost anything for a while."

"For a while isn't good enough. And I don't want a marriage dependent on leaves and fungus."

When the pain in Richard's broken wrist began to diminish, Grania set out in a workmanlike fashion to reestablish a marital atmosphere at Rockfleet. She had Evleen put flower petals in the bed, she brushed and pinned her hair with jewels, and she even rubbed potions onto her face to make the skin softer. Iron Richard was treating her like an unwelcome stranger in his house, with no more than icy civility, but the situation could not continue indefinitely and she knew it. The man had too much pride—he did not want his retainers sniggering about him in their cottages, or his hired gallowglasses strutting around in their long mailcoats and helmets and winking at each other when their lord's marriage was mentioned. A man who could not hold the respect of his private army could hold nothing else.

One night Richard came to bed in a slightly more mellow mood than he had previously shown, and they were actually able to speak to one another about the day's events—a good saddle mare giving birth to a foal in the bawn, a petty war springing up to the north after one Gaelic clan chief had raided another's cattle.

When the small stock of conversation was exhausted, Iron Richard reached out and put one hand on Grania's breast.

He was not sure just how he wanted to approach the issue. Should he be aggressive and have her fight back again? Should he be a supplicant suitor, a country lad with cap in hand?

No—that was not an appropriate role for the Burke tanist. He determined to be firm, to demand his rights and settle for no further nonsense from the woman. His mother, Finola, had played him like a fish on a line, keeping him in constant uncertainty as he tried to deal with her whims and moods on any given day. He had never been able to overcome the habits of a lifetime with his mother, but he was starting fresh with this new wife. He would show her no deference, he would not be tyrannized. A wife was not a mother, but a possession to be used as a man saw fit.

He rolled heavily on top of her without saying a word.

Determined to uphold her part of their bargain, Grania did not fight him; she did everything she could to accommodate herself to him. But as she had already discovered, they did not fit well together. His rhythms were different from hers, the bony surfaces of his body ground against her own, even the natural smell of his skin was offensive to her when heightened by the heat of passion. She had wanted to be with a man again, to find what she had discovered with Huw, but Richard an Iarainn summoned no response from her body at all.

She felt like one forced to dance in an unfamiliar set where none of the steps were known and the music was off key.

From the way Richard pounded away at her she could have been any woman, or even a soft-buttocked boy. What truly made her Gráinne Ni Mháille meant nothing to him when he bedded her. His only awareness was of his own bodily sensations, and these he pursued single-mindedly, pulling and tugging at her with hard hands to make her body meet his needs.

He was virile, there was no question of it, and he was lustful enough to ignore the occasional white lance of pain in his wrist as he grappled the woman into various positions. He was aware that he was using her. He wanted to use her.

At last he gave a mighty grunt and rolled away from her, panting. Grania knew that Huw would have held her even more closely, letting the sweet throbbing die away slowly through their linked bodies. But Richard Burke, once satisfied, seemed eager to be clear of her. He lay at the far edge of the bed and said nothing; did not touch her in any way. His breathing was harsh, and the smell of him was alien to her nostrils.

So this is my new life, Grania thought. I should have bedded him first, and saved us both disappointment.

"You've never had a better man. Admit it," he finally said into the darkness, in his beautiful deep voice.

But Grania never answered.

Time passed, and each time they coupled the results were the same. They were two people who shared nothing but their bodies, briefly. Grania felt no desire and experienced no pleasure. Only sometimes, after he had turned his back to her and begun to snore, did her most private parts ache with a sweet remembering that had nothing to do with Richard an Iarainn. She lay with clenched fists then, trying to will away the unsatisfied, unsatisfiable longing.

When she woke in the morning and found him still beside her, mouth open, eyes gummy, twitching in some private dream, the thought came to her that she would far prefer occupying Rockfleet without him.

In October The MacWilliam Iochtar summoned Richard Burke and his men-at-arms for a campaign against the MacJordan lordship in the east. Grania's husband gave her the news himself. He was not a sensitive man and he did not think quickly, but even he had realized by then that the marriage was not going well. Any hope he might have had of dominating her had evaporated, but he was not anxious to lose the power and prestige she represented or the force of men she commanded, so he made one tardy effort to repair the gap widening between them. He neither knew nor understood the nature of the gap; it did not matter. Woman's foolishness. But he did not want to march away until he was sure of her.

"We are only married a few months," he said, watching closely for her response. "I am sworn to The MacWilliam's support, of course, but if you want me to stay here with you awhile longer . . ." He smiled. He stroked his drooping Gaelic-style mustache. He was trying belatedly, in his ponderous way, to be charming.

"You have obligations," she reminded him, "as I do myself. I have let my enterprises suffer from neglect, I fear, so while you are away I will go to Clare and tend to my ships and crews. This will be a good opportunity . . . and we may board a merchantman or two," she added, as bait.

"Ah, yes. The sea-lanes will be busy." He sounded relieved, for in truth he was as anxious to be away from her as she was to be rid of him. There were always women available to a man of rank; no one expected him to limit himself to a wife who had proved rather a disappointment. A noble lord marching through the land behind his piper and his banners attracted many admiring eyes.

Iron Richard's smile deepened in anticipation. There were plenty of women more easily subdued, more satisfying to his nature, than Grania.

He and his army were scarcely over the first hill when she was setting sail for Cliara.

In her absence, Ruari Oge had commanded her fleet and taken a season's worth of fish from the sea. Magnus' oldest son had remained at Rockfleet as her boatman, and it was he who ferried

Grania and Evleen back to the guardian island in the mouth of the bay.

As soon as they were on open water, Evleen began straining forward, as if she could power the boat herself instead of relying on wind to fill a sail. When they entered Cliara harbor she was leaning over the gunwales, and she was ashore even before Grania, running like a young woman into Ruari Oge's outstretched arms.

I have been selfish, Grania thought as she watched them. I will not separate those two again.

If her expression was wistful, there was no watchful Tigernan to notice or care.

She thought of Tigernan often, however—she could not leave the portal of the tower house without seeing the peak of Curraun rising across the bay. Sometimes she thought of him with anger and sometimes with puzzlement; sometimes she just thought of odd things, like his gingery hair or the shape of his ears—almost pointed, like a satyr's.

Foolish woman! She laughed at herself. You have so much; why torment yourself over one deserter? Or a husband who is not what you hoped to find. Or children you will never know.

She went to the cove again. The day was soft with mist and cloud, the sky gray, the sea gray, the ocean booming hollowly among the caverns. Gray sweet dark Gaelic melancholy rose in Grania, and she surrendered to it—briefly—needing it to balance her nature. Such occasions were rare, but when they occurred they were total, for it was not in her to do anything by halves. If she was going to allow herself to feel sad she would sink like a stone to the lightless depths, float in sorrow as in the womb, and then when she was surfeited rise to the surface again, seeking light and laughter.

Laughter. She came up from the cove laughing. It did Evleen's heart good to hear her.

"I'm a foolish woman, Evleen," she said aloud. "I rule a kingdom any chieftain would envy and yet I always seem to want something . . . more."

"We all do," Evleen told her.

"You, too?"

"Life is a flowing river; it's not meant to be a stagnant pool."

"Either you are becoming less cryptic or experience is better equipping me to understand you," Grania commented.

From Clare island one could not see Rockfleet, even on the clearest day. The vast blue bowl of Cuan Mó lay between them. Grania could almost forget Rockfleet existed at all—but she did not want to forget it. It was only Richard who displeased her.

She sent for a brehon to have the laws pertaining to Gaelic marriage explained to her again, in careful detail.

She had barely finished her conference with the brehon when another arrival reached Cliara. Grania's son Murrough stepped off an O Flaherty boat with a scowl on his face and demanded to see his mother immediately. She ushered him into her hall and offered warm scented water for washing his flushed face, and a bowl of broth for warming his belly, but he brushed aside the amenities and got right to the point.

"My brother Owen is talking about submission!" he cried in a bitter voice. "He married that kinswoman of The MacWilliam Uachtar almost as soon as we got back from Margaret's wedding, married her in haste without even arranging a festival and inviting his clanspeople, and already she is working him like beeswax. The rest of her family has long since bent the knee to the English, and she's convinced Owen it's the only way to peace and prosperity."

Grania raised her eyebrows. "What do you expect me to do about it?"

"Force him to support the claim of Donal Crone to the chieftainship of the O Flaherties. You have the power."

"No, Murrough, I don't. Oh, I could stop trading with Owen, but that would accomplish no more than turning him against me. And would you have me come march into Iar Connaught to attack the English choice, Murrough of the Battle Axes? If I commit such an open act of war, I might well bring the Tudor woman down on me in all her fury, and her military might is infinitely greater than mine. I could not beat her on land in Iar Connaught and she would take Clew bay from me as well. I won't do it, Murrough."

He was trembling with anger. "Donal an Chogaidh was your husband, Iar Connaught became your home . . ."

"Clew bay is my home. This much I can keep safe. This much I can keep Irish, for Margaret's children and grandchildren and yours and Owen's as well, when the day comes that the English finish overrunning Iar Connaught altogether."

"That day will come soon if your son Owen has his way. You abandon us." He spat the words at her.

I see fragments of myself in all my children, Grania thought. Owen is obviously playing a game, trying to survive. He is weak and he gives away too much too soon—I must talk to him about that—but at least he is maneuvering. As I have often done. And Murrough has my hot temper, my impulsiveness I regret afterward. . . .

A vision flashed behind her eyes, that of a man in a monk's robe holding a knife on her son.

"I did not abandon you, Murrough," she said aloud. "When you were attacked that day at Belclare I saved your life."

"What are you talking about?"

"That friar you hit was carrying a concealed English knife, and from the glance I got of his face he would have enjoyed killing you."

"An Augustinian monk?" Murrough asked, dumbfounded. "Why didn't you say something to me then? I never saw a knife, I didn't realize . . ."

"Thinking about it afterward, I came to the conclusion he was probably no monk at all, but someone put there to spy on us."

"You should have told me. I'd have skewered his guts."

"I know. That's why I didn't tell you. I told no one, I just became more watchful. I've seen what open warfare does, Murrough; I watched it destroy your father. I'm trying to learn a different game."

"If you won't take sides in the struggle in Iar Connaught," Murrough warned his mother, "you can't expect any of us to come to your aid here. You talk about holding Clew bay for your grandchildren, but what's to keep The MacWilliam Iochtar from going over to the English as the southern Burkes have done? Then this Iron Richard you married will kneel to the English Crown like my brother Owen and you'll have Elizabeth Tudor for your neighbor at Rockfleet."

"Oh no I won't," said Gráinne Ni Mháille.

But in the night she awoke, chilled, fighting out of a dream in which a pair of malignant eyes glared at her from beneath a monk's hood, and she knew her impulsiveness—Murrough's impulsiveness —had made a deadly enemy.

18

Richard an Iarainn returned from his campaign a weary man. He had been away from Rockfleet for months, yet did not find himself eager for his new wife's embraces. He tarried along the way to visit his three sons and daughter by his first wife, to pay a call on his younger brother Ulick and another on his brother William, who was known as the Blind Abbot.

William was domiciled in a small friary hidden away in a dark glen where no news of the larger world should have intruded, yet blind William in his doubled darkness always seemed to know everything that was happening.

It was he who informed Richard, "The O Malley was stricken with a seizure and lies paralyzed and useless at Belclare, and his tanist, Cormac, was recently drowned in a storm at sea while fishing. The O Malley chieftainship can be considered vacated for all practical purposes, but the brehons are reluctant to call for an election to name a new tanist. It seems the whole tribe already follows the banner of Gráinne Ni Mháille. Under Irish law a woman cannot be captain of her nation, yet your wife serves in that capacity and no one wants to challenge her. The income she brings to Umhall through her seafaring is too important; too many depend on it."

Richard scowled. "They may follow her, but they will never formally acknowledge her. She is just a woman; whatever power she wields will never be credited to her in Ireland. Women sully themselves when they meddle in men's business," he added, thinking of his mother, who had been up to her wriggling hips in intrigue until her health failed.

William, born of the same Finola, nodded. "I agree with you. At least we shall never see women in positions of power in the Church."

"The Protestant Elizabeth of England titles herself head of her church," Richard reminded him glumly.

"She is an unnatural creature," his brother replied, "who makes trouble only because she is thwarted from fulfilling her natural functions. The best way to handle women," advised the Blind Abbot, who never handled women, "is to keep them busy producing children. A queasy belly will put an end to any woman's misplaced ambition."

The rest of the way to Rockfleet, Richard Burke was thinking in slow, thoughtful stages of the plan he meant to pursue with Grania. If she now ruled her clan in fact if not in name—as well as controlling Clew bay—and if she got pregnant, would it not be her husband's duty to relieve her of the burden of her obligations and fulfill them himself?

Iron Richard might not have to wait for Shane Oliverus to die before he, too, ruled a vast territory. Marching with his men-at-arms around him, Richard felt increasingly confident of his future. He saw a certain justice in maneuvering Grania out of her position and assuming it for himself—his own mother had manipulated the lives of all her sons, turning Ulick into a feckless fool, William into a celibate, and Richard himself into a cold man who simultaneously lusted for and despised women. Now he would order the life of another woman to his own advantage.

The priests would support him. The brehons would support him. Both parties had a stake in returning to the natural order, where men held all authority. The terrible example of Elizabeth Tudor and her malevolent influence over Irish affairs was enough to convince any thinking male of the mistake inherent in allowing women power.

Once pregnant, Grania would be forced to loosen her hold. And in spite of her disclaimer, Richard had no doubt he could get her pregnant and keep her perpetually in that state for some years to come, long enough to consolidate his own rule. No woman as healthy as Grania, with three living children, was likely to have gone barren for no reason. He just had not bedded her enough, a failure he determined to rectify as soon as he reached Rockfleet.

But as he and his men broke out of a patch of sheltering woodland and saw the dark tower of Rockfleet rise before them, Richard an Iarainn received a shock. The Burke banner with its crimson cross and sable lion no longer flew from the battlements. Instead, Grania's personal flag floated on the wind.

Richard reined his horse back on its haunches and stared in astonishment.

Rolling his eyes to one side without moving his head, he saw a new forest surrounding the tower of Rockfleet: a forest of men, not trees. Camped across the hilly greensward and all along the brook were Grania's followers, well-armed men with weapons both native and Continental. Their fires smoldered everywhere, evidence of groups sleeping each night in their heavy mantles beneath the stars, keeping watch for Gráinne Ni Mháille within the fortress. Hundreds of men, drawn from the vast body of support Grania had built herself in the Clew bay region by sharing her prizes from the sea with an open hand.

Richard Burke's hired army lost its forward momentum.

The piper who led the march went on playing, a droning wail that hung, disembodied, in the air.

Putting the spur to his horse, Richard galloped to the portal and called out his wife's name. "Open to me!" he commanded.

A pair of tall guards wearing O Malley colors stood beside the door, spears at the ready. They had pistols in their belts, and they looked at Richard an Iarainn as if they did not know who he was.

"Grania!" he shouted more loudly. "Let me in!"

Rockfleet possessed a Gothic-arched aperture on the landward side of the tower, high above the portal. With a block and tackle, heavy furniture that could not pass up the narrow inner stair could be lifted through this opening into the apartment within. As Richard continued yelling, Grania opened the wooden shutter and leaned the upper portion of her body out the arched window.

"Richard Burke," she cried, "are you aware of the passage of time?"

"It is almost summer," he replied.

"It is; a year has passed since we married. You spent a long time away from me; I trust your ventures were profitable?"

His horse would not stand still, and he swore at the animal. "We did little looting," he called to her. "Shane Oliverus marched against MacJordan, you know that. MacJordan raised a rebellion and threatened the peace of our eastern borders."

"Which you and The MacWilliam Iochtar defended," Grania replied. "As the English wished you to do."

"We weren't fighting on the English side," Richard denied for all to hear.

"Weren't you? Isn't it true they are beginning to call your chieftain Elizabeth's loyal subject? Does he plan a formal submission?"

"He hasn't discussed it with me," Richard answered testily.

"If he submits the Tudor woman may take this land away from you and not give it back," Grania shouted down to him.

Richard an Iarainn could think of no good answer. "Let me in and we'll discuss this in the hall together," he called up to her.

"Not in my hall," Grania told him.

"What do you mean?"

"I mean," she shouted, raising her sea-trained voice to its full power so there would be plenty of witnesses, "that we have been wed for one year's term under Brehon law and now I dismiss you, Richard Burke! And I claim this land along Clew bay as my own, not to be bartered away to foreign powers by any clansman of yours!"

Her erstwhile husband felt struck by a bolt of lightning. In one move the woman had set him aside and robbed him of his principal stronghold. "Pirate!" he yelled, shaking his fist at her.

But Grania had already slammed the shutter.

Her men formed a circle around his, with weapons at the ready. So many men—with so many families at home living in well-furnished cottages, eating good food, wearing O Malley wool on their backs and O Malley leather on their feet. The weight of an entire clan faced him, and Richard did not command a sufficient force to summon against them. He knew instantly that Shane Oliverus had his own affairs to handle, and would not come to fight the O Malleys over one tower house and a bit of shoreland. Shane was a country man, not a sea man, and control of harborage on Clew bay was not important to him.

One of Grania's captains, a huge burly fellow with grizzled hair and an expression Richard Burke interpreted as ferocious, stepped forward. The man caught Richard's horse by the rein, and the animal calmed instantly, adding to its rider's annoyance.

"None of you have any right over what is mine!" Richard protested.

"This land is held by Gráinne Ni Mháille now," Ruari Oge told him. "You should be taking your soldiers away unless you have a taste for a pleasant little war."

Richard made a quick effort to estimate the size of Grania's forces and found the attempt disheartening. Behind him, he heard an unhappy muttering from his own soldiers.

"I'll go," Iron Richard said at last. "But I'll be back."

"Come any time," Ruari Oge invited with disarming joviality. "I'm certain you'll always be welcome as a guest in Grania's house. She has a fine reputation for hospitality."

The Gaels around him laughed.

There was nothing for it but to leave—or suffer a humiliating defeat which would close the incident beyond hope of repair. If he left peacefully now without angering Grania, Richard hoped he could yet persuade her to reconsider. Time and tact might somehow regain Rockfleet for him.

He was so furious, that his men stayed out of his reach as he ordered them to a smaller holding of his farther inland. Some of his retainers accompanied him. Many of them, however, had already given their allegiance to his wife and stayed behind.

He wondered if they were laughing at him as he rode away.

I could kill her, Richard an Iarainn said to himself. I should kill her. Surely someone will. She's a rogue and a thief.

He hated her. Yet some secret part of Iron Richard could not help admiring Grania, perhaps as a concomitant of that hatred. When it came to women, his emotions were peculiarly knotted together.

When Ruari Oge came up the stairs, Grania's first question to him was, "Is he really gone?"

"Like snow on a hot rock."

She had been standing, white-faced and tense, just within the window opening, peering through the cracks in the shutters. When she heard Iron Richard had departed she sank onto a bench with a shaky laugh. "I didn't know if he would give up that easily. I didn't want any of our men killed."

"If what you've told me of him is true, he formed an early habit of obeying women and has yet to break it, no matter how hard he tries," Ruari commented. "I can't imagine such a habit myself."

Grania grinned at him. "Of course not. But I'm thankful he's gone with no trouble. And he didn't suspect a thing, did he?"

"He might have," said Evleen, "if you'd leaned any farther out that window. Richard Burke would surely have noticed his wife has grown surprisingly stout."

Grania splayed her fingers over her mounded belly, measuring its size. "Can you believe it, Evleen? I'm really going to have another child at last. My own child."

"And that of Burke," added Ruari Oge.

His commander frowned. "My own child," she said with greater emphasis. "I set him aside as my husband; I will allow him no rights over this infant. When it is born it may bear the Burke name, but its childhood will be spent with me."

"You would even take the man's son from him?"

"It's been done to me," Grania replied grimly.

In one dashing stroke, Rockfleet was hers. Every harbor and inlet and rivermouth, every island and strand and anchorage around the perimeter of Clew bay, was now under her control or that of her ally, the Devil's Hook.

"Leave me for a while," Grania requested.

Alone in the chamber, she slowly paced the room, measuring its distance from one side to the other stride by stride. She wanted to savor every detail of her new possession—the window used as a loading bay, the loopholes in the walls for the discharge of musketry, the concave stone ceiling between the third and fourth floors, the splendid view from the parapets above the hall.

Clare island had always been in her family, had always, to some extent, been hers. But Rockfleet was a new possession, one she had taken with her own wits. Like a rich prize seized from a merchantman, it brought her the satisfaction of solid accomplishment.

I will build more strongholds, Grania promised herself. I will ring Clew bay with them, so everyone may know this place is mine.

She immediately sent word south, to both Owen and Murrough, that Rockfleet was in her possession and would be available to either of them if they ever needed it. She was also careful to remind Owen of the Hen's Castle and its defensive potential, and to offer both young men the expertise of Ruari Oge if they needed to fortify their positions.

They were on separate sides now, Owen and Murrough, one against the Tudor queen and one with her—but Grania wanted them both to survive.

"You win the game every day you stay alive," she wrote to each of her sons.

And my children and their children will live long after you are dust, she said in her head to Elizabeth Tudor. Men fight for honor, but women fight for survival. My blood will win by outlasting yours.

Stimulated by her success at Rockfleet, she was eager to go back to sea again. Any other woman heavy with child would have dreaded stepping into a skiff, but Grania longed for the familiar roll and pitch of an oceangoing vessel. She wanted this child to be born to her world, to know it intimately as she did.

August was a trading month, and having left a sizable force of men-at-arms to secure Rockfleet, Grania returned to Clare island to accompany several of her vessels south on a trading venture. Pregnancy had made her heavy and robbed her of her agility, but it also gave her a ferocious energy and an appetite to match. She meant to enjoy every moment of the voyage and drive a very hard bargain in the port of Waterford before charting a course back to Clew bay.

"Ruari Oge, I want you to stay on Clare with Evleen and secure the island for me," Grania ordered.

As she had known he would, the old pirate immediately protested. "You have never set sail without me or Tigernan or both in your vessel. This is no time to start!"

"Magnus will captain me—don't you trust him?"

"I trust no one but myself," Ruari growled.

"Exactly. That's why I want you here, keeping a sharp lookout."

She did not tell him the real reason. He was limping more of late, from some old wound he never discussed, and she had noticed Evleen giving him quick, concerned looks when his back was turned. She wanted the two of them together from now on. She was almost superstitious about it. Someone, somewhere, had to have it all—and Ruari and Evleen did. She would keep it for them as best she could, as long as she could.

"Take good care of him," she told Evleen before she left.

"Always," the little woman responded.

The voyage went well until they left Waterford and headed for home. As they passed the Old Head of Kinsale, ageless landmark for mariners, Grania felt a deep clenching in her belly.

Wait, she ordered. Wait until we get back to Cliara!

But even she could not order nature.

The pains quickened. Magnus noticed her pallor and saw her clench her fists. As captain of the refurbished carrack, with a fine cargo in its holds, he was mindful of many responsibilities at once, and a woman about to give birth immediately slipped, in his mind, from commander to burden. "If your time is on you, go below," he told Grania as an order rather than a request.

She lifted her chin and glared at him. "There are Turks in these waters, pirates so savage they make us look like sparrows. Would you have me helpless below in case we encounter them?"

"You will be helpless in any case," Magnus pointed out, "until the child has come. But look: the sea lies quiet and the only ships in sight are trading vessels like our own. We will reach the Kerry coast soon. There are plenty of inlets there where we can escape any possible attackers; I know all those waters well."

Grania's keen eyes swept the sea and the land beyond. It was quiet; too quiet. She had a sudden sense of foreboding. Not yet! she cried again to the unborn child, but she was answered by a pain that doubled her over and left her gasping.

Motioning for help, Magnus wrapped her in his own cloak and began trying to maneuver her to her cabin. At this moment he regretted the ancient tradition that denied women the sea, for Grania would need a woman to attend her. But though her crewmen would follow her anywhere, it had always been obvious they wanted no other women aboard. Even as paid passengers females were merely tolerated, and men watched them covertly. The sea was a jealous female, some claimed; she would not tolerate another woman.

Only Gráinne Ni Mháille was exempt. But she needed a woman now, and none was aboard. She had never brought a female attendant; she lived a genderless life as commander of the fleet and meant to keep it that way.

"Who do you want with you?" Magnus asked after they got her into her narrow bed in the cabin. She was not a young woman, and it was obvious this was going to be a hard birth.

"Evleen . . ." Grania gasped.

"Evleen's on Clare, damn it. You should have brought her."

"No . . . Evleen told me the baby wouldn't be born for another fortnight. We were so sure . . ."

"Women can be as wrong as anyone else," Magnus observed. "I've misjudged more than one sea myself. I'll get the O Lee—he's our ship's physician, and at least he can . . ."

"Tigernan!" Grania called, her body writhing.

Magnus stepped back from her in surprise. "She's out of her head," he said under his breath to the nervous first mate who had been helping him. "Quick, get Aidan O Lee and get back here. We'll have to secure her somehow in case we hit rough water—

this coast is notorious for sudden storms. And I'm needed on deck."

He made a hasty exit. The cabin was stifling and smelled of blood and pain.

Once on deck, he ordered the ship's lanterns to signal Grania's other vessels nearby. Several galleys had accompanied the carrack and were also laden to their gunwales with goods, cramping the floor space between the oarsmen.

Grania screamed, once. At the sound, Magnus closed his eyes. "Head for the nearest anchorage," he shouted to his helmsman. "This is one storm I mean to ride out in the shallows."

The labor was protracted and terrible. One scream was all Grania allowed herself, and the physician Aidan O Lee had, at her order, fastened a piece of cloth around her head and between her teeth to keep her silent thereafter. She did not want the men to hear her.

Aidan gave her knotted ropes to pull upon and was horrified by the bloody mess her palms became. Like the other men who followed Gráinne Ni Mháille, he had never imagined her as ill, as fragile . . . as mortal. Her incandescent energy and fierce determination were like the sun, beyond human limits.

Now she convulsed in labor like any other woman. She stank; she rolled her eyes in agony.

The precincts of physician and midwife did not overlap. A midwife's duty was to participate in the entirely natural and healthy act of delivering a child; a physician was for the sick and wounded. Aidan O Lee had rarely seen childbirth and never assisted in it, and what he did he did clumsily, hurting Grania more than he helped. She was aware of him only as hands touching her and a voice that occasionally said things she could not understand. He was not with her in any true sense of the word. She was alone in red darkness, being torn in two between opposing forces who had chosen her as their battlefield.

This was not like her earlier births. She was younger then, slimmer, in practice. Years on the sea had given her a muscularity that worked against her in this peculiarly female endeavor, multiplying the pain instead of speeding the birth. When her body contracted she felt as if she were breaking her own spine.

Because she would never surrender to pain, she tried to find something beyond the labor to hold onto, some talisman to grasp.

Between contractions she struggled to envision Clare island, or her new treasure, Rockfleet . . . or other strongholds she meant to build, symbols of invincibility.

Huw's face appeared briefly in the crimson well engulfing her. She tried to reach out to him, smiling because he was alive after all. I knew it, she thought she said aloud. I knew you had not died. I'm having your child . . .

No. My child. Not Huw's, but Richard Burke's.

A child, a child.

The men faded from her thoughts. The child beat its way out of her, ripping her apart.

Aidan O Lee fell back on prayer, standing beside the sweat-soaked bunk in lanternlit gloom, his head bowed and hands folded. "God's will be done . . ."

The bloody package erupted from between her legs, and the physician leaned forward to take it, marveling at the size of the newborn child. "A boy, Grania," he called to her through the dimness surrounding them both. "A great big lad with a head of black curls on him already."

She gulped for air. Aidan removed the cloth from between her teeth. "I said, you have a son."

Grania tried to smile at him, but she was too weary. Her ears, her fingers, her very hair seemed exhausted. She lay in a puddle of warmth, and the thought came to her that she was probably bleeding to death. Somehow it did not matter very much. The faces she had pictured earlier came back again, fainter, as if they were fading away. Richard. Huw.

Then one sharp and clear, homely and fierce. Ginger hair and a crooked jaw. He was saying something sarcastic, something foolish. . . . All at once, Grania felt safe. Her eyes closed and she drifted into sleep.

"I thought we would lose her for certain," Aidan subsequently reported to Magnus. "Blood was pouring out of her; she was as white as fresh milk. Then the bleeding stopped and she relaxed all over. The next thing I knew she was sleeping as peacefully as her child, and I swear to you she is lying in her bed smiling. I did not have the heart to move her or try to clean her up, though it should be done. Would you . . . ?"

Magnus took a step backward. "Not I! And I think she would not welcome having anyone else see her like that, either. Go back to her, Aidan, and stay with her. Do whatever is necessary. We'll remain here at anchor until her strength comes back and she can at least stand up; then we'll know she's all right."

They waited at anchor throughout the day and a long night. Aidan had cleaned both Grania and her child and put the infant to her breast, but his only reward was a weak nod of her head. The baby was healthy enough, the mother spent. Not until the gray dawn of the next day did she pull herself up into a sitting position in the bed and begin to take an interest in the world around her once more. Her first act was to summon her captain.

"We're at anchor, Magnus?" Her voice was a tired whisper.

"We are. When the child began to come I ordered it."

"You mean we are pinned helpless in these waters? Are our galleys around us with plenty of fighting men?"

"Some," he admitted. "A couple of ships have already weighed anchor and headed on west. If you're better I think it's safe now to follow them, but I did not want to go around Fastnet rock and Mizzen head while a woman on board was giving birth."

Her eyes flashed. "Did you think I couldn't take a little rough sea?" Then her stern features relaxed a little. "I know, you were being considerate, and I appreciate it, Magnus, though I've never asked for special treatment. But I assure you I am myself again. We must hoist anchor and continue. A becalmed vessel in these waters is like a bleeding fish in a shark pool. Go back on deck and tell my men I'll join them soon."

Magnus paused at the doorway and asked Aidan in a low voice, "Can she?"

"Certainly not. But I wouldn't begin to tell her that. Best do as she says and get underway."

Magnus gave the orders and the crew sprang into action, but before they could move out into deep water again the hounds were upon them.

19

Roving bands of Turkish pirates had been the terror of the seas for generations, not only savaging Mediterranean shipping but carrying their menace up the Spanish coast and well into northern European waters. Piracy in the sixteenth century was almost a noble profession, with great buccaneers elevated to the status of national heroes and their skills in seamanship highly sought by their own governments. Countless coastal towns throughout Europe sought to enrich themselves through independent acts of piracy. As a result, protests against pirates were making up the largest item of ambassadorial routine in many noble courts, and corsairs had come to be considered an uncontrollable plague in many quarters.

For sheer ferocity, the Turks were second to none.

The dreadful state of English roads had made the sea the easiest and cheapest means of transport, encouraging not only the great pirate combines of Cornwall and Dorset to plunder but also luring such predators as the Turks from great distances. Elizabeth Tudor had begun strenuous efforts to limit and control the problem, with mixed success, but as a result, privateers were becoming increasingly active in areas somewhat removed from her immediate strength—such as the southern coast of Ireland.

The four galleys that closed on Grania's flagship were of Mediterranean origin, carvel-built by skillful shipwrights in Genoa; long, lean ships with closely grouped oars manned by five men to each oar, giving the ships great power. Turkish pirate galleys were not easily maneuvered in the long Atlantic swells, but in coastal waters they were dreadfully efficient, their crews long drilled in rowing in close formation without fouling their oars.

The main gun carried by these galleys, known as the corsier, was placed in a recoiling carriage and flanked by two pairs of smaller guns, ten- and four-pound sakers. In addition to these forward-firing cannon, the pirate crew was armed with crossbows and other Turkish bows of iron, scimitars, beechwood lances, a wide variety of pistols, and the ubiquitous grappling hooks of their profession.

Unlike the relatively mild Irish pirates of Connaught, the Turks almost invariably slaughtered the crews of ships they boarded and destroyed anything that did not strike their fancy.

Grania's carrack, gleaming with new paint and riding low in the water, must have looked like a singularly attractive target, protected only by a few equally burdened Hebridean galleys rigged for trade rather than war.

In her cabin, Grania heard the lookout's cry and the first boom of cannon. She grabbed her infant to her breast and cast a horrified look at Aidan. "We're attacked!"

The cry from above was clear and horrifying. "Turks!" A single word, enough to chill the belly and freeze the heart.

Grania lay still for only one moment before she began to flounder in her bunk, trying simultaneously to get up and to shield the baby with her body. "They'll kill my child," she gasped. She was pale, her eyes staring in hollow sockets, and Aidan was afraid she would start the hemorrhaging again. "You've got to lie down," he insisted as he struggled to keep her from leaving the bunk. "There's nothing you can do now but take care of yourself."

"I've been a reckless fool," she muttered. "Always . . . it's cost others their lives . . . but I must . . . I must . . ." A wave of dizziness washed over her, and she let Aidan push her back onto the bed as they heard the first unmistakable thud of a grappling hook on the gunwales.

"The infidels are boarding!" Aidan cried in despair.

Shouted profanities rang the length of the ship. The Turks had managed to come alongside before the carrack could effectively discharge its cannon. Almost at once the battle became a matter of hand-to-hand conflict. Swarthy Turks wearing voluminous trousers in every color of the rainbow swarmed onto the deck of the carrack. The element of surprise was in their favor, for Grania's crew had been distracted during the preceding hours by the drama taking place, unseen, in her cabin; the men had unwittingly let down their guard and were far from the emotional pitch needed for battle. Accustomed to being the attackers, they were ill prepared to defend. The larger, more heavily manned corsairs soon gained the upper hand over the lightly armed Irish galleys.

One of Grania's galleys managed to escape from the pack and began a desperate run west along the coast, hoping to hail a seafaring ally in those busy waters who might be willing to join the fight. Meanwhile, however, things were going badly aboard the carrack. Grania's men fought but were outnumbered; they began to fall back, and the cries of the dying echoed through the ship.

The Turkish pirates swarmed from bow to poop, hacking at the defenders with scimitars. Pistols fired and recoiled; the smell of gunpowder mixed with the smell of blood. In the wild scramble every man grabbed for whatever he could get his hands on to flail away at his enemy.

On board Grania's galleys, there was no foot space for fighting, because the open vessels were overfilled with merchandise from her successful trading. Men could not stand to give battle when they were struggling not to fall over bales and crates. Had they been better prepared, they would, at Grania's order, have thrown the goods overboard rather than risk losing their ships. But Grania was not available to issue such an order, and confusion reigned in her absence.

In her bed, Grania sensed the battle as surely as if it were taking place in front of her eyes. Aidan had barred the cabin door and stood ready to defend her if necessary, but the recent childbirth had so weakened her she could not summon her energy back in this desperate moment. She could only lie waiting like any other helpless woman.

But she was not any other woman.

Fists pounded at the door, and Grania exchanged a quick glance with Aidan, who held a loaded blunderbuss in uncertain hands. He was a physician, not a warrior. But he was spared having to use the weapon when Magnus cried through the door, "Let me in, for the sake of God!"

Aidan quickly opened to him. Grania's captain burst into the room, wild-eyed, a streak of blood running down his jaw from an ear half sliced away. "The battle goes against us on every deck," he panted. "The men never took heart for it. But if you could come— if they could just see you . . ."

The pale, haggard woman on the bed stared at him, then her parched lips opened and widened into a smile, into a grin, into a painful, coughing laugh. But it was a Grania laugh, sending strength flooding back through her, because with laughter there was no room for fear. "A sevenfold curse on your head a year from now, Magnus," she said to him, "for not being able to spare me this one day. But I'm not surprised. Hear, Aidan, give me that gun before you blow a hole in my cabin with it. Hold my son instead. If anything happens to him in my absence you'll pay with your life."

Somehow she was on her feet. She swayed but steadied herself before either man could put out a hand to help her. She was dressed only in a blood-soaked shift, so she seized the blanket from her bed and tossed it around her shoulders as a bloody mantle. One step and then another, and she was at the doorway, ducking her head for the low lintel.

"You can't let her do this," Aidan cried to Magnus.

"There's no choice—we'll all die anyway if she can't turn the tide."

Grania emerged on deck to a scene obscured by gunsmoke. The sails were still clewed to their yards, and a slaughtered boatswain had left the anchor partially raised, setting the carrack adrift as her crew fought for their lives. A Turkish vessel was grappled to her side, vomiting more men onto her decks. A quick glance astern showed the remainder of Grania's fleet similarly engaged with pirates and losing the struggle.

Infidels, Grania thought dizzily. Then she remembered that she too paid little attention to the God of her childhood; his priests had turned their backs on her and she on them. Infidel meets infidel, she thought, and somehow found the strength to laugh.

The woman who stepped, blinking and laughing wildly, into the spring sunshine was like an apparition to the men fighting on the deck. Her appearance was so unexpected those nearest her lost the rhythm of their battle for a moment to gape in astonishment. Her face was livid, her unbound hair streamed in black tangles over her shoulders, and in two bloodless hands she held and lifted and aimed a heavy pistol. Pointing it at the nearest Turk, she screamed, "Take this from unconsecrated hands!"

Her voice was like no other on the deck that morning, so strident it commanded attention above the sounds of battle. She thought her scream split her throat, but the sound was sufficient to have an effect. As the Turks had benefited from the surprise of their attack, so Grania benefited now from the surprise of her appearance. The attackers were thrown off stride and could only stare in disbelief, first at finding a woman aboard the carrack at all and then at her bizarre appearance—and the confident way she handled the weapon. The man at whom she fired fell dead. She gave him not another glance but strode forward, uttering a harsh string of oaths in Gaelic.

Her men responded with glad cries and redoubled their efforts against the Turks. Who could fall back when Gráinne Ni Mháille came from childbed to fight beside him to the death? In her face was no possibility of surrender. They had no choice but to fight with her.

Inspired by her appearance, the Irish seamen fought with a savagery to match that of the Turks and won back the carrack, step by step, deck by deck. On board the galleys the effect was similar, for when it became apparent the corsairs on the flagship were losing, their companions began falling back as well. The mood of a battle could shift and swing, affected by something as small as a man's fleeting thought—or a woman's courage.

When she saw her men were going to make a good fight of it after all, Grania allowed herself to feel the weakness in her knees. Turning, she stumbled to the nearest companionway and left the deck. When she found a dark corner she slumped there, her ears ringing. She was dizzy and nauseated.

"Tigernan?" she heard herself say in a faraway voice.

Then the splintered planks of the decking came up to meet her.

She returned to consciousness to find herself still alone, staring through a gray fog at the brass rim of a keg of nails not a hand's distance from her nose. If she had pitched forward just a little closer to it, she could have split her head open.

She lay summoning her strength. Sounds from above filtered down to her. The Irish voices were yelling strongly now, and the gibberish of the swarthy southerners sounded high and fearful. Running feet thudded overhead. A hawser grated through a cat's-eye. The motion of the ship altered.

Grania got to her feet. Keeping one hand outstretched to brace herself, she made her way slowly toward her cabin. No howling Turk met her on the way, but one of her own men soon caught sight of her and hurried forward to help her.

She brushed his hand away. "I'm all right. You do your job and leave me to mine."

The cabin door was still whole, unsmashed, and when she went inside she found Aidan O Lee sitting on her bed and holding her newborn son, still sleeping in red-faced contentment.

Grania sat down first before she held out her arms for the baby. After all this, she did not want to drop him. She was surprised to find enough strength in her arms to support his weight. She cradled him against her body for a moment, then slumped forward and collapsed onto the mattress, curling herself protectively around her child. "They didn't get you," she whispered very softly. "No one will ever get *you* away from me," she promised the baby. "You are the future. It is for you I hold my kingdom in trust. Even Elizabeth Tudor cannot say that."

Her exhausted smile was triumphant.

✠

She was allowed to sleep awhile in peace, and when she wakened her ships were underway again, headed for home. Wind creaked the sails of the carrack, and the ship's motion lulled the baby, who seemed a quiet and easily placated child.

"Have you a name for him?" Aidan O Lee asked. "A Burke name, perhaps?"

Grania's dark brows drew together. "He'll carry a name of his own. He was born just before we were attacked by the Turks in their long galleys, and he goes to his home for the first time accompanied by my own galleys, his heritage. I will call him Tibbot, a name no other man of his immediate family bears. Tibbot na Long. Tibbot of the Ships."

The defeated corsairs, their ships seized, plundered, and burned by the outnumbered Irish, smoldered in Grania's wake, and people who lived along the southern coast waded into the shallows to rip the Turkish galleys apart for building timbers. Their surviving crewmen were treated no better.

The harvest of the sea was the property of anyone strong enough to claim it.

Grania's fleet returned to Cliara with no further incident, though they gave the bay of Galway a wide berth to avoid possible confrontation with the English there. In the hold of the carrack, by the wavering light of lanterns, Aidan O Lee worked with his collection of physician's tools, his chisels and wooden mallets and metal syringe from England, in an attempt to patch the men who had been wounded in the fierce battle. Some would die before they reached Clare island, in spite of his best offices, but when Grania came below, carrying her nursing babe at her breast to cheer them, several of the most seriously injured rallied.

Afterward, with young Tibbot still at her breast, Grania ordered one of her followers who was famed for his skill at gaming to join her in her cabin for a conflict over a backgammon board. She was too weak to stand in the prow as was her wont; she would not like her men to have ample opportunity to observe her pallor in a strong light. But she could appear very strong indeed sitting cross-legged on her bed, trouncing an opponent and laughing.

"Did you think motherhood would weaken my head, Turlough O Flaherty?" she teased the man she had just beaten. "There is a full measure of O Malley salt in my veins. No small inconvenience like childbirth or a sea battle is sufficient to ruin my game, I assure you!"

Though she would admit it to no one, however, the near escape had shaken her. She had never felt so vulnerable in her life as when she lay cowering under a blanket with a baby in her arms, leaving the defense of both their lives to others.

No sooner had they reached Clare than she began issuing orders. "Send a message to my son-in-law the Devil's Hook at Curraun that I mean to build a stout tower to guard the entrance to Achill sound. That is his territory, and he will have the holding of it for me. And we need another stronghold on . . . on Inishbofin, I think, to watch for vessels coming up from the south and warn us by means of signal fires. I want no one near this bay unless I know of it well in advance."

"Curraun. Inishbofin. It sounds as if Tigernan is in her thoughts," Evleen commented to her husband.

Ruari Oge gave a dismissing shrug to woman's fancies. "Not a bit of it. Those are strategic locations, and she is wise to fortify them. It's the sort of move you would expect from a woman who just helped herself to Rockfleet."

In her absence, the shock wave radiating from that acquisition of Grania's had reached as far as the lonely fisherman on the beach below Curraun, and Tigernan leaned against his overturned curragh and laughed until tears came to his eyes. "Threw her lord out and kept his castle," he repeated again and again, shaking his head in admiration. "That's Grania!"

✠

Even for Ireland, the year following Tibbot's birth was a wet one. And cold. Rain billowed in sheets across the land. Papers mildewed. People sickened.

In Dublin castle, Sir Henry Sidney had a new woe to add to his other afflictions. A disease known as the Irish ague was affecting numbers of the English troops in their various garrisons around the island. As usual, too little money had been allocated and there were not enough men to begin to keep peace in turbulent Erin, much less to extend her majesty's dominion—and the soldiers who were there were being decimated by the illness.

The Irish themselves, however, whether Gael or Norman, seemed immune. Sidney, in uncharacteristically peevish humor, commented to an aide, "Men who have been in hell long enough get acclimated to it."

The hardy Irish, used to being outside in all weathers, might not sicken easily, but as their land became a sea of mud and flooding rivers much normal activity was curtailed. Forced to shelter beneath roofs, men became irritable. Talk in the fortresses and cottages and bruighens turned to politics, then poverty, then rebellion.

Reports reaching the lord deputy in Dublin castle were increasingly ominous. The Norman lords of Munster were on the verge of revolt against the Crown, and for once it looked as if some of the Gaelic chieftains might stand with them, both united in outrage against an authority attempting to take their land from them.

Sidney was deeply concerned by the threat in the south, but he remained committed to the policy that had been his from the beginning. He was convinced the plantation of colonies of English loyalists in Ireland was the surest way of making Ireland pay the exorbitant costs of supporting an English government on her soil. Further, he believed that the appointment of presidencies for both Munster and Connaught would take the last remnants of power out of the hands of the old landowners and help to avoid the constant rebellion that seemed forever simmering in the north, in the ancient kingdom of Ulster.

Fertile Munster and wild Connaught must be freed from the grip of Gaelicized Norman and Catholic Gael and made English, through the introduction of sturdy Protestant farmers who could survive the cold, west Atlantic winter that dragged on and on.

Unable to leave his bed at Belclare, Dubhdara O Malley felt his
lungs filling with fluid. His physician worked over him tirelessly,
but it did no good; nothing did any good. His legs were useless
logs—"They would do me more good if we burned them on the
hearth to keep this chamber warm," Dubhdara managed to joke
with a show of his old humor—and he knew he was dying.

"Send for Grania," he ordered at last.

She came down the bay with all flags flying. Propping himself
on one elbow, Dubhdara could look through his window and watch
her coming. The glazing in that window was a luxury he had
imported for Mairgret long ago, but almost everything else in the
chamber had been provided by Grania's shipping trade, including
the food he ate and the luxurious covers piled atop his body in a
futile effort to keep him warm and alive.

When Grania strode into the bedchamber and saw the wasted
figure of her father, she did not allow herself to flinch. The Black
Oak was felled, but she would not punish him with pity.

"You have a son I have not yet seen," Dubhdara told her.

"I have been busy. But I brought him with me; I take him
everywhere." She had the child carried into the bedchamber and
held him down so his grandfather could study the plump little
face.

Tibbot cooed and gurgled; he drooled onto the bedcovers. When
his eyes met those of Dubhdara the two looked for a long time at
each other across a chasm of years. A flight of yesterdays was
trapped in the O Malley's wrinkles; a promise of tomorrows dimpled Tibbot's cheeks.

"He is a strong boy," Dubhdara said at last, pleased. Then the
ache in his lungs clawed at him and he turned his face aside to
cough.

An attendant whispered to Grania, "The O Malley's son Donal
is outside, wanting to see him before . . ."

"I am with my father now," Grania interrupted in a cold voice.
"This is a small room; there is space for only one of us at a time.
Tell him he is welcome to come in when I have finished."

Dubhdara looked back at her. "You sound angry," he said. "You
always sound angry when you are with me. I don't know why."
He coughed again, and the physician leaned over him, but
Dubhdara waved the man aside with a weak gesture. "My little
girl," he said. "My little girl." He seemed to drift into sleep, and
Grania started to leave him to rest for a while, but then he spoke

in a stronger voice, "Why are you keeping my son away from me? I want my son now. . . ."

"*You have always had your son,*" she told her father through clenched teeth.

She stalked from the chamber, brushing past the waiting figure of Donal O Malley as if he did not exist.

The surface of Clew bay resembled hammered lead. A lonely wind wailed over the numerous small islands freckling its eastern shore. Grania went to the very edge of the water and stared down at it, ignoring the bitter cold that seeped even through her woolen cloak.

A tiny green crab floated dead in the clear water where land and sea met. Grania watched as an equally tiny fish darted in to nibble on the crab, then brisked away with renewed strength.

The tide came in, the tide went out.

Movement caught her eye, and she looked out across the bay to see a curragh approaching with its sail set, driven by the wind from the ocean. The boat skimmed over the water. As it neared the shore its solitary occupant stood up to lower his sail, and dark though the day was, his posture and the color of his hair were unmistakable.

Grania plunged up to her hips in the icy water to seize the line he threw her and help Tigernan beach his boat.

He vaulted overboard on the side opposite her, and together the two of them pulled the curragh out of the sea and secured it on shore. Several retainers from Belclare saw and came running to help, to turn the boat over to drain it, and carry its contents, a sea chest containing all of one man's belongings, up to the fortress for safekeeping. With one accord, the tall woman and the red-haired man walked a little distance away together before either of them spoke.

"After the way you deserted me I never expected to see you again," Grania said in a guarded voice.

"I found better fish at Curraun than Clare," he replied, with equal care.

They walked farther, climbing the hill toward Belclare. Boats and nets and the refuse of generations of sea trade littered the muddy slope. The grating voice of a male corncrake sounded from the damp herbage of a low-lying field nearby.

"Birds should all go south in such weather as this," Grania commented.

"Some birds don't know where their best interest lie," Tigernan said.

She turned abruptly and faced him. "Why did you come?"

He did not meet her eyes. "I heard Dubhdara is dying. I owe him honor; he gave me my first position on a real ship."

"And you've thrown it away to go back to a small curragh and one fishing net."

"I heard you threw away Richard Burke."

Grania's lips twitched with a suppressed smile. "We didn't suit each other. I did him a kindness."

Tigernan gave her an appraising look. "You've taken some weathering since I saw you last. How many men would you suit, now?"

She laughed. "Consider yourself, Tigernan. I haven't seen women standing in line to stroke your mustache."

He shrugged one shoulder. "My keel is still sound, and there's no dry rot in me."

"Nor in me!" Grania burst out.

There was a surprisingly uncomfortable silence between them, as if both felt the conversation was leading into dangerous waters. They turned and walked a few steps more, shoulder to shoulder. Then Tigernan asked, with a jerk of his head toward the stone tower of Belclare, "Is it true he's dying?"

"It is."

"And there is no tanist?"

"No."

"What of Donal of the Pipes, from Cathair na Mart?"

"He is nothing and no one," Grania said with conviction. "And I have let it be known that if he is given rank he does not deserve, I will withdraw my support from the clan."

Tigernan whistled. "You are a vindictive woman. What do you care if Dubhdara had women aside from your mother? Every chieftain does it."

"I don't care at all," Grania told him. "He could have bedded a thousand and my blessing to him, if he had enjoyment from them."

"Then why do you raise a shield against your own half brother?"

She started to answer him but found no words to convey her thoughts. She hesitated, cleared her throat, tried again. "Donal is not aggressive enough to be chief of the clan. He's ideally shaped for what he is, a man who loves his comforts and plays his music and goes under a roof when there's a storm. My daughter Margaret is the same; whatever makes an O Malley has skipped over her."

"Who will you support for chieftain, then, when Dubhdara is dead?" Tigernan asked.

When Dubhdara is dead. Just a few words to describe an event long expected, but even as they were spoken Grania saw a figure emerging from the distant gates of Belclare. She watched with the chill of foreknowledge as her half brother, carrying his beloved bagpipes slung from his shoulder, climbed a rise near the fortress and turned to face across Umhall.

Donal stood immobile with bowed head for the amount of time it took to draw three deep breaths. Then he put the blowpipe to his lips and began the dirge for a dead chieftain.

As the pipes wailed, every O Malley within earshot of their uncanny carrying power signed the cross on his bosom and prayed for the departed soul of Owen Dubhdara. The Black Oak.

Grania turned back to Tigernan. "In answer to your question," she said in a tight voice, "I will support no one to succeed my father. He was the last of his kind."

Then, to the surprise and horror of them both, she began to cry.

part four

---

philip

20

Grania did not cry as another woman might, weeping prettily and dabbing at her face with a square of perfumed cambric. Her tears broke free in great gulping whoops of pain, twisting her face into a grimace and convulsing her body. She could neither speak nor catch her breath. She could only stare helplessly at Tigernan as her hands clawed the air.

Parentless, parentless. The chains that bound her to her history forever broken. Step to the head of the line, Grania Mhaol; it will be your turn next. And a great bleeding wound inside herself where nothing could ever be fixed; the words that might have helped and healed could never be said now. *No! No! No!*

In one stride Tigernan had his arms around her. His calloused hand cradled the back of her skull as it had done once before, and he pressed her face into his shoulder, hiding her agony from the world. He rested his chin on the top of her head, gazing beyond her with unseeing eyes as he rocked gently back and forth, embracing the woman, murmuring to her. Letting her cry.

She could not have said just why she wept. For Dubhdara . . . Huw . . . her children . . . herself. So many reasons. The tears flowed from many sources, and she could no more stop them than will her heart to stop. It was like being in labor, her body fighting with all its strength to expel something.

She was not, for a time, aware that Tigernan held her. She never felt his lips brush her hair, gently, gently.

When at last her storm subsided, Grania was exhausted. Then she felt Tigernan's arms holding her up and was grateful. Without him, she could not have stood.

"I don't know what came over me," she said in a strangled voice. Her nose was running. Her eyes were streaming, but at least she could breathe normally again.

"It's all right. It's all right."

She pushed free of Tigernan's arms, and he let her go. She wanted to depend on her own legs, her own strength. She wanted him to see her stand erect and square her shoulders proudly . . . but then the hiccups caught up with her and her puffy, reddened eyes opened wide at the sudden sound she made.

Before she could recognize the expression on his face, Tigernan disguised it with a laugh.

"Oh, don't . . ." Grania pleaded as she hiccuped again, but she was laughing too, on the verge of hysteria, making everything worse. Tears and laughter choking together and Tigernan holding out his arms once more and her going back into them gladly because there was no place left to go.

He stood tall and strong and held her with his eyes closed like those of a man in prayer. The expression on his face was exalted.

When they separated at last, however, she would not look at him. She was dreadfully embarrassed. "I have to get to the castle," she managed to say, pressing one hand against her aching diaphragm. "Dubhdara . . ."

"I'll go with you," Tigernan told her.

"Will you?" She still did not look at him.

"I will." He spoke the words as a vow.

In a brief space of time, Tigernan had received more than he ever hoped for. He was a man who had learned early in life to be content with small pleasures, for his existence had promised him no large ones. A good meal, a warm fire, the company of friends. These were Tigernan's treasures.

Now he added to them the moment when Gráinne Ni Mháille had wept in his arms. That much of her he had; he doubted any other man had ever possessed it.

A magnificent Celtic cross was carved for the O Malley's tomb, and the chieftain of Umhall was buried with great ceremony. From as far away as Tyrconnell other chieftains came to pay him honor.

And as far away as Dublin castle the news of his death was received with satisfaction. "The O Malley made little trouble for us, but his failure to submit set a bad example," the lord deputy reported to the Queen's Council. "Now that he is dead we must finish eliminating the power of Irish law in Connaught so another strong man is not elected to replace him. The priests . . . yes, the priests may hold the answer. The Roman clergy is still very influential in Connaught; they must be persuaded—bribed or coerced or forced—to speak out against the Irish lawyers. What are they called again? Ah, yes, brehons. . . . The priests must denounce the brehons as remnants of paganism and encourage the people to turn away from them."

The lord deputy had reason to think this could be done. He had reports on his desk showing that many of the Catholic clergy in Ireland had already formed the habit of obeying English authority, either for their own protection or to safeguard Church property for a little while longer.

Calvagh of Bregia did as he was told. The people of Umhall heard him speak slightingly, then scathingly, of the old Brehon law, using Grania's irregular marriage to Richard Burke as an example of the faults inherent in the system. "A woman should not be allowed to take a husband on a temporary basis," he cried from his pulpit. "This is a purely pagan custom and abhorrent in the eyes of God! If we wish to keep the lantern of true faith burning strongly against the heresies of the Protestants, we must cling to the teachings of the Church as never before. The Pope will be our salvation—our Catholic friends in lands such as Spain will not let us be overrun—but we must demonstrate our piety in order to earn their support. Turn your backs on the brehons, turn your backs on these pathetic remnants of heathenism and embrace the true faith!"

Within a year, it became obvious the O Malley brehons would not be able to gather enough support to hold a new election fo fill the chieftainship. The English had unintentionally made Grania the only remaining leader of her people, a responsibility she felt in every bone of her body. She would never bear the title, only the weight, but she did her best. She did not know how to do less.

Under her watchful eye, strongholds were built ringing Clew bay and its approaches. The new stone tower house of Kildawnet was given into the keeping of the Devil's Hook, who mounted his own guards on its battlements and held Achill secure.

Ruari Oge was in command on Clare island. Grania spent less and less time there; when she was not at sea, she made Rockfleet her principal residence.

"There are so many memories on Cliara," she explained to Evleen. "And I don't want to be trapped by them, thinking sad thoughts. I have too much to do to spend my time that way."

"Won't you need me with you at Rockfleet?"

"I need you to be with Ruari Oge," Grania said. The two women exchanged a glance of mutual understanding. "You and Ruari are family to me, closer than clansmen. I made a promise to myself that I would not separate you again, and I intend to keep that promise."

"You know he will not live too much longer," Evleen said, as a statement of fact, not a question.

"I sensed it."

"Yet you entrust him with Clare island?"

"So that he will *live* until he dies," Grania answered, "with work to do that is important. I give him what I hope for myself."

Tigernan accompanied her to Rockfleet. Tigernan accompanied her everywhere. He captained her flagship; he was never so far away she could not call him by raising her voice. Neither of them mentioned the day she cried, and he told no one of it. Their relationship picked up where it had left off, with Tigernan as her captain and Grania the star that guided him. He attempted no intimacies, and it never occurred to her that he might.

Only when he was certain she was paying him no attention did Tigernan dare to look at Grania as a woman. Sometimes, when he was alone, he remembered the way she had felt in his arms.

Richard Burke had settled into quarters at Burrishoole, and from time to time he paid a formal visit to Grania and Rockfleet. He did not want her to think he considered the connection between them irrevocably broken, but neither did he want to challenge her power. Upon his arrival, she always welcomed him exactly as a Gaelic chieftain welcomed any guest, with food and drink and a cushioned couch to recline upon during the meal, with fodder for his horses and ale for his men-at-arms.

Tigernan never left the hall when Burke visited, nor did Grania dismiss him during those times. He stationed himself at the edge of Iron Richard's vision and stood with folded arms, watching.

Richard Burke invariably left Rockfleet in a state of frustration. His reputation as a man of bad temper grew; in time he came to be known as plundering, warlike, rebellious . . . but always as Gráinne Ni Mháille's husband, for he never admitted to being anything else.

The MacWilliam Iochtar was becoming more open in his sympathies with the English. "Elizabeth will soon have all of Ireland in her farthingale," some said. Ruari Oge made a journey to Tyrconnell to see his kinsmen once more—once more before he died, though that was never mentioned—and reported back to Grania that even the north, since the death of Shane O Neill, seemed relatively resigned to Tudor rule. "The family trees of the Gaelic clans are intertwined like brambles that have never been pruned," Ruari said, "and O Neill has some living kinsmen who do not even bear his name but still support his cause against the Tudor woman. Others, however, in Tyrone, are coming to various accommodations with the English, making friends with the sasanach in order to preserve a bit of land to farm, or a bruighen where a man can have a tankard of ale with his friends and sing a song or two. Sir Henry Sidney himself, it seems, has taken a nephew of Shane O Neill's back to London with him to convert him into a tame ape on an English chain, a savage to be displayed in royal courts. And his family let him go."

"What would you have done, Ruari?" Grania asked.

"Once I could have answered you easily," the old pirate told her. "Now—I cannot. Ireland is chaos. There are no unshakable loyalties left to count upon—except perhaps those you hold, Grania. It seems to be a matter of we must each save ourselves, and perhaps clan O Neill is right in trying to make a strategic connection with the she-king and her lord deputy. Who can know?"

"I cannot quite see you allowing yourself to be paraded through the Tudor woman's court like an ape on a chain," Grania commented with some amusement.

"Not I, but I am thrice-blessed," Ruari told her. "I have my Evleen, I follow your banner, and I will be dead and out of it before things get any worse."

"Dead, but not out of it," Evleen said softly, putting her hand over his.

"What does that mean?"

The little woman gave her husband a look both sorrowful and proud. "Your spirit will never leave Ireland," she said to him. "At least, not for very long."

Tigernan, sitting with them in front of the hearth in the tower house on Clare island, made the sign of the cross on his breast, though he could never have explained why.

Sidney had, indeed, taken young Hugh O Neill to England, where the stocky, handsome boy with his shock of red-gold hair was as much a contradiction to the expectations of the English as

Shane O Neill had been before him. The Irish were always pictured as uncouth barbarians to be exterminated like vermin if they showed any refusal to become obedient and docile to their conquerors. Terrible tales were told of them, and the English believed those stories. Yet Shane O Neill had arrived in London with suits of velvet and an education equipping him to correspond personally with the King of France. And young Hugh, trained as a Gaelic nobleman, had grown up in an atmosphere of raid and counterraid, conspiracy and violence, but also in a country where learning was prized and every petty Gaelic chieftain had his historians and poets and even many of the common folk were literate.

While Gráinne Ni Mháille was attempting to consolidate her strength in the west of Ireland against an unknown queen in a distant land, the boy Hugh O Neill was observing the English at close range and drawing his own conclusions about the best way to deal with them.

His background, his experiences, and his own brilliant mind would combine to give Hugh O Neill a far-reaching understanding of the chaotic Irish situation and its potential, an understanding the more provincial Gaelic chieftains would never achieve. But Grania, who had sailed into foreign ports and had her own experience of the world, was less than naive herself, and as Hugh O Neill was making preparations to deal with the English in his own way, Grania was similarly laying plans.

Some of them went against her grain. But she had spent too many years at sea to be other than pragmatic; English power in Ireland was a fact and would remain so. She had staked her claim to Clew bay and meant to hold it for herself and her posterity, and that could well mean she would someday need friends among the sasanach.

The first time she said such a thing to Tigernan, he was shocked. "You can't make alliances with heretics!"

"I already have certain alliances with Englishmen," Grania reminded him. "From time to time I have shipped cargo for Thomas, Duke of Ormond—you captained the last such shipment yourself."

"Black Tom engages in trade with Spain that the English consider illegal but we do not," Tigernan said. "If you did not haul his goods for him, some other Irish shipowner would."

"Perhaps. Perhaps not. I went to considerable trouble to arrange that partnership, and it is an alliance I mean to keep in good repair.

Clan O Neill may have a voice in the Tudor woman's court, but someday so shall I. Ormond is well liked there."

"You play a treacherous game," Tigernan warned her.

"I know," she said with a laugh. "That's what makes it interesting."

England tightened her stranglehold on Irish ports, endeavoring to ensure that no valuable cargoes set sail for anywhere but England herself. Elizabeth's economy was perpetually hard pressed, a gigantic maw into which all Erin's resources must be poured. Individuals throughout Ireland reached out individual, desperate hands, seeking aid abroad, but such efforts were fragmented and lacking in leadership. Each person saw the situation increasingly in terms of his own survival . . . and Tudor policy constantly worked to undermine any efforts at unity among the Irish clans.

To survive, Grania engaged more and more in outright piracy.

"I walk on the surface of a shifting bog," she told Tigernan. "I have to grab for whatever I can that is solid."

Yet she loved bogland. The rich green blanket bog that rippled across Ireland, a shimmering green-and-gold sea in the springtime, flowered with white cotton sedge in the summer, flaming red and russet as the daylight dwindled toward winter. Unstable, quivering underfoot, challenging, the bog was as much a part of Ireland as the political landscape, or the surrounding sea. It could furnish peat to warm a million Irish; it could hide Bronze Age treasures lost for millennia; the bog lived, like Ireland, like Grania.

But she loved Clew bay more. And her son, the son she got to keep, she loved most of all. The son she must protect.

Once, when the wind howled beyond the tower walls, she awoke to find herself drenched in cold sweat.

"Dar Dia, that nightmare again," she moaned, cradling her body with her arms and trying to stop shaking.

She threw aside the covers and went to stare out the chamber's narrow loophole of a window at the clouded sky beyond. Through gray veils a few stars glinted over the bay. Two of them, close together, might almost be eyes watching Grania . . . eyes straight from her nightmare, peering at her with deadly intent and an almost unnatural hatred from beneath a monk's hood.

In the morning she sought out Evleen, whom she found in one of the stone outbuildings, grinding grain on an old-fashioned stone quern.

"You understand dreams," Grania said. "I have had nightmares of an enemy who watches me."

"You think too much about the English she-king," Evleen said without looking up. "You think she pays specific attention to you, which I doubt. She probably doesn't even know we exist."

"She sends men to spy on me; she knows I exist, all right," Grania replied, stung by the inference that she was of little importance. "But it isn't her eyes I see. I've never met her, and I have no idea what her eyes look like. This dream shows me the face of someone who hates me personally. Elizabeth and I are adversaries, but the eyes in my dream are those of a true enemy."

Evleen looked up. "Someone you know?"

"Someone who would enjoy killing me. He almost killed my son. What I saw in his face was a hatred for the Irish like the hatred of a terrier for a rat. It chilled my marrow, Evleen, and though I have never seen him again I keep dreaming of him."

"Then he is thinking of you," Evleen told her regretfully. "Beware," she added, whispering in a voice that slithered around the stone walls, echoing and echoing.

Grania stiffened. "I won't let him frighten me! I won't let anyone frighten me! Here, Evleen, move over and let me help you grind the grain."

Grinding grain by hand in a quern was one of the lowliest of household tasks; in noble families it had formerly been the job of a bondwoman. But by Grania's decree, whoever could turn his hand to a job must do it; she believed like every good seaman that a person must be able to perform as many tasks as possible. So she took her place across the stone quern from Evleen, and together the two women ground oats into meal.

The quern was very old; Evleen had brought it with her, a legacy from her mother's mother, she said. Home grinding of grain was outlawed in many parts of Ireland now; the sasanach insisted farmers bring their grain to English mills and have it ground for a fee.

On Clew bay, Grania's people ground their own.

The quern was rough stone, two pieces fitted together with an opening in the center of the upper stone, through which the grain could be poured. Handles allowed one or two people to push the grindstone back and forth, and the flour thus produced flowed out at the edges onto clean cloths. It was a tiresome task, one that clogged the throat with fine particles and made the nose itch unbearably, but Grania did not mind. The oats they were grinding this day would be served to Tibbot in a meal tomorrow; she was producing the food that would build her son.

It was not always that easy to feel in control anymore . . . not when the nightmares came. . . .

On trading missions where she anticipated no danger, Grania took Tibbot with her in her galley. But simple trading missions were becoming rarer and more hazardous. Every change of the moon saw more English ships off the west coast, often sailing openly through O Malley waters without deigning to stop and pay the traditional licensing fee. More than once Grania's vessels were hailed, boarded, and searched. She learned how to become even more evasive.

She ceased taking Tibbot with her.

She did not like leaving him behind in a stronghold without a commander, either, and so eventually—with great regret—she made arrangements for him to spend some time with a petty chieftain at Castleaffy near Burrishoole, and later with Miles MacEvilly in his richly appointed stronghold at Kinturk. Both chieftains were allies whose ties to Grania were further strengthened by having her son in their care.

Donal an Chogaidh would have understood.

But Grania never considered these visitations as fosterages, though the chieftains involved bragged later of having fostered her son. She relinquished not one moment of Tibbot, not one hair of his head.

In August she seized and boarded a galleon off Inishkea South and found it carrying a cargo of Catholic monks, supposedly bound for an isolated island monastery farther south. The men in their brown robes made Grania nervous.

"Have each one of them come in front of me with his hood thrown back," she ordered the ship's captain, who was protesting angrily that this was nothing more than a passenger vessel and he had no loot for pirates.

She stalked along the row of friars, peering into every face. They stared back at her. Most of them were bland of visage and mild of eye, the gentle ascetics who had always been drawn to the lonely worship of God in the lonely places of the earth. Grania saw no familiar, furious glare. Only one of the group seemed out of place, a lean man with a weathered complexion and features more Saxon than Gaelic. Grania stared at him so hard she roused something reciprocal in the monk and saw his jaw muscles clench.

"Are you sasanach?" she demanded.

His mouth gaped open. "I am not! I come from a good Gaelic family where decent women do not wear trews and steal cargoes!"

She almost slapped his face, but then she caught herself. He had been no more than candid, and Grania had already learned that giving way to such impulses could buy more trouble than one could afford. She had angered too many men; it was time to think first and act later, slower, more deliberately.

When the captain's words were proved true and there was no salable merchandise found in his hold, Grania released the ship to go on to its destination.

When they returned from that expedition, Grania sent Tigernan to escort Tibbot to her. They would have some weeks together before she put to sea once more, and she meant to make the most of that time by checking on her son's progress in learning his letters and by taking him rowing on the bay. She had had a new little coracle made, a lovely thing of wood and canvas, light and small enough for a seven-year-old boy to maneuver under his mother's watchful eye.

✠

On the strand road, Tigernan's party encountered a pair of traveling friars. Though he did not know the reason for Grania's intense scrutiny of the monks aboard the galleon recently, instinct told Tigernan that she must have a good reason—one she would never share with a subordinate, knowing her. So as a matter of routine he challenged the pair and was instantly alerted by their reaction. When they learned they were facing Gráinne Ni Mháille's men they glanced at one another fearfully and cleared their throats too many times.

"Search them," Tigernan ordered.

The reports intended for the lord deputy in Dublin were contained in a tightly rolled scroll bearing the seal of the abbot of Murrisk. Tigernan squatted in the road and slit the seal with his shortsword.

He did not read well; he had picked up only a few words by stealing glances at Grania's books over the years. But he had the Gaelic passion for learning which could infect even a fisherman's son, and he was able to recognize Grania's name again and again on the elegantly scribed pages. He turned angrily to the two men in clerical garb. "What are all these references to Gráinne Ni Mháille? Why is so much information about her being sent to the English within the Pale at Dublin?"

He got no answers, so he turned around and marched the pair back to Grania at sword's point.

By lamplight, Grania slowly turned the pages, reading with an increasingly somber expression. Tigernan waited nearby, shifting from foot to foot.

The papers contained extensive reports on the size and success of her fishing fleet, her cargo vessels, and her pirate ventures, as well as an accurate assessment of the number of men-at-arms she could command. And Calvagh's signature was written large across the bottom, a bold dash of black ink.

At last she sighed and pushed the pages away from her. "I've known this in my bowels for months. Maybe for years," she said wearily.

"Known what?"

"That we were being spied upon. I've learned to keep as much to myself as possible and avoid revealing any more than I had to. I don't even go to confession anymore, though there are other reasons for that as well—though I know you disapprove, Tigernan. Don't frown at me like that.

"But these dispatches prove my worst suspicions were well founded. There is a spy in Umhall at its very heart. A man made sacrosanct by his profession. And do you see this name here? Richard Bingham? He is some sort of English sea captain who is obviously involved in this. Very likely we have passed him and his ship a dozen times. Out there . . ." She waved toward the bay. "Watching."

She grew very quiet; very tense. "Watching," she repeated softly, remembering the eyes.

"Spies for the English she-king!" Tigernan said, doubling one fist and pounding it against his open palm.

"Only in the broadest sense," Grania told him. "Elizabeth of clan Tudor probably never reads reports like these; she has plenty of underlings to take care of such matters. Unlike Gráinne Ni Mháille, who must deal with everything herself," she added with a touch of bitterness. "No, Tigernan, these papers were not directed to Elizabeth but to her lord deputy. And even more than he, I think I must beware of this Bingham—and Calvagh, of course. Their enmity is more personal.

"Listen to me, Tigernan. Say nothing of this to anyone. I don't care where you send them, but get those two men from the abbey onto a ship and dispatch them as far away from Umhall as possible. The abbot's reports will not reach Dublin, and I don't want his agents turning up there, either."

"What of Calvagh? Aren't you going to confront him with this?"

"I want to go over there today and bash his head in," Grania said in a voice of deceptive calm. "But I won't. It is better if he never knows I have learned his game. We will just intercept his messengers from now on. That way calls less attention to ourselves."

Tigernan was seething with outrage. "I don't understand how a man of God can be involved in something like this."

"The abbot may think he's justified. Men usually believe themselves justified in whatever they do, haven't you noticed? Very few set out to be evil for evil's sake."

"How can you defend him?"

"I'm not defending him. But I've learned this much, Tigernan: there are more views of life than mine, and the ones I think most wrong are sometimes the very ones I am eventually forced to adopt myself. Making that discovery has been a sobering experience for me. I'm not as quick to judge others as I used to be; I've had to trim my sails to a new wind too many times."

Tigernan was outraged by the abbot's treachery; it flew in the face of everything he held purest and most sacred. The tug and pull of the various factions struggling for control of Ireland seemed to be introducing chaos even into man's relations with God. Grania was an example, letting her faith slip through her fingers, going to church no more.

At least she still had enough reverence to keep her from attacking an abbot, Tigernan thought. That was good.

But the abbot represented a terrible danger to her. And that was bad. He would not have her doom her immortal soul by injuring a man of the cloth, however foul that man might be, yet it seemed clear to him Calvagh must be more than circumvented. He must be stopped forever.

Tigernan saw things both clearly and simply; he came from a clear and simple world of rock, sky, sea, and fish. And the hard sacrifices people make to survive.

The next day found Tigernan visiting the Augustinian abbey. From its battlemented walls—and why should a friary require battlements? Tigernan wondered for the first time—men could easily spy on Belclare and the eastern reaches of the bay. Yet the abbey was as beautiful as God's house should be; it boasted a famous window with interlacing bar tracery above the main altar and housed the Black Bell of St. Patrick. Consecrated ground.

Sanctuary for Grania's enemy.

Tigernan felt as if he were being torn in two.

He had been born to a poverty so extreme he had not even known he was poor, for everyone on Inishbofin lived the same. Their tiny chapel had been their mutual wealth, its few treasures the only beauty they claimed. God's love had been the one bulwark the islanders had against the wind and the sea; it was his beneficence that put fish in their nets and wrested a few vegetables from their barren soil.

No matter what else changed in his life, Tigernan had thought his faith unshakable—until Calvagh of Murrisk betrayed Gráinne Ni Mháille.

And there was something, he, Tigernan, could do about it—if he was brave enough, and careless enough of his own soul.

He made several visits to the abbey until he had learned exactly when what entrances were open and which passageways led where. As a man noted for his piety, Tigernan was not questioned when he knelt at odd hours in the chapel, seemingly lost in prayer while he observed the routine of the Augustinian abbot.

Calvagh, he soon learned, was a man of fixed habits, performing the same duties at the same times every day, week, month.

At each dark of the moon, for example, Calvagh arranged for a small, almost unnoticeable door to be left unbarred, one located at the rear of the abbey close to the abbot's private apartments. And Tigernan observed that on certain occasions a slender young boy approached that door in the dark of the night and crept within, emerging several hours later carrying a small purse of coins.

Monster, Tigernan called Calvagh to himself. You deserve to die.

He sought out Evleen. "Do you have a potion for sleeping?"

Her eyes glittered. "You do not sleep well? A woman in your bed would cure that for you, Tigernan."

"I don't want it for me. I need enough to put twenty men to sleep and keep them asleep until well after cockcrow."

Evleen's eyes twinkled with fun. "What trick are you playing on your friends?"

"No trick," he told her. His face was set in grim lines; there was no innocent mischief there. "Something needs to be done for Grania's sake, and I don't want her to know about it. I don't want anyone to know about it. The blame is to be on my soul alone; all I want from you is a powerful sleeping potion."

She looked into his eyes with a sudden, fixed stare, and Tigernan had the disturbing impression she was looking all the way through them and into the brain behind. The sensation made him uncomfortable, but he stood his ground and let her do it. They worshiped different deities, he and Evleen, he thought, but they had Grania in common.

Besides, his own God might soon reject him forever.

Evleen nodded to herself, satisfied. "Be careful," was the only advice she gave him. She placed a little pot in his hands, a vessel so old and pitted it might have been fired clay or it might have been porous stone, water-hollowed by nature. Within it was a fine powder the color of ashes.

"In the wine," Evleen said.

That afternoon a solitary coracle left Clare island, departing from a tiny bay out of sight of the harbor or the tower house. Tigernan had been so busy among the ships earlier that every man had seen him at least once and would believe he had been there uninterruptedly.

The prevailing wind was kind, and Tigernan knew the currents of Cuan Mó as a tree knows its ground. His boat moved swiftly over the water, unnoticed among the flotilla of canoes and coracles and curraghs fishing the bay.

He beached on a deserted strand near the inlet where the abbey stood, and, wrapped from head to heel in a nondescript mantle of dark wool, made his way to his destination without attracting any attention. From a distance away he could hear the voices lifted in chanting within the walls of the abbey. The monks were at vespers. Without exception, at this hour everyone was preoccupied with prayer.

Tigernan made his way around the handsome tower built with O Malley money and slipped through the small wooden door he had noticed earlier. It was unbarred and unguarded, and he smiled to himself at the success of his reconnoitering. Still unobserved, he made his way to the kitchen and into the small buttery, where the evening's measure of wine had already been poured, waiting to quench the thirst of the good friars now singing like angels in the chapel.

It took but a moment to lace the wine with Evleen's sleeping potion, though he glanced over his shoulder anxiously when he thought he heard footsteps approaching. No one came in, however, and he finished his task with a sigh of relief. Every man who drank that wine would sleep well past cockcrow next morning.

And one would sleep longer than that.

When the wine had been drugged, Tigernan tiptoed back and barred the door by which he had gained admittance. Let the lad come to his rendezvous; let him steal away in disappointment. Or perhaps in joy. Perhaps he only suffered Calvagh in order to provide a little extra money at home. Such arrangements were not unheard of, though as long as Grania's ships had returned laden with goods such measures had not been necessary in Umhall, even among the poorest families. Times were growing harder, though, even here.

He heard the sounds of feet in the stone passageway. Tigernan raced for the stair that led down to the cellars, where he meant to conceal himself until everyone above was asleep.

How easily it had been accomplished so far! He could have killed them all if he had chosen; poisoned their wine instead of merely putting a sleeping drug in it. But Tigernan could not let himself believe there were other men as guilty as Calvagh, and he meant no harm to innocent friars. It was only the abbot he wanted.

21

The cellars were cool, but Tigernan was sweating by the time he heard the sounds of the abbey above him cease. Only a porter at the main entrance would be left awake, and he too had surely drunk his measure of evening wine; he would be nodding over his post before long.

Tigernan waited until some inner instinct assured him, then he slipped from his hiding place and made his way up the wooden ladder to the main floor of the abbey.

The building was beautiful. There were vaulted ceilings even in passageways where simpler construction would have been sufficient, and the most inconspicuous pier was carved by master stonemasons. Clan O Malley had spared no expense in furnishing a fine structure for the Augustinians. Flowing curvilinear carving bespoke the Gael in chapel and cloister as if defying the spare, stripped religion of the Protesters.

But there was a Protester here, Tigernan reminded himself. If not in name at least in sympathies, a man who had chosen to side with Tudor against O Malley. He had to keep reminding himself to keep his anger at fever pitch, for the deed he had come to do terrified him.

Tonight he would lose his immortal soul. Of that he was certain. More courage was required of him tonight than Tigernan had ever known he possessed, and he summoned it with desperate urgency, in Grania's name.

He would not let them crush her.

Outside the door of the abbot's private chamber he hesitated. There was still time to go back.

He did not know if God or the devil whispered that suggestion in his ears.

Grania had spoken of justification. A simple fisherman from Inishbofin might not be familiar with that term, but Tigernan had sailed with Grania a long time, and some of her education had rubbed off on him. He knew what justification was. Perhaps he was using it this night to excuse himself from doing the devil's work.

He was a humble man; he did not dare hope he was doing God's work in rooting out an evil within God's own house.

He put his shoulder to the abbot's door, and the heavy oak panel gave, swinging inward on its iron hinges.

Calvagh of Bregia liked comfort, and comfort did not include squeaking hinges. The iron was well rubbed with grease; it did not betray Tigernan.

The interior of the room was not completely dark. A candle guttered in its own remains in a silver candleholder near the bed, clearly revealing the occupant of the chamber. Calvagh slept with his back toward the door. For some reason Tigernan had imagined him lying on his back with his hands folded in eternal prayer, like a tomb effigy, but the abbot slept curled in a ball like any other man on a chilly night. An embroidered silk coverlet was uppermost on his bed, concealing several layers of warm woolen bedrobes.

Calvagh was very comfortable.

Two long strides were sufficient to carry Tigernan across the room. From beneath his cloak he took the shortsword—a quieter, surer weapon than any handgun. Its handle and blade were purely Gaelic, engraved with Gaelic designs. Nothing foreign polluted the weapon, Tigernan thought with satisfaction. Like Grania, it was all Irish.

Calvagh snorted in his sleep and half rolled, revealing his face. The likeness to a wolf was more marked when he slept, with gravity pulling skin and flesh down from the sharp features. Some pleasant dream flitted through his drugged brain, and he smiled, briefly.

Tigernan thought it a gloating smile, and it freed his hand.

The sword rose and fell, once. The thrust was expertly made; the abbot died soundlessly in his bed.

Tigernan turned away only to have his legs collapse under him with no warning at all. He fell to the floor as if he had been clubbed.

He did not know how long he crouched there, shivering uncontrollably like a man with the ague. He was nauseated and terrified. With one swordstroke he had cut himself off from God. He was doomed. Damned. The consequences of his deed, which he had mentally held in partial abeyance until this moment, washed over him with their full horror.

This was not a death rendered in battle—Tigernan never doubted that God understood about battle, since He allowed so much of it.

This was murder. The murder of an anointed man.

Tigernan doubled his fists and beat them against his forehead.

Time passed. Blood from Calvagh's wound ran down his out-thrown arm and dripped from his fingertips onto the flagstones. The dead body spasmed once, knees rising, then lay still.

The blood splashed on the floor like pellets of lead.

Afterward, Tigernan could never remember getting up or methodically looting the chamber so that it would appear the murder was the result of a burglary. He took all of Calvagh's treasures and wrapped them in his cloak, and for good measure he stole some silver cups from the refectory on his way out, leaving the rear door ajar as an explanation of his entrance. There were always thieves; even a friary could be victimized by other than the Tudor queen's agents.

He did not remember running with pounding heart through the night, feeling the stars watching him like the eyes of God as he hugged the loot to his breast. He did not remember selecting a large stone to weight his cloak, or tying the whole parcel together with a length of rope, or dropping it into deep water when he was well out in the bay again.

Ever afterward, in his mind, it was as if he thrust his sword into the sleeping throat of the abbot of Murrisk and then instantly turned aside to put his foot into the shallows of Cliara, and pull his boat ashore behind him as a red dawn flamed in the east.

The sky was like blood, and Tigernan bowed his head, interpreting it as God's sign.

In truth, it signaled three days of unrelenting rain that kept Grania's fleet in the harbor while Tigernan frantically made himself conspicuous.

When the weather eased they carried a fine cargo of dried beef and leathers to waiting customers in several ports, then returned to Umhall in time to hear, with horror, of the desecration of the Augustinian abbey. Tigernan was loud in his protests against the foul deed—so loud that Grania gave him a speculative glance, once or twice, though she said nothing.

"At least that takes care of your problem," he told her at last when the excitement had died down. "Now all you have to do is use your influence to see that a more . . . ah . . . well-disposed abbot is installed, someone who can be trusted to support the Irish and the true faith against all foreign influences."

"I think I can arrange it," Grania replied. "But . . ."

"But what?"

She narrowed her eyes. "Calvagh had reasons for doing what he did. Murrisk was almost the last abbey on these shores to be left unconfiscated by the so-called new state religion. Now that he is gone . . ."

She left the thought hanging in the air, and Tigernan stared at it, seeing for the first time ramifications he had never considered. Yet, like the martyrs, he had made a sacrifice, and once having made it he chose to remain committed with his whole soul. If he was still in possession of his soul.

✠

A new abbot was indeed installed as keeper of St. Patrick's Black Bell, but no sooner was he in place than Protestant bishops throughout Ireland began complaining of the friary as a hotbed of revolt and rebellion, a Roman remnant in need of seizing and cleansing. By the end of 1574, Murrisk abbey was offically suppressed, and the saint's Black Bell was gone.

But the entire decade was one of such turmoil throughout Ireland that the loss of one more Catholic abbey was hardly noticed. Even on Clew bay, events forced change after change, whether Grania willed them or not. All she could do was adjust her sails to each change of the wind; plan, modify, defy, or accommodate in turn, as seemed expedient.

And her most trusted strategist was gone.

Ruari Oge had died abruptly while Grania was away at sea. Word had reached Clare that the Carmelite abbey there was "officially suppressed" like the Augustinians', and Ruari Oge, in anticipation of an English attempt to come ashore on the island and force the issue, had sailed to the mainland to bring back additional armed men to reinforce Grania's stronghold. As his vessel returned to Clare he noticed a sudden, savage pain in his leg but thought it just a recurrence of the old wound that had left him limping the last several years. But by the time they were entering the harbor the pain had centered in his groin and was agonizing.

He could not leave the boat under his own power. Men carried him on a plank, and Evleen was out of her cottage and running, already halfway to the beach to meet him before anyone went to take her word. The plank was laid on the white sand, and Ruari Oge saw his wife's face bending over him as mists swirled around her.

Fairy mist, he thought. The pain was terrible.

His hands scrabbled at his chest. Agony moved, like a white-hot finger.

One look at his face told Evleen. She pressed her mouth to his ear and called urgently, "Don't forget me! Watch for me!"

And then he was gone. But she thought he said something to her first; she thought he understood.

When Grania returned to Clare they told her, or rather, Evleen told her. None of the others wanted to; they passed the onerous task back and forth among them, finding countless reasons to refuse it. Ultimately Evleen came down to the harbor, again, and met Grania, again, and told her of death, again.

But this time it was Evleen's man who had died.

Wordlessly, Grania put her arms around the other woman.

"He should be entombed among his own people," Evleen said at last.

"We can build him a fine tomb right here," Grania replied. "This was his home."

"You don't understand about Ruari Oge," Evleen told her. "His home is with his people. He comes from a noble family; his bones should rest with theirs."

"We'll take him to Tyrconnell, then. And you . . ."

"I won't go with you."

Grania looked at the other woman in surprise. Evleen was suddenly old. Her hair had grown white while no one noticed; her mouth had collapsed over shrinking gums. "We can make the journey in easy stages," Grania assured her. "I still hold Doona; we can put in there and rest a day or two. And the body . . ." Delicacy prevented her from finishing. The body would be packed in salt. If the weather was cool, they just might reach Ruari's sept before his corpse totally surrendered to the fate of all temporary housing.

"What you will take to Tyrconnell is not important to me," Evleen told Grania. "I would prefer to wait here for you."

"But the funeral ceremonies, the mourning, the waking . . ."

Evleen shook her head. "I have done what mourning I had to do already; I have no desire to give over more days of my life to satisfy conventions that are not mine. I am of the old religion, Grania; we do not believe in death. And so we do not allow it to triumph over life and twist and torture the living. There is bread to be baked and clothes to be washed and lifework to be done here. You take Ruari Oge's body to his people; there are alliances in the north you need to strengthen anyway. I will be here when you get back."

On the cloudy morning they placed Ruari Oge's body in the prow of his galley, Evleen watched from the shore. She said nothing, she made no gesture, and no one spoke to her. She did not seem to be in the same world as the rest of them. Grania looked back at her as the fleet rode out on the tide and found Evleen's figure hard to see, though others standing nearby were clearly visible.

"She almost . . . shimmers," Grania commented aloud to Tigernan, who as usual stood near her.

"Why isn't she going to Tyrconnell? I don't understand. Two people as close as Evleen and Ruari Oge . . . I thought she would crawl into the tomb with him."

Grania was silent for a time before she answered. "Evleen told me that since she does not believe in death, she will not allow death to triumph over life," she said at last. "I think for her, Ruari Oge is not dead, will never be dead. Our funerals are meaningless to her. And perhaps she is right," she added, thinking of Huw.

Tigernan stared at the coastline slipping past them, thinking of his old friend Ruari and trying to imagine him as Evleen must think of him. Immortal?

Death must not be allowed to triumph over life.

But Calvagh's death was surely exacting a sort of triumph over Tigernan's life. He bowed beneath the secret weight of his crime. Without guessing the reason for it, Grania had noticed over the last years a grave, almost tragic dignity growing in the homely lines of his face. The melancholy becomes him, she thought, believing it to be aggravated now by grief for Ruari Oge.

Grania's galley sailed north up the coast, while O Malley and Burke musicians on board played Gaelic dirges with pipes and drum and bardic harp, to inform spectators on shore that this was a funeral cortege and not a war party. They were scarcely out of

Clew bay before they encountered the first ship flying an English flag, and Tigernan saw the way Grania clenched her hands at the sight of it. But they were not challenged.

I wonder if that is Richard Bingham's ship, Grania thought to herself.

The English lined the rail to watch the Irish fleet pass.

Grania stood in the prow of her flagship with her head high, defiant and proud.

Past Killala and Sligo they sailed, toward ancient Ulster and the land of Tyrconnell, headed for the port of Donegal. Unlike most of the port towns ringing Ireland, Donegal was entirely Gaelic in language, dress, and sympathies. The stronghold of the O Don-nells, it had put fishing fleets to sea for centuries, and the arrival of the English had done little to change its basic character. The air still smelled of salt and herring and the docks still swarmed with men in full-sleeved saffron tunics and shaggy hooded mantles, high-colored men with strong proud faces.

Runners were sent inland to inform Ruari Oge's sept of his death and the arrival of his corpse. Soon a large party of his clansmen appeared to accompany him to entombment in the monastery where so many of his family lay. Tigernan was impressed by the high rank of the mourners. Chieftains of major septs wept openly at news of Ruari's death.

"No one will mourn me like that when I die," Tigernan said to Grania.

"You're not going to die," she told him. "I won't allow it."

"Not ever?"

"Not until I'm ready to go myself."

The one-sided smile he gave her was sardonic. "Then you'd best never die, Grania—I don't think I'll ever be ready to face judgment."

His tone of voice was too serious for the light banter of the conversation. Something was troubling him and therefore troubling Grania as well. Only since he had come back to her did she realize how fully she relied upon him, how necessary his presence was to her. Not to take orders and give them, not to command or obey—just to be.

"If you have a problem, Tigernan, tell me and I'll try to fix it for you," she offered.

He shook his head. "It's already fixed. There's nothing anyone can do now—even you, Grania Mhaol."

And when Ruari Oge lay under a silken mantle before the high altar in the monastery of Donegal, Tigernan did not kneel with the others attending the Requiem Mass. He stood outside the chapel with his sword drawn. "I will be a guard of honor," he told Grania. "But out here, not in there."

The weather had been kind, and cold, but even salt could not preserve a body for very long. The mourners in the chapel held cloths over their faces for most of the service, and it was with a visible sigh of relief that his O Donnell kinsmen at last consigned the mortal remains of Grania's captain to his tomb. But the occasion was not ended; these were Gaels. The dead man must be remembered and remarked upon and enjoyed for a length of time commensurate with his stature, and, as the she-king of Clew bay, Grania was expected to remain as a guest of the clan chieftain until the obsequies were completed.

Hugh Dubh O Donnell ruled the northwestern corner of Ireland in the ancient style of a Gaelic prince, though that style had been somewhat diluted during the last few generations by an admixture of English and Continental customs. Still the dwindling number of bards could sing of his Tyrconnell stronghold:

> *A row of fragrant apple trees,*
> *An orchard in its pink-tip't bloom,*
> > *Between it and the hill.*
> *A forest tall of real leeks,*
> *Of onions and of carrots stood*
> > *Behind the house.*
> *Within, a generous household,*
> *A welcome from red, firm-fed men*
> > *Around the fire.*
> *Seven bead-strings and necklets seven*
> > *Round each man's neck,*
> *And the dispenser I behold,*
> > *His flesh-fork on his back.*

Black Hugh O Donnell could welcome guests with bacon and butter, and offer them fine hunting of red stag and wild boar. His territory had once been part of the old kingdom of Ulster and tributary to its kings, the Ui Neill of Tyrone. Isolated by natural barriers of mountain and bogland and water, Ulster had supported the Gaelic life-style long after it began to collapse elsewhere in Ireland under the relentless pressure of the English. But even in Ulster, things were changing.

Tyrconnell and Tyrone enjoyed a traditional rivalry over the fertile river lands along their borders, and men aspiring to the chieftainships of clans from both sides had begun to see the English destruction of the Brehon system of election as a way to gain ascendancy for themselves. Even in the north, submissions to the Crown were becoming more frequent, ripping apart the fabric of Gaelic life.

Shane, The O Neill, was dead, and claimants to his title such as young Hugh O Neill had brought Tyrone to the brink of internecine war.

No sooner had The O Donnell welcomed Grania to his castle than he was explaining the situation to The O Malley's daughter. The opportunity for forming an alliance with her was too good to miss—though like other Irishmen, he was taken aback by her unconventional behavior. Still, there was no ignoring the size of the fleet she had sailed into Donegal bay to return Ruari Oge to the land of his birth.

Gráinne Ni Mháille was a power, and The O Donnell needed more power.

He entertained her in a large rectangular thatched hall adjacent to the stone tower that served as his stronghold. The hall was less permanent in structure but more flexible in use; it could feast many guests at a banquet or be turned into a stable in severe weather. And if someone had too much uisquebaugh, the Irish beverage flavored with imported spices and called whiskey by the English, and so set the hall afire through careless use of torch or rushlight, at least the main part of the castle would not burn too.

Grania declined The O Donnell's offer of uisquebaugh in favor of a tankard of ale, which she drank so quickly she left a mustache of white foam on her lip. The man they called Black Hugh looked at her with appraising eyes.

"Now you do resemble a she-king," he remarked. "But a handsome one!"

He was deliberately flattering her and she knew it, but she did not mind. If The O Donnell was measuring her, she was also measuring him. He was as dark as her own father had been, though fleshier of face, with the quick eyes of a man who has survived many battles and the solid belly of a man who eats every chance he gets, never knowing how long it may be before he can stop to eat again.

Hugh Dubh O Donnell was the legitimate survivor of the pre-Christian warrior society of the European Celts, a man who could justifiably claim the hero's portion of a roasted boar, a man who could lounge in luxury amid his poets and harpers, his wives and concubines and a constant underfoot babble of children, while guards stood at his gates with two-hundred-year-old swords in their hands.

In his own setting, Black Hugh was splendid.

Under Elizabeth, England was taking her place on the world stage as a united kingdom with a sense of national purpose. Ireland remained what it had been for two thousand years, a collection of clans ruled by individuals, each man a king on his own portion, finding the concept of organized bureaucracy as alien as Tudor officialdom found Gaelic culture. Black Hugh O Donnell epitomized that culture.

And two leaders of the Gaels sat together in Black Hugh O Donnell's hall, discussing the form of conflict they were most familiar with—not nation against nation but tribe against tribe, the ancient competitions by which Celtic peoples proved their manhood.

"I have a young son by my most recent wife," Black Hugh was telling his guest, "a boy with hair that burns like a victory fire. Already they call him Red Hugh, and his mother is ambitious to see him elected chieftain someday. He might make it—just this morning he punched me so hard in the small of the back it took my breath away, but when I turned on him he never flinched. I doubt any sept of the O Neills has sired his equal."

"You should see my sons," Grania could not resist saying.

"I hear one rebels against the English in Iar Connaught."

"He does," she agreed. "And the other has gained a reputation for being a supporter of the Crown."

Black Hugh stroked his luxuriant mustache, drawing it aside when he spoke to reveal red lips and strong white teeth. "So you have a foot in either camp," he said. "Clever, I think. One cannot be too careful in dealing with the sasanach. I myself, for example, have hosted many of them in my guest houses as they journey up and down the coast. They leave an English stink in the thatch, of course, but I smile at them and profit from their trade. And they're not all so bad, Grania. Do you see that young man over there, for instance? The one just entering the hall?"

Following the direction of The O Donnell's gesturing hand, Grania saw a slim young man with a fair Saxon face and a suit of elegantly cut dark velvet, beruffed at neck and sleeves.

"That is Philip Sidney, son of the lord deputy himself," Black Hugh said with some pride. "He travels west from Dublin to Galway by way of the sea route, and his father sends him to visit with me along the way and enlarge his education as to Irish ways. I have found him surprisingly agreeable, actually. He claims to be something of a poet, though what poetry the sasanach can string together is probably not worth hearing."

A poet. Grania stared intently at Philip Sidney, remembering another poet.

The O Donnell beckoned to Sidney to join them. When he was introduced to Grania, the young Englishman obviously returned her interest in full measure. He had seen nothing like her before, and her reputation had preceded her.

Sir Philip Sidney, preparing for his stay in Ireland, had made a sincere effort to learn enough Gaelic to converse with the natives. The two aristocrats eyed one another with a certain wariness as they launched into the shallow waters of casual conversation.

"I am told you sail your own ships?" Sidney asked.

"You can be told many things about me," Grania replied.

"Are any of them true?"

"Absolutely none. And probably all," she answered with a disarming laugh.

Hesitantly at first, Philip Sidney laughed with her. He was not quite sure he understood her, but there was no mistaking the human warmth of the woman. She was big and brawny and brimming with zest, a vivid and exotic creature to his eyes.

He did not realize how exotic he himself seemed to the Gaels in their natural setting. The etiquette of Elizabeth's court was out of place here; his every gesture was strange to Grania. Yet there was an undeniable elegance about him that appealed to her. Huw had been a mariner; this Philip Sidney was a landman through and through, different from any man she had ever known. That difference appealed to her—that difference, and the dangerous fact that he was both English and the lord deputy's son.

Flirting with him was like holding your hand in flame, gambling that you could snatch it away before it was burned. I should not be doing this, Grania told herself as she lowered her eyes and then looked up at him with a very womanly smile. He's young enough to be . . . my nephew. And he's sasanach.

The man in the monk's robe was sasanach. The man who hates me. If I could win this one, perhaps I could somehow learn enough about his kind to overcome the hatred a man like Richard Bingham feels for me.

I wonder if Philip Sidney knows Richard Bingham?

Her smile grew wider, demonstrating strong white teeth. Many Englishwomen had rotten teeth almost as soon as their breasts budded so Philip stared at her in admiration. His voice became softer, his laughter more frequent—and the conversation moved toward more personal areas with surprising speed.

Hugh Dubh O Donnell observed this with interest. The O Malley's daughter had definitely taken to playing the political game, he thought to himself. Women had an unfair advantage in that arena if they chose to use it. And she would be resented, if she used that advantage too blatantly.

Nevertheless, he admired her style.

Tigernan, also watching, had very different feelings.

"What do you think of our Ireland?" Grania was asking Sidney. "Has it been good to you . . . so far?"

"The land is beautiful," he replied. "I like to play with words, and it inspires me. I have a friend, Edmund Spenser, who claims his best poetry comes to him out of the air around him. If that is true, I may write something splendid here."

"Is your poetry as good as this Spenser's?" Grania asked with interest.

"It depends on the inspiration, as I said." He leaned forward.

So did she.

Tigernan scowled.

Better not let this man think he could move too far too fast, Grania reminded herself. She had fished with hook and line; she knew how to play her catch. "Ireland is not always beautiful; you would do well to be warned. It can be brutal here."

Sidney sat up abruptly. "I know it. The head of a Gaelic chieftain named Shane O Neill was put up on a pike over the gate to Dublin castle just before my father last returned to London. He told me The O Neill's own distant kinsmen lifted his head and sent it to the English authorities."

"Such things don't happen in England? Your people do not ever betray one another to gain some advantage for themselves? Your monarchs never sent their kinsmen to the block?"

Philip Sidney narrowed his eyes. They were blue, Grania noticed, and the whites were very clear. His skin was probably smooth all over; his hands appeared free of calluses and the nails were neatly trimmed. She found her mind wandering and called it back, sharply.

"I do not associate with the kind of men who betray one another," Sidney told her with great dignity.

Grania laughed. "Nonsense. Everyone does, or we would have no friends at all. I cannot believe the English are any more honorable than the Gaels."

"What is honor to a Gael?"

Her eyes flashed. "Everything," she told him seriously. "But we may not always interpret it as you do. My people and yours are very different, Philip Sidney."

Philip watched her back arch with pride. Her figure might have graced the prow of a warship; her eyes tantalized and challenged. He had never had such a conversation with such a woman before, and it was affecting him like heady wine. He was young; this was his first trip to Ireland. "I am like any other man in all the ways that count," he said.

"All the ways?" Grania asked with a lift of her eyebrows.

"In some of them I am even better equipped than many," he boasted. Surely she had noticed the splendor of his velvet codpiece. He had come here for experience, and it occurred to him this woman would be quite an experience.

Their host was watching this byplay with amusement. He felt certain he and Gráinne Ni Mháille would agree to a mutually profitable alliance before she left his territory. She needed an ally on the north to watch her borders, and he needed a skillful sea captain to ship the fighting men known as kernes, or the mercenaries called gallowglasses, to Tyrconnell, together with weapons and gunpowder and all the accoutrements of battle. The English would not allow such articles to be brought to him from Scotland, not if they knew about it, but Grania's reputation for evading capture and search of her ships was without equal in the west. He would not expect her to actually declare war on the English in his behalf, of course—nor would he do so in hers. Neither of them wanted open rebellion at this time. But they could help each other to survive, The O Donnell and Gráinne Ni Mháille—until such time as neither had to be superficially polite to the sasanach anymore.

Black Hugh smiled beneath his flowing mustache. Grania was being more than superficially polite to the elegant English nobleman.

Tigernan was having the same thought. He seized a roast rib of meat from a nearby platter and ripped into it with voracious bites, his gaze never leaving Grania and Sidney. How could she appear so relaxed, as if she were enjoying herself, in the company of an Englishman?

Tigernan left teeth marks on the bone.

"I am staying in one of The O Donnell's castle chambers," Philip Sidney was telling Grania. "At first I thought he would put me in one of those little round houses beside the wall, but when he learned who I am, at least I got a decent bed under a timbered roof. I've never slept in a thatched Irish guest house and I do not know if I'm prepared to start."

"You'll be comfortable enough upstairs," Grania assured him. "Which chamber is yours?"

"The one I understand lies directly below yours," he replied, being careful to make his meaning clear. His Gaelic was improving.

"Ah." She smiled. "And do you sleep well?"

"No. Sometimes I . . . walk in my sleep."

"Seeking inspiration," Grania finished for him. Her smile deepened.

He was not Huw, though he claimed to be a poet. Not Celt, but sasanach. Yet he was young and interesting and fresh as a west wind. And Evleen had said death must not be allowed to triumph over life.

I will be done with all forms of grieving, starting tonight, Grania promised herself. She lifted her arms and stretched, feeling the healthy muscles slide smoothly beneath her skin.

Sir Philip Sidney watched in fascination.

"I think I will go to bed early," she announced in a carrying voice. "We have had a long journey and undergone a sad ceremony; my men can stay here in the hall and enjoy themselves as long as they like, but I will seek my bed."

Black Hugh nodded. Grania stood up, and Philip Sidney rose with her, as smoothly as if they were joined at the hip. Tigernan uttered a strangled curse. The sasanach was taking hold of Grania's arm as if she were an old woman and he were a blackthorn stick for her to lean upon! Was that some English custom, insulting the strength of women? Or did he mean to grab her and make off with her?

Grania had feasted lavishly at The O Donnell's table. When she rose from her bench, the woven girdle around her waist—which was already rather worn—parted. Evleen would have noticed the girdle's disrepair and mended it, but Evleen was not present. And Grania did not wear the girdle often, for it did not go with trews.

When she stood up and walked from the hall on Sir Philip Sidney's arm, the broken belt dropped unnoticed to the floor behind her.

One person in the hall noticed, however. From a dozen paces away, Tigernan saw. Shaking his head to clear it of whiskey fumes, he strode to Grania's vacated bench and stooped to pick up the girdle. But as he straightened, his eyes looked the length of the hall and saw Grania in the doorway with Philip Sidney, laughing into the young man's face and . . . and letting her hand slide down his back in an obvious caress.

"Dar Dia!" Tigernan dropped the broken belt back onto the floor and gave it such a vicious kick the garment flew halfway across the room, landing in the fireplace amid a great uprising of sparks and ashes, startling those nearest the hearth.

"If that woman thinks I'll run after her and fetch her broken tacklings she's sadly mistaken!" Tigernan proclaimed aloud for all to hear.

He went to the hearth and watched the girdle burn. Flame followed the silk embroidery first, the interlaced green leaves and stems and Celtic birds and beasts that wove a tenuous line between reality and fantasy. One man nearby came forward and reached to save the pretty thing from the fire, but Tigernan intercepted him.

"Let it burn," he said in a voice no one cared to challenge.

Grania and O Flaherty, Grania and the foremastman, Grania and Iron Richard . . . and now the sasanach, Sidney's son. After what Tigernan had done in secret to protect Grania from the English, this last was too much to be borne. Always Grania and somebody. Her appetite was too hearty, she was too blatantly alive. . . .

I love the life in her, Tigernan admitted to himself.

But if she's determined to walk right into the arms of the English, let her! I will not go running to save her, not this time!

He hunkered down on his haunches and stared fiercely into the flames on the hearth.

22

In her chamber, Grania removed her clothes and lay down naked on the bed. She did not extinguish the fine beeswax candles The O Donnell furnished. By their light she could make out the carving on the posts of her bedstand, and she let her eyes lazily follow the twists and turnings as she waited.

She did not have to wait long.

"I cannot sleep," said Philip Sidney softly from the doorway.

"You are not used to the chill of an Irish night," she told him. She was delighted with herself. How smoothly she was playing this game, as if she had done it all her life! She wondered if Dubhdara, wherever he was, was watching, seeing his daughter as feminine after all.

With a twist of her wrist she flung back the covers of the bed. "Get in here with me and I'll warm you, Englishman," she offered.

At the last moment, Sidney hesitated. He had been raised on tales of Irish treachery, and his tardy imagination furnished him with a horrifying vision of the door bursting open and warriors falling upon him at that moment when a man was most vulnerable.

Grania sensed his hestiation and chuckled. "No one will bother us."

"Can you promise?"

"I give you my word. I told you that honor is important to us." She moved in the bed so he could hear the sound of her body on the linen sheets.

Philip Sidney was young, and far from wife and home. The stone-walled chamber of The O Donnell's stronghold seemed like another world, a place where anything might be done, any fantasy acted out. He felt his feet carrying him across the floor toward the bed, and in the candlelight he saw the woman lying there, naked, opening her arms to him.

She was not beautiful by an Elizabethan standard of beauty. She was something much more dramatic, a robust female at the peak of her powers and fully aware of her abilities, and Sidney could no more resist her than he could walk through a stone wall. As if from a distance, he watched himself remove his clothes and fling his body onto the bed beside her.

His skin was as soft as Grania had imagined; the English nobility took care of itself. Yet he did not smell clean, as did Gaelic folk, who bathed daily according to their traditions. The scent of his skin was pungent and overlaid with perfumes that made Grania wrinkle her nose. She had never been so close to an Englishman before, and she was not certain she liked the sensation. Could it be that the sasanach, who pretended they were better than everybody, were not even clean about their persons? Even the poorest Gael washed his skin with water, heated or cold, every day that the sun rose, as his Celtic forebears had for thousands of years.

Holy water. The words flashed through Grania's mind. They meant one thing to the Catholic Church and quite another to Evleen, who insisted all water was holy and bathing was a ritual intended to keep one in touch with life's sources.

The thought of Evleen brought Grania back to the chamber and the strong male body pressed now against her own. Philip Sidney was murmuring something, a phrase he found poetic, a bit of sonnet had Grania recognized the form. But she did not, and the English words sounded harsh on her ears.

With an effort of will she made herself yield to him. In a sense, this man was enemy territory and this was her opportunity to study the land, to find its weaknesses and strengths and gain insight for setting her own future course.

But when Philip's hands moved over her body, Grania discovered that all human landscapes have a certain similarity. She knew his touch as male, and hungry, and when she returned it in kind she felt a familiar rising response that flattered her and made her eager for more. Within the bed they did not seem to be foreigner and Gael. They were just man and woman, enjoying each other.

Enjoying. Yes. If I stop thinking of who and what he is, I can enjoy him, Grania told herself, throwing her head back so he could plant a series of long, drinking kisses down the length of her throat.

Grabbing a handful of Philip's blond hair, Grania pulled his face to hers and tasted his mouth. A memory of Irish beef lay on his tongue, and uisquebaugh. He returned her kiss in full measure, stimulated by the unexpected sensation of sea-chapped lips.

They strove to get closer to each other. Everything about her that was Gaelic and unfamiliar excited him; everything about him that was English and unknown excited her. He was not rough, or coarse; he did not perform the perverted acts some called "the English addiction." And she was not coarse, though she was stronger than any woman he had ever bedded and had no hesitation about demonstrating that strength in the most delightful ways.

Sir Philip Sidney possessed an essential decency, almost a sexual delicacy, that came as a surprise to Grania. There were moments when he seemed shy, reminding her that he was younger than she, boyish in the presence of a more mature woman. She was tender with him then, and generous.

In Grania's mind she had never framed a view of English sexuality, though had she done so it would have been colored by her view of the sasanach as an enemy. Philip made such an opinion irrelevant, at least for a while.

Then she felt his bodily rhythms start to speed up and his breathing became labored. With a pang of disappointment, Grania realized her own body was not keeping pace. With Huw she had discovered what a man and woman could accomplish together when they were perfectly matched, but her pace and Sidney's were not the same. He would go on without her, and she feared being left behind, unsatisfied. With a wordless cry she wrapped both arms and legs around his laboring body as tightly as she could, almost forcing the air from his lungs as she commanded her muscles to clench and throb into the familiar spasms, the longed-for, long-needed relief.

Almost, but not quite. Philip collapsed against her, panting, and Grania lay tense behind her closed eyelids. She felt his heart racing. Her own beat more slowly.

But his arms were warm. His body had thawed and melted the long season of frost gripping hers. Even if she had not soared with him, she realized that the touch of his flesh comforted her, and she had indeed experienced pleasure, the pleasure of giving and taking and sharing one another, of surrendering the last barriers to intimacy with another human being.

Grania snuggled into the Englishman's embrace and fell asleep.

Her last conscious thought was, "I have welcomed your emissary most graciously, Elizabeth. . . ."

She slept, smiling.

Awaking well before dawn, Grania found herself clear-headed and thinking even before she opened her eyes. Her body felt wonderfully used. All the joints were oiled. But Sidney had to be gotten out of her chamber and back to his own, and quickly.

She shook him awake—gently, gently—and urged him into his clothes. While he dressed, she made the most of the opportunity to talk to him in a low voice, seeking what informtion she might glean while his own thoughts were still fuzzy. Did he sail often? Who was his captain for this voyage? Did he happen to know any of the men she knew . . . a Richard Bingham, perhaps?

No? Ah, that was all right; the sea was a wide place and many never met. . . .

But she was disappointed. She had hoped to learn something more than simply how a woman needs a man from time to time.

At the back of her brain she heard Evleen say, very sharply, "That is a major lesson—be thankful you've learned that one."

Nevertheless, until he slipped out of her door and was gone, Grania continued to talk with Philip Sidney in order to gain knowledge that could help her navigate the shifting political currents. Nothing could be simple anymore, not in Ireland. Even a night in bed had many meanings.

✠

Tigernan, sleepless and hot-eyed as he lay wrapped in his mantle in one of the guest houses beyond the castle, knew only one meaning for a man and woman together in bed. He simmered in rage throughout the night.

A faint false silvery light painted like a wash across the eastern sky as Tigernan extricated himself from his bedding and began searching among Grania's crewmen who slept around him.

Tigernan spoke no English and was proud of it, but he knew which among his seamen did. Taking a sleepy interpreter in tow, he coached the man in what he wanted said and then led him to a position near the castle portal, waiting to waylay Sir Philip Sidney whenever that young man appeared in the morning.

Morning was damp in Tyrconnell. Ruari Oge had bewailed the loss of Ireland's timber, but near The O Donnell's stronghold yew and oak still held the dawn mist in their crowns. Small fields, stone-bordered, nurtured crops for the castle's table, and men and women were already at work in them, their brightly dyed woolens and homespuns dotting the landscape with color as thrushes and chats lifted their dawn serenade to the lowering skies.

Sir Philip Sidney emerged from the castle, yawned, stretched, and looked around with interest, mentally shaping a bit of poetry to capture this highly unusual occasion. To capture it in the most circumspect fashion; he would not have them laughing in London about his savage Irishwoman. Not that Grania was a savage—she was . . .

Two men approached him. One was round-faced and nondescript; the other was a tall and glowering fellow with a broken jaw that had healed unset, and rusty-colored hair hanging in barbaric braids around his face. The first man called Sidney by name, with a most humble "milord" prefacing his speech; the second man dug his elbow in the ribs of the first and was obviously controlling the conversation.

"Milord, were you in the presence of Gráinne Ni Mháille last night?" Tigernan's interpreter inquired.

Sidney was instantly on guard. "In The O Donnell's banquet hall."

"And after?"

The Englishman tightened his mouth to a thin line. "Who has the right to question me in such a fashion?"

The elbow in the ribs again, and a quick reply. "Ah, 'tis for your own safety, milord. There are many in Ireland who would not want to see harm come to Lord Deputy Sidney's son. And there are many who know things about that woman you may not— terrible tales, milord."

Sidney was simultaneously repelled and intrigued. Like any man who has just slept with a woman, he thought he knew her. But the dramatist in his soul was always interested in a bit of color. "What things are you talking about?"

"She has had . . . any number of men, it is said. And they're all dead now."

"All of them?"

The man nodded. "All of them. She sees to it. Everyone knows. She's under some kind of a curse; she cannot suffer a man who has lain with her to live long. A dreadful thing, milord, a dreadful thing. Everyone knows," he added again before Tigernan could nudge him, fearing he had overdone it.

It occurred to Sidney, who was not a naive man, that the Irish meant to have some fun at the ignorant foreigner's expense. Grania was a magnificent creature who had surely inspired legends already, but he was not going to be so easily taken in as this. Tricky devils.

"I vow I'll be careful and keep an eye on her," he said, making his face as solemn as possible. "And I will pass on your warning to any man I think may be in need of it."

The crooked-jawed fellow with the braids did not seem satisfied. His interpreter listened to a harsh whisper from him, then said aloud, "And for yourself, milord . . .?"

"I?" Philip laughed. "I am an English nobleman. I have no desire to get out of a bed with Irish lice on my skin."

The remark was insensitive and out of character for Philip, but it made a sufficient point. Tigernan was reassured . . . for almost half the day. Then he began worrying again. And getting angry again.

Sir Philip Sidney, still musing over his first major adventure in Ireland, sailed aboard an English ship from the port of Donegal late that same day. And on the next morning's tide Grania and her men left for Umhall, with Tigernan sullen in the prow beside her.

Grania seemed in a high good humor that added to his irritability. When he did not joke with her, she complained. "You are as dull as dirty water, Tigernan, and I'm tired of seeing your face folded. Ruari Oge was a sick man and he died. Will you go through the rest of your life curdling the milk with your sourness because of it?"

"Ruari Oge is not the source of my misery."

"Ah, you're seasick then and have been hiding it from me all these years. I always suspected." She grinned at him, daring him to smile back.

But he could not. "It is the Englishman, Grania. I never expected to see you treating familiarly with . . . with one of the sasanach, particularly a son of Ireland's tyrant."

She turned to face Tigernan squarely, though the wind rising out of the west blew her dark hair across her eyes and into her mouth, so she had to constantly brush it back as she spoke. "I learned something valuable from Philip Sidney, my friend. He is a nice man. Do you hear me? He is English, of the class that rules in that land, but he is a nice man."

"You've dealt with English before," Tigernan reminded her.

"You've traded with them in the Welsh ports and had them board your ships; you cannot roll over in your own shadow in Ireland any more without coming in contact with some Englishman. So why did you have to study one up close? And what is so important about his being . . . what did you call him, nice?"

She who could see beyond the far horizon determined to be patient with Tigernan, who apparently could not. "England is our opponent," she reminded him. "I spend my life struggling to hold Clew bay free from the grasp of Elizabeth. If I am to play the game well, I need to know all I can about those who represent her here, the people I will have to outmaneuver. Sir Philip Sidney is as close as I've gotten to the highest level of authority, and it came as a revelation to me to find I could actually like the man. If all the English were monsters I would deal with them one way. Since they are not, I will deal with them another."

"Some of the sasanach are worse than monsters," Tigernan muttered darkly.

For just a flicker, Grania imagined the eyes watching her. The eyes of the false monk; the eyes she had long been convinced belonged to a man named Richard Bingham. Eyes brimming with hell.

"Yes," she agreed slowly. "Some of them are."

"So that's what you were doing with Sidney? Spying on the sasanach?"

"Not spying, exactly. Measuring might be a better way to describe it."

Tigernan's temper flared. "And what exactly is it you were measuring, Grania Mhaol? To what part of Philip Sidney did you apply your measuring standard?"

She slapped both hands against her thighs and roared with laughter. "You're jealous, Tigernan!"

He drew himself up with excruciating dignity and turned his shoulder on her. "I do not care if you bed all the pigs in Ireland."

He stalked away, hearing her laughter follow him.

Then the laughter died. If he had turned, which he could never bring himself to do, Tigernan would have been surprised by the speculative look Grania was giving him.

In the days that followed, Grania would think from time to time of Tigernan's jealousy and the emotions it betrayed . . . and think also of Philip Sidney, the Englishman, kind and decent, who had pulled the covers over her when the night grew cold and he thought she slept.

✠

Before she left Tyrconnell, Black Hugh heaped the leader of the O Malley fleet with gifts, an assurance of continued alliance. But Grania had noted that he earlier showered similar gifts on Philip Sidney as the young man departed for Galway.

"The English are very afraid that clan O Donnell will settle its long-running quarrels with clan O Neill and rise against the she-king's authority," Black Hugh told Grania when she remarked on his generosity. "My tokens are meant to reassure."

"There is no possibility of a united rising of the northern chieftains, then?"

Black Hugh narrowed his eyes. "There's always a possibility. As there is of a further union including O Malleys and your northern Burke kinsmen. The English fear that mightily; why else do you think Sidney sent his own son to my court to befriend me?"

And me, Grania thought silently. But she did not feel betrayed. The time she had spent with Philip Sidney was a time outside of politics, and they had both known it. If it colored the future to some degree, she would deal with that when it happened.

Back down the coast Grania sailed, but this time instead of a dead hero's body she carried northern cargo for trading in the south. They swung round Achill head and put in at Curraun to see Margaret and her husband, and as Grania had expected, Margaret quickly relieved her of the prettiest of her merchandise.

"Oh, Richard, look at this lace!" she exclaimed, holding up a bit of silvery cobweb.

The Devil's Hook smiled indulgently. He was openhanded with his pretty wife and they both enjoyed it.

"You're spoiling her," Grania told him.

Margaret rounded on her mother. "Would you have me go back to Clare island and sit in a dark chamber listening to the wind howl?"

How lovely she is in anger, Grania thought, seeing Margaret's cheeks flame. "No," she said. "You belong where you are, and it's glad I am to see you here."

Margaret pouted, because she knew she looked charming when she did so; she practiced in front of mirrors. "I belong in a palace," she told her mother. And then that which was Grania surfaced in her for the first time, rising at last with maturity. She threw back her head and laughed.

Her husband and mother exchanged delighted glances and laughed with her.

"I love her and I hate her," Grania told the Devil's Hook as she bade him farewell later.

"So do I," he replied.

Grania returned to Rockfleet in time to learn from a diligence of messengers sent by Donal, her half brother, that a president named Perrot had been installed by the English in Munster and the province had broken into open revolt. Buildings were being burned, people slain, blood was running in rivulets over land that had been bloodied before. In the Pale, the walled and guarded area around Dublin that sheltered the queen's Loyalists, men shivered with fear and demanded the rebellion be contained before it reached them.

"If we are asked to stand with Munster, refuse," Donal pleaded with Grania.

She sent him an angry reply. "My father sired only one brave child, and you are not that child." But she had already determined to take no part in the warfare turning Munster into a wasteland. The English were adopting savage policies of conquest and repression in the south, turning Ireland into dry tinder. All traces of "Irishness" were being outlawed. Families were being slaughtered wholesale, down to the youngest baby, and the English phrase of justification, "Nits make lice," was repeated with horror the length of Ireland.

Grania did not want to bring such butchery into Clew bay. Her people depended on her for protection.

But the most ancient part of her, the unreconstructed Gaelic warrior, itched in silence to pick up sword and shield and fall on the English with terrible cries. Except for people like Philip Sidney, perhaps . . . and Elizabeth of clan Tudor, whom Grania had come to think of as her own image, reversed in a dark mirror.

23

The Year of Our Lord 1574 dawned with sunny skies for a change, but bitter cold winds. Nevertheless the bay teemed with fish, and Grania could hear the fishermen singing in their curraghs as they returned with their catches.

But prosperity was not so easily taken, nor held. Connaught had a president of its own now, the Englishman Sir Edward Fitton, who subscribed to many of the repressive policies being carried out by his colleague in Munster.

Owen O Flaherty sailed north from Iar Connaught to urge his mother to ship more of his sept's wool. "You sought an alliance with the English," she reminded him in the hall at Rockfleet. "Why don't you apply to them for permission to sail your own trading galleys out of Galway?"

Owen looked sullen, an expression Grania remembered too well from the face of Donal an Chogaidh. "I already tried that. I was told it would set a bad example to favor me while my brother Murrough stands with the rebels."

"And you accepted that decision?"

Owen held out his hands, palms up. "What else could I do?"

"Probably nothing, by now. But you gave in to the English too easily in the beginning, Owen. You compromised without a struggle, showing them that you were no one to respect. Now they need give you nothing."

"Would you prefer I anger them as Murrough does, risking the lives of my family?"

Grania sighed. How could she pass on the wisdom—learned at such great cost—to the deaf ears of the next generation? "I don't want any of you in jeopardy. But you did not make friends with the English, you just rolled over and showed them your belly."

"Are you saying you want me to befriend the English?"

"Of course not, Owen! We are Gaels; we need not embrace the

sasanach!" She thought for a flicker of Philip Sidney and almost smiled, but stopped herself. There were exceptions for every rule, she noted. "I'm merely saying you made a strategic mistake in submitting so readily. You threw away your bargaining power."

"Where were you when I needed someone to teach me?" Owen asked. Something cunning peeped at her from behind his eyes, trying to manipulate her with guilt. And there was a tone in his voice she almost recognized, a hint of a voice long stilled perhaps —just in the inflection, the roundness of the vowels. . . . Mairgret! Grania realized suddenly. It was the echo of her own mother's voice she detected when Owen spoke, though the words came through lips shaped like Donal O Flaherty's. And that diffidence of his—was it a transmutation of Mairgret's contemplative nature, her quickness to tears, her acceptance of the guilt the priests taught as being the human condition?

Grania studied her son afresh, seeing the lines that led from him back through her and to the generations before them.

We are tied in time, she thought.

Owen returned to Iar Connaught in a state of confusion. He had made a mistake, he saw that now. And he did not know how to rectify it, nor did he dare ask Grania. This was a problem he must work out for himself, to prove his manhood. On his own, he must move his relations with the English to different and more profitable footing.

There was an English sea captain who often put in to Galway harbor, a man said to be asking many questions about the Clew bay region and Gráinne Ni Mháille. Bingham, Owen thought his name was. John, or Richard . . . some name like that, foreign and hard. Perhaps this Bingham would be interested in meeting one of Grania's sons. Perhaps he could even be charmed, with a full and calculated measure of Irish charm, into putting in a good word for Owen with President Fitton.

I can play the political game every bit as well as my mother, Owen told himself. And no harm will be done; I will be very careful in what I say to any Englishman.

Sir Richard Bingham had finally attained his captaincy and was striving for more. A minor title did not satisfy him either—not when men like Francis Drake were the heroes of the day and all the glory was going to them. Bingham redoubled his efforts to call favorable attention to himself. He made it well known in Dublin castle that the woman the English referred to as Grace O Malley, in the region Anglicized as Mayo, had amassed considerable personal power. She seemed to conduct herself as she saw fit along the coasts of Ireland, Scotland, and the southern routes, trading and pirating and occasionally indulging in a brief spate of feuding with other Gaelic clans—whom she subsequently manipulated into alliances with herself. The woman appeared to subscribe to no law but her own self-interest, and Bingham described her as unpredictable in the extreme.

Dangerously unpredictable.

She did not seem preparing for all-out rebellion, but with her Burke and O Donnell connections she could not be trusted to maintain the peace.

Sir Edward Fitton conferred with the lord deputy and decided there was only one answer to the problem of a Grace O Malley.

"Our agent Bingham tells us this O Malley woman has one son who is loyal to the point of servility and another who is an outright rebel and will probably never be subdued," Fitton told his aides. "So she could go either way. Best we teach her a valuable lesson right now—attack her and rout her out. When they see her defeated her clansmen will calm down soon enough and accept the inevitable."

Richard Bingham expected that assignment; he had worked long and hard for it. When it went instead to a sea captain named William Martin he was furious.

"That woman is mine!" he complained angrily to his brother John, who was also doing a tour of duty in Ireland. "She owes me a debt I will never forgive. She prances along the seaways as if she had a man's balls, John, and by the bright blue eyes of God, it should be my hand that grabs those balls of hers and crushes them."

John Bingham, a coarser-featured, heavy-bellied version of his brother, drawled, "I suspect our President Fitton just owes more debts to Martin's family than he does to ours."

"My time will come," Richard Bingham promised himself.

"Perhaps. But right now you and I are both wanted in London. Drake is talking of putting together a fleet to sail around the world, and if we step smart we might be part of it."

For a brief and shining moment Richard Bingham's hatred of Grania fled from his mind entirely.

✠

Grania and Tigernan had just returned from a trip to Clare island. As so often of late, Tigernan was quiet and withdrawn, brooding over some private melancholy of his own, and Grania was chiding him about it. She missed his former self, sarcastic and merry.

"Pull your feet out of that wet sand and move quickly, Tigernan," she shouted at him as they worked together to beach the boat. "I am getting very tired of your . . ." She stopped and straightened, shading her hand with her eyes against the dazzle of March sunshine reflected from the water.

By the stiffness of her spine and her wide-planted feet Tigernan recognized the onset of some sort of trouble. He turned to follow the direction of her gaze and saw several warships approaching, flying Tudor colors.

"To the castle, quickly!" Grania screamed to the crewmen still spilling out of her boat and wading ashore. "This is why I have Rockfleet," she panted to Tigernan as they ran together toward the portal. "No vessels can enter the inlet without being seen; at least they cannot take me by surprise."

She and her men were safely within Rockfleet's walls long before Martin's warships, abristle with guns as a gorsebush is with spines, reached firing distance. Only the black stones of the fortress greeted the English.

Grania had pounded up the stairs to the roof and out onto the parapet, with Tigernan behind her. She watched the invaders keenly. As she had known from the first time she saw Rockfleet, warships of any substantial size could not turn broadside in its limited channel and fire cannon directly at the fortress. They would have to risk shooting across their own bows with smaller guns, and the massive walls of the castle were thick enough to withstand a considerable barrage.

But it was not cannon she needed to fear, because the ships carried a more menacing cargo. Men lined the decks, looking eagerly toward land and their first glimpse of the infamous pirate of Clew bay.

"Tigernan, how many men do we have available to us here?" Grania demanded to know.

"Not as many as we're going to need," he told her. "Much of the fishing fleet is still out, and they won't come back with English ships blocking the harbor. They can beach elsewhere and come overland, but it will take a while. And they'll have to prepare themselves for battle, which may take still longer."

"Then we will make what men we have suffice. Get fresh water from the stream, and hurry; get others to help you fill every container you can find. And snatch up all those little green crabs you can see, and the dulsc in the shallows. We may have to live on crabs and seaweed if our food supplies run low and we are besieged."

She was not frightened; she was thinking too fast for fear to catch up with her. On the contrary, she felt exhilarated, as if at the back of her mind she had always anticipated this test, from the first time she determined to claim Rockfleet as her own.

The English warships anchored and put down boats filled with armed men. Grania spun around and went back down the stairs to ground level and the guardroom there, currently manned by a woefully small number. But at least plenty of weapons were stacked in the niche beside the stairwell door, and the base of the castle boasted a unique feature that would enable a mere handful of men with firearms to repulse a much larger attack force.

Rockfleet's only entrance opened into a tiny cramped hallway that let onto the stairwell rather than directly into the guardroom. The wooden ladder on ground level could be drawn up, rendering the upper stairway inaccessible. At the same time, anyone coming in through the door would find himself facing directly into the guardroom itself, thanks to an aperture in the wall of the entryway, a rectangular opening allowing men within to fire at point-blank range straight into the faces of invaders.

Grania loved Rockfleet.

Captain Martin aboard his flagship watched through a spyglass, counting heads as Grania's warriors ran toward the castle from their camps and cottages, nearby. "I doubt she has three dozen soldiers to defend her," he crowed. "This is almost too easy a victory."

But Grania was marshaling her troops to mount the most efficient defense possible. Men were posted to the turrets to rain arrows and stones down upon anyone who rushed the walls, and Grania regretted that she had no boiling lead prepared for a similar purpose. If Ruari Oge were alive he would have seen to it, she thought.

Martin deployed his troops along the shore and sent them inland as well, hoping to surround the castle and cut off the approach of any reinforcements. At the same time, within Rockfleet Grania was taking stock of her weapons. There was enough powder and shot to last quite a while, if she was thrifty with it, and every man in her retinue was well supplied with blades of various descriptions, from old-fashioned two-handed iron swords to fine Italian cinquedeas with double-edged blades, along with Tigernan's latest treasure, a combination pike and wheel-lock pistol of German origin. In addition there was a large pile of throwing stones and the usual collection of clubs, skullbreakers every one.

Grania did not let herself think about what sorts of weapons Elizabeth's warriors might be equipped with; since there was nothing she could do about it, it did not matter. She would win with what she had.

Martin threw up his siege with professional skill, though his survey of Rockfleet and its surround had daunted him. The place could scarcely be more impregnable. He tried his shipboard guns, but as Grania had foreseen, it was not possible to get a telling shot with a large enough ball to breach her walls. The English force with its superior size was able to overrun the defenders outside the fortress, but once they attempted to fight their way inside they were stymied at every attempt. On the third day of the siege, at Grania's order Tigernan deliberately opened the great oak door a crack and then stepped back as several Englishmen rushed it, shouting. The door swung inward, and the trio crowding through it promptly had their heads blown off by a volley of gunfire.

The English ardor for frontal assault cooled after that.

The siege of Rockfleet was mounted on the tenth day in the calends of March. A fortnight passed without Martin gaining any appreciable advantage. From time to time the strapping big black-haired woman he had come to kill stepped into one of the turrets at the top of the castle and shouted highly colorful insults at his men below, goading them until they lost their heads and came too near the tower; then her own warriors cut them down with gun and javelin and arrow. Even men well shielded by good chain mail suffered crippling wounds to face or knee, for the Irish had sharp eyes and aimed their missiles with deadly accuracy.

"Grace O Malley is a crafty devil," Captain Martin was forced to admit with a certain reluctant admiration. "Perhaps we made a miscalculation in trying to trap her here; it might be better to lure her into some other place where the advantages are on our side and seize her there."

But such a policy was not within the range of his orders. He must attempt the capture of Rockfleet until the matter was decided, and as the days passed and Grania hung on he felt victory slipping away from him.

Her men began returning. At first they were easily defeated by the element of surprise and his own numerical superiority, but some always escaped and ran for more help. The Irish began coming out of the trees, it seemed, more and more of them every day, brandishing weapons and eager to assail any enemy of Grania's.

A balance shifted. Defenders became attackers. Sixteen days after the siege had begun, Martin was forced to order his men back into the boats and beat a hasty retreat, narrowly escaping with his life as he encountered well armed Irish galleys converging on Rockfleet in response to signal fires Grania's followers had lit.

Though they had gathered beyond Rockfleet harbor in an ideal position to ambush the English ships, Grania's vessels withheld their fire for the most part, mystifying Martin. He could not know how many times she had stressed not engaging or enraging the English more than was necessary for survival.

As the defeated attackers sailed out into Clew bay, Tigernan went looking for Grania. He thought to find her elated and in a mood for celebration. Her begrimed and exhausted warriors certainly were; the portal of the castle had already been flung open and the small garrison room was crowded with men pounding one another on the back and sharing jugs, while the overflow cheered outside and began their own festival. Encamped around Rockfleet once more, Grania's army was both mourning its casualties and celebrating its survival.

But their commander was nowhere to be seen. At last Tigernan climbed the recently replaced wooden ladder to the first floor, then followed the circling stone stairs up toward Grania's chamber. He found her sitting on the top step with her head in her hands.

"Are you all right?" he asked anxiously.

"I am," she said in a muffled voice. She would not lift her face and look at him.

"You're tired. The English have gone."

"I know. I watched the last of them leave from the window in the privy room. I keep throwing up my food."

He was immediately concerned. "You're ill. You should have told someone. Let me send for Aidan . . ."

"No, no, I'm not sick. Truly, Tigernan. Here, just wait with me a minute. Then I'll go down and congratulate the men. They have been splendid. I hear them shouting out there; I should be with them."

But she did not move. She sat hunched on the cold stone. Tigernan edged past her and then tried to catch her by the shoulders and lift her to her feet, but she shook her head. "Not yet, not yet."

He did not know what to do.

At last she got up, slowly, and made her way into the hall. No fire was burning; the supply of firewood was exhausted and there was no peat. Nevertheless Grania sat down on a low bench close to the hearth and wrapped her arms around herself as if she were trying to get warm. Sensing Tigernan standing beside her, she suddenly leaned her head back against him.

"I was afraid," she said in a voice so low he could hardly make out her words.

"You . . . afraid? The wind is more easily frightened."

"I was. The last few days before our men started getting here, when I thought perhaps they'd all been intercepted and killed—I thought I'd never see Tibbot again, or that new child of Owen and Katharine's. Or the bay. We were almost out of fresh water, you know that. Men were drinking their piss to save what little was left for me."

"Who told you?" he asked angrily.

"No one had to tell me. There are few secrets in a tower house this size. That's when I really began to be afraid. Do you think anyone knew?"

"I'm sure they did not," Tigernan told her.

✠

The episode served to warn Grania that her situation was under constant peril, and to show the English that she was not as easily dislodged as one might think. This was proving true of many of the Gaels, and the costs of warfare throughout the land were being bitterly criticized in England.

Sir Henry Sidney decided to try some less costly diplomacy.

In the winter of 1575 he toured both Munster and Connaught, and the annalists of the day gave him credit for dealing fairly with both Gael and Anglo-Norman, so long as they promised loyalty to the Crown. In Munster he even promised to protect the lesser nobility against the alleged tyranny of the Earl of Desmond. This stratagem of promised military protection relieved minor chieftains of keeping armies of their own, opening the door for still more English soldiers to arrive in Ireland and keep the peace on behalf of all.

Sidney then moved on to Connaught, which was writhing under the grip of a very military government. There the lord deputy met with his son Philip to discuss the situation, in a handsome timbered house in Clare temporarily commandeered as headquarters for Ireland's governor.

The elder Sidney was a distinguished and precise man, and when Philip arrived the house was already ordered. Plate gleamed on the tables; fresh rugs hung from the walls. "We must make some effort to bring this wild west country under civilized control," the lord deputy told his son. "You have traveled here. What do you think of my plan to hold court in Galway city and summon all the region's chieftains to attend? On a friendly basis, rationally, man to man?"

Man to man, thought Philip, seeing Grania in his mind's eye and smiling. He had not told his father about his relations with Grania. Philip believed in keeping a man's private affairs private. "It is a superb notion," he said aloud. "Holding court—the Gaels always respond to pageantry. And will you invite the O Malley woman and her Burke husband from Mayo?"

The lord deputy nodded. "After she handed us such a defeat I'm most anxious to get a look at the creature."

A great number were soon planning to converge on Galway city. The Earl of Clanrickard was expected to attend, along with many Gaelic chieftains. Men who sought to retain control of old holdings or acquire new ones would be very much in evidence, as would minor nobility both Norman and Gaelic, hoping for English support to improve their status. Men who had been taxed to poverty and clerics whose monasteries had been seized also made their way toward Sidney's court, each with a claim to make.

Hiding his embarrassment behind an attitude even more surly than had become customary for him, Iron Richard paid a visit to Grania. "The MacWilliam Iochtar plans to go to Galway and make a formal submission to the English," he told her, looking everywhere but in her eyes.

Grania pursed her lips. "It was only a matter of time."

"The dean of Christchurch persuaded him. Once he converted to the English religion they had him by the nape of the neck. The English will take this land clan by clan and make it part of their world, mark me."

Her eyes flashed. "The English world! What do I care for that? I do care for Clew bay, which is *mine*, and Rockfleet, that protects me. Shane Oliverus cannot surrender that to the English because Rockfleet is no longer a Burke holding, remember?" Her eyes lit with triumphant laughter.

"Rockfleet is mine and you are my wife," Iron Richard replied stubbornly. Yet in his heart he knew what her response would be, and he was secretly glad; glad that all was not yet lost to the English queen.

"Not under any law the sasanach accept!" Grania cried. "I did not marry you before a priest; they would not consider us married if the matter were taken before one of their courts. But you did surrender this stronghold to me, and I hold it free of any Burke claim, free for your son Tibbot and his heirs. I will never turn it over to the Crown of England and then go crawling on my knees, begging to have it given back to me under Surrender and Regrant."

Richard said, "I understand clan O Malley finally has a new chieftain. A male . . ."

"Melaghlin," she answered, refusing to be goaded. "A kinsman of mine and a far better choice than Donal of the Pipes."

"Be that as it may, your Melaghlin will soon be under great pressure to recognize that he holds all O Malley lands subject to the Crown."

"Lands perhaps, but not the bay," Grania insisted. "I have won territory and built strongholds in my own name, and my shipping interests are protected by Cliara and Inishbofin and Kildawnet and half a score of other holdings on island and headland, property The O Malley has no more control over than you have over Rockfleet. They and the sea between them are mine."

"If Shane Oliverus succeeds in getting the English to give him back the lands he surrenders, and I follow him as MacWilliam Iochtar, someday I will have all your north shore," Richard reminded his erstwhile wife.

She shrugged. "Someday has as much weight as sea mist. But . . . I might even be willing to help you. You want to be in line for the MacWilliamship, and if I keep my strength I can be a power in the land, supporting you."

"What do you want in return?" Richard asked, already expecting the price to be high. As always, his perpetual anger with Grania was tempered by fascination. She manipulated him and he took out his rage on others, but he invariably came back to see what she would do next. For eight years he had watched her occupying the fortress he thought was his and had never dared openly challenge her for it, because he was clever enough to know that Grania was cleverer.

She proved it now. "I want you to go to Galway with me and tell the lord deputy how Rockfleet was lost to me; prove it stands beyond Oliverus' claim."

"And even if I do that, how do you propose to get the English to leave you alone here? They may not attempt Rockfleet again, but sooner or later they will fire on Cliara or your ships at sea, you know it."

Grania lounged back comfortably on her padded bench, propping her feet up, knees apart, thoroughly at ease. "I am going to surprise them. Surprise always disconcerts. The English are stretched thin around the coasts of Ireland, and they can certainly use the services of more skilled seamen, particularly since they are in such constant fear of a Spanish attack. I will go to Sidney in Galway, and before any demands can be made of me, I will offer him three galleys and two hundred fighting men to be used at his discretion."

Richard could only stare at her in admiration. She had it all planned, every step . . . and must have done so long before he arrived, the moment she received word of the lord deputy's summons to Galway. She had foreseen with calculating certainty that Shane Oliverus would submit, and found a way to use even that in her own favor.

"You play a dangerous game, Gráinne Ni Mháille," Richard said. "Some will call you traitor for this."

He saw the spark of rage in her eyes and saw how quickly she extinguished it, though her cheeks caught the fire and burned red. "Let people think what they like," she said. "The reward of winning will be to keep at least this much of Ireland Irish, for my children's children. I do not care if I am hated; I do not care if I am misunderstood. I will hold Cuan Mó for my people if I have to kiss the lord deputy on the mouth to do it!"

part five

tigernan

24

"There came to me also a most famous feminine sea captain called Grany Imallye, and offered her services unto me, wheresoever I would command her, with three galleys and two hundred fighting men. . . . She brought with her her husband for she was as well by sea as by land well more than Mrs. Mate with him," Sir Henry Sidney wrote of his meeting with Grania in Galway. "This was a notorious woman in all the coasts of Ireland."

The lord deputy had been both astonished and impressed by the tall woman who came bursting into his chambers demanding to talk with him. He had already seen a parade of Irish chieftains and landholders, presenting him with an assortment of attitudes ranging from scarcely concealed hostility to embarrassing obsequiousness.

But Gráinne Ni Mháille treated him as her equal.

From the first she led the discussion, stating her offer and making her demands. She made it clear she understood the English desire to control Ireland's coastal waters, and she had exact figures as to crew size and armament of English-controlled ships available for that purpose. The skill and experience of her seamen were well known; there could be no denying they would be an asset to the English on the west coast of Ireland.

For the time being, Sidney decided, since he had so many problems in other parts of Ireland, it might be expedient to make the arrangement the O Malley woman wished, at least on a temporary basis. A few barren stone towers around a remote fishing bay— they did not matter that much, not now, not yet. He would soon have the submission of the new O Malley chieftain, and that was what he wanted most from the area. If the land was loyal to Elizabeth, a few square miles of sea and rocks could be spared, for a while, and remain in Gaelic dominion.

He had held court in one of the guild halls in Galway, rimming the room with men-at-arms intended to impress the outlanders. But Gráinne Ni Mháille swept in without so much as a glance to left or right, as if no amount of weaponry could abash her. She had stridden up to Sidney and only submitted to using an interpreter when it became apparent he could not understand her heavily ac-cented attempts at English.

"I can understand her," Sidney's son Philip said. "I will interpret for you."

Grania had been surprised to see the young man here. Surprised, and pleased. A friend at court . . . perhaps. Or another spy who might have whispered to the lord deputy about her possible in-volvement in various conspiracies in Ulster.

But one glance at Philip Sidney's face reassured her. His smile was without guile; even Evleen would see no betrayals lurking there, and Evleen with her ancient wisdoms could see deep into the soul. "Watch the dark centers of the eye, Grania," she had instructed as the party was preparing to set sail for Galway. "If any man means you harm, that black hole will shrink when you stare at it."

Philip was equally pleased with Grania's appearance. Seen in the hastily thrown-together background of English authority, she still possessed both power and a certain dignity, an assurance as regal as a crown. She had captured every eye from the moment she entered the room, sweeping past the ranked sycophants as if they were so much furniture. When she saw Philip he caught a twinkle in her eye and realized she was enjoying herself.

The redheaded man at her back, the one with the broken jaw whom Philip remembered from Tyrconnell, did not seem so pleased. He was glowering around at everyone as if he expected an attack on his female chieftain at any moment.

After Grania had made her statement and her offer, and Richard Burke had corroborated her explanation of the ownership of Rock-fleet, Sir Henry Sidney beckoned his son aside. "Did I understand you correctly?" he asked, going over the issues.

"You did."

"This Grace O Malley offers men-at-arms and ships—and God knows we could use them right now—in return for being left alone? And the man called her husband lets her do the speaking?"

"I think," Philip hazarded, watching Grania and Iron Richard out of the corner of his eye as they waited with their attendants, "that the relationship between Grace and her husband is a little, ah, irregular, to say the least."

"To say the least," his father echoed dryly. "Barbarians indeed. You seem to have a favorable impression of this woman, Philip. Have you met her before?"

"Would I be likely to forget her if I had?" Philip Sidney countered. "But I would recommend you give her what she asks."

"Do you think that she-wolf can be trusted to keep a vow of alliance made between us?"

Philip turned and looked straight at Grania. Her black hair was braided with golden balls as ornaments; her heavy mantle was rimmed with fur. She was tall and splendid, and her eyes were commanding.

"I think," Philip said, measuring his words, "that honor means a great deal to her."

Sir Henry Sidney, who did not always ascribe virtues to the Irish, snorted. "On your word, then, we will give the Mayo woman a try—and welcome the use of her men and ships. As long as she causes no trouble I will order no further attacks against her —but be certain she understands that, Philip. This arrangement is contingent upon her good behavior."

As they left the guild hall and were making their way back through the narrow streets of the city toward the harbor, Tigernan felt the top floors of the two-storied houses leaning toward one another over his head, like giants about to fall on him. He hated cities. And he particularly hated the grim gray look of this one, this town crouched on one of Ireland's loveliest bays and flaunting its foreignness. For all its lovely Gaelic name, Galway was as Norman as any town. Sasanach, Tigernan thought.

A Tudor flag, honoring the queen, fluttered from a window, and Grania noticed it. I am in one of Elizabeth's cities, she said to herself.

Feet came pounding after them on the paving stones. Tigernan wheeled around, a shortsword already in his hand, and the rest of Grania's armed escort followed suit. But it was Sir Philip Sidney who came running up to them, flushed and panting, his fair hair disordered. He flung a graceful bow at Grania and said, "My Lord Sidney requests you to take him on a tour of Galway harbor so he may view the city's defenses from the sea."

Grania grinned. "Did you put him up to that?"

Sidney bowed again. "Your obedient servant."

"I think I have a friend in you, Philip Sidney. Very well, return to the lord deputy and tell him Gráinne Ni Mháille would be honored to have him as a passenger aboard her flagship. I will give him a tour of these waters he will never forget!"

"You will not do anything rash?" Sidney asked, suddenly concerned. He had only meant to give Grania a little additional time to win his father to her side more fully, but all the reports he had ever seen on this woman described her as unpredictable.

"I will do your father no harm," she promised.

Nor did she. The lord deputy's party boarded her favorite galley warily, but they were treated with the most exquisite courtesy for an entire day while Grania pointed out every aspect of the view from the sea, leaving an indelible impression of her knowledge and her intelligence carved in Henry Sidney's brain.

When at last Grania's fleet set sail for the return to Clew bay, Tigernan was fairly quivering with anger. As soon as the opportunity to speak to Grania presented itself he burst out, "I knew there was something between you and Philip Sidney!"

She stood in the prow, watching the massed buildings of Galway and its forbidding walls recede into the distance. "What do you mean?" she asked in a casual tone.

"Perhaps Iron Richard didn't notice, but then he never notices anything about you," Tigernan replied with contempt. "But I stood close beside you and saw how Philip Sidney devoured you with his eyes while you were pointing out the sights to his father. He's made every effort to give you a good smell in English noses, and I know why."

"You would prefer the English all hate me?" she asked, glancing at him sidelong. "I can think of one or two who do, and I consider that enough enemies. I like spice in my life, but I am not ready to be stabbed with a thousand spears at once."

Suddenly Tigernan chuckled. He did not mean to, he wanted to stay angry with her, but she was Grania. "I loved the look on the lord deputy's face when you presented him with a bill at the end of the ride," he said.

"I don't take any passengers for free, even Elizabeth's men," Grania replied.

The change in Grania's status was news that traveled as swiftly as the sea wind. Many saw her galleys circle the harbor at Galway with the lord deputy himself standing beside her. Almost before she returned to Clew bay the whole west coast was aware her ships were welcomed in Galway and her fleet was expecting little English interference in the future. The MacWilliam Iochtar and then The O Malley joined so many others in submitting to England's power, but Gráinne Ni Mháille remained independent, a law unto herself.

Murrough O Flaherty, son of Donal an Chogaidh, heard the news as far inland as the rough mountain country north of the Twelve Bens, where he and his wife and small children were living almost as outlaws with a band of Donal Crone's partisans.

Murrough laughed when he heard the tale of Grania charging Sir Henry Sidney for his boat ride. "That's herself," he said admiringly.

"You don't think she's gone over to the English side like your brother Owen?" someone asked him.

At the mention of Owen the smile faded from Murrough's face. Owen was living in comfort in the castle at Ballinahinch, considering himself a friend of the authorities and making sociable little visits to this or that English home. "I don't think Grania is anything like Owen," Murrough said aloud. "Owen lets the sasanach come into his halls and eat his food and ride off on his best horses and he never charges them a coin, just smiles and nods and says kick me again."

This was not strictly true, but close enough. Owen and Murrough were surviving in totally different ways. But they were both still surviving, and their mother criticized neither of them publicly, being busy enough with her own affairs.

✠

On a radiant summer day, when the sky blazed blue above Cuan Mó and the sun shimmered in crescents on the surface of the indigo water, Grania leaned back against the sun-heated surface of an overturned curragh that drowsed in the heat like a beached turtle. Young Tibbot sat at her feet, chewing on a grass stem. His mother was, as she sometimes did, telling him tales from her own childhood, from Gaelic Ireland as she had known it—stories of booleying, and the summer houses on the upland pastures. Of fairy wells and magic spells and boundless freedom, of smoky halls and rowdy warriors and pipes keening on windy headlands.

From memory she summoned her youth, and the youth of the

generations preceding her, and spun it out for him to see. She sang snatches of old songs for him, and told long and complicated jokes only another Gael could understand. She handed on the stories Dubhdara had once told her of his own childhood to pass the long hours at sea as they sailed together for Spain, and in so doing she thought she caught glimpses of her father in her son's face.

Her precious, precious son.

When the storytelling was done for the day, she buckled on a heavy leather belt and a brace of pistols, hugged the boy farewell, and set off to seize and board a passing merchantman that rode too low in the water from the weight of its rich cargo.

Old Ireland lived in Grania's memory and she would see it lived in Tibbot's as well, but the stomach must have food for the future.

Her success had gone to her head like ale. Each time she pitted herself against the sasanach and won, through strength or cunning, she became more confident of her own abilities and more eager to throw the dice again. Her world, more or less the way she wanted it to be, was intact for a little while longer, and she had accomplished that herself with shrewdness and bravado.

She allowed herself a little boasting in the hall at Belclare, where Melaghlin now resided as chieftain and tried to act as independent and autonomous as she, as if his submission to Elizabeth had never taken place.

"Owen Dubhdara was the last of his kind," Grania said often and pointedly.

She was riding a cresting wave, lifting up, up . . .

Under her command the galleys set out, flaunting her banner, on numerous missions of trade or piracy up and down the west coast. Wherever there was an advantage to be seized, Grania seized it; wherever there was an opportunity for profit, Grania took it. Under English control the rest of Ireland grew poorer, but there was still food on tables in Mayo and tools and weapons and imported cloth.

She had stood on equal footing with Sir Henry Sidney, looked him in the eye, and gotten what she wanted from him—she would not shrink from anyone. When various chieftains along her way contested her rights to fishing grounds she cheerfully brought up warriors and subdued them. She had extended her network of strongholds to include Tigernan's own Inishbofin, where from time to time she occupied the old, long-neglected Gaelic fort there and insisted on keeping the islanders' vessels beached while her galleys commanded the surrounding waters.

Seeing Grania rule like a chieftain on the island of his birth gave Tigernan a mixed sense of elation and discomfort. He never questioned the gender of her leadership elsewhere, but having Inishbofin under the control of a woman seemed to tilt the world as he knew it, the traditional hard world of the sea-ravaged islands where brave men went out in frail boats and a woman's place was to keep the peat burning on the hearth in the tiny house, and keen when her man's boat did not return.

There was no keening, no wailing and mourning, when Grania was on the island. There was laughter and purpose, and if she saw someone with the troubles of the world etched on his face she chided him for it. "Everyone has miseries," she would say. "But you don't have to be miserable. You're alive and your legs work; smile over that and get on with your life."

And then Tigernan heard her discussing, in the most casual of conversations, the possibility of extending her triumphs still further and doing a little raiding around the mouth of the Shannon, in the territory of the Earl of Desmond.

"You go too far!" he told her.

"Everyone hates Desmond," she replied. "He has made a career of bullying his neighbors, and he has some fine fat cattle down there in Munster."

"He also goes to the English court and is supposed to be a subject of Elizabeth Tudor. If you attack him . . ."

"Subject of the she-king! When the Desmond rebellion has set half of Ireland aflame? You think the English will care if we help ourselves to a little of the fat from Desmond's broth?"

"You are daring too much," Tigernan said with conviction. "Why do you do this? Don't you care if they . . . if they kill you? They might, you know."

She gave him a hard look. "Everyone dies, Tigernan. But I mean to live while I'm living, and if I take joy in victory would you deny it to me?"

"You take too many joys," he said.

"What do you mean by that?"

He could not keep the lid on the pot any longer. "Men! The men you take to your bed as if you were . . . as if you were . . ."

She was standing on his island, with the rocks he had clambered over as a boy and the wrinkled dark ocean he had always loved and feared as her background. She wore her trews and a heavy shaggy cloak, and the wind whipped her hair like a black flag. "As if I were a man helping myself to a woman I desired?" Her face set in the lines of challenge. "And why should I not, Tigernan? I do everything else as I please, why not that?"

Her doubled fists were on her hips, and her dauntless eyes were daring him. In his place, on his island. They stood just outside the rough stone fortress, one step away from a gaping door, a worn stair, a dark upper chamber where Grania kept a sea chest and a bed.

He had lived his life for her and, he thought, probably sacrificed his immortal soul by killing Calvagh; he had laughed with her and been laughed at; he would cheerfully die for her. But she had said, "I mean to live while I'm living," and suddenly Tigernan knew he needed to live completely too.

He grabbed her by the wrist. Grania's eyes widened with surprise, but she did not pull away. There was a curious look of waiting on her face, and a great silence seemed to settle around the two of them. Neither heard the pounding sea, or the gulls, or the shouts and calls of Grania's men as they loaded her galleys with the silver wealth of a good September run of herring.

"Grania Mhaol," said Tigernan, his voice hoarse and deep in his chest. He tugged at her arm, and she came after him, through the gaping door, up the worn stair, into the chamber that smelled of time and the sea.

Her bed waited as she had left it in a hurry at dawn, with the coverlet thrown back. A robe Tigernan had never seen her wear was flung across the sea chest, a fine woolen fabric dyed in the fashionable color known as goose-turd green. No candles were lit, for Grania brought no attendants to this outpost. In such places she preferred to take care of herself, and travel unencumbered.

"Who do you wear that robe for, Grania Mhaol?" Tigernan heard himself ask as if he had the right.

"Myself alone," she answered. "The nights are cold here, and I get cold more easily than I used to."

"You will not be cold tonight," he told her.

He stepped so close she could feel his breath on her face. The broken, homely face she had taken for granted seemed, when seen so near, to have taken on a stern dignity that was very attractive.

How can he be ugly and beautiful at once? Grania wondered. This is not Tigernan.

But it was. The eyes were his, green as the tide on the Kerry coast in late summer. He did not bathe in perfumed water, nor groom his warrior's mustache with perfumed oils. His jaw was clean-shaven but already rough with tomorrow's stubble. He seemed larger than she always remembered him; he loomed over her.

His face was naked with desire.

Generosity was second nature to Grania. The woman in her, that longed to receive, was instead compelled to give, to be responsible, to help, to care. With a flashing look back at their years together she realized how little she had actually given Tigernan and how much he had given her, from saving her life to making her laugh when she thought there was no laughter left in her. He was like the planks of her ships, she thought: absolutely trustworthy but needing some attention and maintenance from time to time, and not to be taken for granted.

She began it as a generous gesture, reaching out to a fellow human being. She lifted one hand to his stubbled cheek, and her eyes softened. "I know something has been troubling you for a long time, Tigernan. If you want to talk to me about it . . ."

"I am no good at talking," he replied. "I am clumsy at so many things."

Her hand moved tenderly down his face, and all his control slipped away in a moment. His arms closed around her with more strength than even he had known he possessed. He could feel the creaking of her ribs. He thought he might break them.

So did she. She could not breathe.

His mouth was savage. He gnawed her lips until she tasted blood. If he had been a different man she would have been groping for the knife that always lay within easy reach beside her bed. She actually tore one hand free and clawed the air with it, but instead of wielding a weapon the hand closed on Tigernan's shoulder, squeezed hard, then opened to slide down his back.

Tigernan expected almost anything but that. Yet when he realized she was returning his embrace some corner of his mind was not surprised. She fitted into his arms as if she had always been there. Surely he had known from childhood, as flowers in their tight buds anticipate the touch of the sun, what it would feel like to hold Grania.

He had known the depth of his own desire, too. Had known it and fought it and whispered, shamefaced, in the confessional of his lust for women, had begged for purgation and peace. And found none, even in the thundering silence of his hut at Curraun.

He could have tumbled the country girls as other men did, or satisfied himself with a dough-faced daughter from some social level equal or even below his own, where no claims might be made. He could have taken a wife and sired a houseful of children, as the priests urged. He could have done many things but in the end had done nothing, contenting himself with being Grania's captain.

"You should have gone into the priesthood, Tigernan," Magnus had once told him. "There's the place for a man like you."

But with Grania in his arms he knew the priesthood had never been the place for him.

They were on her bed together, though he did not remember how they got there. He did not remember removing clothing, but he could feel her bare skin against his.

Tigernan's whole being seemed to have centered itself in the massive erection he was pressing against her belly. Like a knife, like a sword . . . like a standing stone from some ancient ritual where Evleen might have worshiped. He felt Grania's hips move, pushing even closer.

Her head was thrown back and her eyes were closed. In the dim light filtering through the loophole he could see the lines of her throat and the vulnerable windpipe, successive rings of cartilage forming a column beneath the skin. Skin roughened by time and exposure, but beautiful, because it was Grania's skin.

He kissed her throat, and the violence ebbed in him. All the pent-up frustration and anger and longing melted into something quite different, a rich outpouring of emotion that seemed to fill him with a golden light.

She squirmed beneath him, and he realized she was lying at an uncomfortable angle, her spine pressed against the wooden slat at the side of the bed. He half rose and lifted her with him, shifting her into a better position. She weighed nothing in his arms.

She let him manipulate her body until they were both settled comfortably. At first his daring had surprised her, and her own response had shocked her, but that was over. She just wanted to get closer to him, to soak up the feeling of him.

Tigernan was not inherently graceful as Huw had been. He was a man of knotty musculature and sturdy peasant frame; he had not trained, as had Philip Sidney, in court dances or swordplay as an art. Whatever he did was done honestly and with straightforward determination. He went about his lovemaking the same way. He was not skilled, but he was earnest—and there was no mistaking his joy.

Joy. It came again to Grania, as it had once before, with Huw, and this time she recognized its face. With Huw she had taken what she needed, but with Tigernan she was giving in response to his need, and the pleasure she received in turn was just as great. His hands caressed her with delight, and she luxuriated in his admiration as he kissed her breasts, her belly, murmured something that might be flattering and might be merely incoherent as he pressed his hot face to the curling black hair triangled above her thighs.

He wanted to look at and touch all of her at once. It was as if he, sinner that he thought himself, had bypassed the purgatory the priests claimed existed on some half-mythical coastal island and had entered heaven direct—a heaven he thought lost to him. He must explore every path and byway, peer into every aperture. But he did it with such reverent admiration that Grania opened to him unashamedly, giving, giving.

When she smiled up at him and returned his most intimate caresses he could wait no longer.

He entered her with a confident plunge, then tried to hold back, because it seemed the heat would boil over, the moment would be past before he had time to savor it. There had been occasional furtive instances long ago to give him some intimation of the possibilities of sexual pleasure, but with Grania everything was amplified beyond his imagination's reach.

Tigernan braced himself and tried with all his strength to regain mastery of a body that would no longer obey him.

Grania's fingers dug into his back. "Don't stop," she whispered.

He heard himself start to laugh, helplessly. "I can't. Jesus and Mary, how can I stop now?" His hips slammed against hers, and Grania felt the laughter run all the way through his body and into her own where they were joined, so she experienced laughter in a way she had never felt it before. The laughter and the motion and the deep strong tide that flowed through both of them were creating something that wasn't Grania and Tigernan, but one single blissful creature with one immortal soul for that brief space of time. What one felt the other felt; he knew when her climax began though he had no prior knowledge of such a phenomenon in a woman. She knew the moment of his because it was simultaneous with her own, one the part of the other, shared like the laughter.

At last, panting, Tigernan rolled over onto his back. He stared up with sightless eyes and felt the woman move to cover his naked body with her own, keeping him warm while the sweat dried on his skin. She covered almost his entire length; she was a mantle of bone and muscle and softness. I will never need a cloak again, Tigernan thought, his eyes lazily following patterns smoke had made on the planked ceiling. Grania's heat will warm me forever.

He must have fallen asleep. He awoke with a start and could not imagine where he was. He lay in a carved bedstead such as he had never known in his life, and there were linen sheets . . . and a woman's rhythmic breathing beside him . . . !

Tigernan almost leaped from the bed before it all came rushing back to him. Dawn light showed pearly through the chamber's single loophole, revealing the planes and lines and disordered hair of the face beside him on the pillow. Grania had one hand under her cheek as she lay on her side, facing him. Her eyeballs moved behind her closed lids, following some dream, and she was smiling.

Gráinne Ni Mháille.

Outside the fort, her men would be up and about already, hawking and spitting and listening to their bellies growl, complaining of the cold, damp night or bantering with the island women who would bring their morning meal to them.

Who could possibly imagine where I am this day? Tigernan thought with wonder.

Grania opened her eyes and looked at him. For a moment she seemed disconcerted; then she chuckled. "It wasn't a dream."

"It was not. Or we both had the same one and you're trespassing in mine."

Her hair was tangled, and wrinkles had been pressed into her face from the night's sleeping. Tigernan had never seen anything so lovely. He envied the silver tongue of her dead foremastman, who could have articulated his feelings. "Did you sleep well?" he managed to ask.

"Wonderfully. Until I awoke sometime in the night with a bladder full to bursting and was forced to remember there is no privy chamber in this fort. Then I missed my own Rockfleet."

"I couldn't find a corner with straw in it, either," Tigernan confessed.

"That's no way to behave in a woman's bedchamber, you ignorant fisherman!" Grania told him, doubling her fist and aiming a playful punch at his shoulder.

He caught her wrist and prevented the blow. "I know how to behave in a bedchamber," he said, the expression in his eyes changing.

Grania ran her tongue over her lower lip. She could feel the delicious slow warmth seeping back into her body, making it heavy, languorous. "You do indeed," she murmured.

They rose together, much later, and dressed together too, like comrades. Tigernan could not helping taking one last proprietary look at her body before she covered it in cloth, however, and she saw the look and laughed.

When they went out into the misty morning, Grania stretched and filled her lungs to their very bottom. "I feel new," she said. "I feel that I can do anything." Her lips curved mischievously. "Even raid the Earl of Desmond, Tigernan . . . unless you're too fearful for it."

"I am not!" he said quickly. It was easy to be reckless on such a morning—regrets were for later.

25

Grania's first raid on Munster was most successful. She caught Desmond's clansmen by surprise and relieved them of a full cargo of good beef, and no sooner was that accomplished than she encountered two Spanish merchantmen coming north along the coast, straight for the offshore waters of Cliara. With nine galleys and a full complement of warriors, Grania surrounded the Spaniards and seized one of their ships. An Atlantic gale overtook them before they could capture the second, however, and the heavily laden vessel foundered and sank off Achill head in its attempt to escape. But Grania returned to Clew bay with enough loot to feed and support her people for quite some time.

"Take care," Evleen warned her, watching the galleys offloading. "Never try to grasp more than your two hands can hold."

Grania tossed her head. Her cheeks flushed with success, and she felt good; she felt wonderful. "Elizabeth of clan Tudor has sent a man named Francis Drake on a voyage to sail around the world and undoubtedly try to claim all of it for the English," she told Evleen. "Why should I not help myself to just a little for our clan before it is all eaten away?"

She sent presents to Margaret and her children and to both Owen and Murrough and their families. She dispensed largesse throughout Umhall so openhandedly her stores were soon depleted, but she did not care. She could get more. She was strong, she had Sidney's tacit support, and the horizon seemed limitless.

Late one night Tigernan found himself still awake and restless long after Grania had fallen asleep beside him. They had spent the day together supervising the recrating of a shipment from Tyrconnell, and they were both tired—though not too tired to let their eyes lock over a pile of glossy furs from some lonely northern woodland. She had winked and he had grinned and they had taken the furs to her chamber to warm them properly, flung down upon the floor with two hot bodies atop them.

Yet afterward, sleep eluded him. Moving carefully so as not to awaken Grania, Tigernan slipped from the chamber and went outside to crouch at the water's edge, sorting through a rubble of thoughts.

Stars glittered above Cuan Mó and slipped from the sky to splash soundless onto the water, where their memory glimmered in pinpricks of light. Looking at them, at so many of them, Tigernan found himself thinking of the men who had known Grania. He had no idea how many, she never spoke of it, but surely they were all of noble blood. Even that foremastman, he added to himself with grudging honesty.

So what was a coarse-fibered, lowborn fisherman doing with Gráinne Ni Mháille?

Simultaneously he had a sense of being very out of his place and also of being exactly where he belonged, and the incompatibility of the two cut him loose from the world as he knew it, leaving him floating, as alien as a fish in a pasture. Perhaps, he thought, that disjointed sensation had begun with the killing of Calvagh, an awkward murder by an awkward man who had been damned lucky no one caught him. Awkward . . . yes, that was how he felt, spreading out the knotty fingers of his capable hands and looking down at them in the starlight. Too awkward ever to dare aspire to the love of a chieftain's daughter.

Yet he would move the stars in their courses above if she asked it, and put them together again into whatever pattern she desired. With the memory of her body still imprinted on his, he believed such a miracle within his abilities and longed to demonstrate.

He just could not tell her such a thing. His tongue would never shape fancies to present to her like the trinkets everyone bestowed as if by divine right on Grania's daughter.

"It hurts, sometimes," said a soft voice behind him.

Tigernan jumped to his feet before he recognized that voice as Evleen's. "What are you doing out here?"

"Do you think you're the only one who can never sleep? Do you think there are never nights when I dream of Ruari Oge?"

His heart went out to her. "That's what you meant by hurt; it hurts to love."

"Yes. If you really love."

"Then why does anyone ever want to do it?" Tigernan burst out.

Evleen put her small hands on either side of his forehead and squeezed gently, as if she would squeeze the pain from his skull.

"Because we are, none of us, complete creatures, Tigernan. Even Grania in there—she is only part of something. Like the rest of us, she longs for more, for that she cannot even name. Right now she thinks her hunger can be satisfied by things, by winning, by seizing, by material wealth. She is wrong, of course, but she must learn it in her own time."

Tigernan crouched down again and lazily spun a stone out across the surface of the water, watching to see which incoming wave gobbled it up. "Tell her that," he suggested.

Evleen scissored her legs and sat down beside him with a move too sprightly for her years. Not for the first time, Tigernan had the peculiar impression that Evleen was not simply an aging and ordinary woman. She was more like . . .

As if she could read his thoughts and wanted to turn them in a different direction, she interrupted by saying, "Stay close to her, Tigernan, and guard her well. Our Grania is in great danger."

"And that is news, isn't it? She's been in danger almost as long as I've known her, and if she isn't she goes out and finds some."

"Listen to me. There are forces too strong for her, and clouds gathering she knows nothing about. I smell it on the wind. She thinks she moves the pieces over the chessboard, but there are others to whom she is only a pawn, and if she is in the wrong place they will take her out of the game."

He twisted his head to look at Evleen face-on, seeing only a pale glimmer instead of features he could read. Some trick of the moonlight blurred her face. "I didn't know you played chess."

"You've never seen me do it. I bled in my cycle throughout my youth but you never saw me do that, either. Heed my words, Tigernan. Stay close to her."

Evleen's voice was so intense it became a command, and he made every effort to obey it.

In fact, he hovered too close to Grania and it began to get on her nerves. One day she snapped at him, "I cannot take a step without finding you standing on my shadow and holding me back, Tigernan! Are we to be yoked together like oxen? Do you think me incapable of minding my own affairs?"

"Every woman needs a . . ." he began, but she interrupted him angrily.

"A man, is that what you're about to tell me? If that is the set of your thinking I warn you to forget it. I may enjoy you and your company, but I belong to no man and wear no fetters. I've tried Christian marriage and I've tried Gaelic marriage, and I'm done with marrying forever."

Tigernan straightened his spine to its longest so he could look down into her eyes. With the great dignity of a simple man, he replied, "What makes you think I would want any kind of marriage with you at all, Grania Mhaol? A well-used woman like yourself and me accustomed to my freedom?"

She stared at him with lifted brows for a moment, and then she laughed and clapped him hard on the shoulder.

✠

Though Grania did not realize it, Evleen's foreboding was solidly if intuitively grounded in the fact that her mistress was contributing to a growing English determination to control the seas and safeguard critical trade routes. As Grania became more bold in her piracies, her name appeared increasingly in dispatches of complaint sent to Dublin castle.

And even as a voyage of honest commerce took her to the Welsh ports, Sir Richard Bingham was returning to Ireland with anger burning in him like a tumor, sick to the depths of his soul that he had not been included in the crew of Sir Francis Drake's epochal attempt to sail around the world. While Grania was arguing the cost of iron and flannel in cramped medieval towns with streets like alleys, running with sewage and rats, Bingham was returning to the Erin he hated, a land exemplified for him by his remembered image of strong, wild, vivid, unconquered Gráinne Ni Mháille.

Headed for home once more, Grania put in at Dublin to replenish her supplies. She did not much like Dublin. In the heart of the Pale it was too Anglicized altogether for her taste, its Viking origins submerged in a Tudor building boom. She went no farther into the town than its docks, then told Tigernan she had a notion to spend the night as a guest of the lord of Howth instead of aboard her galley, or in one of the reeking inns near the harbor.

"O Malleys have traded with the lords of Howth for generations," she said. But when she arrived at the castle held by Christopher St. Lawrence, latest in an ancient Anglo-Norman line, she found the gates barred to her. The lord of Howth was very aware that Grania was out of favor in Dublin and was looking to his own safety.

"How dare he shut me out and deny me traditional hospitality!" Grania cried, fine in her fury. "So be it, Tigernan; I will sleep aboard ship after all, but when St. Lawrence next wants some goods shipped without the English hearing of it and taxing them, he will have to apply to a different sea captain!"

She turned away from the closed gate, then paused. A flash of movement caught her eye. "You there . . . you lad lurking behind that holly bush. Come forward and tell me why you've been following us!"

A slender youth emerged from among the shrubberies beside the high stone wall. He wore a shirt of fine Holland cloth with an English ruff, but his hair was tousled and two merry eyes sparkled in a face full of freckles. For a moment Grania thought she was seeing Fergal the long-lost ship's apprentice again after so many years.

"Who are you?" she demanded to know.

"Someone who likes boats and the sea," he told her. "I saw your galleys come in down at the harbor and their looks pleased me. So when you headed here I . . . I suppose I followed, because I was curious about you and why you should come to my father's castle."

"Your father . . . the lord of *Howth?*"

"He is," the boy said with a nod. "I am Nicholas St. Lawrence."

"Are you now?" Grania grinned. "And you like the sea, is it?"

"I do. But my father refuses to allow me to sail out on a ship. He won't allow me to do anything I want to do." From the way he spoke Grania realized young Nicholas had little fondness for his sire—a feeling she shared in full measure at that moment.

Her eyes glinted. "Would you like to come to sea with me?"

"Are you serious?" He was suddenly as quivering and eager as a hound puppy on its first hunt.

Tigernan put his hand on Grania's arm. "You can't kidnap a lord's son, Grania Mhaol! We've stolen many things, but . . ."

She shrugged off the cautionary hand. "I said nothing about stealing him. The boy has a taste for the sea, and we're short a crewman, since Liam has the stomach complaint. We can give young Nicholas a fine boatride as far as Clew bay, by which time he will have a set of sea legs under him and a good tale to tell his children someday. And if his father wants me to send the boy back, then he can give me his promise to keep his doors open at dinner for all eternity, so *my* sons and their sons will always be assured of a meal and a bed when they visit this region!"

The prank was so typical of Grania that Tigernan could only shake his head as he joined in her cheerful gale of laughter.

Nicholas St. Lawrence looked from one to the other. "Is she serious, sir?" he asked Tigernan at last. "Nothing would give me greater pleasure than to sail around Ireland. I would leave this minute, but I won't be teased."

The ginger-haired Gael winked down at him. "I assure you our Grania is serious. Don't let her laughter mislead you; she means what she says."

Nicholas began to grin too. "I would love to see that old fart's face when my father learns I've gone off on my own . . . and when he hears what it will cost him to get me back!" With no further hesitation, he swung onto the path beside Grania and Tigernan and turned his face toward the sea.

✠

Young Nicholas was bright and bold. He was quickly seasick and quickly over it, entering wholeheartedly into the adventure. He could almost have been my son, Grania thought to herself, watching him. All the bold and merry lads of Ireland could be my sons, this Norman included. It is not the blood, but the spirit that is the strongest bond.

A wind came up as they were off Drogheda, filling the sails so the oarsmen could rest on their oars. One promptly brought out his tympan and began to play it, drawing first a bow and then his fingernails across the strings. A second man joined in with a single pipe; the resonant beat of a bodhran soon followed. The sun was setting. Once Nicholas came aboard, Grania had determined to sail immediately rather than waiting for the next day, when her plan might be discovered and the fine fun thwarted.

They would soon be sailing at night, but she loved sailing at night. Leaning against the mast, she felt the powerful tug of the sail. She smiled, and saw Nicholas smile back at her. She reached up to rumple Tigernan's hair as he passed her on his way to the stern.

[335]

I have all I can ever hope for, Grania thought. It's a fortunate woman I am. I must remember exactly how this feels, as you need to be able to remember a full belly when you're hungry.

Evleen had told her that, once.

When they reached Clare island a messenger was sent east, carrying word of Nicholas' safe arrival and the ransom wanted for him to his father. In due course the lord of Howth sent Grania a heavy ring in pledge of his honor, and she returned his son by way of the southern coast, obtaining a ride for him on an O Flaherty galley.

"I will be sailing almost in your wake myself," Grania told him as she bade the boy a fond farewell and sent him home showered with gifts. "I plan another visit to the Welsh ports soon and may stop at your father's stronghold to be sure he lives up to his part of our bargain. But first I mean to visit a place where I have had good fortune of late and do a little raiding along the banks of the Shannon."

The remark meant nothing to Nicholas. But he innocently repeated her words to a sailor aboard the vessel that carried him home to his angry father—who would never forgive Grania, and had told the lord deputy so, in yet another of the complaints being lodged against her. And the O Flaherty crewman to whom Nicholas mentioned Grania's plans repeated it to a friend, who repeated it to another friend when they put in at Liscannor bay for fresh water. A disease spread by mouth, the word traveled.

Grania almost took Tibbot with her on that voyage to build his sea legs, but at the last moment the boy came down with a fever, and she left him to Evleen to nurse with herbs and broths. Then, with a high heart and the anticipation of a goodly haul, Gráinne Ni Mháille set sail for the coast of Munster.

The Earl of Desmond, of the family Fitzgerald, was a man torn by conflicting loyalties. Like the other Anglo-Norman lords, the Fitzgeralds had given nominal allegiance to the English monarchs since they first came to Ireland, while building feudal kingdoms of their own and becoming Irish, they thought, in every sense that mattered. But English authority was attempting to strip them of their lands as surely as it was confiscating the lands of the Gaels, and the two old enemies at last united in a revolt of the southern Geraldines that laid waste to most of Munster.

The English had responded with measures of such brutal retaliation that even many of their own number were appalled. Babies were slain as ruthlessly as warriors; the rotted flesh of Munstermen stank in open fields and hung swaying from nooses.

When the rebellion faltered, Desmond decided his current self-interest lay in reestablishing some sort of amicable relationship with the English. They were winning; they would win. They had an endless supply, it seemed to the Irish, of both men and arms. Even Desmond, who frequently visited London, did not realize how thinly that army was stretched. To keep what lands he had while he quietly rebuilt his strength, Desmond planned to offer some propitiatory gift to the lord deputy.

When he received word that the galleys from Mayo were planning another raid on him, he went straight to his private chapel and thanked God for a plum dropped into his hands.

With her banner floating proudly above her and a fair wind lifting her heart, Grania sailed toward the south. The cresting wave on which she had ridden for so long rose up, up . . . and curled over.

And began to fall.

Desmond's soldiers were waiting for her at the mouth of the Shannon.

✠

The morning had been shrouded in fog with a feeble, shifting breeze, and even Grania's experienced captains were not always certain of the shore and the shallows. They had made a cautious approach to landing and were just stepping onto dew-wet grass when the attack came.

This was not to be a sea battle, with the barking voices of culverins and falconets to punctuate the action. Muskets roared and kicked instead, while blades flashed and men screamed and yelled and swore. The fog crouched low upon the earth, as if to enfold both sides in an unreal blanket of gray protection. But there was no true protection. Men died on the bank of the Shannon and their blood soaked into land that had already been well watered with blood, generation upon generation.

The air was acrid with the smell of gunpowder and bowels opening in the spasm of death. Tigernan fought with the strength of three, but Grania's forces were so badly outnumbered even his passionate ferocity could not save her. He stood back to back with her until the end, however, neither of them aware that the order had gone out to take her alive at all costs. For that reason no guns were aimed at Grania, a factor that probably saved Tigernan's life as well. But at last a sword thrust broke through his tiring defenses and laid open his thigh to the bone, narrowly missing the artery. He fell sideways with a groan of anguish, one hand reaching for Grania.

She screamed in rage as they closed in on her, Desmond's men. Anglo-Normans, Gaels bought with the earl's money, imported Scots mercenaries like the ones Grania smuggled in for The O Donnell. So many men, grabbing for her, beating at her . . .

The bards of Ireland, now hunted and in hiding because the English feared their ability to inflame with verse and vigor, composed ballads to commemorate Grania's capture so future generations would hear the truth of it. In firelit circles in secluded glens they sang for the bold souls who dared listen:

> *Intermarriage is high treason, Gaelic names*
> * forbidden be.*
> *Even Desmond, once a hero, to the Saxon bends*
> * the knee.*
> *With his guile and with his gun*
> *Was his treacherous triumph won*
> *Now Gráinne Ni Mháille is not free.*
> *Desmond's prize to Limerick prison was delivered,*
> * bound in chain.*
> *Henry Sidney would not free her; Connaught's*
> * loss was England's gain.*

Philip Sidney himself pleaded for Grania's release, highly incensed that she had been offered like a bribe to win back the favor of the English for Desmond. "A man who would capture and imprison a woman just to gain an advantage for himself does not deserve to have that advantage," he argued with his father.

But the lord deputy was in no mood to listen. There had been too many complaints about Grania, and she had, after all, been taken in the very act of raiding. "Let her remain where she is," Henry Sidney said. "And concern yourself no further about her; she's only Irish. Besides, I have decided the three boats and handful of fighting men she put at our disposal are in no way worth the trouble she causes in paperwork alone. Have you any idea how many complaints I've had to read about the woman?"

She's only Irish. Hearing those words, Philip Sidney vowed to return to England, to his own home and his own wife. To a land less likely to break your heart with its strange magic.

Grania's cell in Limerick prison was one pace wide and a pace and a half long. A tall man—or Gráinne Ni Mháille—could not stand upright in it. The walls were slimy, the air fetid, no window admitted light.

When the door first shut behind her and she heard its iron bar drop into place, Grania refused to be frightened. She had seen dungeons before; almost every stronghold had them, including those of the O Malleys. She would just wait; surely they must let her out sometime . . . as soon as Sidney learned of her capture. . . .

But time passed and she was not released. Occasionally a coarse hempen rope was fastened around her neck and she was walked in a small walled courtyard, where she saw no one else but her guard. Her questions about her men were never answered; indeed, she heard no Gaelic spoken. And after too short an interval beneath a small patch of open sky she was thrust back into the cell.

In time, a dreadful sense of her own helplessness began to overpower her. Action had always been her answer to every trouble, and now she could not act. She could do nothing on her own behalf.

Helpless. Captive.

Sweet Jesus, I am so afraid!

Her heart began to pound in her breast like a netted trout. The sound of the door closing behind her, the iron bar falling, was like a wound that went through to her soul. She began to have trouble breathing. Sometimes she lay at full length on the gritty floor and bit her fist to keep herself from screaming. And then she found herself beating from wall to wall, flinging herself against unyielding stone until she was bruised and bloody in her frenzy to find the freedom that did not exist.

Stop it! She ordered herself. Stop it! But it took a long time to get control of her mind and still longer to control her body, to make it cease its destructive struggles.

Sit down, she told herself. Be calm, Grania. Think.

The trembling started, and she fought it back, step by step.

Be calm. Think.

She had not done enough thinking of late, she realized tardily. In the darkness of her cell she saw with embarrassing clarity the recklessness that had brought her here. If you gamble long enough you are certain to lose sometime, she reminded herself—and those who follow you must lose as well.

Tigernan . . . oh God! Are you alive or dead? "Tigernan!"

Her self-control broke then, and she pounded her hands against the indifferent walls until her flesh broke and ran red with blood, but only the echoes answered her.

✠

A day might have passed, or perhaps even two. Grania had no way of judging the time. When at last exhaustion overtook her someone opened the door and put in a basin of wheat and weeds boiled together to serve her for a meal. The filthy stuff was inedible, but she drank the puddle of liquid in which it swam and that at least eased her parched throat.

So someone, she reasoned, must have a way of watching her that she had not detected, and had been aware when she slept. She resolved to stay awake after that to deny them the satisfaction of seeing her vulnerable and unaware. From time to time she heard a rumble of English voices beyond her door, as guards passed by and hailed one another. English.

No Gael would have treated a hostage as she was being treated. Prisoners were traditionally shown the same generosity as guests under Gaelic law, for what man could predict when the situation might be reversed and he find himself a prisoner? Therefore a Gael treated his prisoners well indeed. The English did not.

They will let me die here, Grania thought.

She did not want to give the English the satisfaction of taking her life from her like this, in squalor, like some animal.

Will Elizabeth order me killed? Grania wondered. Have I at last slapped her face so hard she felt it, clear across the sea?

In Dublin castle, no one had any intention of executing the Mayo pirate. The lengths to which the queen would go to avoid ordering the death of another woman were well known. Grace O Malley was not worth stirring up that hornet's nest; she was no Mary Queen of Scots, no threat to the throne.

But she was a problem.

She was summoned before first one official and then another, and questioned repeatedly about her activities and her alliances. No matter what she said, it was obvious the English chose not to believe her. They accused her of being locked knee to knee in a conspiracy with the northern clans to rise against Tudor authority and set all of Ulster ablaze.

On a day of damp drizzle she was led into the courtyard once more and met there by a man in a broadcloth coat and wrinkled hose, a sour-smelling man who would not speak to her but only attacked her head with a pair of shears while four guards held her. Grania felt the thick hair slide down as she was shorn; she heard its soft rustle as it fell at her feet. She saw, in the eyes of her captors, the pleasure they took in thus humiliating her.

She flung up her head and bared her teeth at them, and let loose a great scream of defiance. Startled, the barber paused for a moment but then resumed his work, keeping one eye on the guards to make sure the woman did not break free until he had her shorn.

Grania Mhaol.

Oh, Tigernan, she thought. Do you live? Do you know I live?

Somewhere in the corners of her soul she was aware of his continuing presence, as if his crooked smile reached her through layers of darkness.

Perhaps he was still alive . . . somewhere.

She had been questioned and accused by Desmond shortly after her capture, and at last it was the turn of the English. A guard took Grania from her cell and conducted her to a bleak chamber with only two arrow slits and a smoky lamp for light. There, in the face of the man who waited to interrogate her, she saw an echo of features she recognized and felt a spear of ice run through her body.

Like his brother Richard, John Bingham had been disappointed at not being assigned to Drake's expedition. Sullenly he accepted the first post offered him instead, one which required he examine the Crown's prisons and prisoners and report on the status of both.

He looked at the latest captive brought before him with unconcealed disgust. Another lice-ridden Gael, and a woman at that. According to the charges he held, this was the notorious Mayo pirate his brother had mentioned to him in scathing tones. He was not inclined to be gentle with her. "You are charged not only with piracy and raiding, but also with conspiring against her majesty with certain northern warlords. Have you anything to say about this?"

She was tired and terrified, but she would not let him see either. The man spoke to her in a rough mixture of English and Gaelic, showing long familiarity with Irish administration, and she answered him in kind. "I demand only to know the fate of my men, and to speak with the lord deputy."

John Bingham worked a gob of spittle around in his mouth and then shot it into the air so it landed almost upon her. "You will not see Sidney," he said with conviction. "You have betrayed by your thievery the trust the lord deputy placed in you, and you can expect no quarter from him now. But if you will tell me the names of those with whom you conspire in rebellion—and also give me lists of the weapons you have illegally shipped into the country for them—I might be inclined to at least spare the life of that wounded captain who is identified as coming from your own flagship."

Grania could not control her swift intake of breath. Tigernan was alive, then! And she could barter for him. . . .

She could betray The O Donnell and the others who hoped to stand against the might of Elizabeth Tudor. . . .

In a land that had seen too many Irishmen turn against each other, Grania could not add that particular betrayal to her list of crimes. She was no longer always sure what honor was, but her Gaelic heart still loved it and must be true to that love.

"I can give you no information," she said. "But I warn you of this: if any man of mine still living is hurt by your order, I promise to call the great chieftains of the north to fall upon you and all your kind with such fury as you have not yet seen in Ireland!"

She was bluffing; neither The O Donnell nor Hugh O Neill was obligated to her to do any such thing. But she had gambled all her adult life and knew how to be very convincing, and she saw John Bingham hesitate in the face of that threat.

"Furthermore, I demand to see my captain," she added while Bingham was sifting her words. "If he is not brought to me I will . . . I will go back to my cell and refuse to eat." She drew on the ancient Gaelic culture there, the time when a man could destroy another's reputation forever by starving at his doorstep in response to an injustice. But her words triggered a light of alarm in John Bingham's eyes. His orders had been explicit; Grania was to be held alive.

"You will not starve!" he thundered. "You will eat if a guard has to ram the food down your throat with his fingers!"

She allowed herself a small and secret satisfaction. Unwittingly, the man had put a weapon in her hands by telling her her death was not desired. So she had the smallest of coins for bartering, and was just a little less helpless. "Let me see my captain and I will eat." She folded her arms.

The next day, the door to her cell grated open and Tigernan stumbled in as if pushed, with an oath wrung from him when he put too much weight on his wounded leg.

"Tigernan! Is it really you? Are you all right?"

"I am grand," he growled. "They have hacked my leg almost off and I have been dead these nine days, but I am just grand."

She knelt beside him on the filthy floor, hugging him, searching his face and body with her fingers in the darkness of the little cell. She knew that mustache, that skull shape, those shoulders . . . his chest was too bony. And bandages bulked his thigh, stiff with dry blood.

"You're badly wounded," she whispered.

"And didn't I tell you that myself? But at least you're alive, Grania Mhaol." He was touching her too, his fingers stroking her shorn skull. "You're alive." She could tell from the tone of his voice that he had thought her dead.

"I mean to stay that way, Tigernan, and you will too."

The door opened, and she sensed rather than saw guards crowd into the cell. They pulled Tigernan away, and Grania swung her arms wildly, hoping to hit one of her captors in the face. Then Tigernan's familiar hand caught one of hers and squeezed it, hard, once before they hustled him out the door.

The prison walls closed in on Grania with a terrible rush. "I want to see your magistrate again!" she screamed. "Tell him I must talk with him!"

In the corridor beyond her cell, an unfriendly voice laughed.

✠

She did not see Tigernan again, but the next day she was moved to a slightly larger cell with an arrow slit and a pile of almost clean straw for bedding. Though she did not realize it, this was to be her home for the next year. John Bingham had closed the book on Gráinne Ni Mháille and moved on to his next post, leaving her to await whatever disposition Dublin ultimately chose for her.

She was in Limerick jail so long she came to know her jailers of necessity, for people could not see each other every day without at last speaking. So it was that she learned Tigernan had finally been released because he was deemed too injured to be dangerous and too minor to be of political value. If she had felt like addressing God, Grania would have offered a prayer of thanksgiving at receiving such news. But she was not in a mood to speak to God, who seemed to have forgotten her altogether.

The winter was bitter, and the clothes she wore provided all the warmth she had. Her light summer sea cloak served her as an inadequate blanket, and she lay curled beneath it dreaming of great shaggy Gaelic mantles with heavy hoods, warm, warm.

Her body, accustomed to strenuous activity, screamed for exercise. Like watching at a friend's deathbed she observed the growing flaccidity of her muscles. She was not a young woman, but her way of life had staved off much of the aging process until she was imprisoned; then it began to catch up with her with frightening speed.

And she was helpless. Her death was the only threat she could make, a threat that came to be meaningless even to her as she endured the living death of captivity.

Imprisonment was a horror beyond anything she might have imagined. Every day her eyes opened to sameness, to a stolid and gray discomfort that eroded both strength and will. She was always hungry, for the boiled weeds and stringy meat they gave her provided inadequate nourishment. She was always filthy, which made her more miserable than the cramping in her belly.

And she could do nothing.

At night she tossed and rolled, feeling the hard floor beneath the straw on which she lay, longing for the escape of sleep but falling instead into troubled dreams where she rarely experienced the freedom of the sea. Instead she dreamed of the men who had died in her service, or of her children in some strange world she did not recognize, in troubles she did not understand.

I shook my fist at God and thought myself self-sufficient, she whispered in the night, and He reached down to pluck me out of life and drop me in this dark hole forever.

Terror lurked at the back of her mind, always waiting to open up and swallow her.

I could spend my life like this.

With nothing more than this.

Ever.

Once more she bit her fist to stifle her screams.

✠

There was always trouble in the west, and in time even Limerick prison was not large enough to hold all the Crown's accused. In November of 1578, Lord Justice Drury, president officer of Munster, informed the Privy Council in Dublin that he was sending to Dublin castle "a woman of the province of Connaught . . . famous for her stoutness of courage and person, and for sundry exploits done by her by sea."

It was time for Dublin to take some responsibility for the continuing problem of maintaining and controlling Gráinne Ni Mháille.

She was to be transported overland to the prison in Dublin, that being deemed the safest way. Too many of her followers still roamed the western seas; it was better they not know of her transfer in case they attempt a rescue. Tigernan, upon being freed, had scoured Mayo for fighting men to stand with him in an effort to attack Limerick jail and free Grania, but the mission was suicidal, and he had won few converts to the cause.

Iron Richard Burke was the most blunt about it. "She got herself into this, let her get herself out."

"But she's your wife," Tigernan protested. "Or so some still call her."

Burke's expression was sardonic. "She doesn't think so. She has used me and I have used her, but I feel no obligation to her now. If she wants to buy her freedom, let her offer the English Rock-fleet."

"Never will she do that," Tigernan told him.

He went farther afield in search of help, but neither Owen nor Murrough was forthcoming. Both expressed sorrow though not surprise about their mother's imprisonment; each was busy with his own affairs, and each considered Grania capable of taking care of herself without involving them.

"She would be better off with goslings for children," Tigernan told them darkly, glad for once that he had no ungrateful offspring of his own. He wished that the boy Nicholas of Howth were Grania's son, for there was a boy who would come after her with all flags flying, even if he was not a Gael.

For her trip to Dublin, a fettered Grania was put into an open cart pulled by a team of sturdy Irish ponies. On the morning of her departure she found herself reunited with at least a few of her men, for Turlough O Flaherty, the brothers MacShea, and young Cormac Downe were brought from their cells to go with her. They exchanged warm greetings, each delighted to find the others still alive. All five were tightly secured, and the trip across Ireland promised to be most uncomfortable.

Guards on foot and horseback accompanied them with surly resentment for the long journey. The road they followed was hardly a road at all, often disintegrating into a treacherous track through bogland or outlaw-haunted woods. As they moved eastward, Grania began to see what years of warfare and rebellion had done to the rich meadows and valleys of Munster. Crops had been burned, houses pulled down, carcasses of Irish cattle left to rot in the fields, their stiffened legs pointing the way from one scene of devastation to the next. From the south, those people still strong enough to travel were pouring into the midland, their eyes permanently haunted with memories of rebels hanged or pressed to death and women and children left to starve.

"This is not the Ireland I knew," Grania said in a horrified whisper to Cormac Downe.

Overhearing, the nearest guard reined his horse closer to the prisoners' cart. "You should see what it's like farther south. All the Geraldine lands threaten to turn into one vast boneyard, no matter how hard Desmond tries to win his way back into Elizabeth's favor. The bailiffs and sheriffs of Munster show no mercy to any Irish person. I've seen people so desperate for food they ate carrion. Any patch of cress or shamrock is a banquet, and hundreds of people descend on it, stripping out even the roots to eat and leaving the poor earth all but bleeding. And it will get worse. Beaten as they are, there are still a few who resist surrendering their holdings to English authority."

Grania's eys swept the man's face, the wide-set eyes, the broad cheeks, the gentle curve of a mouth forced into uncharacteristic grimness. "You're Gaelic," she said.

"I am. And you want to ask why I ride guard on you for the lord deputy? For the same reason you tried to make an alliance with him once, Gráinne Ni Mháille. I don't want to live on cress and carrion."

She looked down at her bound hands and made no reply.

The cart jolted on.

As they drew nearer the Pale, they met increasing numbers of English soldiery in the roadway. Every fold in the hills seemed to shelter a garrison; every ford across a stream was guarded.

Within the Pale itself the landscape changed. Farms were prosperous compared to those they had seen before, and houses stood unburned, many of them with slate roofs instead of Gaelic thatch. There were live cows in the byres and clots of sheep blocking the roadway. Few people bothered to watch as the prisoners passed, for such sights had become common on the road to Dublin.

When the cartwheels clattered onto the first of the city's cobbled streets, young boys ran out, hooting derision and throwing stones. "Pagan Papist heathens!" yelled one lad, intoxicated with his own daring. In his home he heard the teachings of both Luther and Calvin debated, but one fact was essential to both views of Protestantism: he had been taught to hate the Catholic Irish on sight and hate them forever.

They rounded a corner onto a slightly wider street just as someone threw a pail of slops from an overhead window, to the accompaniment of raucous laughter. The mess rained down onto the unprotected head of Turlough O Flaherty. He could not lift his shackled hands to wipe the filth from his eyes and mustache. He could only stand rigid, and endure.

I could have been with Tigernan in a cottage at Curraun, thought Grania, helping him mend his nets. We would be trading insults and telling fine rare stories. . . .

Digging deep, she found the threadbare remnant of a smile and spread it across her face.

After so many months of imprisonment her bones stood out sharply through her pallid skin, making her smile a ghastly parody of itself. Those who saw her as she passed by never forgot that brief, wild vision: the tall woman in the cart, wrapped in stained and threadbare Gaelic garments, her spiky hair streaked with gray, her colorless lips drawn back in a skeletal grimace.

The cart passed through the arching gateway of Dublin castle beneath the heads of rebels rotting on poles, grinning that same terrible grin.

Grania had been kept in isolation in Limerick, but in Dublin she was thrust into the heart of a teeming crowd whose crimes ranged from purely political to murder and worse. In such a subculture, every day was a fight just to stay alive against the menace of those who would kill you for the food in your bowl or the use of your body. But at least Grania's men were with her, and they afforded her the best protection they could. They also made it mandatory that she wear a brave face, a heavy responsibility she had not had to bear in solitude.

The prison was never quiet, and they were constantly aware of other captives being added or subtracted. Some few were released for reasons no one knew; others went to their deaths with curses or hymns on their lips, and those who remained behind jeered or wept to see them pass.

Many were Palesmen, loyal to the queen, who were now called traitors simply because they could not pay the ruinous taxes imposed upon them by a perpetually money-poor monarchy.

Taking pity on one kindly old fellow whose only crime this was, Grania promised, "I will speak to Sir Henry Sidney if and when I get to see him on my own behalf. We have an understanding; I may persuade him to help you."

"Don't you know?" the man asked. "Sidney has been recalled to England."

"Then to whom can I appeal?" Grania wondered, throwing out her hands as if she must grasp something, anything.

The poor farmer shook his head. "I do not know," he sighed. "A new lord deputy will be appointed in time. Then . . . who can say?"

Who can say.

The dungeons of Dublin castle were perpetually damp, with a pervasive stench of human excrement that eventually became part of one's hair, one's clothing, one's taste buds. And there was always a sound of water dripping somewhere, onto stone.

During the day the usual prison noises drowned it out, but in a night punctuated by groans and curses, the repetitive drop, drop, drop dominated consciousness.

No one knew where it came from. No one seemed particularly interested in stopping it, for each prisoner had more urgent troubles. But Grania came to dread the nights with a new sort of horror because she knew that sound would erode what remained of her sanity.

Drop, drop, drop.

She imagined the dripping noise was creating a web of fissures throughout her head, like the cracks in the limestone of the Burren. If she heard just one more drop fall, her skull would split wide open.

Drop, drop, drop.

Rumors floated on the stagnant air of the prison:

"Queen Elizabeth has had a bastard child and strangled it."

"Desmond has risen in revolt again and his old rival Ormond is coming back from England to stand against him."

"A new lord deputy has been named and is on his way here."

It might all be true, or none of it; Grania had no way of judging. But some seeds of truth were there, for a new lord deputy was indeed on his way to Dublin—a man named Arthur Grey de Wilton, selected by the Privy Council simply because he had no Irish experience and might therefore operate more objectively than others who had become baffled and bemused by the land.

But before leaving England, Grey had spent an evening with a young friend of his, son of the former lord deputy—just to familiarize himself at second hand with his new post. And Philip Sidney had made a most surprising request.

"There is a woman, one Grace O Malley, being held as a prisoner for piracy and conspiracy," Philip told Grey over a meal of boiled eels and stout. "She has a following in Connaught and would be more valuable to you alive and loyal than imprisoned and dead. I would urge you to win her support and free her."

"Why did your father not free her, then?" Grey wanted to know. "Or is he . . . not as moved by a woman's charms as you, my randy friend?"

Philip flushed but held firm. Meeting Grania had changed his life in some indefinable way, for in her he had encountered for the first time a woman who met him on equal footing in every aspect of life, socially and intellectually and sexually, with a healthy vigor that made the powdered creatures of Elizabeth's court seem pallid by comparison. Philip found himself recalling Grania's athletic body and great boisterous laugh at the oddest times, as if a fresh wind had suddenly blown through his memory.

The thought of her still captive haunted him.

"As a favor to me, Arthur," he pleaded.

Lord Grey snorted. "Sometimes I wonder why I am fond of you, Philip. You can be a perfect fool."

"But I added my voice to those recommending you for this post," Philip Sidney reminded him. "You owe me."

26

The new lord deputy of Ireland had a finely modeled head and wispy hair as fine as a girl's. When talking to someone, he had a habit of tilting his head to one side and squinting astigmatically down his nose.

He was squinting now, trying to interpret what he saw.

For Grania's audience with him one of her jailers had given her an alum-dyed gown to replace the remnants of her skirt and trews. The dress was of poor-quality linen, too tight across her rib cage and too short to cover her ankles, but at least it was female garb. Grania had accepted it gladly, and even gone so far as to try to twist her growing-out hair into a skimpy semblance of a married woman's braid. When she asked for water to bathe in, however, she was rewarded only with laughter. No one bathed in the dungeons of Dublin castle.

News that she was at last to be able to see the lord deputy had put a little strength back into legs wasted from inactivity, and she walked with a hint of her own stride down the long hallways to Grey's offices.

From whispered rumor, she had learned that Grey was a nobleman, but little else about him. "I know an English nobleman," Grania had said. "Sir Philip Sidney, a decent enough man altogether. It could be this Grey is of the same tribe, and if so . . ."

She truly wanted to believe that not all of Elizabeth's men were monsters. She could not bear thinking Ireland was being subjugated by a cruel and vicious race.

Her first instinct was to go swaggering into Grey's presence in spite of her weakness, showing him that nothing the English might do could intimidate the woman she was. Showing him the pride of the O Malleys. But as if whispering from the shadows of her cell, she heard Evleen's voice very clearly: "Wait. Feel him out. You have made too many angry already. Do not head into the storm with all your sails spread."

Grania glanced around in surprise at the familiar clarity of that voice, but all she saw was bare stone wall. No Evleen. Yet somehow the woman was with her, urging sensible caution, her soft Gaelic voice running like water over pebbles even in that harsh dungeon. Ireland, seeping through the stones.

She walked upright into Grey's presence, scorning to lean on the guard who accompanied her. But she did not swagger.

The new lord deputy gave her one piercing look and then dropped his gaze to the papers before him. He was, though he did not want to show it, surprised by the natural majesty of the bedraggled woman who faced him.

"You are charged with piracy and various felonious raids on loyal subjects of her majesty," Grey read aloud. An interpreter at his elbow chanted the words after him in a bored and indifferent Gaelic.

When the reading of the charges was completed, Grania summoned all the English she knew to reply, slowly and carefully, "I am a sea captain and ply that trade in the traditions of my clan, supporting myself and my people as best I am able. I have never declared war on Elizabeth Tudor, nor attacked her through her subjects."

She had no sooner begun speaking than the interpreter's voice overrode hers. She frowned and tried to raise her poor prison-rusted vocal cords to a louder pitch, only to see Grey slam his open palm on the polished oak table between them and point sternly to the interpreter.

Grania understood. There was to be no direct conversation between them; no way for them to come to an understanding at all. She knew her English was poor and this man surely had no Gaelic, but if he had been willing to try they might have found a few words to narrow the gap between them.

But Lord Grey had no intention of trying to narrow that gap. He had not come to Ireland to understand, merely to serve the interests supporting him.

Ignoring her as if she were not in the room, Grey remarked to his aide, "I doubt this creature has any capacity to appreciate the charges brought against her. And looking at the scrawny wench, I also doubt she is quite the unholy terror described in these papers; my predecessors here must have been easily frightened. So . . . the council whimpers over the cost of every crust of bread that's fed to the prisoners here, and the best way to cut that expense is to either free them or hang them. As a favor to a friend, I am inclined to free this one and let her go home to die in peace."

Grania, who had been straining to understand his words, could not contain herself any longer when she heard that last phrase. Forgetting Evleen's warning, forgetting everything but her own desperate need, she ran forward crying out hoarsely, "Free me! Free me!" Her fists beat on his desk.

The lord deputy looked up and met the full force of her eyes then. They blazed out at him from the hollow caverns of their sockets with such intensity that he felt the hackles rise along his neck. *Irishwoman!* he thought. This is what these people are, a force of nature that threatens orderly civilization!

In that moment the core of the new governor's policy for Ireland was formulated, though he was not yet consciously aware of it. He thought he was seeing a different species from his own, one conforming to no patterns of behavior he recognized. His atavistic dislike was immediate and intense, and would be permanent. He regretted having given Philip Sidney his word in the matter of Grace O Malley, because now he knew he would sleep better if all these creatures were exterminated forever. But he had promised Philip, and whatever else he did, Grey prided himself on being a man of honor among his peers.

He would find a way to release this one. But let the others tremble, for there was a new governor in Ireland.

Grania, meanwhile, realized she had made a mistake the moment she saw Grey's face pale and his eyes turn hostile. Fighting to regain control of herself, she tried to get back to the bargaining position she had thought out during the long hours in her cell. She grappled with her fear, her exhaustion, and her helplessness, as she expressed her offer to the interpreter, and then waited while he repeated it to Lord Grey.

The lord deputy looked at her down his nose, considering. He had not come to Ireland totally unprepared, and he had already learned something about tribal relationships and the various Burke rebellions in the west country. The suggestion Grace O Malley made was a viable one, and one which made it easier for him to accede to her release. She was a woman and an ignorant Gael into the bargain; he did not suspect cleverness of her, but took the offer at face value.

"Very well," he said at last, summoning his secretary. "Let it be shown that the woman Grace O Malley of Mayo has agreed that if she is allowed the Queen's Pardon and given over into her husband's custody, she will urge that husband, Richard Burke, to demonstrate appropriate loyalty and gratitude to the Crown."

Grania had kept her face absolutely sober and serious as she made the offer, though she could imagine Tigernan howling with laughter at that phrase "given over into her husband's custody." As if Iron Richard could exert any control over Gráinne Ni Mháille! But obviously the offer was sufficient, and Grey felt the risk of releasing her was outweighed by the chance to encourage further submission in Mayo, among the troublesome Burkes.

Grania's words had very carefully not included submission, however. She had a Gaelic appreciation of language. She had only offered "appropriate loyalty and gratitude," knowing full well that what she deemed appropriate was very slim indeed, and also knowing Grey would interpret that offer quite differently, as she intended him to. She had said exactly what she meant and would abide by that and that only.

The agreement was drawn up and she was summoned again to have it read to her, preparatory to Grey's affixing his seal. One phrase she heard made her stiffen with suspicion. She was to agree in addition to everything else to "relinquish her career of maintenance by land and sea."

She gave the interpreter a sharp look. "I do not understand exactly what the lord deputy means."

The man was tired. He had endured a long day and had a chill in his back. He did not feel up to the task of clarifying so English a term as "maintenance," nor was he himself quite certain what Grey meant in this instance. "You are to give up piracy and raiding, of course," he said shortly, anxious to be done with the business and get home.

Grania was also tired, and the idea that Grey meant her to give up all seafaring was beyond her ability to imagine, for the sea was her life and without it her freedom meant nothing. So she accepted that narrowly erroneous definition, telling herself she could survive by trade alone if she must. She was shown a place on the document where she could make a mark signifying agreement, but she scornfully wrote out her name, Gráinne Ni Mháille, in a trained hand.

And as she was led out the door she turned and said directly to

Grey, in clearly enunciated Latin drilled into her long ago by the Augustinian friars, "I bid you welcome to Ireland and thank you for your courtesy."

Grey stared after her in astonishment. Recovering himself at last, he directed an aide, "Get her out of here at once. Send her home the quickest way possible. . . . Does not Richard Bingham have a swift new vessel at anchor in the harbor? See her aboard that with orders that she is to be transported immediately! I want her on the farthest reaches of the most isolated part of Ireland."

They led her, with a rope around her neck, to the harbor. And the wind from the sea came singing up to her.

I am going home, thought Grania, blinded with tears that might or might not be no more than the wind watering her eyes.

✠

Then she saw Sir Richard Bingham, in clothing almost too elegant for any ship's captain, come forward from his new vessel, the *Swifture*, to accept charge of her.

There is no end to it, Grania thought in a daze of horror. I am to be clubbed and clubbed and clubbed just because I am cursed with enough strength to survive.

Bingham smiled narrowly at her. "You recognize me, then," he said. "We have met before, Grace O Malley. And you are in my custody now."

He was very pleased with the turn fate had taken. Being given this assignment indicated that Grey, at least, might recognize in Bingham a quality he most admired in himself. Too many men sent out from England had succumbed to the peculiar glamour of this eerie frontier, but Bingham knew himself to be too tough-minded, too filled with hatred to let Ireland seep into his bones and influence him. He would never be found wearing Gaelic clothes or letting that cursed accent seep into his speech. He would not be corrupted as had so many before him and wind up fighting the guerrilla warfare of bog and forest in the old Irish style. Ireland was insidious; London was furious at the way the island had befuddled each new wave sent to subdue it. But Bingham would not be conquered by mist and madness and the likes of Grace O Malley —whom he now had in his hands like a ripe plum.

"This woman may not reach the coast of Mayo alive," he told his officers. "The seas are rough along the way. There is every

chance she may fall overboard, if she happens to be exercised along
the rail at the right moment."

To Bingham, Grania's fate had been sealed long ago on the first
occasion of their meeting, and soon her death would be no more
than a footnote in a report, one of those commonplace tragedies of
the sea which would give a peculiarly intense satisfaction to a man
who deserved some satisfactions.

His men had orders to wait until they were out of sight of any
possible hostile observation from land, which meant until they
were well down the wild west coast. They brought her up on deck
of the square-rigger as they were clearing Slyne head—and the
moment Bingham had anticipated with such delight was suddenly
snatched from his hands.

Grania saw them first. More than saw them—she felt them as
she had sometimes felt the coming of a storm in the air over the
rim of the world. Then the lookout in the crow's nest of the
Swiftsure shouted a warning and there was instant activity on
every deck.

The O Malley fleet was advancing toward them, with red boar
and white seahorse floating from every masthead. A large fleet of
strong and sharp-eyed men bore down upon just one English ship
that could not possibly hope to sink them all, even if it had time to
maneuver its cannon into firing position.

Sir Richard Bingham, who had savored the moment of his victory over Grania for so long, deliberately delaying it until the
ultimate moment so he could enjoy the anticipation a little longer,
uttered a terrible oath of outrage.

No helpless woman would be thrown overboard into the sea this
day.

As the galleys drew closer, he saw the guns and spears the Gaels
held waiting in their hands.

As Grania's own flagship came alongside the *Swiftsure*, the air
between the two vessels crackled with tension and the potential for
violence. A word, a gesture from Grania and her men would attack
without hesitation. She could see it on their faces, their dear and
familiar faces. *Tigernan.*

He was there in the prow, grinning at her. Ready and eager to
kill for her. But Grania had lain in the dungeons of power, and the
weight of that power still pressed down upon her.

Grimly, loving every Irish face she saw and not wanting to

watch one more convulse in death, Grania gritted her teeth against the adjustments that must be made to ensure survival. The lowering of expectations, the acceptance of inevitability. If not submission, at least acceptance.

"Put down your weapons," she called across the water to her men. "I am being returned alive to you."

In the final moment before she was ushered from the deck of the *Swifture*, Grania looked once more into the eyes of Richard Bingham.

They stared at each other with the fascination of mortal enemies, creatures in whom a natural enmity is bred in the bone. She saw a tidy, sharp-featured man with a neat spade beard and a fine laced doublet, the stamp of England firm upon him—Elizabeth's England, an empire borning, and Sir Richard Bingham fairly quivering with his desire to be one of its builders.

He saw a big gaunt woman with freedom like a light in her eyes, freedom leaping with a triumphant glory she could not hide. Beyond her all of Ireland waited, hunch-shouldered with mountains wreathed in mist.

"I will have you yet, Grace O Malley," Bingham vowed in a near-whisper. "No woman has ever bested me and none ever will."

She could not help herself. With freedom only a step away if she retained her caution, she felt the rope of self-control slip just a little, crucial notch, and Grania laughed in Richard Bingham's face.

Then quick as a harried fox she was over the side and gone, leaping down into the water and swimming with sure strokes the short distance to her galley, unwilling to wait another moment.

Bingham watched her go as intently as a lover watches his lady, though something murderous rather than worshipful burned in his eyes. "Let the filthy bitch go . . . for now. I will have my day with her yet," he said. "I will have my day, Grace O Malley," he breathed in the way a man takes a solemn oath before his God.

Beneath her own banners, Grania was laughing and hugging each of her men in turn, pounding their backs as they pounded hers, all of them yelling and whooping and swearing with joy.

Tigernan stood to one side, waiting his turn. Dar Dia, how bad she looked! he thought. Pallid as mutton tallow, her hair chopped short and lifeless. He wanted to gather her into his arms and bare his teeth at a world capable of doing this to her.

The same thought occurred to her. Her feeling of relief was so strong it almost broke her; she longed just to collapse in his arms and rest her aching head on his shoulder. But she was Grania. She smiled instead when she came to him, and grabbed his hands as one grabs a long-lost friend. "It was a close thing there," she said. "For a minute I thought I heard spears singing through the air."

"It was sheer luck we intercepted you here," Tigernan told her. "We did not know you were being freed. Ever since I was freed myself I've been trying to recruit enough of an army to come after you and rescue you, but . . . you know how it is."

Grania nodded. "I do, I know how it is. Murrough and Owen were doubtless busy with their own troubles, and there was the herring run, and the plowing. There is always some struggle more immediate and closer to home."

Tigernan, ashamed of those he could not unite on her behalf, dropped his eyes. "The Devil's Hook promised to join us, though," he said.

"And what of the man the sasanach call my husband?"

"Ah, that one! I myself shamed Richard an Iarainn for not going to your defense. At first he said it was on your own head and he would have nothing to do with it. But I kept after him until he boiled over and went off on his own to attack the English wherever he could find them. Making it all worse, probably. He took a band of gallowglasses and kernes and got himself involved in the latest outbreak of rebellion in Munster. One of the Geraldine lords, a man called Fitzmaurice, was supposedly given a mission by the Pope to lead a war there against the heretic she-king and restore Ireland to the true faith. But it is said Fitzmaurice was killed and Iron Richard was turned back—he's supposed to be plundering somewhere now along the borderlands.

"I . . . I tried to rescue you, Grania Mhaol. But I just could not organize an army sufficient for the task."

She put her arm around his shoulders, comforting him instead of seeking comfort for herself. "As easy to comb the sea as to organize the Gaels, Tigernan. As it happened, I think I helped get myself out with my own wits, though my foolish tongue came as close to getting me hanged as I care to get.

"But ah, what terrible things I have seen, Tigernan. I was taken the width of Ireland in a cart, like a beast to the slaughter, and along the way I saw people starving in the midst of fine rich grass-lands that should have fed a hundred cows. And that hundred cows sent off across the Irish sea to fill English bellies instead.

"I saw sweet-faced Gaelic women with their features like crumpled linen, their mouths collapsed in grief over teeth rotted away because they have no bones to gnaw to keep them strong. And no milk to feed the infants who paw at their stringy dugs. I saw men, tall broad Irishmen, walking the streets the English have paved and keeping their heads down, trying to look smaller than they are. Trying not to attract the unfavorable attention of some Englishman. And them grand high-colored men who should never look down except in the presence of God Himself!

"We may not be broken, Tigernan," she said, "but we are very badly bent. Myself included. The day dawned when I thought I would say or do anything, anything at all, just to get out of prison. It is a terrible thing to find one's own breaking point, like looking ahead to the hour of your death and seeing the rot waiting for your body."

"But you didn't break," he told her savagely, willing it to be true. "Nothing could ever break you!"

She could not meet his eyes. "I hope not. But if I were in danger of being held captive again . . ." She did not finish the thought.

✠

In the months that followed she seemed—almost—to assemble her old self again. Only Tigernan, watching her closely, thought he sometimes detected a small piece missing. She no longer tried to force things with the strength of her belief in her own invulnerability, and she was more patient with the failings of others than the Grania he had known. Many might call these changes improvements.

Tigernan, who had thought Grania perfect, resented even the smallest alteration in her and added it to the stock of his angers against the English.

His greatest disappointment came when she announced they would engage in no more piracy but would support themselves and their followers by trade alone. "But the sea trade is only providing a subsistence living," he protested, "now the English claim so much of it for themselves. Without piracy we will be . . . poor."

Grania laughed. "I never thought you cared about being rich or poor."

"Nor do I. But your daughter Margaret does."

"Ah, yes, Margaret. The Devil's Hook has grown very dependent upon the stolen wealth we bring into Clew bay, hasn't he? Margaret will scream like a stoned gull, I expect. But there will still be food on the table, Tigernan, and bread in the oven, which is more than many in Ireland can say these days."

"Why are you doing this? Are you afraid of the English now?" he asked, challenging her.

Grania's jaw muscles tightened. "I am not. But I gave my word. In order to gain my freedom I agreed to relinquish something the English call maintenance by land and sea, which I was told meant my raiding and piracy. I would have given up more, Tigernan, to get out of Dublin castle."

When the Devil's Hook heard Tigernan's version of this conversation, he was worried. "Maintenance by land and sea . . . it sounds to me as if they meant her to abandon commercial trade, too, in which case we have a problem indeed."

"Grania asked and was assured it just applied to piracy," Tigernan told him. Yet both men worried; they knew the English were famous for pulling words out of shape altogether.

Meanwhile, Iron Richard Burke had been enjoying a fine war, plundering Connaught and attacking lesser English strongholds until at last the full force of the queen's soldiery was brought to bear against him. Even then Richard fought on with a stubborn, cold defiance, in spite of the fact that most of clan Burke was now on the other side.

When Grania learned that Richard and a small contingent were now hiding out on one of the islands off the coast, living off seal meat and sheltering amid blue slate and limestone boulders, she knew the time had come to fulfill the rest of her agreement with Grey.

She sent a messenger to tell Richard an Iarainn she strongly urged him to make his formal submission to the Crown while he was still in a position to do so voluntarily.

Richard had always, subconsciously, counted on her support and the power implicit in her reputation, and when he learned she no longer stood behind him, he accepted with ill grace the futility of further opposition. He made his formal submission to the governor of Connaught—but he did not think to ask if Gráinne Ni Mháille had likewise made a formal submission.

She had not, of course.

✠

On the calends of November 1580, Shane Oliverus died. The bards in hiding in the west of Ireland praised the late MacWilliam Iochtar for his noble character and generous nature; the English lauded his loyalty to Elizabeth. And his brother laid claim to his vacated title.

Richard an Iarainn was furious. "I insist you support my claim to the title of clan chieftain as you once pledged to do!" he demanded of Grania. "Shane's brother has no right to it!"

She had indeed given her word to Richard. She had also made an effort to effect some degree of peace between him and the English, for the sake of both his clan and her own. From what she had seen elsewhere in Ireland she knew an outbreak of war in Connaught would reduce the land she loved to the condition of raped and ravaged Munster.

Tibbot came to his mother's chamber in Rockfleet to ask if she supported his father's claim. He filled the stone-walled, tapestry-hung room with his presence. The lad was a child no longer; the set of his shoulders was manly, and the line of his jaw was firm. There was something of his mother in his quick and candid glance —and something of Grania's mother, too. And Dubhdara, and so many generations long gone.

Looking at him, Grania's mind went racing over the water to that other she-king who had no sons. Gloriana, they called Elizabeth now. The Virgin Queen, as if being shriveled and barren was an accolade.

I am fighting to keep a small kingdom for my kin, Grania thought. For whose sake does Elizabeth of clan Tudor do battle? We are so different, fertile Gael and barren Saxon. . . .

Yet simultaneously she sensed, as always, the peculiar tug of sisterhood between herself and that other woman who lived a sort of parallel life, defying convention, leading men, making compromises, planning strategies. Winning and losing and outwitting opponents so she might win again.

"Will I support Richard an Iarainn?" she repeated aloud, echoing Tibbot's question. "I've always supported him; his whole clan eats from the fish I catch. But if you mean do I intend to encourage his battling now, I do not—and it is as much for your sake as his that I say it. If he goes marching across the countryside with an army at his heels to threaten Shane's brother, the English warlord who currently has soldiers stationed here will be forced to intervene. And he well may take Shane's brother's side, or announce abolition of the chieftainship altogether. Better there be no fighting over this, Tibbot."

"Are you afraid to stand against the English now?" the boy asked, a note of truculence creeping into his voice.

His mother's teeth grated upon one another. "I am not!" she flashed—too quickly, an older and more perceptive person than Tibbot might have noticed. She must show him she was brave; Grania would rather die where she stood than have her son think her a coward in even the slightest respect. "I like to fight far too well," she went on, "but I have learned over the years that sometimes the most crucial battles are fought with the mind rather than the sword. Though after being imprisoned by the English I have no desire to be within arm's reach of any sasanach, I will go to their warlord Malby myself and try to dissuade the man from preparing for war against the Burkes. I will urge him to support Richard's claim to the MacWilliamship, and if he accepts I will then go to Richard and urge him to subside peacefully."

"How do you know that either man will listen to you?" Tibbot wondered.

She grinned. "Malby will accept because his supply lines are stretched thin right now and the winter is almost upon him; I doubt he had much heart for fighting. And Richard will calm down because he will have gotten what he wants. You can always get someone to listen to you, Tibbot, if you appeal to his self-interest, and this happens to be a time when I know the self-interest of both men."

"So you will go to Malby personally," Tibbot said, impressed. He could imagine the depth of courage that decision revealed. He could not imagine himself going voluntarily to the English if he had been treated as his mother had been. Then he scowled. "And will Tigernan go with you?"

"Tigernan usually accompanies me. I rely on him."

The young man flushed darkly. "But you have a husband, my father. It is not right that you . . . that you . . . spend all your time with some other man."

Grania bit back an amused smile. He was growing up, her Tibbot. "That bothers you?"

"It does not!" He blushed harder than ever. "I don't care how many men you have around you. You're Gráinne Ni Mháille—everyone knows you make your own laws."

"Ah, Tibbot, Tibbot." Grania stood up and crossed the room to stand beside him, putting her arms around his sturdy fourteen-year-old body as if he still were a little boy; she tousled his hair with her hand. He suffered it patiently. Such encounters were rare and brief and he enjoyed them more than he would ever admit. "No one makes his own laws, Tibbot," Grania said, "though it sometimes seems otherwise. Even Elizabeth of England has laws she must follow that are not to her liking, I am certain. We get old; that is a law. We must learn to deal with other people; that is a law. Change what you can when you are a man, but I tell you the wind and the sea cannot be changed."

"And that is as it should be," echoed a soft voice from the doorway. Tibbot started and pulled free of his mother's embrace and she let him go without hesitation. He spun to face Evleen, who had an uncanny knack of appearing silently, like a spirit sprung from a fairy well.

✠

Evleen was in the chamber some weeks later, laying fresh rushes on the floor, when Grania, with Tigernan, reported to Tibbot on the success of her mission. Open warfare had indeed been averted by her skillful negotiations, for Malby had been impressed by Grania's bold intercession and her clear evaluation of the situation. Richard an Iarainn, though his mouth was set for battle, had been content with the English-supported chieftainship instead, and the brother of Shane Oliverus had dropped his claim because he dared not pursue it without Malby behind him.

Grania's interview with Malby had been very different from her interview with Grey, for she had arranged to meet him under an open sky with Ireland all around her and empty space at her back, an open stretch between her and the sea. Without walls to hold her, she had proved a competent and persuasive negotiator.

"So there will be no battle over the chieftainship," Tibbot was saying. He sounded a little disappointed, though he was glad his mother had returned to Rockfleet safely and enjoyed the bright color in her cheeks betokening what she considered a small triumph.

Evleen stooped by the hearth and poked at a dying flame. "There will always be battles," she said. And her voice was the voice of the rain, dripping forever on cold stones. "We are a warrior race; how else do we define ourselves? That is our glory and our tragedy." She looked at him over her shoulder, and he could have sworn she was smiling. And crying. "Immortality is born from glory and tragedy," said Evleen.

Tibbot did not understand her, but he believed no one understood her. She was a mystery.

The room smelled of Grania's freshly washed hair. She could never get enough of bathing after her captivity. The fragrance of peat smoke also hung on the air, for with the vanishing of the timber the Irish were being forced to burn the very earth itself for fuel. A brace of pistols waiting for Tigernan to clean them lay on a carved oak bench blackened by the centuries. The dull glow of random bits of pirated gold still shone from a few shelves, though its massed amount was greatly diminished since the days of unlimited seafaring. The hall at Rockfleet was a mixture of rough lime-washed stone and brightly dyed woolen wall hangings, of imported glass in the loopholes and lice-ridden wolfhounds dreaming all aquiver near the hearth. Of ancient mysteries and modern worries. . . .

Suddenly Tibbot experienced an almost physical jolt, as if he had taken a step backward—though his body had not moved. But his field of vision widened until he saw the three of them, Grania and Tigernan and Evleen, as if they were welded into one icon whose meaning was obscure to him, but whose power resonated through his soul. Indomitable Grania, Tigernan the warrior, and Evleen of the mysteries. He felt some unseen door swing slowly shut, even as he watched, leaving him forever outside, destined to find his own way in a very different world.

Then he saw Grania catch the hem of her sleeve in her fingers and lean toward Tigernan, using the soft fabric to wipe a bit of matter from the corner of his eye. The homely, thoughtless gesture, and the way the grizzled warrior bent his head to let her do it made Tibbot ache with jealousy and love.

His mother caught his expression and smiled at him. "Let's feed the lad, Evleen," she said, "before his bones burst through his skin altogether. I do not like to see one of my own with a starveling look."

Then she glanced back at Tigernan, and her eyes held a specific promise.

27

Tigernan had long since moved his few belongings into a cottage near the walls of Rockfleet, a location close enough to allow him to be on constant guard but far enough away to allow Grania the illusion of privacy—another condition she cherished after her confinement in the crowded and stinking depths of Dublin castle. She wanted no one with her inside Rockfleet at night, though Evleen was tolerated and two men-at-arms maintained a firmly entrenched position at the portal.

But sometimes she summoned Tigernan by ways only the two of them recognized, and on other occasions she went to him, going out into the night with brushed hair and jewels on her hands like a woman who needs reassurance of her own female power.

At such times—and this night was one of those times—she was voracious. She rode him like an unbroken horse, her sweat-glazed body plunging eagerly to meet every movement of his. Then passion leaped between them like a flame, leaving them both shaken.

Tigernan's fading hair and gradually stooping posture had never bothered Grania, for she barely noticed them. But in the morning when she awoke to find him propped on one elbow, studying her in the revealing daylight, she grabbed for his blanket to pull over the damage time had done to her body.

Tigernan grinned and caught her hand before she could complete the gesture. "I was just envying you that fine set of shoulders," he said.

So she left the blanket down.

On other occasions, however, she sought him out almost diffidently, wanting nothing more than to meander along the shore or sit under a tree chatting about household trivia. Was the quality of the new tar up to standard? Was there enough wool for the winter's weaving? Were more stones needed for the seawall?

This, too, was a vital part of Grania's relationship with Tigernan as it had been with no other man. She shared both the large and the small of her life with him, and he in turn gloried in his possession of the whole woman . . . or as much of her as Grania would ever allow any man to possess.

As the two of them walked along the shore of the inlet one day, watching an overturned curragh go down to the water on six human legs, Grania remarked, "I have abided by my agreement with the sasanach, Tigernan, but for my reward I seem to be getting poorer. There is no spice in this way of living, and no pleasure in seeing my people suffer for my caution. Malby liked me, I could tell it—maybe he would not notice if I extended my activities a little bit. He may be the governor of Connaught now, but he has better things to do than to watch every seafarer up and down the coast, eh?"

Tigernan understood. Her memories of prison were fading at last and her own adventurous spirit was demanding expression once more. She was tired of being frightened, and Grania's characteristic response to being frightened was to go on the attack.

The old days, the good days, of daring and raiding and an occasional looted merchantman were coming back.

She might be killed for it and so might he, but in that moment Tigernan did not care. His Grania Mhaol was back again, full-strength.

Carefully at first, under cover of fog and mist, Grania slipped out past Achill head into the shipping lanes and took first one small and relatively minor vessel and then a second. Her success was met with rejoicing around the perimeter of Cuan Mó, and Margaret immediately let her mother know that she would not scorn some new fabrics from the next Flemish trader Grania appropriated.

The day would come when a new song would be sung of Gráinne Ni Mháille:

> . . . *Sped before a driving blast, by following*
> *seas uplifted,*
> *Catch, from the huge heaps heaving past,*
> *And from the spray they drifted*
> *And from the winds that tossed the crest*
> *Of each wide-shouldered giant,*
> *The smack of freedom and the zest*
> *Of rapturous life defiant.*

Tigernan's dwelling at Rockfleet was a stout round building of wattle and thatch, but after they began sea raiding again he found he preferred to sleep right on the shore, beneath an overturned curragh. From such a vantage point he would be one of the first to notice any English attempt to come up the inlet to Rockfleet. He slept like an ascetic, wrapped in his shaggy mantle. When he awoke with stiff joints and aching muscles he experienced a moment of near-religious ecstasy, having sacrificed his comfort for Grania's safety.

But she made it plain she would not join him to couple beneath the black shell of the boat. "I learned to appreciate beds in prison," she told him.

"It's just as well," he replied with a shrug as he assembled his gear for a day's fishing. "Now that I think of it, it would do me no good to be seen thrashing around under a boat with some old woman. People would think I was mad."

"Or drunk," she added amiably, holding up one of his fishing lines so she could worry a knot out of it.

He began to come to her, mounting the stairs to the chamber Grania had once shared with Richard an Iarainn, and finding the door open to him, the candles burned low in their holders. Or sometimes on star-splattered summer nights they rowed out together in Tigernan's little boat to a sheltered strand no one visited, and returned at dawn with the tumble of Grania's bedclothing piled in the prow.

And all the time Tigernan was waiting . . . waiting for the blow he felt must inevitably fall.

✠

Richard Burke proved loyal enough in his submission to win a knighthood for himself in 1581—that was a bad year for herring, Grania noted—though he continued his feud with the brother of Shane Oliverus. He was invited to attend a gathering of the loyal Irish nobility in Galway city soon after, and Grania attended on his arm as the wife of The MacWilliam Iochtar, dressed in the most opulent of her pirated finery and walking with a straight spine, daring anyone to mention the ships she had seized before and those she still meant to capture.

No one did. Connaught was relatively quiet, and Malby wanted to keep it that way.

Once safely back aboard her own galley, Grania described the event for Tigernan, punctuating her narrative with much laughter. ". . . and we were such an assemblage as I think the English have not seen together in one hall before, Tigernan. They fairly gaped at us, even Malby. The man the sasanach made The O Flaherty was there, and I spoke to him with as smooth a tongue as if he had not robbed my husband Donal of his rank. Every chieftain in the place wore gold, and their wives dressed in silk and laces. The court of the clan Tudor could not be more splendid, I think."

She had actually enjoyed herself, Tigernan realized with some difficulty. He would have been acutely uncomfortable in such a gathering. He derived great satisfaction out of seeing her walk away from Richard Burke on the docks of Galway harbor without a word of goodbye, and come straight aboard her galley to him, to inquire about the fishing fleet.

She was playing a reckless and dangerous game, was Gráinne Ni Mháille. And she was determined to enjoy it. She had broken free of the paralytic pall of fear her captivity had cast over her step by step, first with the Malby negotiation and then with her return to piracy, and she had promised herself never to let fear torture her again. The only thought that could make her heart thunder, in fact, was the idea of a second imprisonment, but she had decided she would take her life with her own hand before allowing that to happen. No one had to bear the worst that could befall them twice in one lifetime, she felt. Surely not.

She was always busy. Life on Clew bay arranged itself to the rhythm of moon and stars and seasons rather than arbitrary human dates. When Grania arose at dawn, sometimes she went out with Evleen and the two of them knelt and put their ears against the ground. In the ringing silence between earth and heaven they heard the sounds of the new day being born.

That was the only passage of time Grania acknowledged.

But mortality has its own clocks. In the spring of 1583, Richard Burke, Iron Richard, was dead of natural causes. The Irish annalists would describe him as an unquiet and rebellious man, and he was not excessively mourned, but Grania was unexpectedly saddened by his passing. "All his life, some woman herded him around," she commented to Tigernan. "He had good reason to be a sour man. His mother ordered his existence until she died, then he ran afoul of me and it cost him Rockfleet and much of his self-respect. If I had it to do over again . . ." She narrowed her eyes in speculation.

"Would you do it differently?"

Grania threw back her head and laughed. "Not for a minute!"

But when Malby sent formal condolences to "Lady Burke," as he had always called Grania, she withdrew into Rockfleet and flew a flag of mourning from the battlements, seeing no one for ten days.

When she emerged, she immediately gathered all her followers from Clare island and added them to the community at Rockfleet, ordering cottages built for them and roads inland secured. "With Iron Richard dead," she told Tibbot, "I must reestablish and strengthen my claim to Rockfleet and its holding as quickly as possible. According to the Brehon law a chieftain's widow is entitled to a third of her husband's property, but under that same law I am not really Richard's widow. And besides, Brehon law has little power left in Connaught; it is the English voice we hear now."

"Curse the English," Tibbot said as casually as many said it a dozen times a day.

Grania was instantly alert. "You will not curse it, you will attend to your studies with the monks and master the English tongue! Back to the friary with you, lad; you must be properly prepared for whatever is coming next."

No one could say for certain what laws were valid and what claims would be upheld. Ireland had become a strange new place.

Grania was grateful for her good relations with Malby, but the president officer of Connaught, like Iron Richard, had numbered days. Within less than a year she received word that he was dead.

And Sir Richard Bingham was coming to Connaught to succeed him.

The messenger who brought the news to Grania arrived redfaced and breathless, but obviously enjoying his role as the carrier of bad news, as some people do.

The news that Richard Bingham was now governor of the west frosted the very air of Rockfleet. And as if that were not bad enough, the messenger added with obvious relish, "The new governor is already said to be drawing up an agreement known as the Composition of Connaught, affixing new rents to be paid to the English Crown for every foot of arable land in the province."

Grania heard a cold iron bell toll in her heart. Richard Bingham. Richard Bingham.

With bribery and bludgeoning, the new governor forced first one Irish chieftain and then another to agree to Composition—because it was becoming painfully clear that the chieftains still retained their holdings at all only through English tolerance and English law, both of which could be revoked at any time.

But Grania, who held Rockfleet in contravention of any law the English accepted, did not sign. She spent most of her time in the remotest reaches of her territory or on the sea-lanes, avoiding Bingham as best she could while continuing to live a life of daily more narrowed horizons.

Yet narrowing horizons focused one's attention more sharply on what remained, and she lived each day with a fierce joy, draining every cup to its dregs and enjoying every bite of food and every change of light.

Meanwhile, with unprecedented cruelty, Sir Richard Bingham marched armies across Connaught, slaughtering and pillaging. He had killed a number of Irish and had an appetite for killing more—one in particular. Gráinne Ni Mháille could not stay out of his reach forever.

Grania's caution was more for her people than for herself. She would not let Bingham cow her, or reduce her to a frightened widow unable to leave her hiding place behind stout walls. So she continued to conduct herself as the she-king she had become, though she was careful to arrange her adventures in areas far removed from Bingham's activities of the moment.

One such occurrence took place at Kinturk castle, where reprisals were called for because the Staunton family of that holding had waylaid and robbed some of Grania's own clansmen. With battle of one sort or another always on the horizon now, Grania took Tibbot with her to Kinturk to assess his own fighting skills firsthand.

"This will be but a small skirmish," she explained to him, "as I have no desire to slaughter Irishmen when there are so many Englishmen anxious to do that job. But I would like to see if you have a warrior's heart."

"I do," the young man affirmed with his chin up and his eyes burning.

So off they marched to take part in the sort of exercise every strong leader needed to engage in from time to time, in order to keep the respect of the neighbors. And the Stauntons met them happily, ready for battle. But in the thick of the fray Grania was astounded to find Tibbot maneuvering to stay behind her, shielded by her body.

She whirled on him in a towering rage. The fury with which she attacked the Stauntons was nothing compared to the way she meant to savage her own son. "Trying to hide behind my backside, are you?" she yelled at him above the din of battle. "Would you crawl back like a puling infant into the place from which you came?"

Her powerful voice carried for a great distance. Everyone heard, and Tibbot was disgraced, knowing he would be the object of much scorn for a long time to come. With a face as red as if he had taken a bloody wound upon it, he stepped forward then to fight at her side for the rest of the brief and successful engagement.

But she neither spoke to him nor looked at him. She treated him as if he did not exist until long after they had returned to Rock-fleet.

"Tibbot is not meant to be a warrior," she said sadly later to Tigernan.

He shook his head. "Perhaps the days of the warrior are passing away, Grania Mhaol."

Her lips tightened into a thin line. "Not as long as foreigners claim our land," she replied.

The foreigners had no intention of leaving, and their grip tightened day by day. Richard Bingham's brother John took advantage of the improvement in his brother's status to mount an army of his own and lead a looting foray as far north as Grania's Umhall, where there were still some fat cattle left grazing on the green hillsides. His scavengers arrived at a time when Grania and her galleys were far out on the trade lanes and even Tibbot was not in residence at Rockfleet, having been sent by his mother to the monastery to polish his letters—since he did not appear to be equipped to become a warlord.

Like insects stripping the bones of a fallen deer, John Bingham's men rampaged through the countryside until they encountered the small Papist friary tucked away in a forgotten glen. At first the English laughed at the poverty of the place, and were inclined to let the monks alone simply because there was nothing of value to steal from them—until they saw the young man who stood among the robed and hooded friars but wore a gold chain around his neck.

"Your name, Papist!" Bingham demanded with a sword's point at the young man's throat.

Tibbot had learned courage in a hard school, and recently. He would not hide now. "I am Tibbot Burke, son of Iron Richard Burke and Grace O Malley," he said in a firm voice, calling upon the very English language the monks had drilled into him at Grania's request. "Prepare my son for the future," she had ordered.

For the future when the English will stand with one foot on the neck of the Irish, she had thought silently, with fearful prescience.

Now it was Tibbot's neck pressed to the earth beneath an English foot.

John Bingham laughed aloud when he learned what prize he had taken. "We will deliver this whelp to the governor and hope to flush out the bitch that bore him! My brother will not be displeased with this day's hunting."

He immediately sent word to Rockfleet that Tibbot was an English prisoner. Then he waited.

When Grania's flagship sailed into the inlet at Rockfleet to receive the terrible news, Tigernan did not happen to be with her. He had taken another vessel and gone farther down the coast to deliver supplies to Grania's adherents on his own Inishbofin and Inishark. By the time he returned to Cuan Mó it was too late, of course.

With her unbound hair streaming down her back and her eyes red-rimmed, Evleen met Tigernan at the landing and told him of Tibbot's capture. "Grania threw away her caution like an outworn garment," she said, "and has gone to save her stolen cub, with just what warriors were at hand and her banners flying and her piper playing the war-pipe."

Tigernan squatted on the rocky shore and beat his fists against his skull. "They will kill her!" he cried in his pain. "And me not there with her!"

John Bingham waylaid Grania and her small troop in a narrow wooded valley that spilled into bogland, leaving little room for battle or escape. She fought through a long and bloody morning, but by the time the sun stood overhead most of her followers were slain and Grania herself was trussed with rope and slung from a pole like a stag being carried home after a day's sport.

"Muzzle her and wrap her claws in leather," Bingham ordered. "Just don't break anything that will not mend. I want to deliver this parcel to my brother in prime condition."

She was carried to Galway city and dumped, literally, at the feet of Sir Richard Bingham.

"The last time we met you were very arrogant, madam," the new governor of Connaught remarked, nudging his tightly bound captive with the toe of his boot as she lay on the stone floor. "Will you be as haughty now, I wonder? Listen—you can hear the sound of my carpenters hammering your gallows just outside the window."

He ached to see her cry as another man might lust for a woman or hunger for a fortune. He even ordered the gag removed from her mouth so she could beg for her life, but Grania chewed on the dust-dry lining of her cheeks until she summoned enough spittle to spew a gob at him.

He would have kicked her to death as she lay there, if he dared. But he could not forget the clemency that had been shown to this particular woman—inexplicably, from his point of view—before. To excecute her outright without gaining some sort of permission from Dublin could amount to career suicide, and Richard Bingham's ambition stayed his kicking foot.

But his leg quivered with the need to lash out and hurt her.

He sent word to Dublin that he had captured the pirate who continued to ply her trade in direct defiance of her agreement with Lord Grey. He sought permission to execute both Grania and her son as an example to others who scorned English authority . . . but his request arrived in Dublin at a bad time. The lord deputy was not, at that particular moment, anxious to throw fuel on the fire for a new rising in the west country.

"There are too many reports coming in already of Bingham's brutality since he became governor," he told the next meeting of the council. "Connaught has been relatively quiet for a time—in thanks, to some degree, to this O Malley woman, who seems to have urged her clansmen to more peaceful pursuits. If she is executed there will doubtless be a whole new rebellion in response and we will have to spend a fortune on troops to put it down."

"A fortune we do not have available to us," one of the queen's councilors reminded him.

While Sir Richard Bingham waited for formal permission to kill her, Grania waited alone in yet another prison cell.

This time, she promised herself, I will die. I will find some weapon to end my life; if nothing else I will claw my wrists open with my own fingernails.

I will get out of here. Be free again, as free of this body as the sea eagles are free of the earth. Not hurt anymore. Not fight anymore. Not make any more mistakes, or watch everything I know and love shrink away. . . .

I will just die.

The sweet seduction of it beckoned strongly to her. Death at her own hand would give her yet another victory over Bingham.

The second captivity was more than twice as bad as the first, because she knew what to expect and also because she knew that Tibbot must be sharing it with her, locked frightened and alone in some other stinking hole.

Did he feel the same rising panic she did? Were the walls closing in on him too? Was he, like his mother, one heartbeat away from being overcome by a screaming terror Grania feared she could not fight back again?

Not again, not again.

A captive in a cage, *again*.

I will die before they can kill me, she promised herself. And a sea eagle will come for my soul.

✠

So she and Bingham waited in their separate ways, but Tigernan was not waiting. He did not expect to be able to get aid from either of Grania's grown sons, or from the man who was now The O Malley and had signed the Composition of Connaught to protect his own neck. But he knew where there was a full store of courage he could summon.

He burst into the fortress of Kildawnet shouting and waving his arms in the air.

The hall of the Devil's Hook's stronghold was handsomely furnished with good wooden pieces from a dozen different ports, and silk-embroidered wall hangings from as many different lands. Grania's treasure.

Margaret managed to calm Tigernan enough to settle him on a bench close to the hearth and get a tankard of ale in his hand. She and her husband listened as Tigernan recounted the tale of Tibbot's capture, and then of Grania's; from time to time their eyes met over the head of the distraught man. "This does not really surprise me," Grania's son-in-law said at last. "She has sailed too close to the wind for too long."

Margaret nodded. "She has that. And I cannot understand why, with a fine strong house where she could be comfortable, she needs to wear a man's trews and go out on a slimy, pitching ship . . ."

Tigernan looked up and scowled at her. "You are not big enough to understand anything about your mother at all," he said.

Margaret's eyes flashed, but her husband broke the tension by saying, "How can you expect to rescue her, Tigernan? Everyone in Connaught owes her something, I grant you that, but no two clans will stand together; each is involved with its own self-interest right now. You can gather no big army of fighting men to batter down the gates of Galway city, and you know it—and there's no other way to get her free."

His back bowed into a sad curve, Tigernan buried his chin in his chest and gazed at the fire. "And I thought the Demon of Curraun, at least, would help me."

"I will. If you can tell me how we can actually do it. But I have children of my own and people who depend on me, Tigernan; I cannot just march off to commit suicide."

"Grania did that very thing to try to save her son Tibbot. And she would do it for you, too," Tigernan added, throwing a glance at Margaret.

He had never approved of Margaret very much, and so on this occasion she surprised him. "Grania would do that," she said in a low and thoughtful voice. "For me. She is . . . she is a mother, whatever else she is. If the mothers of Connaught could fight for her . . ."

Tigernan jumped up from his bench with his jaw agape and a wild gleam in his eye. "We cannot summon enough warriors, but what about the women? There are enough females on the shores of Cuan Mó to make an army twice over, and every one of them has put in her child's mouth food provided by Gráinne Ni Mháille!"

The Devil's Hook raised one eyebrow. "You can't make an army out of women, you fool. Gaelic women haven't borne arms in more generations than I can count, back to pagan times, most probably."

"And don't I know that? But do the English know it? And how

are they to recognize a woman at all, unless she's dressed in a long shift and has her apron on? We might not be able to get enough fighting men to intimidate that English bastard in Galway city, but suppose we could at least get enough *people* . . ."

The fire on the hearth crackled and spat as the three gazed at each other in speculative silence. In the shadows beyond their vision, ghosts of ancient Ireland stirred, and warrior women strode forward with their men to brandish swords long gone to rust.

28

In her cell in Galway city, Grania heard the small wooden panel at the top of the door slide back, allowing someone to peer into the room through the grating. Whoever it was breathed heavily but said nothing.

She got to her feet and peered at the dark, shapeless head of the observer, silhouetted by the light from the lamp an attendant held aloft behind him. Grania's cell was dark; looking into that light made her blink. "Who's there?" she wanted to know.

Silence answered her. Only silence, and the heavy breathing. Then the panel slid shut again, but not before she knew.

Richard Bingham had come to gloat over his captive.

Rats scurried in the straw, waiting to take bites out of her when she grew too weak to fend them off.

Anger beyond anger and pride beyond pride began toughening the fibers of her body as if rich new blood were pumping through her veins. Irish blood that would never surrender to the sasanach, nor give him any reason for pleasure at all.

"I will not die to set myself free, Richard Bingham," Grania vowed to herself through clenched teeth. "You would be too happy to see me dead upon this floor, even if you had not put a noose around my neck yourself. No . . . I will live. I will survive, and that will be my revenge upon you."

She could not set her soul free yet, then. It must remain captive with her body, defying him. Giving back hatred for hatred. Challenging the deathbringer with her own indomitable life.

This was a game no longer, nor even a duel between equals, but something bitter and ugly and unnatural, for Grania knew no honorable Gael would have reacted to a prisoner as Richard Bingham reacted. He was not just an enemy, he was a curse.

She had somehow never thought of Elizabeth Tudor as an enemy, but rather as an honorable opponent, a person who played the game by rules of a sort and was subject to the same forces Grania understood—politics, luck, weather, greed, the limitations of cleverness.

But Bingham was different. His enmity stank of bloodlust.

Each time the panel opened and the silent watcher watched, Grania stood tall, with her hands on her hips and defiance in her face, letting him see that she would not be broken.

So he gave the order that her food ration was to be misdirected and never reach her, and her water was to be cut to a few pitiful drops and forgotten on some days altogether. He would see her crawl yet.

When her belly screamed too loudly, Grania trapped a rat by throwing her shirt over it. She slammed shut the door in her mind that would have allowed her to think too much about what she was doing, and ate the warm meat, letting its blood moisten her parched mouth. On other days she cupped her hands and caught her own urine to drink when there was nothing else to sustain her dehydrated body.

Richard Bingham watched and waited.

She did not die.

Driven to seek her core, Grania was finding the tough, residual elements from which she and all life had been created: earth and air, fire and water. The enduring clay from which she was formed was the earth of Ireland, imbued with its own relentless will toward continuance.

She kept on living and Richard Bingham kept on waiting.

And when he thought he could bear it no more, when he thought surely she would starve or he would break into the cell and throttle her with his bare hands, word came from Dublin that the lord deputy refused his request to execute the O Malley woman, for fear of reprisals too widespread through Connaught to be managed at the moment.

The new governor of Connaught—who counted among his many frustrations the fact that he had been given that title and not that of president officer—stalked from his chambers black-faced with anger. Aides and underlings ran after him, but he ignored them. He wanted one thing and one thing only: to lose himself in the most squalid inn in the narrowest alley of the town, and there gulp liquor until he was insensible. He knew no one would dare laugh at seeing his mightiness drunk.

No one in Connaught dared laugh at Richard Bingham at all—except for Gráinne Ni Mháille.

He was still nursing a hangover so terrible he could hear the film forming on his teeth when sentries brought word from the sea wall that a fleet was approaching Galway harbor. An obviously Gaelic fleet composed of galleys and curraghs, a wallowing old carrack, and a pair of splintery hybrid three-masters, each vessel sporting an overlapping of battle shields along its gunwales. If most of those shields were scarred and faded from long neglect, none of the stunned inhabitants of Galway who observed their approach noticed the telling detail. What they did see was people, countless Irish people in hooded shaggy mantles and brandishing spears and swords and axes as well as occasional firearms. A whole army of warriors crowding the decks of the Gaelic fleet descending upon Galway city.

The alarmed Galwegians fled to their homes and barred the doors, praying the English authorities would protect them from the long-dreaded Irish reprisals against the city. Even Bingham's strong new walls and sentried gates could not be expected to repulse so many Irishmen, and all of them ready to fight together.

"The Irish have at last risen to throw off our control!" one of Bingham's officers reported to him with great agitation. The man's face was paler than it should have been, and his hands twitched.

"You fear those rabble?" the governor snorted.

"Of course not, but . . . but there are so many of them on the boats, my lord. Our garrison is outnumbered, and they have already put some of their number ashore to circle the city and prevent us sending for outside reinforcements."

Richard Bingham bit his lip. He wished—oh, God, how he wished!—he did not have such a thunderous hangover on this day of all days. But there was nothing for it; he gave the order to prepare for an attack and began arming himself. He who had been so vicious to them could expect no quarter from the Gaels.

But the warriors packed aboard Grania's fleet made no move to come ashore. They waited in the harbor, keeping enough distance between themselves and observers that no one could get a clear look at their faces. And so the English were unaware that many of those faces were the wrinkled old countenances of grandmothers, toothless and scrawny, brandishing spears for the first time in their lives and safely disguised in male attire.

And some of the warriors were younger women, even nursing mothers who held babies to their breasts beneath their woolen cloaks while stamping their feet on the decks just as if they were soldiers itching for battle. Some of the warriors were no more than children, standing on casks to appear taller. Some were girls too young for marrying but not too young for bravery, who giggled and winked at one another behind their hands and had no idea what to do with the firearms belted to their slender waists.

And some of the warriors—though not nearly enough to sack a city—were men, clansmen and admirers of Gráinne Ni Mháille who had been able, briefly, to set aside their various feuds with other clansmen, just for the glory and danger of this day.

The ships were filled with fighters; that was all the English could tell. And though they cleverly stayed just beyond cannon range, the Gaels were beginning a low, ominous chant that carried clearly over the water and boded no good for the queen's loyal citizens in Galway.

In command of the motley fleet, the Devil's Hook waited long enough for Bingham and his forces to grow very nervous indeed, and then he had a boat put down and came ashore. In a voice that would brook no refusals he demanded to see Governor Bingham and insisted the truce flag he carried be honored.

It was Richard Bingham's day for surprises. He had Grania's son-in-law shown into his office, into a room ringed with armed guards who seemed to impress the Gael not one whisker's worth. The Devil's Hook got right to the point. "I come to offer myself as a hostage in return for the release of my wife's mother, Gráinne Ni Mháille," he explained. "I am a powerful warlord with armies at my command"—he made a vague but chilling gesture in the direction of the harbor—"and I offer myself as security for her good behavior. We are kin by marriage, and more important, we are friends. I would not have her harmed further."

Bingham found the whole concept of an exchange of hostages primitive and baffling—as baffling as this cleft-chinned, blue-eyed Burke chieftain who stood before him, obviously no longer a young man but dangerously vigorous. In the courtyard beyond this room the gallows still waited for Grania—and among the papers on Bingham's desk was a message from the lord deputy denying him the pleasure of executing her.

Of course, he could always claim he had not received the message in time. He could always claim he had killed her hastily when a Gaelic attack was imminent, as a sort of reprisal in advance. . . .

Thinking fast, Sir Richard Bingham looked into the eyes of the Devil's Hook and tried to assess his chances of getting out of Galway city alive.

Aboard the galleys, Margaret Burke's patience was wearing thin. She complained to everyone within earshot, "This terrible mantle stinks and I can't see from under the hood. When is my Richard coming back? I hate the feel of homespun on my skin. Do you think we will actually have to sleep aboard ship until this matter is decided? He said we must not land, no one must see us up close . . . but my stomach is beginning to heave again. Dar Dia, I hate the sea!"

She complained without cessation until those nearest her edged away and found business elsewhere, but Margaret never failed to hold her spear up so its thin black line could be clearly seen.

The gulls shrieked and circled, and a soft wind moaned the length of Galway bay. The sky was the color of a dove's breast.

The tension had long since passed the point of being unbearable when the Devil's Hook and his party came back down the stone-paved streets to the quay, walking like victors. Margaret thought she saw the figure of her husband himself leading them, and held her breath as he got into the little boat waiting at its moorings to return him to the galley.

Behind the Devil's Hook came Tigernan, and cradled in his arms was the emaciated but living form of Gráinne Ni Mháille.

Once safely aboard the Gaelic vessel and rowing out of the English-held harbor, the Devil's Hook explained the situation to his followers. "Meaning to insult me, that toad who calls himself governor said I was too old to be a useful hostage. He did demand my pledge of loyalty and good conduct on behalf of both Grania and myself, of course—and went to great pains to remind me that breaking that promise would be a capital crime meriting execution."

"He released Grania just in return for your promise?" Margaret asked in wonder.

Her husband's face darkened. "Not entirely. All the cattle of Umhall were confiscated by his brother, of course, and they mean to keep those. And . . ." He hesitated, glancing over his shoulder to the place where Tigernan had made a bed of furs and blankets for Grania and was kneeling beside her, rubbing her hands. "And he is holding young Tibbot still. It seems the English have this idea that they can keep the sons of Gaelic chieftains in their own households until they shapechange them into Englishmen." His mouth twitched with contempt. "It will probably work, with some," he added.

"With Tibbot?"

The Devil's Hook shrugged. "Who can say? To my surprise, Grania offered no opposition to the suggestion. I suspect she wants her son to survive at whatever cost, even if it means making an Englishman of him."

Thinking of her own children, Margaret closed her eyes.

Grania opened hers and looked up into Tigernan's face. "You again?" she asked him in a rusty voice.

"It is."

She ran her tongue over her lips, trying to lubricate them enough to form more words. Tigernan offered her a cup of water, and she drank deeply, then pushed it away. "Was I dreaming, or did I see my own girl's face when you brought me aboard?"

"You saw it. Margaret came with us, wearing a warrior's garments and carrying a spear."

She managed a very small chuckle before falling asleep again in Tigernan's arms.

✠

They took her home, and Evleen wept and swore at the sight of her and immediately began cooking rich broths to strengthen her. Being Grania, she did not stay in her bed as long as anyone thought she should, and soon she was going down to see the galleys again, and railing against the English for having robbed her clansmen of their cattle. She did not mention Tibbot, and no one dared mention his name to her, for fear of hurting her—yet in all other ways she seemed almost her old self again. Almost.

Only those closest to her knew she could not bear to sleep alone now, and only Tigernan knew how many times she cried aloud in her sleep, or came leaping out of the darkness of nightmare to clutch at him, the pounding of her heart shaking her body.

"This time they have broken something in her I cannot fix," Tigernan mourned to Evleen.

"They have not," she contradicted him, willing it to be the truth. "They have not."

The comfort of the flesh was all Tigernan had to offer, but he gave that gladly. When she seemed ready he covered her with his body as with a shield and entered her swiftly, plunging and plunging until he felt her warm around him, beginning to respond. Then, and only then, could he relax into tenderness with her, his rough hand pillowing her head, his husky voice murmuring a wordless croon. His strength was the strength of the pounding sea and his voice was the softness of seamist then, catching her between the two and holding her pinioned there until all else was swept away and she could relax, shuddering, against his chest.

"There now," he would whisper to her afterward. "There now, little girl."

He would lie holding her clasped in his arms until she slept again, but his unsleeping face remained fiercely vigilant.

✠

Two signal fires blazed from Cliara, and a galley went out from Rockfleet to bring back a messenger from Flaherty territory with dreadful news.

On July 30, Sir Richard Bingham, who had hardly drawn a sober breath since Grania's release, had tried and hanged Edmund Burke, leader of the most recent Burke rebellion. This time Dublin did not demur. The caution that prevented the lord deputy from allowing an Irish noblewoman to be executed did not hold for Edmund, who had openly declared war on the Crown. Edmund Burke died nobly, the Irish annalists would record—still cursing the sasanach.

Captain John Bingham then marched through Iar Connaught and into the heart of Owen O Flaherty's holding. Because Owen's wife Katharine was the dead Edmund's daughter, they seized property in sufficient amount to "make restitution" for Edmund Burke's crimes.

"Like the noble prince he was," the messenger, one Teigue O Flaherty, reported to Grania, "your son Owen met with John Bingham and treated him as if he were an invited guest instead of an invader. But in the night, after they had enjoyed your son's hospitality, Bingham's soldiers seized and bound Owen and his retainers and stole his cattle, his personal horses, all the portable property he possessed. They hanged his men without trial, even Tibbot O Toole, a man near ninety years of age who had merely been Owen's house guest on that unfortunate day.

"John Bingham imprisoned Owen himself in your own bed-chamber at Ballinahinch," Teigue told Grania, though he could not meet her eyes as he said it for fear he would cry and be unable to continue. "They put a heavy bar across the door and stationed a guard outside, and then sometime during the night a false alarm was raised and the guard ran outside to see what was happening. When the chamber was opened in the morning Owen O Flaherty lay dead inside it, with a score of wounds on his body. But John Bingham denies any knowledge of the murder."

In my bedchamber at Ballinahinch, Grania thought. He was probably conceived there.

Her mind would only snatch at random details; it would not yet absorb the whole.

But she had absorbed enough pain already in her life; it was a familiar element. She knew better than to take it in all at once and let it crush her. Better to allow it to flow through her and away, to accept it and let it go, a little at a time.

Owen. A big, handsome man with an indecisive mouth. A lad who saw no reason to save the lock of hair his mother once sent him. Owen. First born, first lost.

Grania insisted on accompanying Teigue back to Clare island on his way south to Iar Connaught, and there, in azure twilight, she visited the tiny cove that would always be hers and Huw's in memory. If she wept, she wept there where no one could see her —even Tigernan was under orders to remain in the harbor, with her galley.

Alone among ghosts, Grania remembered a fragment of old bardic poetry:

> . . . *Melodious is the crane*
> *In the marshes of Druim du Thren,*
> *But she cannot save her nestlings*
> *Once the red fox has torn them.*

And when the ritual of mourning was complete, she turned her back on the sea and looked at the island itself, at Cliara, scoured by wind until she was as bare as an unpainted face, but made beautiful by the underlying structure of her stone. The shoulders of Cnoc Mór defied the Atlantic gale. The surging sea sent its long rollers past the island as it had done before the first Gael came to Erin, and as it would do when even the last Gael was gone.

But it will be a long time before the last Gael is gone, Grania whispered to the night wind. There are black-haired O Malleys all over this west country now. And O Flaherties everywhere in Iar Connaught, some with my Owen's blood in them to pass on. Elizabeth of clan Tudor will be childless dust, but you will still see my eyes in the faces of my descendants in a Spanish port or a Danish harbor . . . or even in the New World, I wager. Yes. Certainly in the New World.

Yet no proud face will look upon the New World through *your* duplicated eyes, Elizabeth. You shall not win forever.

The O Malley motto sounded like music in Grania's brain, the beat of a war drum that would not be silenced. *Terra Marique Potens.*

Powerful by Land and Sea.

From Galway city, letters began arriving from Tibbot. They were obviously well examined before they reached her, but Grania did not complain; she was pleased they reached her at all.

"The English want me to see how civilized my son is becoming under their influence," she told Tigernan. "What I see is that he is learning lessons even I could not teach him. He is learning how to be accepted among the sasanach as Owen and Murrough never could be, and perhaps all his children will live to see their own grandchildren."

"Do you not hate thinking of Tibbot living in the household of Richard Bingham?" Tigernan wanted to know.

She grinned. "Bingham did that deliberately to hurt me, so I won't allow myself to be hurt by it. Rather I am thankful my Tibbot is getting such a close-up look at the workings of the English nature. The knowledge will serve him well someday."

Closing her mind on the thought of Tibbot in Bingham's house, Grania went down to the beach to haggle with a fisherman over the price of his catch—and when she made a good deal Tigernan heard her laughter ring out, free and clear.

Small things, she knew from long experience, could sustain her. It was not the great victory, the transcendant moment of rapture, that nourished one through the long days and the dark nights. No, for those rarefied moments were as fleeting as life itself, beyond recapture even as they occurred.

What lasted, what she could truly count on, were the pinpoints of light dancing on the surface of the bay as the sun glittered on wind-whipped wavelets. The well of warmth waiting when she crawled back into bed after getting up to relieve herself on a cold night. A tankard brimming with ale. A wager won. A joke shared with Tigernan.

An eagle flying overhead, carrying her heart up with it in lazy spirals. *Huw* . . .

In one of his letters, Tibbot happened to mention that Queen Elizabeth kept an Irish bard in her court to entertain her—after having outlawed the bards in Ireland as a dangerous and disruptive influence. When Grania read that passage aloud to Evleen and Tigernan, the latter jumped to his feet.

"The hypocritical she-dog! She thinks the Gaels good enough to sing and recite for her, to play the harp and play the fool beneath her rooftree, but not good enough to be allowed to go on living in their own style in their own land." A vein throbbed visibly in his temple. "Let me summon the Devil's Hook, Grania, and we'll set sail for Galway city before the moon changes. We'll batter down the gates and bring Tibbot out of that nest of corruption and . . ."

Grania silenced him with a long, sober look. "You're howling into the wind," she said.

The unexpected streak of pragmatism that ran through her was the one element of her character which most baffled Tigernan. It caused her to make decisions that were incomprehensible to his way of thinking, but as Grania herself told him more than once, "My strength may lie in my inconsistency. I am happiest when people do not know what to expect of me; it gives me an advantage."

But he knew she was not as strong as she wanted everyone to believe. Once she asked him, "Do you still have that little hut at Curraun?"

"I do have it."

"And if you retired there to live out a simple fisherman's life, would anyone bother you?"

"I doubt it. There is a farmstead or two inland, but no one pays much attention to a solitary fisherman."

"Or his family?"

"Or his family," Tigernan replied in a suddenly hoarse voice, not daring to hope.

Grania stared past him into some distant othertime. She did not bring up the subject again but left it shimmering on their mutual horizon. If the English ever broke her completely, Tigernan thought, she would be content to give up Rockfleet and the galleys and go with him to Curraun; shelter there in his arms for the rest of their lives.

If.

29

A party of Englishmen with time and mischief on their hands came ashore from a pinnace in the territory held by the Devil's Hook. They raped every woman and child they found over the age of four years, and burned every building they saw.

In rage, Grania's son-in-law rose in rebellion. The promise of good conduct he had offered to ransom Grania was forgotten in his anger. Margaret and his own children had escaped unscathed, as they were visiting Grania at Rockfleet when the incident occurred, but they might not be so lucky next time.

Warfare blazed on the west coast as the Devil's Hook attacked every English garrison for miles.

"I will hit you over the head again if I must," Tigernan told Grania, "but I will not see you stay here. If the fighting grows much worse, even Rockfleet will no longer be safe, and the Binghams will slaughter us all to get to you. I have asked you for nothing in this life, Grania Mhaol—but now I ask you to withdraw to some place of safety, or prepare to die and see Evleen and me die with you."

She propped her chin on her hands and looked at him without speaking for a long time. Then she shrugged and gave the order: "We'll take those who want to go with us and sail to the only refuge that might yet welcome me, the north country. Tyrconnell and Tyrone; Ulster. There are, bless Mary, more Gaels than Englishmen in Ulster."

But as they sped toward Donegal a vicious gale blew off the Atlantic, battering Grania's fleet. She and her men made it safely ashore, but they were forced to watch helplessly as the sea slammed the galleys against each other and against the rocky coast until the surf was filled with wreckage.

"My galleys were all I had left," Grania said in a small voice. "My seabirds . . ."

Black Hugh O Donnell offered her hospitality, but no lumber to repair her ships. His son Red Hugh, whom Grania remembered as a mere lad, had grown into a splendid young man his admirers called the Eagle of the North, and it was Red Hugh who seconded his father's words. "The only timber left in Donegal is saplings the English did not want, Grania," he said. He was a white-skinned, handsome man with a square jaw and a hard hand, with clear gray eyes and flaming red hair, and Grania had liked him on sight.

But his words did not please her. "Your tribe has an alliance with Hugh O Neill of Tyrone that has given you a degree of strength unequaled in the rest of Ireland," she told him frankly. "Surely you are not without resources."

"No one in Ireland can be sure of his resources; you yourself are proof of that, Gráinne Ni Mháille. Even the great Earl of Desmond, once a welcome guest in the English court, was hunted down like an outlaw several years ago in the Kerry mountains and slain by a bounty hunter, and his Munster has been carved up like so many pieces of a pie. That is the best treatment any of us can expect as long as things remain the way they are."

Something in his tone alerted her. "You expect things to change?"

Red Hugh's face might have been carved of stone, but something smoldered in his eyes, like fire burning deep down in the peat. "You spoke of Hugh O Neill. We expect him here soon, in Donegal; we have matters to discuss with him."

"You have trouble to make with him," Black Hugh O Donnell spoke up.

His son threw him a warning glance. "Old dogs hate the changing of the moon. But O Neill can change everything, if he gets enough of us to stand behind him." The young man's voice began gathering momentum, and Grania found herself leaning forward, listening to him as if she herself were young, and eager.

"Hugh O Neill is a man who truly deserves the hero's portion, the roasted haunch of the biggest boar in Ireland," Red Hugh was saying. "He intends to make of Ireland a nation, as England claims to be; one land under one king, with one purpose, and one army to stand together and fight to defend it if need be!"

He finished in a breathless rush, and his father's voice cut in immediately. "The part about *one* king, that's where the cattle will tear down the fence. We were all raised to be kings; we are a race of chieftains and warriors, not followers."

Red Hugh turned his back on his father. "Will you stand with us, Grania? Will you wait here and at least talk to Hugh O Neill?"

She gave him a bitter smile. "My timbers are full of dry rot, young Hugh. But yes—I will wait and speak to this hero of yours. The sun will never rise on a day I did not hunger to meet a champion."

"We may be allies for the moment," muttered Black Hugh O Donnell to no one in particular, "but the sun will never rise on a day when I myself will grant an O Neill the right to be the only king in Ireland!"

And there is the trouble, thought Grania to herself. There, indeed, is all our trouble.

Hugh O Neill of Tyrone arrived in Donegal attired in European clothing, accompanied by a large retinue of fighting men carrying imported weapons. A Continental polish gleamed; a strong trace of English accent lingered about many who had accompanied Hugh O Neill to Elizabeth's court in the past.

But their leader's face was purely Irish.

He was not a tall man, Grania noticed immediately. Yet he gave an impression of latent power, and his ruddy coloring spoke of hot blood. Grania's eyes scanned the man appraisingly as they were being introduced, and Tigernan commented angrily about it as soon as they were in bed together later. "You make a great fool of yourself, slavering over a man young enough to be your son," he said.

His jealousy amused her. "Do you think I want to see nothing more in my bed for the rest of my life than wrinkled skin?"

"My wrinkled skin can still make you cry out with pleasure!" Tigernan flashed angrily.

With her interest thus heightened, Grania took a long second look at Hugh O Neill the next day. Her eyes measured the breadth of his shoulders and the weight in the English codpiece he affected. But she found him most attractive that night, when he put aside his foreign clothing and entered O Donnell's hall dressed as a prince of the Gaels, with an ancient gold torc encircling his thick neck. In the smoky gloom it was like seeing Brian Boru come marching out of bardic time. Grania forgot both O Neill's age and hers.

Glancing at her, Hugh O Neill caught an expression on her face as readable as a footprint in fresh snow. He smiled, slowly and with interest, and Grania smiled back the same way.

Silly old woman, she scolded herself, vastly pleased.

She found time to talk with Hugh O Neill over a banquet of
eggs and mutton and lobster and gooey sweetmeats from abroad,
so chewy they made Grania's teeth hurt. The other women in The
O Donnell's retinue were served at separate tables, but she had
automatically taken her place with the chieftains, and no one dis-
puted her.

"I've heard many things said of you," Hugh O Neill told her.
"Even in the mountains we know of your exploits as a leader of
men."

"I did not intend to become a leader," Grania replied. "I just
went in the direction I chose, and when I looked back they were
following me."

The chieftain from Tyrone let out a hearty bellow. "That's the
best definition of leadership I've heard yet! I hope it will apply to
me someday."

That night, as Evleen was helping her prepare for bed, Grania
repeated something of the conversation to the other woman. "Hugh
O Neill belongs to the Morrigan," Evleen said, shaking her head.
"It is not a happy marriage."

"The Morrigan? The war goddess of our ancestors? That
shouldn't be such an unhappy thing—if he wins."

"Those who belong to the Morrigan know no happiness in this
world." Evleen said. "Stay clear of him, Grania. Or, else watch all
your grandsons march after him. Hugh O Neill may be a hero, but
heroes and survivors do not come from the same egg." Her eyes
brooded.

"Yet your heart leaps to the hero, as mine does," Grania pointed
out, remembering Ruari Oge.

"It does. It does." Evleen's misty eyes broke Grania's heart.

Hugh O Neill liked Grania, and his words had weight in Tyrconnell, where young O Donnell was his strongest admirer. And
so, in spite of the shortage of lumber available for ship repair,
Grania noticed loads of timber beginning to arrive at Donegal castle
—timber well suited for the repair of wrecked galleys.

The price of the timber was made known to her in due time. "I
always need to import iron and various, ah, tools, from abroad,"
Hugh O Neill told her. "Some for myself, some for allies of mine
such as The O Donnell's son. And men . . . Scots mercenaries in
need of work so they can support their families at home, of course."

"Of course," Grania agreed. "I know well enough how to hide a man or two—or a crate or two—in a load of harmless trade goods."

"I thought you did," said Hugh O Neill. "But I trust you will be very careful, once your ships are repaired."

"I have been careful never to declare a formal war on the English she-king," Grania replied, "and when the current roolya-boolya dies down in Connaught I think I may slip safely home again and take up my old trade, at least to some extent."

"There is said to be a price on your head right now," Black Hugh O Donnell warned her, but Grania just laughed.

"I had rather surrender my head to a bounty hunter than lay it down on a prison floor again," she said.

She could not resist throwing the dice. She could not stay out of the game.

When Mayo seemed quiescent, she returned. The Devil's Hook had retreated to Kildawnet to lick the wounds inflicted upon him by an overwhelming English force, and Grania's clanspeople were on the verge of starvation with neither cattle nor fishing fleet. So Grania was soon hard at work at the only trade she knew, and it seemed as if a few of her years fell away from her once her body was active again.

Surprisingly, the English did not seem inclined to bother her at the moment. Their attention had been drawn elsewhere.

In Spain the keels of an awesome number of new ships had been laid down, according to reliable reports. An armada was being readied to attack England.

Grania's own son Tibbot brought her the news. He was a man full-grown, in his twenties and solid through his torso, like his father before him. He arrived at Rockfleet with an English wardrobe and a good English horse, but when he saw his mother he ran to her without hesitation and gave her a good Irish hug.

"Sir Richard's name seems to have acquired a bad smell as a result of his policies in Connaught," Tibbot explained to Grania. "His superiors have reposted him to Flanders, for the time being, where he will not be able to stir up the Irish against the English and encourage them to take the Spanish side. In the meantime his household has been dispersed and I find myself my own man at last."

"You are Irish," Grania told him. "You are always your own man."

She served a banquet in his honor, though in truth the food on her tables was not adequate for such an occasion in either quantity or quality. But she dispensed it without apology, and the feasting lasted late into the night; it was dawn by the time the last bones were thrown to the dogs.

Tibbot was anxious to get on with his own life in what little of Burke holding remained to him, but he had hardly begun to do so when sad news came from the north. The passionate life of young Red Hugh O Donnell had flamed to a climax. The Eagle of the North had been lured into a trap and taken by the English to imprisonment in Dublin castle, a move designed to forestall the long-planned rebellion in Tyrconnell. Without his energetic leadership, the O Donnells would subside for the time being and Hugh O Neill would have to seek support elsewhere.

Several other chieftains were captured with Red Hugh, and some of them could be expected to divulge what they knew of the Ulster conspiracy against English control. Grania's name and activities on behalf of the rebels were sure to be mentioned.

"We must keep the fleet in the bay and attract no attention for a while," Grania decided. "There will be little to put on the table but our own fish—and my daughter Margaret hates fish. She will become a holy terror, that one."

"Like her mother," Tigernan remarked. Grania aimed a blow at his ear but missed. He caught her arm and their eyes met and held.

That night he stood naked in her chamber as she lay on the bed, smiling up at him. Evleen might have left a fire on the hearth to keep the room warm, but they did not notice; they did not need additional heat.

As Grania stretched lazily, preparing to welcome him to her bed, a wicked thought occurred to her. "Would your confessor be shocked if he could see you now?" she asked.

Tigernan had been fully armed for their encounter, but her words wilted him entirely. Aghast, he stared first at her then down at himself. "See what you've done with your tongue, woman. It is a dangerous weapon, a tongue."

"Indeed it is." Chuckling, Grania moved to the edge of the bed and reached out for him, her hands slipping between his thighs to caress the sensitive flesh there. And then her tongue . . . and then her mouth . . . here, there, wherever needed . . .

What would the priests think of this? she wondered but did not say aloud. Gráinne Ni Mháille did not care what the priests thought as she restored vigor to the man before her.

Some might think her poor now, and wrung out, but Grania did not think herself poor. Her mortal enemy was out of the country, and the sky above Cuan Mó arched all the way to heaven.

Then word came that Sir Richard Bingham, having left Flanders bathed in blood, would be returning to Connaught.

Grania sent for Tibbot. "The English will no longer keep Bingham from killing us all; they are too fearful we will side with Spain and let Spanish ships supply themselves here. We must seek special protection before Bingham returns. You are fluent in the sasanach language. I want you to write a letter for me to the lord deputy at once, explaining that I have truly repented my past mistakes and any connection with the Ulster warlords, and begging a royal pardon."

Tibbot looked at his mother with an expression of disbelief she had seen before, on the face of Iron Richard. "You are willing to beg?"

She tightened the loose belt around her waist. Times and people had grown very lean in her territory. "I am not begging and I am not betraying friends. I am merely using a small lie to erect a shield against Richard Bingham. He would do worse than that against me. Only Elizabeth's own pardon can keep us safe now, I suspect."

Tibbot nodded. He had feared Grania would be sacrificially defiant for the rest of her life, and he was pleased to see her taking what he deemed a more reasonable course. Tibbot had observed both Richard Bingham and the English system at close quarters and did not want to see his mother dash herself against the rocks of inevitability.

He wrote the letter as she requested, polishing every phrase, and on May 4, 1588, a pardon was granted to Grania as widow of Richard Burke—and to her son Murrough and daughter Margaret as well. "I must spread my roof over all my family," Grania had said.

The lord deputy dealt with the matter almost absentmindedly, relieved that one of the more troublesome Gaels seemed once more pacified. "I will probably have to alternately fight and pardon this woman until one of us is dead," he remarked, "but at least Mayo will be quiet for a while."

Ulster, too, seemed quiet after Red Hugh O Donnell's capture. For a while.

And in July of that same year the invasion fleet set sail from Spain for England to destroy the heretic queen and take control of her kingdom. For the English, Irish problems quickly faded into the mist of the greater threat.

The Year of the Armada, they would call it later, all those who lived through it and forever after dated things from before the Armada or after the Armada. It had not been a year, of course— just one brief, bright summer, when the sea was the color of slate and every morning dawned oppressively hot and still.

To Hugh O Neill the Spanish invasion was great news, for a victory of Catholic Spain over the forces of Elizabeth Tudor could signal Ireland's freedom from England's chains. The ties between Spain and Ireland were of long standing, bonds of religion and trade and Celtic temperament that O Neill hoped to forge into a powerful alliance once Ireland was an independent land again.

For England, the coming of the Armada signaled the greatest test yet put to the borning empire.

The weather turned unseasonable, with savage storms.

Sir Francis Drake had heard in the spring that between four and five hundred ships, manned by eighty thousand sailors and soldiers, were massing in Lisbon harbor and awaiting word from Philip of Spain to invade England. Terrifying though such rumors were, Drake refused to give in to the wave of fear rolling over England. His own name had proved sufficient to instill a degree of terror in Spanish hearts before this, after such battles as that of Cádiz bay when he sank, burned, or captured thirty-seven Spanish ships. He assured Elizabeth he could repulse any Spanish attack and proceeded, with the reckless boldness that had always characterized his career, to mount the defense of England.

A lifetime spent in privateering could give a man—or a woman —a certain kind of confidence nothing could shake.

Drake relied on such fellow pirates as the notorious Hawkins to help outmaneuver the Spanish fleet, no matter how large. But Elizabeth had placed Charles, Lord Howard of Effingham, as lord admiral of her fleet, and Francis Drake with all his plans and his swagger was intended to answer to someone else.

It was not in the nature of Sir Francis Drake to answer to anyone else, save his sovereign. Gráinne Ni Mháille would have understood that. Whatever internecine battles for authority were fought between himself and Lord Howard, it was Drake's name that would ultimately be trumpeted as the hero of the Armada year.

All Europe seemed to hold its breath that hot and stormy summer as the immense Spanish fleet advanced on the English coast. The size of the forces that would ultimately fight, and the types and numbers of their guns, were unprecedented. Against the massive Spanish ships—a smaller number, to be sure, than those early rumors, but still a vast force—stood the bulk of the Elizabethan fleet, consisting of fourteen of the queen's heaviest galleons and a motley assortment of armed merchantmen and volunteers. Everyone who owned and could man a boat seemed to be converging on the English Channel as the Armada approached.

Signal fires blazed up the west coast of Ireland.

"The Spanish have set sail," Grania announced in her hall.

She, who knew the harbor at La Coruña well, could imagine the great galleys and galleons, the Levantine carracks, the squadrons of hulks which King Philip could have summoned and launched against Elizabeth. In her mind's eye she could follow them up through the treacherous bay of Biscay and into the Channel; what she could not know was the degree to which the weather had turned against them, or the fact that the very diversity of ships composing the Armada had resulted in the fleet's being separated and fragmented long before it reached English waters, where Drake and the defenders waited.

In the year of the Armada most of the Irish were fully occupied with trying to survive, to wrest some sort of living from their pillaged land. Those who knew, or cared, about the war between Spain and England were a small number, and those who might appreciate its ramifications smaller still. Survival was a personal matter; politics was a solar storm causing eddies of wind that eventually reached the individual, but whose source he could not comprehend.

On the thirty-first day of July, as the first great modern naval battle was being joined and the Spanish captain-general was hoisting his banner as a signal to engage off Eddystone in the English Channel, Grania was haggling with a Dutch merchant over the price of sea trout at Cathair na Mart.

"I can get it cheaper from almost anyone else," he told her.

"But you are here and the fish is here," she answered reasonably. "What will it cost you to take your vessel elsewhere and start bargaining all over again?"

She got her price, and there was rejoicing in Umhall. "We will have a few coins left over," Grania said with relief. "Perhaps we can buy a little additional wool from Iar Connaught to clothe my people for the winter."

It was not too soon to start thinking about the winter, even in August. Huge black clouds built up repeatedly beyond Clare island, like massed and menacing armies promising a hard season ahead.

The Spanish invasion fleet was pushed to the back of Grania's mind. When she thought of it at all, she imagined Elizabeth of clan Tudor as a woman much like herself, dressed in trews perhaps, standing in the prow of a war galley and personally commanding the defense of her kingdom as Grania would have done. The image gave her an empathy with the English queen. The O Neill, she knew, desired a Spanish victory, but Grania had felt a relationship between herself and Elizabeth for so long that her thoughts were with the queen and not with the Spanish. No matter who won, she did not see how it would immediately affect Ireland.

Who was it who had once told her that England and Spain slavered over Ireland as a dog slavered over a bone? She did not remember anymore; her memory was overcrowded with too many things, too many seasons and events. Whoever won, Grania thought, would probably continue the conquest and pillage of Ireland. So things would not change very much.

The authorities in Connaught had, some months earlier, passed the word that it would be considered an act of treason punishable by death if any Irish person aided the Spanish, the enemies of the Crown. Grania's only comment then had been, "I suppose this means we should desist from trade with Spain—if we had anything left to ship to them, which we don't anyway."

Even though Bingham had returned to Ireland, Grania had her official pardon, so she was back on her ships once more and engaged in the little trade remaining to her. And the fishing, for the waters of Cuan Mó would at least sustain them when all else failed. She was out beyond Achill head when the Armada ships, pursued by the English, sped up the Channel toward the strait separating Dover and Calais. Both sides had already learned hard lessons in savage fighting. The Spanish had discovered that even when the wind was in their favor they could not grapple the English ships, which were nimbler and swifter and possessed more large guns. The English had learned that for all their skill at sea battles, they could not easily sink the Spanish ships. Philip's invasion force was on a course that would take them to the mouth of the Thames, unless they were stopped.

Grania took a fine catch off Achill head that Saturday, then set her course southward to deliver some provisions to Tigernan's people on Inishbofin. There was always someone, somewhere, in need of something.

England struggled to be in a state of readiness in the event the Spanish succeeded in landing. Elizabeth's subjects, in a white heat of fear, struck out at every foreigner within reach, causing one horrified and sympathetic observer to write, "It is easier to find flocks of white crows than one Englishman who loves a foreigner."

Dispatch riders on fast horses were galloping across Europe, from Calais and Paris, from knowledgeable observers and fanciful rumor-mongers, relating news of the great battle. Europe had been expecting some form of disaster for a long time, as the forces of various kingdoms and interests were pitted against one another to hammer out the dimensions of a new age. Now it was obvious which nations were involved in the most immediate struggle—and now it also became apparent that catastrophe had befallen one of the antagonists.

Wild stories that had been circulating for a fortnight began to coalesce into a clear picture as the skippers of Newfoundland fishing barks began picking up survivors of the final conflict off Gravelines. Sir Francis Drake in the *Revenge* had given the first charge, and the opponents had engaged in a battle marked by skill and courage on both sides. A violent squall had briefly made battle all but impossible, and by the end of the day the Spanish formation had been broken and valiantly re-formed again. But they were almost out of shot, and the northern weather had turned against them. Most of the best surviving vessels were leaking, with spars and rigging littering their decks. There was no safe harbor where they might land for repairs, as the English could. They had been engaged again and again, and in time the effort had taken its toll. Human flesh and blood could only stand so much. The Armada ran up the coast in full flight, desperate, failing, with the English in pursuit, and the rocks and the beaches and the pounding sea waited to claim the losers.

✠

Even in the stone-hugged security of her chamber at Rockfleet, Grania knew long before dawn that a storm was coming. She awoke with the familiar tingling in her joints, an atavistic instinct fundamental to the survival of Atlantic seafarers since the Milesians set sail from Iberia. She lay in her bed with her eyes closed and the smell of her feather-filled coverlet in her nostrils, but she could see the clouds boiling; she could smell the rain.

When she got up Evleen appeared at her chamber door, with peat for the fire. "The autumn storms come early this year," Grania remarked, yawning and stretching.

"They do. It is only the first week of August, but the light in the sky looks like that of November."

The somber greenish light lay over the whole west coast of Ireland that day; that week. In its baleful glow the scattered ships of the Armada were attempting to get home.

Grania had expected to meet an O Flaherty galley up from Iar Connaught with wool that week, and so with Tigernan and a crew she set out from Rockfleet, rowing into the wind. Her experienced oarsmen exerted just the effort needed to send the vessel forward with one clean stroke, then allowed its momentum to complete the glide before they stroked again, making steady headway in spite of the storm. The huge bay seemed uninhabited that day; even fishermen stayed on shore in such weather, mending nets or caulking boats or sitting content before their hearthfires, watching their wives weave and cook.

But Grania was abroad of necessity. The empty bay represented her freedom, to whatever degree she still possessed that treasure. And with freedom came responsibility. As a chieftain's daughter she understood the inseparability of the two. People were depending on her; business must go on. When the galley laden with wool sailed into the small harbor on Clare island, she must be there to meet it.

Like bloated rats pursued by agile terriers, the galleons of the Armada fled the English from the coast of Scotland to Ulster and down the rocky, remorseless coast of Connaught, where, no longer driven by mortal enemies, they encountered a more irresistible foe.

The Atlantic gale savaged them.

Sheltered by the Curraun peninsula and to some degree by Clare island in its mouth, Clew bay did not feel the full brunt of the storm. Grania was approaching Cliara when she caught sight of the towering masts of a great Spanish vessel out on the Atlantic. The ship was obviously being driven straight onto the rocks on the western side of the island and disappeared from view almost immediately.

"That must be one of the King of Spain's warships!" Grania cried to Tigernan. "The battle is over, then. But why . . ."

". . . have they come so far west?" Tigernan finished for her, frowning. "And did you notice they've lost one mast? That is a ship in trouble, Grania."

She did not hesitate. "Row harder!" she shouted to her men.

They reached the harbor as swiftly as possible, and Grania was overboard while the water was still waist-deep. She ran onto the beach, wringing moisture from her clothing without missing a stride. But the harbor seemed deserted. The O Flaherty galley had not yet arrived, and the curraghs belonging to the O Malleys still living on Cliara were all properly beached. No lantern burned by the gate of the tower house. Cottage doors everywhere stood ajar, as if their inhabitants had abandoned them in flight.

From the flank of Cnoc Mór the whipping flame of a signal fire summoned fretfully.

"They've all gone to the western side of the island," Grania told Tigernan, "to plunder the Spaniard."

With her men, she followed as quickly as she could, but she arrived too late.

The splendid ship commanded by Don Pedro de Mendoza had set sail from Spain gleaming with new paint, vivid with bright banners snapping from its mastheads, its many decks athrong with laughing cavaliers anticipating the greatest adventure of their lives. The galleon breaking up on the coast of Clare island bore little resemblance to that earlier self. English cannon had battered it; North sea elements had all but torn it apart. And as its hapless crewmen abandoned ship and struggled through the boiling surf toward land, the Irish met them.

In arrogance and optimism, the Spanish had laden their invasion fleet with riches. By the time Don Pedro's ship broke up on the Irish coast his water casks contained only green and stinking liquid, but in his holds was gold for the use of victorious armies as well as gunpowder, field guns and small arms, lead for bullets, chests of fine clothing, oil and vinegar and bacon and beans. Wheels of cheese, bags of rice. Port and sack and spices. The wealth conquerors would need to intimidate the conquered spilled from the dying galleon into the surf of Cliara, and the O Malleys merely waded in and got it.

When the Spaniards tried to resist they slaughtered them.

The year had been hard, and Grania's kinsmen had not yet grown used to poverty. The treasure thus providentially deposited on their shores was irresistible, and questions of political affiliation were beyond most of them anyway, for Grania had left the island in the charge of a young and hot-blooded chieftain who had never been farther away from the bay than Castlebar.

By the time Grania and her men reached the scene almost three hundred dead Spaniards floated on the water or lay littered along the shore, eyes glazing. Their vessel had all but disappeared; its wreckage was scarcely identifiable as having come from a ship at all.

Grania stared at the scene with the horror shipwrecks must always inspire in any seafarer.

The young O Malley who styled himself the Red Oak came up to her, grinning. "It's a fine haul we're taking," he assured her. "You're just in time to help divide the spoils."

Thinking of Hugh O Neill, Grania replied, "These were King Philip's men, come to attack England. Our Spanish allies, some call them. Perhaps if they defeated the English we would be rid of the sasanach here. . . ."

"They don't look as if they've defeated anybody," the Red Oak said, pushing at a corpse with his foot until it rolled sluggishly onto its back. The satin doublet the dead man wore had been ripped on the rocks, and something gleamed. The Red Oak bent forward, fumbled, tore open padding to reveal a treasure in gold ducats sewn into the dead cavalier's clothing. "Conquering army," O Malley said sarcastically. "Much good their gold will do them now; we might as well have the use of it. And are you so certain they would have been our allies, Grania? Men greedy enough to hide gold like this are greedy enough to loot us as everyone else has. That's why I first ordered my own men to attack them as they came ashore; I thought it might be some new wave of invaders meaning to take Cliara from us."

And perhaps there was truth in the thought, Grania said to herself wearily. Who could know?

She forced herself to consider the reasons why the Spanish ships might be attempting to go south along the Atlantic coast. There was only one real reason she could think of: the battle in the Channel had been lost and the Armada was fleeing around Ireland, unable to return the way it had come because England held those waters secure.

The Red Oak was wading into the surf, plowing the sea with his hands as people were doing all around him. A fine harvest was coming in with the tide. Grania saw him lift a magnificent platter of solid gold, richly embossed and rimmed with a rope design. He waved the treasure in the air and shouted, and his wife went splashing out to join him, carrying an apron she had already filled with valuables herself.

A manic hilarity infected the islanders. The shores of Cliara became a festival ground with fires blazing and people dancing with abandon as darkness fell, parading before one another in water-soaked finery and throwing gold coins into the air to watch them fall like shooting stars, flashing in the firelight.

Grania watched, making no effort to restrain them. They were seizing materials for survival, and she understood. But she did not take part. From her conversations with Hugh O Neill she had some idea what the Spanish invasion might have meant to Ireland, a final overthrow of the Protestant yoke. Perhaps.

Or perhaps the exchange of one tyranny for another. Who could say?

The storm's heart blew past, but the wind howled on.

The great galleons that had carried Spain's hopes and survived the succession of sea battles with the English were, one by one, being pounded to death on Irish shores. In the masses of tangled wreckage men fought for their lives against sea and storm and sometimes against the Irish who came to hack life from them and plunder Spanish property to feed hungry Irish children.

In Blacksod bay a kinsman of the Devil's Hook captured and robbed survivors from the *Rata*, the vessel which had carried the second in command of the Armada expedition. Another ship of fifty-four guns foundered in Grania's own territory, and its survivors were stripped of everything they owned before being set free on Grania's order to make their way inland, trying to avoid English search parties.

They fled to an unknown fate.

But what fate could be predicted, in Ireland?

Grania, gazing eastward on a quiet morning after the storm had long since passed and the beaches were still littered with Spanish wreckage, raised one hand in a silent and unobserved salute to that other woman, across the sea. The woman who had destroyed Spain's greatest fleet.

You have won yourself a war, Elizabeth, Grania thought.

Enjoy it.

PART SIX

ELIZABETH

30

With the destruction of the Armada the political climate in Ireland changed again. Not all of the Irish had pillaged the Spanish wrecks; some Gaels, recognizing acquaintances among the survivors, had hidden them or attempted to arrange transportation for them back to Spain. Men of such diverse interests as the Devil's Hook and The O Flaherty eventually sheltered some hapless Spaniards for a time while the English launched a systematic search for them.

Shortly after his return to Connaught, Sir Richard Bingham proudly wrote in one of his dispatches, "In my province there have perished at least six or seven thousand men." Her majesty's enemies were being hunted down, and no one questioned his brutality now; it had become an asset.

Meanwhile the Gaelic chieftains who had aided the Spaniards introduced some of their homeless guests into their own bands of warriors, where Spanish bitterness fanned new flames of rebellion.

Months passed, years passed, and there was no peace in Connaught.

Bingham never doubted that Gráinne Ni Mháille was contributing to the turmoil, but she had that priceless pardon and he had no firm proof to override it. As long as she had her swift galleys and her countless hiding places if pursued, he could not move against her for fear of suffering yet another frustrating and humiliating defeat at her hands.

But he had no such qualms about attacking her clansmen and allies.

Tibbot na Long, who had developed what his mother considered a valuable gift for maintaining amicable relationships with both the English and the Gaels, came up from a trip to Flaherty territory with disturbing news.

"My half brother Murrough is now speaking out against you,"

he told Grania at Rockfleet, with every appearance of sadness at his own words. "Bingham has finally succeeded in intimidating even him, for he lives too close to Galway city and has a wife and children to protect. The first gray in his hair makes a man more careful. Murrough said publicly, right in the middle of market day where everyone could hear, that Richard Bingham was right in attacking our northern allies, the Burkes of Castlebar, and that your support of them was indefensible."

Grania's eyebrows drew together like storm clouds on the horizon. "I would not quarrel with Murrough for turning cautious at last, if that is the way for him now. But if he publicly speaks against his mother, that is a different fish in the net, and he needs to be reminded of the importance of blood loyalty. We are Gaels, after all. Not English," she added firmly, giving her son a direct look.

"Prepare my galleys for war," she instructed Tigernan. "It may be that the parent is never through teaching the child."

"You believe Murrough has turned against you?"

Her smile was small and sardonic. "I believe Tibbot has learned the lessons of personal survival very well, and there is always the chance he sees an advantage to be gained by causing a rift between me and my other remaning son. We will sail to Iar Connaught, but I will learn the truth of this matter before Murrough feels my hand on his backside."

However, when Murrough O Flaherty learned that galleys flying Grania's banner were approaching his father's old stronghold at Bunowen, where he was in residence, he immediately departed with all his family to spend an unspecified time in Galway city.

His action told Grania all she needed to know. Landing in the familiar harbor at Bunowen, she plundered all the surrounding area claimed by Murrough and then led her men up the Owenmor river to Ballinahinch, which she also looted. In the halls of that castle she found many things she had given her sons over the years, and she reclaimed them all. The jewels, the plate, the Venetian glass.

But she never opened the chamber where Owen O Flaherty had been murdered.

When Murrough finally returned home and found his holdings plundered, he protested to Bingham. Sir Richard promptly sent a letter to the queen's secretary, Cecil, in which he condemned

Gráinne Ni Mháille—an old familiar refrain from him by then—for having "a naughty disposition toward the state."

Privately he said much worse things about her.

"Cecil would send me an order for the O Malley woman's execution tomorrow," he told his brother John, "if it had not been for that unfortunate matter of the Scottish queen. Her majesty was reluctant to put to death another monarch, and a woman at that—particularly after her own mother was beheaded. I believe that is why no one ever agrees to the necessity for killing this wild woman in Mayo. But someday she will go too far; Mary of Scotland went too far. And then I will do her majesty a great favor whether she agrees to it or not!"

In 1592, Red Hugh O Donnell staged a daring escape from Dublin castle, and in Ulster Hugh O Neill rejoiced, certain that with Red Hugh's support he could now win over those chieftains still unwilling to fight with him and effect an overthrow of English control in Ireland. O Neill looked forward to the day when he would don the mantle of Ard Rí, Brian Boru's long-vacated title as King of Ireland.

But meanwhile the Celtic tribalism carried in the blood continued to set one clan at war with another, and the army O Neill could rally behind him remained fragmented and divisive. With a skill to rival that of Tibbot na Long, O Neill managed to maintain a public semblance of fealty to Elizabeth while writing a series of frantic letters to Spain and the Continent, urging another Spanish invasion with Ulster as its landing site.

Richard Bingham, meanwhile, had slaughtered so many of the Burkes of Mayo that Grania's son Tibbot slid almost uncontested into the title of clan chieftain—and promptly proclaimed loyalty to the Crown with the same sincerity as Hugh O Neill.

"Damme if the O Malley woman's son hasn't taken over an Irish title!" Richard Bingham exploded in anger. "And after all the generosity I showed him, feeding him at my own table and seeing that he learned civilized English customs. I do not for one moment believe he will hold the Burkes loyal to Elizabeth; he and that plaguey mother of his will foment a new rebellion before the sun sets."

There was no time to waste, as Bingham saw it. Now that Tibbot had the Gaelic chieftainship he would surely betray his former mentor—Bingham would have done the same thing himself—and use his mother's warships against the English. Without waiting for permission from anybody, Sir Richard Bingham set out to thwart such a possibility in the only way remaining open to him.

✠

The mirror was in the bottom of Grania's sea chest, under a stack of woolens. She found it by accident while looking for a pin to fasten her bodice together. The gown had ripped open as the cloth grew thin with wear. These days, Irish people wore their clothing until it fell off them.

Grania lifted the mirror and carried it to the embrasure, where she could study her face in the light from the narrow loophole. She sat there for a long time, just looking. Then she put the mirror face down and descended the stair to find Tigernan at the portal, talking with two boatmen about the dulsc harvest. Seaweed had by necessity become an important dietary staple in Ireland.

She took hold of his elbow. "Walk with me, Tigernan."

He matched his pace to hers, and they strolled together along the banks of the narrow stream supplying Rockfleet with fresh water.

"Why do you stay with me, Tigernan?" Grania asked abruptly. Most of the Irish circled around and around a subject, enjoying the vagaries of conversation, but Grania tended to go straight as an arrow for the heart of the matter.

"You're a bad habit, and they are the hardest to break," Tigernan told her.

"Seriously."

I will not, he thought. I will not answer you seriously, Grania Mhaol, and stand in front of you like an old fool without even a shield to protect myself. "I gave you the best answer I could," he said aloud.

Grania shook her head and smiled a bemused smile. "I am a woman with a worn-out face and a great amount of wealth," she replied. "You and Evleen, my children's children, Cuan Mó. My ships." Her eyes were tenderest when she named the ships.

Taking Tigernan with her, she went inland to conduct a little trading business with the Burkes while her fleet sailed out to fish. She returned to Rockfleet in time to learn that the galleys would not be coming home.

Bingham had used his most crushing weapon against the woman who had so long defied him. Sailing English warships into the mouth of Clew bay under cover of night, he had waylaid and seized Grania's entire fleet, impounding them in her majesty's name "to prevent their being used in rebellion."

Grania's spine bowed under the weight of the news and her face drained of color. "My ships," she moaned. "My ships!"

In haste she sent for Tibbot. "Write me a letter to the English she-king herself," she ordered him. "You have enough connections to get it through to her without Bingham's knowledge, I should think. Tell her the details of my long-standing grievance with Bingham and implore her to allow me the tools of survival."

Pacing the flagstone floor of her hall as she dictated her ideas to Tibbot, Grania outlined the details of her situation, then paused to argue meanings and correct and amend at her son's suggestion.

"Be certain to point out that I have two living sons who profess loyalty to the Crown," she said, and Tibbot smiled at the quill in his hand. Grania went on, "The Tudor woman must be made to understand that I have a rank in our society at least the equal of hers, for I too am the daughter of a great chieftain and have served as a leader of men. Tell her that, Tibbot. And . . ." She paused, a sly glint creeping into her eyes. "And ask her to grant me liberty during what may remain of my lifetime to invade with sword and fire all Elizabeth's enemies, as one prince defends another."

Tibbot dropped his quill, and it slung a spatter of ink drops on the flagstones. "You would have the effrontery to ask her to rearm you?"

"I have nothing now," Grania pointed out. "So I might as well ask for what I want, and appeal to her self-interest to give it to me. And while we are about it let us ask for a sum of maintenance from the estates of my two dead husbands, since Bingham has robbed me of everything else."

"What makes you think she will grant you any of this?" Tibbot wondered.

The weatherbeaten woman in the threadbare clothing replied, "She is of noble blood, as I am, and on that basis I appeal to her. I have met some of the real nobility—a young man called Philip Sidney, for one—and I know there is decency in some of them. Not like that Bingham, to whom they gave a title the way you put a rug down to hide a dung heap."

The unexpected missive, written in English, eventually reached
Elizabeth, who took an active interest in even the smallest details
of her realm as Grania would weigh a lobster in her hand and
squint her eyes over its size and prospects. The letter, coming as it
did from a woman mentioned in dispatches dating back many
years, intrigued the queen. She promptly had Cecil send eighteen
Articles of Interrogatory to Grania for answering.

Summoned once again, Tibbot read the questions aloud to his
mother. The first several dealt with Grania's husbands and her
families by them; the next probed into the situation of chieftains'
widows under Gaelic law.

Grania was pleased. "She is of royal upbringing and well educated to prove it," she said. "Even the she-king of the English seems
aware that ours is the older law."

"More likely she is just curious about something she considers
an exotic custom," Tibbot told his mother.

Grania frowned at him. "Explain, in our reply, that under the
Brehon law a chieftain's possessions are considered the property of
his clan and not exclusively his. That is where we differ from the
English, who would rob the most needy to give everything to the
sole ownership of the most powerful. Explain also, therefore, that
when a chief of the Gaels dies, no great wealth is bestowed on his
widow for her own use."

Grania went on to tell Elizabeth that when a woman married
under Brehon law—which had always allowed divorce—she was
given securities by her husband for the return of her dowry if he
someday wanted to set her aside. Grania did not bother, however,
to add the small detail of having once divorced Richard an Iarainn
under that same law.

Tibbot Burke was impressed by his mother's canniness, but
from his own knowledge of the English he did not want to
make her appear too proud and thus arouse hostility. He
skillfully worded her replies so she sounded like a helpless widow
who had been badly used, appealing to English justice to override the deficiencies of Gaelic law that would leave a widow so
helpless.

Tibbot had a canny mind himself.

He sent the reply on its way, through a complicated tangle of
Irish and Englishmen, and was returning to Rockfleet castle when
a party of Bingham's soldiers seized him. The charge was simple:

Tibbot, as chieftain of the Mayo Burkes, was accused of taking part in a conspiracy in Mayo to raise support for O Neill in Ulster. A similar charge was simultaneously brought against Grania's half brother, Donal of the Pipes.

Bingham could not put his hands on her, but he could attack her menfolk; he could find other ways to hurt her.

Tigernan was with Grania in the hall when she received the news of Tibbot's capture. Her eyes met his, and a long look passed between them. Grania's mouth twisted. "He should have taken Murrough," she said. "I would not have minded so much."

"If Bingham imprisoned Murrough you would have gone after him no matter how angry you are with him," Tigernan said.

"You know me that well, do you? Ah . . . perhaps you do. But it isn't Murrough, it's Tibbot. And my poor stick of a half brother. And all those who call me friend, I suspect."

Tigernan did know her, after so many years. He knew the one word that never failed to anger her, and he used it now deliberately. "Is it hopeless then, Grania Mhaol?"

Her chin came up. "Hopeless? It is not!"

"Then what will you do?"

Her bitter smile became a bitter laugh. "People always expect me to do something, don't they? And I will again." She sounded very tired. "Because if you don't do something you are dead. They have tied both my hands behind my back, but I still have my tongue."

"So you still have a deadly weapon," he replied.

"I do indeed. And I must put it to service quickly. The time for sending letters and dispatches is long past, for in the number of days it would take a newly written plea to reach Elizabeth I could be there myself and put my case more persuasively."

"You can't go to London! You are surely known in England as an enemy of the Crown!"

Grania shook her head. "I have probably been called that for at least a generation or two, yet I am still alive. And while I am alive I must do what I can. Bingham may have my galleys, but there are a few battered curraghs on the shores of Cuan Mó, Tigernan, and you are skillful enough to sail one down the coast to O Flaherty country even in a rough sea. Some O Flaherty will remember me from the old days and let me have a galley to take around the southern coast and on to England. The waters are kept safer now," she added sarcastically, "by the pirates who are captaining Elizabeth's own warships!"

It would do no good to argue with her, Tigernan knew. Any objection he raised would just confirm her in her determination. But no matter how bold her unvanquished heart, Tigernan wondered if it was strong enough to carry her all the way to London and into the lair of the sasanach monarch. Better than anyone he knew the battering Grania had taken over the years and could measure its toll in the shifting shadows of her eyes.

"I can do no more than cling to her like a burr in a horse's tail," he told Evleen, "and try to guard her back."

"There will be a second burr to keep you company for a while," Evleen surprised him by saying. "I will go with you, for a way."

"To London?"

The little woman's face seemed to fold into its countless wrinkles; her eyes almost disappeared. "Never there," she said. "But as far as Grania needs me."

As she had anticipated, Grania was given a warm welcome by at least some of the O Flaherties, those septs which had not aligned themselves with her son Murrough in the latest squabble. Even old Murrough an d'Tuadh, English-appointed chieftain of the clan, had mellowed sufficiently with the years to extend a formal welcome to Grania. He was willing to allow her the use of a small fleet, though he assured her they would return with no more than her dead body.

"I will die sometime anyway," she told him. "But not until I have looked into the eyes of Elizabeth of clan Tudor. I have seen my own face in the mirror; now I need to know what she looks like."

The answer made no sense to the old man.

They stood together on the shore of Bunowen harbor, surrounded by white sand and black fingers of rock that clawed toward the flat horizon with a desperate hopelessness. Bunowen was not Cuan Mó, Grania reminded herself. Yet there were people here who loved Iar Connaught as much as she loved Umhall, people who drew strength from the tumble of stone and the boggy pools and the long flat expanses of wiry grass.

People who needed hope to carry them through the English twilight descending upon them.

Staring past The O Flaherty into inner space, Grania reflected to herself that Ireland had, in her own lifetime, become a land of lowering skies and hunch-shouldered people. Joyless people on the verge of a permanent bitterness that would make Iar Connaught's landscape seem lush by comparison.

"Someone must represent the Gaels in the English court and let these sasanach see what we really are," she said aloud to The O Flaherty and his clansmen crowded around her. "We have had shame and murder thrust upon us until we have become equally brutal and untrustworthy, and the English find it easy to call us savages. It will make it easier for them to stamp us out like vermin and take our land if they think we are less than nothing.

"But I go to England to show their she-king a real Gael, not one in foreign dress like Hugh O Neill, or some young man taken hostage from his family and raised in the English style. When she looks into my eyes she will know she can never make us into poor copies of herself. She will know that we are still iron-hard and bronze-bright and will be here when she and her agents are dust!"

Grania's listeners absorbed her impassioned speech and gave it back to her with a thunder of cheering. More men stepped forward asking to crew her to England than she could possibly use.

Only Tigernan, watchful as ever, detected the faint tremor in Grania's voice toward the end, or noticed how pale she had become. She was entering her sixties, and life had used her hard. He had often feared her misfortunes would swamp her and always been glad to be proved wrong, but this time was different. The instinct in his bones told him Grania's strength was not sufficient for the task she had set herself, and if she gave way in front of the sasanach she would surely be thrown into an English prison and left to rot. Without him.

Once, Tigernan had made a great sacrifice on Grania's behalf, imperiling his Christian soul and alienating him from God. But the effort had been wasted; the murder of the abbot of Murrisk had not appreciably bettered Grania's position or made her any safer. It had been a pebble dropped and lost in the ocean, making no difference at all.

If he was to sacrifice himself a second time for her sake—as he must sacrifice himself, as his own nature demanded—he would do something that would make a difference.

Fortunately, by now he knew Gráinne Ni Mháille so well he thought he could almost dismantle her in the dark and put her back together again. He knew the one weapon he could give her that would carry her with stored-up strength all the way to England and even, perhaps, bring her home safely again.

✠

When all was in readiness, with provisions for many days securely lashed in place and oarsmen at their posts in Grania's flagship and two escorting vessels, Tigernan made his move. She was about to go aboard and give the order to cast off when he stepped in front of her, blocking her way.

"This is a mistake and I am not going to let you go, Grania Mhaol," he said, folding his arms across his chest and planting his feet.

"What are you talking about now, you old fool? Of course I am going. Stand aside."

"I will not."

"You are my captain! Take your place."

He set himself more firmly. "I will not," he repeated. He had rehearsed his words on the beach, all by himself, struggling with a tongue that lacked polish but must somehow, just this once, say all the right things. Her life might depend upon it.

"I do not mean to let you set sail for England, Grania Mhaol, because I know the Englishwoman will never see you. And even if she did she would never listen to you; you are of no importance to her at all. You are just another Irish person making a fool of herself, and Elizabeth has seen so many of those; she will sweep you aside with a wave of her hand."

Grania's eyes glittered. "You suddenly have a very low opinion of me and what I can do."

He pushed his point further. She could not see the sweat pouring out of his armpits or running in rivulets down his back. "You're a weak old boiled-out bone, Grania," he said in a loud voice, insulting her for all to hear. "Who knows it better than myself, whose shoulder you've leaned upon for years? You can hardly take a step without me. You cannot possibly go to England without me, much less challenge Elizabeth and win something from her. You can do nothing at all without a strong man's help anymore—if you ever could—and I'm not going. So you will have to stay here."

He was not bluffing. His straightforward soul was too honest for bluffing. He would not go to England, and she could read it in his eyes.

[414]

For a moment he thought her shoulders sagged, as if she heard truth in his words and accepted it. That was the worst moment of Tigernan's life—the moment when he feared the Grania he loved was really gone, forever.

But then she balled her fists and yelled at him with a powerful voice, a commander's voice resonant with energy and will, "You miserable coward! How dare you desert me again! And what makes you think I ever needed you for anything? I prefer going to England without you dragging at my heels, and I will accomplish everything I set out to do there, do you hear me? Everything! Watch me, you faithless deserter. *Just watch me!*"

Into her lungs Grania summoned power she had not called upon for years. In rich and lusty Gaelic she cursed Tigernan, calling down invective upon himself and all his line, upon the rocky island of his birth and the ground he walked today, upon all the descendants he would never have. She swore at him from the well-furnished stock of a mariner's profanity until even the hard-bitten men around her were impressed by the range of her curses.

Tigernan stood under it like a man in a rainstorm, with his head bowed. And when at last she paused to draw breath for a renewed assault he made himself turn and walk away.

In all their years together, in all their fond bickering, Tigernan had never accused Grania of impotence or disparaged her abilities in front of others before. It was a cruel and unexpected betrayal. She thought he spoke not only for himself, but for Donal an Chogaidh and Richard an Iarainn and Owen Dubhdara; for all the men who had resented her unconventional life and unwomanly success. The fury she summoned followed him in a raging bellow of profanity until he was nearly to the foot of Doon hill and her voice subsided into a thready croak. Still the anger burned in her. Fueling her.

She would show him. She would show them all.

"I will captain my flagship myself," she told her crewmen.

Evleen came forward at the very last, and reaching up, she put her small brown hands on the taller woman's broad shoulders. "Ruari Oge stands with us today," she said softly. "Go to that foreign court representing both of us and the children of this land who will come after us. And when you are tired or discouraged, send your heart home to Ireland, Grania. We will feel the spirit of you reaching out and we will answer.

"Claim the Christian faith if you will, but remember what I tell you, for I know: Ireland is a goddess, Grania, and from her womb in its painful contractions has come greatness before. Who can say what heroes she may yet bear? The women as much heroes as the men, Grania. Go and be brave."

Evleen's wizened face was illumined by a light almost too bright for Grania to look upon. Suddenly she threw her arms around the other woman and hugged her hard, not caring who saw a chieftain's daughter hug her servant. She, and Evleen, knew that the smaller woman was no servant. She was Ireland.

When Grania at last opened her arms the eyes of both women were suspiciously damp.

I go for all of us, Evleen, Grania thought as the galleys set sail. She stood in the prow and turned her face toward England and Elizabeth.

I am coming, she thought. We have had an appointment for a long time, you and I, for kin must meet. And we are kin whether you know it yet or not. I have watched you from afar too long to doubt that a common thread unites us . . . and I will prove your equal, woman of clan Tudor.

Watch me, Tigernan!

31

The men who accompanied Grania stole glances at her from time to time and talked among themselves. "How can a woman have so many tragedies befall her and still go on?" they wondered. The wind snatched at their words and carried them to Grania.

But she knew the answer. Tragic circumstances need not add up to a tragic life, any more than a few herring made a whole catch. The choice of interpretation was always a human option.

Sorrow, like love, could be embraced or rejected, and the flavor of life thereafter determined by a conscious act of will—even if one had no control over circumstances themselves.

So. So. So Grania could set sail to face the Queen of England, knowing that no matter what the outcome the essence of her life remained hers to choose. And she chose to make it happy.

She laughed into the wind, tasting salt spray on her lips.

From the crest of Doon hill a crooked-jawed man with rusty hair watched the departing fleet until it dwindled to invisibility. Then he dropped to his knees on stony soil. "Go with her," he begged of the God he had insulted by murdering an abbot.

When he got up he hurried to the nearest cottage to ask direction to whatever priest might be hidden and protected in the area. He had dreadful confessions to make and earnest prayers he wanted professionally guided toward heaven. If Grania came back, and if she ever forgave him—and he had doubts in both areas—he wanted to meet her with a shriven and burnished soul.

At Grania's order, her ships hugged the coast, constantly on the alert for English flags that might mean an attack at sea instigated by Bingham. But luck was with her; Sir Richard was busy with another battle elsewhere at the moment and could not turn his entire attention on Grania's undertaking. But he did hear of it, when she had already set sail. And he did make hasty and desperate plans to try to prevent her doing any damage to him with the queen, for he had no doubt she would spread exaggerated tales of his brutality all over England if she had the chance.

"I should have killed her long ago," he muttered in his bed at night, tossing and sleepless. "She has poisoned my life; she has poisoned my entire life!"

Grania had laid her own plans. As she explained to her crews, "We will not arrive in England totally friendless. Black Thomas, Duke of Ormond, owes me a debt or two for shipping some highly irregular cargo for him in the past. As soon as we land we will get a message to him and ask him to smooth the way for me to visit Elizabeth; he is well placed in her court."

Trade, Grania thought with satisfaction, had a way of paying unexpected dividends.

The voyage was completed as successfully as if a benign fate had ordained it, and the Irish galleys sailed into the mouth of the Thames with such brazen aplomb they were not challenged. Unmolested, Grania's trio of ships headed for the docks of London.

The Thames was crowded with vessels of every description. The dark water was an open sewer for the city and smelled like it. Grania pulled her cloak over her nose and mouth in disgust. This was no healthy waterway, swept clean by the wind, but a place of shrieks and clamor and commerce and theft, of hard-eyed men swearing at each other and foreign captains from many ports adding indistinguishable commands to the polyglot of tongues.

And over it all loomed the city. In her career, Grania had sailed into many European harbors, but none of them compared for size or density with London. "I find it hard to believe people would willingly live all packed together like herring in a barrel, amid so much noise and filth," she said to one of her men.

"They probably have no choice," he replied. "I suppose the Tudor woman has claimed all the sweet open country for herself and only left this for the peasantry."

So many strange sights were commonplace in London that Grania and her ships hardly attracted any attention. Grania stared at the gray stone and red brick representing the humming power which was the nerve center of Elizabeth's empire, and wondered if anyone even knew she was there. Or cared.

But Elizabeth would know. Soon.

Rather than seek lodging in the city, Grania chose to remain aboard her galley, and it was there the Duke of Ormond called upon her in response to a message she sent him. Black Thomas, a barely tamed rogue of a man who seemed out of place in his satins and ruffs, laughed lustily when Grania told him of her desire to call upon the queen.

"By God, madam, such audacity as yours deserves a reward! I can get you into court easily enough. I flirt with her majesty almost daily and give every indication I'm hot to bed her dried-out bones. She loves it and currently loves me, or so she claims. But she's as changeable as the weather and a new buck will catch her eye tomorrow, so I had better get you an audience immediately while I'm still in favor."

Grania drew back. "Hurry breaks the eggs," she said.

But Black Tom knew Irish sayings, too. "Catch the egg before it splatters," he replied, making Grania grin. She liked the man. She liked men, and her eyes told him so.

The Duke of Ormond waved to the corps of men-at-arms he had prudently brought with him to the savage dockside area. "I may be staying here for the afternoon," he told them, "and having a cup of wine or two."

Three days later, he sent a messenger to tell Grania she had an audience with the queen in Greenwich. "Her majesty is said to have been impressed by your correspondence and pleased with the quality of your handwriting," the messenger reported.

Grania laughed. That was a mark for Tibbot!

Other letters had been written as well. Richard Bingham had hastily dispatched a furious missive to the queen's secretary, Sir William Cecil, in which he denounced Gráinne Ni Mháille as a towering traitor and the mother of all treacheries in Ireland for the last forty years. He claimed he had enough information about her activities to force her execution and begged Cecil and the queen to listen to nothing she might say against himself.

Fortunately for Grania's peace of mind, perhaps, she did not know the letter had been penned and was racing to England by the swiftest ship.

Had they been treated fairly, the chieftains of Ireland might, in time, have come to an amicable acceptance of English law as tribe by tribe they discovered ways in which it was advantageous to them. But men like Bingham created an undying hatred that would flare up again and again for centuries to come. They never made any effort to understand the archaic but highly complex culture they encountered in Ireland; they viewed the natives as no more than vermin and undertook the destruction of that vermin with an unholy pleasure.

Perhaps there could never have been amity between two peoples as disparate as Gael and Anglo-Saxon, or perhaps the chance was there but already fading past reclamation on the summer morning when Gráinne Ni Mháille arrived at Greenwich palace for her audience with Elizabeth of England.

Grania had hired riding horses for the occasion, because she wanted even the smallest details of her visit to create an impression. So she traveled to Greenwich aboard a mettlesome chestnut mare who tossed her head the whole time and never settled into a relaxed walk. "My bones will protest this jogging tomorrow," Grania remarked to her companions. "The roll of the sea is far more kind."

They journeyed along wide paved highways and avenues lined with trees. Roads in Ireland were generally narrow, muddy tracks; the contrast was just one more example of the difference between the two lands. England was in a period of expansion; Ireland had begun to huddle in upon itself.

Grania held her head high and threw her shoulders back, showing no fear of anything.

Greenwich, as they approached it, proved to be a long palace of irregular shape built near the riverbank, a green and pleasant retreat in the heat of summer. The base of its largest tower was touched by water at high tide, and the sun glittered on countless casement windows.

"So much glass!" murmured Grania, thinking of dark Rockfleet.

And such a large staff, she might have added. Guards stopped and questioned her party with increasing frequency as they neared the palace, and Grania's aide showed the sealed safe passage Ormond had provided again and again. By the time they reached the main gateway, Grania had to admit to herself that her heart was beating hard. But she kept her face composed and her chin up; her hand was steady on the reins.

She was waved through and her companions almost immediately diverted into another area. She would be sent, alone, to confront the Queen of England.

Gates and doorways opened, admitted her, and closed behind her in rapid succession, each passage moving her deeper down the gullet of the palace. Bored attendants mispronouncing her name guided her in this direction and that. Curious courtiers dressed in styles outrageous to her eyes glanced at her with mocking expressions. A balding man in a heavily padded velvet doublet drew back as if her proximity might contaminate him; as if she would stain his silk hose or tarnish his silver shoe buckles.

Then at last a doorway opened and she was admitted to a small inner chamber devoid of windows. A chamber curiously like a cell, with a door that slammed shut with frightening finality.

Grania whirled and faced the door and heard the bolt fall home. Dar Dia!

She spun around again to search the chamber for some other means of escape. The room was lined with polished wainscoting of dark oak, and the ceiling was ornamented with plaster swirls. A few small tables, a carved cabinet, a pair of benches completed the furnishings of the chamber, none of them suggesting it might indeed be used as a prison cell.

Grania took a deep breath and went back to the door, not certain now if she had really heard a bolt fall or not. When she turned the handle, the door gave immediately and a liveried servant on the other side peered in at her.

She pulled the door shut and stepped back. "It's glad I am you weren't here to see this shameless performance, Tigernan," she said aloud in a voice shaky with relief. But just the sound of that human voice steadied her. She made herself sit down on the less ornamented of the two benches and awaited further developments.

As she waited she examined her surroundings with more objective eyes. Even this minor room was lavished with the results of skilled craftsmanship and opulent with tapestries and carving. As she progressed through the palace she had seen such expensive trappings as not even the most lordly castle in Ireland contained, luxury piled atop luxury for its own sake and serving no functional purpose.

"It is obvious to me," Grania said aloud, savoring the cadences of Gaelic in this Tudor stronghold, "that the woman called Elizabeth has spent no time on shipboard or she would not burden herself with so many things she cannot use." She was reminded of her daughter Margaret, who was also driven to surround herself with toys as if to make up for having once seen others favored over her. Clothes and jewels were desperately important to Margaret Burke, who could never get enough.

[421]

Now that Grania had seen Elizabeth's stronghold, she recognized the hunger of another woman who could never get enough.

"You are in a trap," Grania said softly to the Tudor queen, wherever she might be. "You have to hold on to all of this, and none of it important. You have no children; ravens will seize it when you die."

As if in reply to her words, the door opened to admit an elderly man dressed in black velvet with a modest ruff at his throat. His manner was obsequious, his eyes red-rimmed and rheumy. He was accompanied by an interpreter who spoke in the unmistakable accents of the Pale.

"There is a specific court procedure for being presented to her majesty," the courtier explained through the interpreter, and went on to detail a whole long and tedious list of bowings and scrapings, of formalities intended to make any petitioner feel humbled.

Grania felt the anger building in her. She made an impatient gesture. "I will not use an interpreter," she announced.

The man in the velvet suit started to argue, but her voice overrode his, and the aide who spoke Gaelic strove desperately to keep up with her words.

"I have been told by the Duke of Ormond that Elizabeth is as fluent in Spanish as in English, and can also converse in Latin. Is that true?" Grania demanded to know.

Velvet suit affirmed, obviously agitated.

"I speak Spanish myself and was trained in Latin by the friars of Murrisk," Grania told him. "Your queen and I will be quite able to understand one another without having men distort our words through translation."

Velvet suit wrung his hands together. The interpreter looked uncertain and cleared his throat several times.

At that moment a footman entered the chamber to bring word that the queen was prepared to see her visitor from Ireland. Ignoring the two men as if they were part of the furniture, Grania swept from the room at the footman's heels.

✠

A pair of great carved doors was opened from the inside by unseen hands as Grania approached. They swung back to reveal an expanse of polished floor and a dazzle of light. In one quick glance Grania received a confused impression of swaths of crimson cloth with the royal arms emblazoned, of tables laden with baskets of apricots and cherries and crystal liquor bottles, of harp music (a harper, an Irish harper! her indignant mind screamed) playing in a corner, of a swirl of courtiers in brilliant costumes and a gagging overlay of too much perfume. The court of Elizabeth was as loud and colorful as market day, yet the gaiety seemed forced, all a mask assumed because the silent watcher at the far end of the room demanded it.

On a gilded chair of state beneath a canopy studded with gems sat the monarch of England, looking down on her subjects from a raised dais. Once she would have been at the very heart of the crowd, laughing, dancing, fighting a duel of wits with whatever clever man captured her fancy that day.

But she was the same age as Gráinne Ni Mháille, and time had used her hard.

Courtiers crowded around Grania hissing instructions, repeating the orders she had been given in the anteroom. But she did not listen. They were little people, unimportant people, and the rituals they tried to enforce were unimportant rituals. All that mattered was the woman on the other side of the room, the woman who had just looked up and met her eyes.

Grania did not bow. She did not bend her knee or lower her head; she did not contort herself into some posture of humility.

Look at me, Tigernan, she commanded. See what I do.

And you, Dubhdara . . . watch me. All of you whose blood pounds in my veins, you old chieftains, you brave men . . . watch me. My courage did not fail me because I would not let it. I am as strong as any of you.

Holding her head high, she strode across the floor straight toward the Queen of England.

The crowded room seemed to suck in one deep and audible breath.

Grania's eyes devoured every detail of Elizabeth Tudor as the space between them narrowed. For so long she had tried to imagine this woman, to give her a face and a voice and a character one could grapple with. Now she was looking at the reality.

Female king. Thin as a goose bone, she is, Grania thought, and that orange hair is a suspicious color indeed.

Elizabeth's face was as white as linen bleached on summer grass. Old and worn as I am, Grania told herself, I could lift that frail creature in my arms and break her across my bent knee.

Then she met Elizabeth's eyes.

Fierce, opaque eyes; eyes that would dare anything. In those eyes, Grania saw a reflection of her own.

The English queen was dressed in the exaggerated court style which she had created and which had become a veritable caricature of itself over the years. Her white silk gown was studded all over with aglets of black onyx, coral, and pearl, and rose from an elongated bodice to a ruff of muslin that nearly dwarfed her head. Massive skirts billowed from her narrow, brittle waist; her long-fingered hands seemed to struggle to emerge from yards of ruffled fabric.

Elizabeth had powdered her naturally pale face until her feverish eyes seemed to peer from a moon-white sliver of flesh. The finely modeled nose that had given her features distinction in youth had thickened, and she had lost some teeth from her left jaw, giving her cheek a sunken appearance and blurring some of her enunciations. She exuded an air of nervous irritability, like some well-bred, high-strung horse that has been ill used.

"I am Gráinne Ni Mháille," proclaimed the visitor she saw striding across the floor toward her with one hand extended in the style of warlords meeting to show one another they come unarmed.

The queen's colorless eyebrows lifted and quivered like fine antennae. She watched, fascinated, as the apparition bore down upon her, shrugging off the guards who rushed forward to intercept it. The creature was obviously a woman—a woman of incredible boldness and determination.

Elizabeth waved her hand, and the guards fell back.

Grania did not stop until she stood directly in front of the queen.

The Irishwoman was as large and powerfully built as Elizabeth Tudor was small and thin. Her coarse, graying hair had been twisted into an elaborate braided knot and skewered with a jeweled bodkin from the Armada treasure. She wore a pleated linen smock with an overdress of saffron-dyed wool, its sleeves slit to allow the pleated linen beneath to show. Embroidery of red and green silk decorated bodice and hem, and the Irish craftsmanship of the garments was exquisite.

"I am Gráinne Ni Mháille," she repeated, first in Spanish and then in Latin, though the classical tongue did not adapt itself well to Gaelic names.

Her hand remained extended. She obviously had no intention of kneeling, nor of kissing Elizabeth's own hand. She stood waiting with compelling confidence until the queen, unable to bear the burden of passing time, half rose from her seat and touched Grania's fingertips with her own.

The assembled courtiers gasped. It was quite the best show of the day.

Watch me, Tigernan.

Beyond the palace walls, the sky darkened and the sun disappeared behind a bank of clouds rushing from the west. A distant, ominous rattle of thunder sounded, and the first raindrops hit the glass windows like pebbles thrown from an angry hand. The light in the audience chamber darkened perceptibly; servitors hurried to bring more candles.

"I have sent you letters," Grania said, opening her offensive.

Elizabeth was surprised that this exotic woman spoke such civilized languages as Spanish and Latin. She chose to reply in the latter.

"Our secretary has kept us informed," she said in clipped, slightly nasal tones.

"I have made every effort to comply with your majesty's requests, and I fully answered the questions you sent me," Grania said, "yet I have not been honorably dealt with by your agents, and I have no choice but to apply directly to you."

"On what grounds?" The nasal voice was tightly controlled, the eyes watchful and guarded. Grania was suddenly reminded of her husband Donal's hawks in their jesses, enslaved by the very bonds that protected them.

On that day she understood the truth of Elizabeth Tudor, a truth only another woman like herself might fully grasp. This domineering monarch surrounded by her armies, swathed in luxury, was a captive to the very power she wielded. She was, beneath the powder and lace, a raddled spinster who would never walk barefoot along a deserted beach, or nurse a child, or know the tender delight of a mystery like Huw-from-the-sea. Would never have the freedom to live life as she chose without regard for a crushing chain of circumstances.

Yet this was the all-powerful Queen of England, the ban-rion.

In Grania's eyes, Elizabeth was startled to see pity. It threw her off guard, and the painted face was briefly vulnerable.

Grania attacked without hesitation. "I apply to you as one chieftain to another," she said in her most forceful tone. "You rule here, and I am sovereign in my own territory. I ask you to treat with me according to the honor due princes."

For a moment it was as if the ghost of Mary Stuart had entered the audience chamber. The Queen of England seemed to shrink inside her clothes, and those who knew her best could see how her cheeks paled beneath their rouge. But Elizabeth's was no weak spirit, and when she spoke again her voice was as imperious as ever. "You deign to proclaim yourself our equal?"

"I proclaim myself a free Irishwoman of noble blood!" Grania answered her.

The affairs of state were many and pressing, and as Elizabeth had consolidated her reign over the years they had grown even more numerous. At any given moment she had threescore extremely important matters on her mind and an equal number that were absolutely urgent. Ireland, its turmoil and the unresolved struggle to plant it with English colonists, had become such a permanent fixture among her problems that Elizabeth rarely considered it separately anymore. But now her visitor demanded attention for Ireland and the Irish, demanded attention and respect for herself as an individual.

It had never been English policy to consider the Irish as individuals. They were subjects to be subjugated, a faceless mass that merely represented an impediment to English goals and that Elizabeth dealt with only from a distance.

But today there was no distance between Elizabeth Tudor and Gráinne Ni Mháille.

The two women locked eyes.

After a long pause, Elizabeth spoke. "What is it you request of us?"

During the voyage to England, Grania had rehearsed again and again the conversation she would have with the she-king. The words came easily to her now, as familiar as ship's commands. She explained her situation again, in detail, from the most advantageous point of view—grateful to Tibbot for having suggested the right words and phrases. His feet had flattened the path she must walk on now and made it easy for her.

Elizabeth listened with focused interest. She was justly famed for her powers of intellect and her ability to concentrate, and both were brought to bear on Grania. The Irishwoman was a revelation to her, and she was eager to examine every nuance of the other's character. "I have met no one quite like you before," she admitted candidly.

Flattered, Grania smiled. "There is no one like me, any more than there is anyone else like you," she said.

It was Elizabeth's turn to smile. The spectators were surprised at the way the two women seemed to be warming to each other.

With a wave of her hand, Elizabeth summoned a seat for her guest and then a tray of refreshments, though she never took her eyes from Grania's face.

"What can that Papist savage be saying that is so fascinating to our Gloriana?" a spindle-shanked man in peacock satin asked a long-faced lady-in-waiting attired in puce silk. She shrugged and leaned forward, as avid as he to catch some stray crumb of the conversation.

But Grania was speaking only for Elizabeth's ears. "So my marriages brought me little but trouble and sadness," she was saying. Her intuition told her, early in the conversation, that Elizabeth responded favorably to hearing another woman complain about men. The English queen's relationships with the opposite sex had always been volatile; she could be expected to sympathize with a woman whose marriages had been unhappy through no fault of her own.

"I resorted to seafaring to support the kinsmen of my first husband when he did not support them himself," Grania related. "Yet he never thanked me or even acknowledged my contribution."

Elizabeth found herself nodding. "Men are ungrateful wretches," she said. "They expect so much from women that no matter what we give them it is never enough."

You are halfway won to my side already, Grania thought to herself.

Then it was as if she heard Evleen's voice in the back of her brain, cautioning her. Be careful, be careful! This is no easily manipulated female, but a true king who will claim your head as a trophy if you make a mistake with her.

I will make no mistakes, Grania answered in silence to that watchful voice from Ireland. I am impulsive no longer; I can be as cunning as the best of them. The English themselves have taught me that, and taught me thoroughly.

She continued to tell her story, weighting each word with the woe men could bring down on helpless women—yet never allowing herself to sound defeated by it. She held up her uncrushed spirit for Elizabeth to see and recognize.

Admiration grew in the eyes of the English queen.

Grania noticed that Elizabeth surrounded herself with rich foods and fragrant beverages, yet took nothing for herself but a little wine into which she stirred a large amount of water.

No wonder the creature is so spindly, Grania thought. Perhaps she fears poison. How many evil potions might be concealed on the persons of all those fancy birds who strut her halls? Better a clean sword in the open air, or a gun fired at you in the daylight by someone not afraid to meet your eyes. Her pity for Elizabeth Tudor grew.

The audience chamber was stifling. The large room stank of sweat and perfume and damp fabrics and damper hair. Outside the storm stalked the land, growling and flashing fire.

32

One great bolt of lightning suddenly struck nearby. A few people shrieked; Grania felt contempt for them. But as if it had cleared the air the flash cut through the pleasant conversation between the two women and Elizabeth leaned forward to ask abruptly, "What is it you want more, Grace of Ireland? Your ships released to you . . . or the freedom of your imprisoned son?"

It was Grania's turn to be thrown off guard. They had been playing a game after all, she reminded herself; it had been a game from the very beginning, in spite of the pleasantries and the spiced wine, and Elizabeth Tudor had always known the stakes. Now she was offering only half of the pot and expecting Grania to be grateful.

I am glad it is out in the open, Tigernan. Now we will see who really plays the better—the sasanach woman, or I.

"The galleys, as I have explained to you, represent my only means of supporting myself unless you grant me funds from the estates of my husbands," Grania said. "But it is a cruel choice you offer me—my child's life or starvation. I can only ask which you would take under the same circumstances."

The feverish eyes glittered dangerously. "I am not the one who has to make the decision," Elizabeth said. "But . . ."

"But?" Grania sat still; very still. And waited.

"I have no children," Elizabeth said slowly. "I cannot be expected to know how a mother would feel or what value she would place a on a child's life." She did not seem to notice that for once she was saying "I" instead of the royal "we."

But Grania noticed—and chose her next words accordingly, realizing she had uncovered an old wound. "You are a chieftain, as I am," she said. "Therefore you are as responsible for your followers as a mother is for her children. You must understand a mother's feelings very well."

Elizabeth's lips tightened, refusing to smile. This Irishwoman was clever. "Are you saying you choose your son's life above all?"

Grania would not accept the bait. Not now; now she knew her opponent too well. "I am saying," she replied in a measured cadence, "that I leave it to you to make the choice for me. You are my equal in rank and honor and I trust you to make a noble decision no one else could."

She was rewarded by a swift intake of breath Elizabeth could not conceal. Then the queen, to cover her confusion, signaled for more wine to be brought and urged another drink on her guest. Grania downed it easily; thin wine would have no effect on a head trained to uisquebaugh.

Elizabeth sipped from her own goblet, lost in thought. I can outwait you, Grania said to her silently. I have had a lifetime to learn patience and practice for this duel. Then, as the concept of patience flitted across her mind, the image of Tigernan followed it. Tigernan . . . deliberately insulting her at Bunowen bay, then waiting patiently to see how she would react. Why had she not noticed that look of *waiting* in his eyes, and understood? Had she already been too preoccupied with Elizabeth?

Oh, Tigernan, you were playing a game too! You wanted me to arrive here with my sails full of wind and my fists doubled, and I did. I strode into this hall as much to show you as to show the English, armored in the anger you gave me. Your funny gift of love.

Watching over the rim of her goblet, Elizabeth observed a subtle curve form the Irishwoman's mouth. Not quite a smile, it was at once more tender and more ironic.

The queen felt a sting of envy. What could the weathered creature before her, with her life of woe and loss, possess that could bring such a sudden glow to her eyes? A temptation to destroy that visible happiness rose in Elizabeth, who was not happy, who no longer believed in even the possibility of happiness.

"We will be pleased to make the choice for you," she told Grania. "And you will be bound by our decision. We will weigh your son's life against the value of your ships and your husbands' property; we will consider all you have requested from us. And we will choose." Her voice was cold.

Grania met her eyes without flinching. This was the last throw of the dice. See me as I am, she cried out silently to Elizabeth, pouring all her strength and will into her naked face. *See what I represent and give me the honor one king may demand of another!*

The force of her personality burned through her eyes. It leaped out at Elizabeth Tudor like a generation of warriors brandishing proud swords.

Bend to me, Grania silently challenged. Accede to my will, for I am your equal in every way that matters save one: on this day, at this hour, I am stronger than you! Give me what I ask!

Their eyes locked. Thunder boomed and crashed and rain pelted the roofs of Greenwich. A terrible tug of wills continued in the audience chamber while the queen's courtiers watched uncomprehending.

Time stopped, and Grania's heart with it, as she waited for the final move of the game.

Court life swirled around them and the buzz of chatter droned on, but neither woman paid any attention to it. Without words, they spoke. Without words, they asked questions and answered them.

Ireland and England. Two she-kings. One ostensibly supplicant, the other ostensibly all-powerful. But in the hall of Greenwich the real essence of power, that unremitting energy which builds empires and defies fate, was being measured by two tired and aging women. On this day, at this hour, for a brief space of time, one must surely yield to the other.

Grania was standing now, her feet braced wide apart. Unyielding; proud. She did not look like a supplicant, but a monarch.

Elizabeth shifted on her seat and made a vague gesture with one thin hand. "You must excuse us now," she said wearily. "There are more pressing matters demanding our attention. You will stay as my guest until I have reached my decision; then you will be notified."

She meant it as an act of dismissal. She had already begun to turn away, to look elsewhere—when to her own surprise and everyone else's, Grania sneezed. A great whoop of a sneeze with nothing dainty about it. At once one of the queen's ladies-in-waiting was at her elbow, offering her a square of cambric embroidered with silk. Grania accepted it, blew her nose long and thoroughly, then wadded the handkerchief into a ball and tossed it toward the nearest hearth.

Elizabeth saw the gesture. "In England we know enough to put our handkerchiefs into our sleeves," she said patronizingly.

Grania flung back her head and laughed the big booming laugh that was hers alone, its vitality reducing Elizabeth's thin voice to a wasp-drone. "In my land," she cried for all to hear, "we would have nothing but contempt for those so filthy they returned soiled linen to their persons. *We* are a noble race!"

With a great swing of her shoulders she faced about, turning her back on the Queen of England, and strode from the hall.

Elizabeth sat on her throne like a carved image, staring after her. Shocked into silence, the queen's courtiers waited, exchanging looks with one another. Would her majesty order the impudent woman seized and flung into prison as she deserved? Or better yet, since she was only Irish, executed for insulting Gloriana?

They looked at one another and they looked at the queen, but her face offered no clue. She stared at the doors through which Grania had made an uncontested departure. Only those closest to Elizabeth, those who knew her best, might have interpreted the dawning light in her eyes.

✠

The queen held no more audiences that day. Instead she retired to her chambers and spent considerable time gazing out the great casement windows at the pelting rain and the broad curve of the river. She interrupted her vigil for a conference with Cecil but was soon back at the window again, lost in a sort of melancholy that discouraged even the most persistent of her attendants from talking to her.

Late in the day, as the light began to fade from the leaden sky, she noticed another woman framed in a window of the palace, clearly visible to her because of the angle where she stood. A broad-boned woman with natural color in her cheeks.

They eyed each other across open space, through spears of rain. And at last it was Elizabeth who turned away.

"Will we be held prisoner here?" Grania's men had been asking her all afternoon. "Are we in danger, should we try to escape?"

"No," was all she said. "No."

If they were imprisoned, if they were in danger, then the game was truly and finally lost and she did not want to attempt to play it anymore; she would welcome death in such an event, and be done with it.

And if the game is won, she promised herself, I will go home. I will go home to Cuan Mó and Evleen . . . and Tigernan. I will give him the rough side of my tongue, the rogue, for as long as it pleases me, and then I will pour him a great flagon of ale with my own hand and we will sit down together while I tell him the story of my adventures. And we will drink a toast to the English queen together and invent wonderful new curses to apply to Richard Bingham. . . .

If I have won. If only time would flow past as swiftly as that river out there, and I could know.

The night seemed endless. The Irish guests were entertained in the banquet hall together with a vast assemblage of other people of varying rank and importance, many of whom did not know each other and did not seem to care. But the queen did not put in an appearance.

"Her majesty is not as strong as she used to be," someone said.

"Nonsense!" another replied. "She will still be awake and working when the rest of us are long abed."

The night seemed endless and the rain never stopped.

By dawn, however, a watery sun broke through the clouds. Soon the air was steaming as clouds of vapor rose from every tree and shrub. Mist hung over the river, reminding Grania of home.

She had slept fully clothed and ready for anything. She longed to get back to her ships and put on her oldest, most comfortable trews. And let her hair down. And have a real drink. She fought to keep the tension locked inside herself where none could see.

And at last there was a knock at her chamber door.

An aide of Cecil's entered, carrying an olivewood casket. He opened the box for Grania so she might see the scroll lying inside, fastened with ribbon and sealed with the queen's own seal.

Grania took it out herself, trying to keep her fingers from trembling though they were very cold.

The document was written in Latin. When Grania saw that, she felt some of the blood return to her limbs. Had it been written in English she would have known at once that all the doors were shut against her.

She carried it to the nearest window and spread it out so she could read it, lingering over each word. She read it once silently while her men breathed down her neck and shuffled their feet and cleared their throats. Then she read it again aloud, the carefully scribed words penned in Cecil's polished style.

At Elizabeth's order, the widow of Richard Burke was to receive an almost unprecedented clemency. Her kinsmen, including her son Tibbot, were to be released from captivity. She was forgiven her acts against her son Murrough O Flaherty, described as now being a loyal subject of the queen. She was to receive sums for her maintenance from the properties that had once been held by each of her dead husbands.

And as long as she remained Elizabeth's "dutiful subject," she was empowered to prosecute by means of arms and men anyone deemed an enemy of the queen in Ireland.

"We will be given the war galleys back," one of her officers said joyfully.

"I trust Richard Bingham will have a seizure when he learns his sovereign's order," Grania replied with a grin so broad it was like the sun rising over the Irish sea.

"Now we go home!" announced Gráinne Ni Mháille.

✠

From her window, Elizabeth of England watched the jubilant departure of the Irish. She knew, as they could not, that all victories are temporary and Ireland would continue to be a battleground, where loyalties would shift and change as easily as fortunes, and glorious causes would drown in blood and mud.

But she also knew, for the first time, that she was not quite so alone in the world as she had always believed. Mary of Scotland had been a great disappointment to her cousin Elizabeth, for though born to be a monarch Mary had never known how to act like one except at her own death.

In Greenwich, in the Year of Our Lord 1593, Elizabeth Tudor had at last met another woman like herself, with the soul of a king.

She would not forget Grania.

epilogue

The two she-kings had another decade of life left to them, and their fires faded in the same year. Elizabeth's support had turned many of the Irish chieftains against Grania, but she lived her life and fished the bay and had Tigernan for company in the long silver twilights, and her grandchildren to visit.

Many grandchildren, many bright faces with sea-colored eyes and the zest for life blazing in their cheeks.

And she had Cuan Mó and the vast arching sky.

When she fell so ill that neither Evleen nor Tigernan could help her, they sent for the nuns from Cliara to nurse her. Tigernan could not stand by her bed and watch her fade away. He was a brave man, but the greatest courage has limits. He waited until God's women were crowding around her, praying her soul toward heaven—though he knew she would always prefer Clew bay—and then he got into his curragh and set out for Curraun.

He did not let himself look back. Grania would not have looked back.

He only rested on his oars once, to mark the passing of an enormous sea eagle winging inland from Achill as if it had some urgent appointment to keep.

✠

The nuns stood in sober rank around Grania's bed with their hands folded like those of stone-bound saints and their mouths downturned.

They thought they watched a sinner's end. The notorious Gráinne Ni Mháille was dying with little to show for her days of rebellion and high adventure; she possessed only a few battered galleys in the harbor and the dark stones of Rockfleet. But everyone knew she had been wicked in her day. The younger nuns whispered behind their hands that she had slain "any number of men, and some of them were her own husbands!" The older nuns frowned at the gossip and kept quiet, for Grania had always seen there was food on the refectory table, even if she rarely appeared in chapel.

But she was a sinner, no doubt of it. She took lovers, she looted and plundered, her own son had turned against her. She drank and swore like a man and was a notorious gambler. Surely none of a female's tender virtues could exist in such a creature. God's mercy was her only hope.

Poor, pitiful woman. Such a tragic life and such a tragic end to it, the pious faces said in a white-lipped silence. They poured their pity over her like sacramental oil, easing her passing from a cruel world.

✠

Dying, Grania stood in the prow of her flagship again and felt the exultant sea lift her. She sensed the strong muscle in her arms and back and the nimbleness of her brain. The blue vault of the sky above was the dome of a cathedral, stretching on and on. Beckoning.

She heard the warm whisper of Huw's voice, reciting poetry to her. Not dead, never dead; Evleen had understood. But waiting for her somewhere, to be joined with her and the others as rivulets run together to meet the sea.

She felt the soft lips of her babies fumble at her breast, all innocence. So sweet and dear, the little downy heads! Live, she urged them. Live.

Life was its own imperative and there was no end to it, she knew full well; there was only an ebb and flow.

Dying, she thought at last and forever of the fierce, funny joy of Tigernan . . . Tigernan, Tigernan . . .

. . . and turned her face to the wall, and laughed.

acknowledgments

The author gratefully acknowledges the immeasurable assistance given her by Cornelius Howard, whose enthusiasm and support helped make this book possible. Also, a special debt is owed to Dr. John De Courcy Ireland of the Maritime Institute of Ireland for his great generosity in sharing his knowledge of Ireland's seafaring history.

Last but by no means least, I wish to thank those many friends in Ireland who contributed in ways large and small to the research required. Their greatest gift, however, has been their kindness to myself and my husband over the years, and for that no words are sufficient to say what is in my heart. Thank you.